APHRODESIA

Also by John Oehler

Papyrus

Tepui

APHRODESIA

John Oehler

CreateSpace

Cover design by Dorothy Oehler

ISBN-13: 978-1477680308

PRINTED IN THE UNITED STATES OF AMERICA

Dedicated to my wife, Dorothy, and to Jean Kerléo

ACKNOWLEDGMENTS

The basic idea for APHRODESIA came to me during an interview with Jean Kerléo when he said that creating a true aphrodisiac would be a triumph for any perfumer. Kerléo, a master perfumer and the founder of the Osmothèque, gave me an education in the perfumer's art, a tour of ISIPCA (the world-renowned French perfume school in Versailles), and a rarely granted tour of the vault that houses the Osmothèque's unique collection of fragrances. *Monsieur, merci beaucoup.*

Gaining a knowledge of perfumes is altogether different from turning that knowledge into a gripping novel. For tremendous help in refining the story—for offering suggestions that ranged from word choice to adding whole new chapters—I sincerely thank my critique partners: Chris Rogers, Stacey Keith, Rodney Walther, Charlotte Jones, Chuck Brownman, Marcia Gerhardt, Sarah Warburton, Bill Stevenson, Vanessa Leggett, Heather Shelly, Michelle Devlin, Rebecca Nolan, and Jack Thomas.

For help with modern laboratory techniques, I thank Mary Jo Baedecker and a person in the perfume industry who wishes to be unnamed.

Most of all, I am eternally grateful for my wife, Dorothy, the woman I married in Kathmandu more than forty years ago and who continues to be the best thing that ever happened to me.

APHRODESIA

Prologue

In the flickering light of a hundred oil lamps, Balquees stood in her bath, trying to conceal her anxiety from the servant girls washing her. She had journeyed long across the desert to this strange kingdom where people worshipped an invisible god. She had brought gold and jewels and rare spices from her dominions in Sheba. Solomon had received them graciously and inquired with great interest about her land. Three days she and her entourage had occupied a wing of his palace. Three nights she and the king had dined before dancers, musicians, wild beasts brought to heel. But not once had Solomon invited her to his bed.

Balquees glanced down at herself. Just twenty-three years of age, she was still slender, her legs and stomach firm, her breasts full. What about her did not appeal to a king renowned for his love of women?

There could be only one explanation. She dismissed the girls and, still dripping, turned to her vizier. "He has seven hundred wives."

"And three hundred concubines, my queen." The vizier, her most trusted minister, spoke softly, his aged face radiating confidence. "Yet had he ten thousand, all would envy you. Your skin is as dark and flawless as the night, your beauty like the sunrise."

"Still he rejects me." Balquees bit her cheek. She needed a son, a successor as wise and strong as Solomon himself, or her empire would be in danger of collapse. But time's sands were slipping through her fingers. According to the moon, tonight would be her last opportunity to conceive this month.

"We have come prepared, my queen." Stepping forward, the vizier produced a golden flask from his robes. "Provided you are willing to endure a rapture so powerful it could consume both of you in its fire."

"I am willing."

He hesitated. "Are you certain?"

Balquees held out her hand. "Give me the fragrance."

Chapter 1

In the lab where students mixed ingredients for their perfumes, Eric Foster proudly unstoppered the project that could catapult him to stardom. Brimming with excitement, he turned to Durand. "What do you think of aphrodisiacs?"

"A mirage. The unachievable goal of fools." Jacques Durand cocked a bushy white eyebrow. "Why do you ask?"

"I'm working on one. It's a reconstruction of the fragrance the Queen of Sheba wore to seduce King Solomon." Eric proffered the vial. "I call it Balquees."

Ignoring the vial, Durand frowned. "Why do you waste your time? Why do you waste *my* time, on a Sunday morning?"

Uh-oh. Apparently Durand was in one of his testy moods, perhaps because of the cold drizzle outside. For a seventy-year-old man accustomed to his villa on Cap d'Ail, Versailles in early April could be a dreary place.

It was dreary for Eric, too. Just this morning, on his three-mile run, he'd gone off the sidewalk to avoid a young girl dressed for church and stepped right into a mud puddle. But Eric had to be here. He was stuck in Versailles until graduation next month when, at age twenty-five, he would finally start working for a major perfume house.

At least he and Durand had the institute to themselves. Durand, who refused to join the faculty but taught an occasional master class, hated the groveling of students who foisted their creations on him whenever he showed up. But Sundays were safe—no students, no staff, the labs spotlessly clean, the air cleansed of experiments by the filtration system humming softly overhead—the ideal day for their fortnightly meetings. And now Eric had unwittingly provoked his mentor's scorn.

Deciding Durand could smell Balquees when his mood improved, Eric replaced the stopper and attempted to justify his so-called waste of time. "I've finished all the requirements, except the final examination. So I have a few weeks to indulge in other interests."

"And this is how you indulge? Butterflying after fantasies?" Durand unbuttoned the jacket of his suit, Armani of course, which he wore over a thin turtleneck the same pigeon-gray as his wavy hair. Seating himself on the adjacent lab stool, he said, "Eric, you have an excellent mind and the finest nose of anybody I know. But more important, you have extraordinary talent. I would take no interest in you if you did not. You should be spending your time on serious creations."

Eric opened the bottom drawer at his station in the lab and withdrew a brown, screw-capped vial. "I finished this last week. For my graduation project."

Durand gave him that skeptical squint that could crush reputations, then selected a *mouillette* from a beaker on the tiled countertop. He dipped the thin strip of white filter paper into Eric's offering, sniffed, and his eyes widened.

"This is good." He waved the *mouillette* in the air, to evaporate some of the top note, and smelled again. "I might even say excellent. But you used real bergamot."

"I know it's been claimed to cause cancer in rats. But almost any organic compound can do that if you rub it on full-strength for several months. My perfume has only a small percentage, and it doesn't smell the same with a synthetic."

"Synthetics never smell the same. Cheaper, more consistent quality. But none of the nuances of the natural. Still, there is strong resistance to certain naturals, especially in Europe and America. You have a risk that this could never go to market without one of those infantile health warnings your government loves."

Eric's ego deflated. "Never go to market" from a man who

had made his fortune and reputation as a master perfumer was equivalent to the kiss of death.

"However," Durand said, dropping the *mouillette* in a waste jar, "this is so good that the synthetic will not hurt it. Congratulations."

Relief swelled in Eric's chest, a physical sensation that made him straighten his posture. Durand had a habit of doing that to you, crippling you one moment, then lifting you back up. Similar to Eric's father, who could grimace at your soufflé or rip apart your sauce, then smile and show you how to fix it. Eric loved them both. But his future lay in perfumery, not *haute cuisine*.

So, synthetic bergamot. Eric's station, like all the others in this lab, had an electronic balance for weighing fractions of grams plus four shelves of deep-sided plastic trays, each tray filled with brown glass vials of extracts, essential oils, and cold-pressed tinctures. The vials were fitted with screw-cap eyedroppers, one drop being one-twentieth of a milliliter. He pulled down tray B from the top shelf and picked out *Bergamot synthétique*. "I'll try it again."

"More than try. You will succeed."

Encouraged by his mentor's confidence and apparently improved mood, Eric returned to his original subject, the whole reason he'd been itching to see Durand today. "Would you smell Balquees now?"

"Were you not listening to me?"

Eric clamped his jaw to keep from swearing. What was wrong with the man? Durand could be stubborn, but never before had he dismissed one of Eric's creations without even giving it a sniff. And this fragrance was possibly the most important in Eric's life. He yearned to be great, to create something that would leave a lasting mark in the world of perfumes. Durand's saying an aphrodisiac was "unachievable" only fired Eric's own belief that Balquees would make that mark. Surely Durand could see Eric's enthusiasm. And just as surely he should be curious, or at least willing, to smell the fragrance that inspired it.

Brushing aside a fall of sand-colored hair, Eric changed tack in hopes of pricking Durand's interest. "I've used an ingredient that's extremely rare. The same one the Queen of Sheba is said to have used. It comes from—"

"I do not care where it comes from. You chase a fantasy."

"Why do you keep saying that?"

Durand shook his head slowly, as though it should be obvious to a student of perfumes. "Because men have tried for centuries. Spanish fly, the crushed powder of a beetle that inflames sensitive tissue, is nothing more than an irritant. Vanilla, sweet amber. Possibly they worked in an earlier age, because women thought they were *supposed* to. But today's woman is more sophisticated."

"What about androsterone?" Eric said, playing along for the moment. "Male perspiration."

Durand blew out a dismissive breath in that manner unique to the French. "For some women, perhaps. For some women, the sight of a man in tight trousers is stimulus enough. Do you wish to cater to such women?"

Spoken with the unwitting arrogance of a man who'd spent his life creating specifically for sophisticates. "But smells can generate so many emotions. So many physical reactions. Why not desire?"

"Eric, you do not strike me as a fellow who needs assistance attracting women."

"It's not for *me*." Eric racked his brain for a different approach but couldn't come up with one. "Would you just smell it? One time, that's all I ask."

Durand stood from his stool. "Come with me."

Exasperated, Eric followed him out of the lab and to the office of Jean Kerléo, founder of the Osmothèque. Billed as the "living perfume museum," the Osmothèque shared quarters with ISIPCA, *l'Institut Supérieur International du Parfum, de la Cosmétique et de l'Aromatique alimentaire*, the world's top school for perfumes, cosmetics, and flavorings. There were roughly a hundred students in each curriculum, and among the perfume students, Eric suffered the segregation of being best—and American.

Durand opened the door and knelt in front of a small safe behind Kerléo's desk. With long, delicate fingers, he turned the combination dial.

Eric stopped at the threshold. Durand never missed a chance to extol the honor of perfumers. Yet here he was, opening the private safe of a man who, for thirty years, had been the master perfumer for Jean Patou and who dwelled among the gods of perfumery just as surely as Durand himself did.

When his mentor withdrew a set of keys from the safe, Eric could hardly believe it. *"Monsieur*, this is—"

"Jean is a close friend. He would lend me these if he were here."

Hoping that was true, Eric again followed Durand, this time down the stairs and out of the laboratory wing into one of the two pink-and-white chateaux that were the public face of ISIPCA. Inside the chateau, Durand unlocked a door, flipped on a light switch, and headed down the stairs into the basement. At a steel door labeled 27, he selected a four-sided, high-security key from Kerléo's ring and opened the lock.

This was the vault, the heart of the Osmothèque's unique collection. Eric hadn't been here since the orientation tour for new students, nearly two years ago. In fact, few people in the world even knew it existed, and fewer still ever got inside.

Eric, just over six feet tall, had to duck his head to enter. The temperature of the room was a chilly fifty degrees Fahrenheit to counteract one of the three enemies of perfume—heat. Of the other two enemies, light was easy to control. The room was kept dark, except when Kerléo was here. Durand switched on the fluorescent lights.

A tile-topped table attached to the far wall provided the room's only workplace. Aside from the table and a small area around it, floor-to-ceiling metal shelves occupied nearly every available space, and bottles of perfume filled the shelves almost to capacity. Several thousand bottles, ranging in size from five milliliters to two liters. Roughly half of the bottles were glass, the other half aluminum.

Nobody except Jean Kerléo ever took a sample from any bottle, and Kerléo only did so after one hell of a good reason had been presented to him. When he did withdraw a sample, he topped off the headspace with argon from a gas cylinder, for the final enemy of perfumes was oxygen. No bottle in this room contained any air. In all cases, what looked like air above the liquid was argon.

"Eric, you are standing among the greatest perfumes ever created. Some of them no longer exist outside this room." Durand leveled his gray eyes. "Not one of them is an aphrodisiac."

"But that doesn't mean an aphrodisiac couldn't join them."

"Never!" As though embarrassed at his outburst, Durand ran a hand through his hair. "I say never because an aphrodisiac, even if possible, would be dishonorable. Great perfumes like these create a mood, an impression. They do not drive a person to sexual liaison against that person's will."

"But something that arouses desire could augment that mood. It doesn't have to be against the person's will. A person might *want* it."

"It would be dishonest."

"Don't you think it depends on intent?" Although it felt like he was getting nowhere, Eric had to keep trying. "If you know the person well, if you're in a committed—"

"Eric, please." Durand opened a binder on the worktable and started flipping through pages of computer printout. "Look at these. Jicky, Mitsouko, Number Five, Joy, Ma Griffe, L'Air du Temps. Here, Sublime by our own Kerléo. All masterpieces. These are the fragrances you should study."

"I *have* studied them." At the mention of their names, Eric could recall exactly how each one smelled. He could summon the fragrance in his mind and discern the ingredients, even the relatively uncommon ones like the opopanax in Jicky and the styrax in Ma Griffe. For a moment, he was tempted to remind Durand that Jicky, Mitsouko, and L'Air du Temps all contained real bergamot. But he held his tongue.

"And if you wish to indulge in re-creations …" Durand flipped through a few more pages. "… consider something useful like this." He tapped one of his manicured nails on an entry that read *Crêpe de chine (1925, Millot) par Jean de Pres.* "Of the original perfume, there is no more. We have it here only because Kerléo recreated it. We know it is perfect because the owner of the formula allowed him to copy it. That formula, and at least two hundred others, he keeps in a safe deposit box. People have given them to him because they trust him to keep them secret. They know he is honorable."

Not very creative, Eric thought. The creativity came when you figured out the ingredients yourself.

"Honor, Eric. You are about to enter the most honorable profession in the world. When you have gained the respect of your colleagues and proved your ability to create fine fragrances, then you will have the right to venture into the realm of recreating lost perfumes."

As usual, Durand had taken the long way around to make a point, going so far as to bring him down here to the *sanctum sanctorum* to do it. But honor wasn't the issue. The issue was having the freedom to create something revolutionary without naysayers throwing up roadblocks every step of the way. And in the case of Balquees, having the freedom to bring the wisdom of the ancients into the Twenty-first Century. If that shattered the mindset of what was "achievable," then so much the better.

"So," Durand said, "you will now concentrate on the important things. Yes?"

Eric nodded with conviction. "Yes, sir, I will."

Chapter 2

At the Palace of Versailles, an hour's walk from ISIPCA, Eric's favorite place was the Gallery of Mirrors. He liked the grandeur and sheer decadence, the long row of twenty-foot-high windows, the duplicate row of equally large mirrors on the opposite wall, the crystal chandeliers that must have weighed half a ton each. A monument to excess, in gold and glass.

But Abby, he knew, saw its gilded statues of women raising candelabras in honor of the Sun King as a disgusting tribute to male narcissism and female servitude. To her, the best part of the palace grounds was this thatch-roofed village called the Hamlet, a folly built for the queen where she could make believe she was just plain folk.

Never mind the overcast sky and threat of more rain. If Abby wanted to come here, fine. All he wanted was to get his mind off the disappointment of Durand's rejection. And nothing took his mind off other things like Abby Han.

As the two of them approached the Watermill Cottage, a cold wind rippled the nearby pond and wafted scents of rosemary, thyme, and dead lavender from last year's plantings. Eric stopped, turned up the collar of his leather jacket, and said to Abby, "I bet I know why you like this place. You picture Marie Antoinette cavorting with her serving maids. Pretending to be farm girls, milking cows, hoisting skirts and dancing jigs until they fall into the hay and have to loosen each others' bodices."

"Jealous?" Abby gave him a sly grin, her beautiful Chinese eyes laughing in that impish way that always charmed him. Slim and graceful, with chin-length black hair streaked red today, she came closer to the French concept of *félinité* than any other woman he'd ever met.

He returned the grin. "Only if there was a man-servant in there with them."

"Dreamer."

She had that right. He dreamed of *her*, a dream only partially fulfilled in reality. For besides being his best friend and the only other American at ISIPCA, Abby was his occasional lover.

Too bad she was also, as she put it, "mostly lesbian."

Taking her hand, he walked her along the path to the stone-and-timber cottage. "What's wrong with dreaming?"

"Mental jacking off," she said with the accent and bluntness of her native New York City.

"Gee, thanks for the image."

She leaned closer and pecked him on the cheek.

Just like her. Crude one minute, cuddly the next. Always toying with him, except when she wanted him in bed. He'd once asked her why, why him since she generally preferred women. She'd answered in a rare tone of true affection, "I like that you adore me. And you don't let up after my first orgasm."

The memory gave him an idea. At the front door of the cottage he jiggled the latch, knowing it would be locked. One evening, when he'd misplaced his keys, she'd opened his apartment for him with her Swiss Army knife. "Maybe you could pick the lock, and we could see if they've spread fresh hay."

"Durand must have put you in a frisky mood. So it went well with him this morning?"

Eric looked aside, then back at her. "About as well as ice water in the shower. I've been trying to reconstruct an old aphrodisiac, and he dumped all over it. Not just *my* effort but the whole idea of aphrodisiacs."

"You mean like rhino horn or tiger's balls?" She squinched up her face. "Frankly, I'm with him. I'd rather see those parts still attached to the animal."

"No. I'm talking about a perfume. And he wouldn't even

smell it. Not one damn sniff."

"My love, who needs an aphrodisiac?" Turning to face him, she drifted a hand down one thigh of his jeans and back up the other. Then she cupped him through the denim and smiled. "See?"

Unfortunately, another couple chose just that time to come strolling down the path in their direction. But it didn't stop Abby. She tugged at his zipper.

Indecision quickened his pulse. Should he let her continue and risk being seen? Abby would love that. And there were times he might, also. But this wasn't one of them, not here.

To stop her hand, he wrapped his arms around her waist and hugged her tightly. "Why don't we continue this behind the cottage."

"Because I'm only making a point." She pushed away and shot a glance around his shoulder as crunching footsteps on the gravel path announced the arrival of the other couple. *"Bonjour."*

"Bonjour," the couple sing-songed before turning to Eric's left to peer into the cottage's windows.

Irked that she'd just been teasing, Eric pulled up his zipper and steered Abby to the right, down the steps to where an old wooden waterwheel stood motionless in the sluice. The breeze down here seemed colder, the scents it carried dominated by the odor of duck droppings and the chlorophyll smell of algae growing at the pond's edge.

"It doesn't matter," he told her, "that some people get turned on easily. It's about the whole idea of perfumes. Attraction and romance. Only this one would go a step further and create sensations that inspired passion."

"Love Potion Number Nine?"

"I'm being serious."

"You're always serious. You should lighten up a little."

"This could make my reputation."

"More dreaming." She took hold of his hand. "In case you haven't noticed, good sex is in the mind. Granted, you can create a perfume that might enhance the mood. But if one person or the other doesn't want to get laid, it ain't gonna happen."

"Don't be so sure." According to the ancient texts Eric had found translated on the Internet, King Solomon had been reluctant to lie with the Queen of Sheba until her fragrance enchanted him. "This thing I'm working on, it started out partly as a whim and partly because the only specified ingredient was something I'd never heard of before."

"Oh, my God, there's something you never heard of? You must be mortal, after all."

Eric strained to control his temper. When she got like this, it reminded him of the French students who hated his guts. Normally he'd walk away, but he needed her to believe him.

"*As* I was saying, the only specified ingredient is the heartwood of a tree that grows on Socotra."

"Socotra?"

"A Yemeni island in the Gulf of Aden. It turns out ISIPCA has a sample of the wood, but they wouldn't let me use any of it. Too rare. Which pissed me off. So I—"

"Now I see." Abby flashed one of her "Aha" smiles. "Someone said 'no,' and you said, 'Just watch me.' That's so typical of you."

"Would you just listen for a second?" If she wasn't going to take his mind off Durand, the least she could do was stop interrupting. "What I have so far really works. At least on me."

"Sweetheart, I think you're succumbing to the power of your own suggestion." In a mocking tone, she said, "I want this stuff to turn me on. Oh my, look, it's turning me on."

"You're wrong." Was there no way he could convince her, short of giving her Balquees, which wasn't quite ready? Maybe her specialty. He should have thought of that before. Abby was, after all, the star pupil in ISIPCA's flavor curriculum. He switched to foods. "How about oysters, dark chocolate, saffron?"

"Give me a break. Have you ever gotten a hard-on eating oysters?"

"Okay, forget it." First Durand, now her. Why was everyone who counted so negative? Never mind. He'd prove them both wrong eventually. "Let's cash out of here and go to that bistro you like."

"You didn't have lunch with Durand?"

"He said he needed to hit the road for a hunting trip in the Pyrenees."

"Well, I'm not very hungry, but I'll have a glass of wine while you eat."

Wine. That gave him an idea. Instead of lunch, he could use the afternoon killing two birds with one stone. He'd show her that scents really can arouse and, in the process, he could try out some additional ingredients for Balquees. "Do you still have that birthday present I gave you? *Le Nez du Vin?*"

"Of course. I love it."

"Then let's go to your place."

"I want to blindfold you," Eric said in Abby's bedroom.

"Ooh, kinky." She gave him a soft kiss, then went to her dresser and removed a black silk scarf from the second drawer. "Will this do?"

"Nicely." Her apartment lent itself to dark, almost Gothic fantasies—two rooms in a 19th-century mansion with wooden shutters, plank floors, and bare stone showing through the plasterwork. Her furnishings were all black, right down to the sheets and bedspread. "Matches my personality," she'd told him. As did the bed itself, a four-poster in heavy oak, positioned like a sacrificial altar in the center of the room. But if she wanted kinky, it would have to wait until later.

He shed his jacket, then unbuttoned her wool coat and slid it from her shoulders. Beneath the coat she wore a cashmere sweater the same blood-red as a Ferrari. Her nipples stood out against the soft fabric. "God, you're beautiful."

She closed her eyes. "Say it again."

Abby, reared by a father who'd treated her like trash, didn't consider herself pretty. Eric never tired of trying to convince her otherwise. "You are beautiful."

As though the words were magic, she opened her eyes and smiled. "And now?"

"And now ..." Glancing around, he spotted *Le Nez du Vin*, The Nose of Wine, on a shelf of the bookcase in one corner. He walked over and pulled out the bright red box, roughly the size and weight of an encyclopedia volume.

"You were serious about a bunch of wine smells?" She gave him a very French pout. "I thought we were ..."

"You'll like it." He laid the box on her bed and flipped it open. Inside were fifty-four small bottles of scents common to wines. The collection was intended for connoisseurs who wanted to hone their appreciation of these subtleties, or impress their friends with how many they could detect. Several of the scents were different from what he had in the lab, and he'd judge from her response whether any of them might work well in Balquees.

When he looked back at her, Abby was gazing up at him with a "take me" expression, her eyes beckoning, her lips moist and slightly parted.

A ripple of desire thrilled him where it counted. In his palms, he could almost feel the perfect smoothness of her face, the silky softness of her hair.

But not yet. He needed to concentrate on Balquees, take advantage of this chance to flesh it out.

He turned Abby and tied the scarf around her head. As he did, he couldn't help inhaling the fragrance of her skin, like cream laced with a hint of violet, that uniquely Abby fragrance he loved. From behind her, he kissed her neck.

"Mmm," she cooed, "that's better."

He removed her boots and his own shoes and socks, leaving them both otherwise clothed. Then he climbed onto the bed with his back to the headboard and guided her into a position so that she sat between his legs with her back against his chest.

"Unless you're a contortionist," she said, "I don't know how we can do it like this."

"Just relax." Looking down at the box of scents, he selected peach for the fruit's resemblance to labia, a similarity many cultures associated with sex. He passed the bottle under her nose. "What do you smell?"

"Peaches."

He drew a fingertip across her mouth. "Peaches and lips."

"Is that supposed to be innuendo?"

Not if he had to tell her. But maybe something similar. He opened the bottle of apricot. "And this?"

"Apricots. Same innuendo. Eric, if I wanted a woman, I'd

have one."

Abby's nipples had become barely discernible under her sweater, the exact opposite of what he was trying to achieve. Frustrated, he surveyed the bottles of other fruit aromas, equivalent to top notes in perfumery. Various citruses and berries, apple, cherry, banana, quince. Prune! That was a possibility, darker and richer than the lighter fruits, closer to a perfume heart note. And this time he'd use a combination, instead of a single fragrance.

To the prune, he added blackcurrant and walnut for their earthiness. Holding the three bottles together, he passed them under her nose. "How about this?"

She sniffed, then sniffed again. "Prunes stewed in Armagnac. How did you do that?"

Another failure. With a sinking feeling, he wondered if he could actually do this, use food smells to arouse a woman whose specialty was food flavorings. But he had to try.

Sticking to heart notes, he selected butter for its warmth, peppercorns for their impression of soil, and cut hay for its slight similarity to the smell of semen.

When he waved them under her nose, her body stiffened for a second. Then she tilted her head up toward him. "Now you're being naughty. Where did you get that boy-girl smell?"

Beneath the sweater, her nipples were more prominent. Finally he was making progress.

He decided to keep the cut hay. The oud in Balquees contained a note that was even more similar to semen, closer to Bisquick dough or diluted bleach. But there was nothing like bleach in this collection, and the closest to dough was yeast. He chose the yeast to enhance the "boy" note and added truffle, a scent that reminded him of nuzzling between her legs.

When he waved the combination in front of her, Abby's toes curled. "How do you do that?"

"I'm just trying to conjure images in your head."

"You're doing a pretty good job of it."

She didn't have to tell him. Her heightened arousal was obvious in the sharp scent of apocrine perspiration coming through her slacks, a scent that was having the same effect on him.

But there was still the realm of perfume base notes. Shifting position so she wouldn't notice the bulge rising against her back, he kept the cut hay, replaced truffle with musk, and added dark chocolate. He held the four together under her nose.

Abby's stomach quaked. She grabbed the cord that tied the front of her slacks and started unlacing it. "Can we just have sex now?"

God, he wanted to. But there was one last thing he had to try. Fumbling with the bottles, he substituted truffle for the yeast.

One whiff of the combination and Abby ripped off her blindfold. She twisted to face him, her eyes ablaze.

As evening darkened her bedroom, Eric cradled Abby in his arms, her soft breath feathering his wrist. Dreamily he gazed at the teardrop-shaped birthmark below her left ear, the only "blemish" on her otherwise flawless skin. Usually she concealed it with makeup. But he'd told her he thought of it as nature's earring. And often, when she knew they were going to spend time together away from other people, she didn't bother hiding it. He was glad she hadn't hidden it today.

With a contented, "Mmm," she uncoiled from his embrace. "That was nice."

For him, more. All of her flavors still lingered on his tongue, her textures on his fingertips. The aromas of her body were so firmly embedded in his memory that he could recapture every moment of their lovemaking. And the events leading up to it.

Propping himself on an elbow, he said, "What's your opinion of aphrodisiacs now?"

"They're in the mind."

"What?" He sat upright, incredulous that she could say that. "I took you through a whole progression of fragrances and never touched you. And pretty soon you're tearing my clothes off."

She smiled benevolently. "I got hot for you at the palace. You blindfolded me. Nice touch, by the way. Then you put me between your legs. What was a girl to do?"

"You're saying the fragrances had no effect on you?" That hurt. Really hurt, physically in the middle of his chest.

Abby pushed herself up and sat back against the headboard. "You want me to say they helped? Okay, they helped. But they wouldn't have made me want you if I didn't already."

Eric swung his feet out of bed and stood up.

"Oh, great," she said. "What are you, angry at me?"

Yes! "No, just frustrated." And now more determined than ever to show her what a true aphrodisiac could do. When Balquees was ready, he'd prove— Wait a second. How could he have forgotten? "Before Durand left, he gave me four passes to a perfume launch in Paris this Friday, at the Panthéon. He can't attend, and wouldn't anyway. I'd like you to come with me."

Her eyes widened. "Which house?"

"Styx."

"Wow. They're big time. A new perfume from them should be sensational. Who are you giving the other passes to?"

"I'm thinking Diego and Marie-Claire." The only other students he considered friends. "I'd like all of you" ... *especially you* ... "to help me test this new perfume I'm working on."

"Your aphrodisiac, so-called?"

"Just wait." If he crafted it right, Balquees would turn his friends into the center of attention, completely eclipsing whatever Styx had to offer.

Chapter 3

In his one-room apartment Monday evening, Eric chopped a handful of dried shiitake mushrooms, scooped the chunks into his coffee mill, and crossed his fingers.

Of the many scents he'd tried on Abby, truffle had been the biggest surprise, until he realized it smelled vaguely anal. The great master, Jacques Guerlain, had famously said perfumes should smell like the "underside" of his mistress. And most good perfumes contained animalic base notes—ambergris from whale vomit, civet from the anal glands of an African cat, castoreum from abdominal glands of beavers, musk from the scent-marking glands of a Himalayan deer—all designed to emerge late in the evaporative sequence, as the evening culminated in sex.

For Balquees, Eric had chosen civet because the cat it came from would have been available to the Queen of Sheba. But if he could achieve the same impression with a plant product, it would be a noteworthy achievement in perfumery.

Fired by the idea, he'd raced from shop to shop in Versailles, buying every variety of mushroom he could find. But hours of subsequent experimentation produced nothing except a string of expletives and a wastebasket full of failures.

"Come on," he growled as he pressed the mill's button. The blades screamed like a dentist's drill.

After a minute or so, he released the button, removed the mill's lid, and sniffed. *Wow, potent.* The powdered shiitake gave off a dense, rich, animalic aroma much stronger than the essence of truffle. This was it.

And it was perfect for Balquees because mushrooms grew everywhere, even in those areas of the Arabian desert that were once part of Sheba. Recharged, Eric popped the cork from a bottle of Saint-Estèphe and poured himself a celebratory glass. "To the lowly mushroom."

Now came the question of whether to boil the powder, do a steam extraction, or make a cold infusion. That was a problem with ancient fragrances—you seldom knew for sure how the ingredients were prepared. But whatever method he chose, it should involve only water, since distillation in alcohol hadn't come into practice until the Middle Ages, thousands of years after the Queen of Sheba.

He rolled his lips in. He could go halfway and do an infusion in wine, as the ancient Romans sometimes did. Wine figured prominently in the Old Testament, so the queen's perfumers might have used it. And the alcohol in the wine would extract a somewhat different set of compounds from those released by water. But any wine, no matter what kind he chose, would impart its own aromas, a complication he didn't need if he were going to have Balquees ready in time for the Panthéon Friday night.

So, yes, best to stick with water.

Which still left the question of method. Eric dumped the powder out of his coffee mill onto a saucer. Boiling or steaming might destroy some of the mushroom's aromas. Cold infusion might not bring out enough. Settling on the Goldilocks solution, hot but not boiling, he was about to warm a pan of water when someone knocked at his door.

He opened it to find Diego Alvarez, dashing as ever in his signature black leather and beaming like a bullfighter who'd just won both ears and the tail.

"You finished your graduation project?" Eric asked hopefully.

Diego's smile wilted. "That is not so easy."

For Diego it never was. Although gifted with a fine nose, he had less imagination than most of the other students and more trouble predicting how different ingredients would smell when combined. Consequently, he tended to build his formulations by imitation or trial and error.

"Well, you still have a couple of weeks." Eric motioned him inside and poured him a glass of Saint-Estèphe. "If you brought it with you, maybe I can help."

"Perhaps tomorrow. You are free tonight? I will take you to hear some music."

"La Bodega?" Eric perked up immediately. Discounting the palace, the town of Versailles bored him, or *had* bored him until Diego took him to a nightclub called La Bodega and introduced him to flamenco. Eric found it mesmerizing. Like a radical perfume born of anguish, flamenco blended the seemingly disparate music of Gypsies, Jews, and Arabs—all persecuted under the Spanish Inquisition—into an art form so passionate it could wrench your heart and inflame your soul.

For Eric, an outsider all his life and never more so than at ISIPCA, the music and the dance struck a deep chord. "I'm always up for flamenco."

"Not tonight. Tonight we go to the cathedral."

"Cathedral?"

"You like organ music, yes?"

"Depends on the music," Eric said cautiously. "You talking Bach, Handel, Pachelbel?"

Diego shook his head. "A Frenchman named Grigny. "

"Never heard of him."

"So it will be new for both of us."

Red flag. In the two years Eric had known him, Diego had never expressed an interest in any organ except the one between his legs. What the twenty-four-year-old did like was women over fifty. "Would we happen to be meeting anyone else there?"

"Who knows?" Diego said with a shrug. "There will be people. We might meet them."

Jesus. "Why don't we talk about your perfume, instead?"

"Tomorrow." Diego glanced at his watch, then downed the remains of his glass. "Good wine. But we must go. The music begins at eight-thirty."

"Diego, there will always be women. Graduation comes only once."

"You hurt me, amigo. You like old churches, so I invite you to an old church. You like organ music, so I invite you to hear organ music."

"My ass. You're inviting me to meet a woman. For some reason I don't understand, and at a time when your project is far more urgent. *More* than urgent. It's crucial."

"But you will help me." He grinned, as if that settled the matter.

For Eric it did not. He wanted Diego to succeed, in part because the Spaniard had befriended him when most of the French students wished Eric dead, but mainly because Diego truly yearned to become a perfumer. Yet despite the countless hours Eric had spent tutoring him, the guy still wasn't qualified. *Mañana* would no longer cut it. "Listen to me. Either you knuckle down now, at the eleventh hour, or you're squandering two years at ISIPCA for nothing."

Diego squinted at him. "What is knuckle down? And why eleven o'clock?"

"What I'm trying to say is I can't help you forever." Eric planted himself on one of the two straight-backed chairs at his tiny dining table. His stomach grumbled a reminder that he hadn't eaten dinner yet, but he put hunger out of his mind. "Think ahead, will you? Graduating from here will get you an apprenticeship at a good house. But then what? What happens when you have to perform on your own?"

"Apprentice is like student. I will have two years, or three, to become better."

More *mañana*. Eric doubted Diego would last six months when his employer found out he couldn't create. Diego might cover his butt for a while by working late and churning through all sorts of mixtures until he came up with something approximating what the house wanted. But long hours in the lab took self-discipline. Not exactly Diego's strong suit.

"Look," Eric offered, "I know some things are tough for you. But maybe we could try a different approach. Principles, instead of specifics. For instance, there's a theory about odd versus even numbers of carbon atoms in fragrance compounds."

Diego's eyes glassed over, a reminder that organic chemistry ranked right down there with self-discipline in his list of strengths.

Then he sniffed the air. "What is that smell? Like shit."

Shit? Oh, the mushrooms. Suddenly it struck Eric that this was a great opportunity. Diego, reared on a horse farm outside Cadiz, was the only other student at ISIPCA who shared Eric's appreciation of barnyard odors, something that brought sneers of derision from most of the students. Eric didn't think the mushrooms smelled like animal feces, but if they did to Diego, then he'd have to find something else for Balquees. At the same time, helping Eric with a fragrance problem might stimulate Diego to concentrate on perfumery.

Eric got up from the chair and went into the alcove that passed as his kitchen. "Come here a second. I want your opinion." When Diego joined him, Eric said, "Close your eyes," then picked up some of the powdered shiitake, rubbed it between his fingers, and held his fingers under Diego's nose. "What does this remind you of?"

"Shit. I told you."

"What kind of shit?"

Diego sniffed again. "Not a bad kind. Cleaner. Like a woman's ... *ano?*"

"Anus." Eric cracked a smile. "That's what I thought, also."

Opening his eyes, Diego backed up a step, a dubious expression on his face. "Where did you put your finger to get that smell?"

Eric laughed. "Don't worry. It's just a mushroom." He pointed to the pale-brown powder.

"More of your experiments?"

"A good one, I think." No, a very good one, he was *certain.* And now was the perfect time to mention something else that might keep his friend centered on fragrances. "I've been meaning to tell you, I have passes for a perfume launch this Friday. At the Panthéon in Paris. Would you like to go with me?"

Diego ran his fingers down the lapels of his leather sport coat. "There will be beautiful women, yes?"

"Tons of them."

"Then I go with you happily."

"Excellent." Eric picked up the wine bottle. "Now let's pour another glass and get back to your project."

"You work too much. Day has enough hours for work. Night is for pleasure."

"Your graduation project—"

"Tomorrow, amigo. We are late for the cathedral."

You win some, you lose some. Bumper-sticker philosophy, but it was the best Eric could muster as he matched strides with Diego down Rue du Parc de Cagny. He could cite Diego's charm and enthusiasm, but the bald truth was that he feared alienating one of the few friends he had at ISIPCA. Still, Eric felt guilty for caving. Guilty, irritated, and hungry.

He resolved to get this over with as fast as possible. A polite "Hello, nice to meet you," and he would bow out, grab a quick meal, and get back to working on Balquees.

Working on Balquees. Eric slowed his pace. Other people were going out while he preferred to stay home and grind mushrooms in his coffee mill? Had he become that much of a nerd? Next thing you knew, he'd be wearing a pocket protector for his pen and a "Kick me" sticker on his back.

"Something is wrong, amigo?"

Glancing up, Eric saw Diego several steps ahead of him. "How would I look with black-rimmed glasses?"

"You need glasses?"

"I hope not." Truth be told, he would have gone readily to La Bodega. "Come on."

At the intersection with Boulevard de la Reine, he and Diego caught a cab to the Cathédrale Saint-Louis de Versailles.

By European standards, the cathedral looked dull and boxy, emblematic of the town. It did, however, boast two pipe organs. And the notice outside announced that tonight's performance would be played on the *Grand Orgue*.

"You will like this," Diego said. "The *organista* is exceptional."

Organista? So the player was a woman. Eric looked again at the notice. Lucie Boutin. "Is she the one?"

"Exquisite. You will see."

Eric bit his lip. Quickly saying hello to a lady in the audience was one thing, but waiting to meet the performer was a different matter altogether. Church concerts usually took an hour or two. "Diego, this is more than I bargained for. I can't wait for her to finish playing. I'm famished."

"But I told you we will hear the music. You agreed." Diego looked crestfallen.

Maybe a compromise. "How about we listen to some of it, then go grab a bite to eat and come back before she finishes. Or *you* could stay, and I could go and come back."

"Amigo."

"Okay, okay." Eric looked around, searching for a shop that might at least sell candy bars. Nothing.

"Come, we are late."

Inside, an audience of perhaps two dozen people sat in silence on wooden chairs. Typical of French cathedrals, the place smelled of limestone and candle wax and the incense used in a thousand masses. On a more upbeat note, Eric considered recreating this combination to take home as a reminder of the happy hours he'd spent spelunking through some of the oldest churches in Paris.

"Let's sit there." Diego walked to the front row of chairs, took an aisle seat, and twisted around to face the big pipe organ ensconced on a broadly arched balcony above the front doors.

Eric had to admit it was an impressive instrument. Nearly a hundred visible pipes, some of them two stories high, stood majestically in roundels and rows set into an altar-like cabinet of dark wood that was carved with angels and topped by a huge clock.

The clock read 8:40. If he got out of here before ten o'clock, he might find a cafe still open. Might but probably not, since Versailles was basically a bedroom community that rolled up its sidewalks when it deemed respectable folks should be home with their families. Kick me.

Resolved to enjoy the music, Eric hooked an arm over the chair back and waited.

At 8:46, a woman walked out on the balcony in front of the organ. Her long black skirt and white blouse buttoned to the neck suggested prim propriety. Her wild mane of silvery hair suggested otherwise.

"Magnificent," Diego whispered, his eyes soulfully admiring.

Without preamble, she disappeared behind the winged coat of arms in the center of the balcony. For several moments, there was dead silence. Then the whole church resounded with the opening notes of a fugue.

The first measures reminded Eric of Toccata and Fugue in D Minor. But the piece quickly degenerated into something he found musically muddy, as though the composer wanted most of the keys and half of the pedals all pressed at once.

The saving grace was the organist who, like a medic delivering frantic CPR, played with a ferocity that kept the fugue alive through sheer force of will.

Face glowing, Diego turned to him. "Such fire."

Like all cathedral organs, this one had a mirror. It hung just below one of the roundels, angled so that the organist could observe the priest and coordinate with him during mass. Eric peered up at it and caught brief flashes of Lucie Boutin's face as she attacked the keyboards. Fiery, indeed.

"She has a passion for her work," Eric said. "You could learn something from that."

"I already have the passion."

Feeling his passion rise again, Diego turned onto his side in Lucie's bed and crushed a handful of her hair to his face. In his mind, he relived how skillful she was, her every movement polished, refined by the kind of experience younger women simply did not possess. He listened to her shallow breathing and pondered whether to wake her, whether to satisfy his own eagerness for more or let her slumber amid dreams of the hours they'd already spent together since the applause following her recital.

A hard decision. But she looked so serene he didn't have the heart to disturb her. Let her sleep. In the morning, he would rouse her the way she seemed to like most. The way he would now forever associate with Eric's mushrooms.

He rolled onto his back. The sky outside her windows was black. As dark, he conceded, as his own prospects in the world of perfumes.

He'd been depressed about it for months, and Eric tonight had only made things worse. Fortunately, thanks to the teachings of a Japanese widow he'd met on Majorca, Diego could compartmentalize his emotions, shut them away in separate drawers where they would not interfere with one another. Without that ability, he might have sunk to the bottom of the well and been unable to perform for this luscious lady lying beside him.

He looked at her contented face, then turned his gaze to the small chandelier hanging from her ceiling. It glowed dimly on the setting she'd chosen in lieu of wasting time to light candles.

Wasting time. Eric thought he, Diego, wasted too much of it, that he didn't take his studies seriously. But he was wrong. Blessed from birth with God-given abilities, Eric simply could not comprehend how things that came easily to him could be so difficult for others.

Diego had read half the books in ISIPCA's library, spent unknown hours in the lab, beyond the hours he spent with Eric. Last August, when everyone else was on holiday, he'd practically camped out in the school's collection of raw ingredients. It was not for lack of trying that he still had trouble grasping everything he needed to know.

He simply was not in Eric's league. No one was.

Still, the two of them had grown close, closer than Diego felt with any of the other students. Like tonight. When he needed to share his admiration for Lucie, he knew he could trust Eric to appreciate her for herself and accept Diego's attraction to her without muttering some snide comment about … what was the American expression? Cougar hunting.

As if responding to his thoughts, Lucie opened her eyes. "You're still awake?"

He leaned over and kissed her, grateful that he spoke French even better than English.

"What time is it?" she asked.

"Middle of the night." He gazed at her face, pleased that what little makeup she'd worn for the recital had since rubbed off. Its absence revealed the natural beauty of her eyes and skin, the charming little lines that spoke of a happy life filled with smiling.

She favored him now with one of her piquant smiles. "Are

you tired?"

"Not at all." He slid a hand down her thigh. "You?"

"Not anymore."

Chapter 4

In ISIPCA's library, the least trafficked room at the institute, Eric sat in a corner and stared at the wall. He wasn't yet satisfied with Balquees, and his test at the Panthéon was fast approaching.

He chewed the cuticle of his thumb. While shiitake nicely rounded out his list of ingredients, he still had to refine the proportions. Which he tried to do by tuning out the tap-tapping of the librarian at her keyboard as he mentally mixed varying percentages and assessed the results.

He wanted Balquees to be unisex, as appealing to men as to women. He'd picked himself as a typical male, and even his early formulations worked like gangbusters on him. But his model for the woman had been Abby, a poor choice since lesbians were usually attracted to the same female odors as men were.

He needed to imagine a more average, heterosexual woman and tweak the formula for her.

Maybe Lucie Boutin, the organist. In her late fifties, Eric estimated, she'd struck him as the kind of woman who spent her vacations scuba diving in the Caribbean or volunteering on archaeological digs in North Africa. She had that look—intrepid, feisty, hungry for new experiences—that seemed to characterize the women frequently profiled on French television. In a word, a pistol.

But was she too much of a pistol? With those daring eyes, she could probably snare any man she wanted, regardless of whether she wore an enticing perfume.

"Eric," a female voice called.

Jolted back to the library, he turned to see Marie-Claire Benoit rounding a display rack of magazines. Plumpish, mousy, and one of the youngest pupils, she had few friends at the institute. But Eric liked her. Her timidity concealed huge talent. Plus her family's perfume business in Grasse assured her future, a fact he truly loved for the envy it sparked among the snotty elite in ISIPCA's student body.

"I need your help." She pulled up a wood-laminate chair like the one he sat on, then unscrewed the cap of a brown glass vial and handed him a *mouillette*. "Does this have too much clove?"

Although he'd holed up here to avoid distractions, he could always make time to help someone with a fragrance. He dipped the *mouillette*, gave it a few quick waves in the air, and sniffed. She hadn't actually used clove oil. "You used eugenol."

"To remind about *Peau d'Espágne*. The *origine*."

Clearly she meant the origin of French perfumery. Grasse, where it all began, first achieved fame in the early 1800s for the quality of its leather, used mainly to make gloves. To soften the leather and counteract the foul stink of the urine-rich tanning baths, they dumped basketfuls of flowers and cloves into the vats. The result, much prized among cultured society of the day, was *Peau d'Espágne*, Skin of Spain.

But eugenol was a distillate fraction that smelled more strongly of clove than clove itself. Eric handed back the vial, happy the fix had come to him quickly. "If you use clove oil and cut back to about half the percentage, you'll bring out the other ingredients and should get the result you want. Which, by the way, is a lovely fragrance. Your graduation project?"

"Yes. And thank you. I will try what you say."

Her ready agreement told him she'd already been thinking along the lines of his recommendation. He should have known. With her lack of self-confidence, what she'd really wanted was confirmation. Then it dawned on him. Marie-Claire, shy and conservative, was precisely the woman he should target with Balquees. If it worked on her—and *for* her, since it should affect the wearer, as well as the person close enough to smell it—it would work on anyone.

He ran some adjustments through his head and decided five percent more oud and five percent less frankincense might just do the trick.

"You are a good friend," she said.

"And so are you." She'd just given him both the woman he needed to imagine and his final formulation. As she rose to leave, Eric stood also. "Wait a minute. There's something I wanted to ask you. Styx is launching a perfume in Paris this Friday. I have some passes, and I'd like you to go with me."

"Styx?" She scrunched up her nose. "Their products smell like a train station."

He laughed. "A lot of them, yes. But I'm not interested in their products. I want to go there to try out something I've been working on. An aphrodisiac. You could help me."

"Aphrodisiac?" She scowled at him.

"It's nothing serious," he said, hoping the idea didn't offend her strict Catholicism. "Just something I've been toying with."

"Aphrodisiac is ... imagination. By men who are ugly, or old." Her expression softened. "Not for you."

From the look on her face, he got the awkward sense that she might still harbor a crush on him. Fortunately, he knew how to redirect her attention. "Diego is going."

"He is?"

"Diego, Abby, me. And you?"

She touched the gold crucifix hanging from her neck. "I am not sure. I will talk to him tonight."

"You two are going out?" Eric realized his eyebrows had shot up and quickly lowered them.

"I make dinner for him," she said with an uncharacteristically puckish smile. "A man's heart is in his stomach, yes?"

Not Diego's, but Eric wasn't about to rain on her parade. "So the cooks would have you believe."

"Ah," she exclaimed, "your father is a cook. A chef *cordon bleu.* You can help me choose the food."

Maybe he should have kept his mouth shut. "I don't know."

"But you do. You know Diego very well." She grasped Eric's hand. "It will not take long. A few minutes in the market."

More like a few hours, given Marie-Claire's penchant for perfection. On the other hand, perfection drove him, as well. The curse of Virgos.

The tap-tapping of the librarian broke into his consciousness again, along with the library's collective aroma of book bindings, industrial carpet, and glossy magazine covers. He'd finished here, and she *was* a friend. "Okay, let's go to the market."

As he reached for his jacket, he realized he was still holding the *mouillette* he'd dipped in her perfume. He was about to toss it into a nearby wastebasket when another thought occurred to him. "Grasse is famous for its lavender. So while you're changing to clove oil, why not switch to real lavender, also? Instead of the synthetic you've used."

"True lavender is much more expensive."

About five times as expensive, which was why eighty percent of perfumes that contained "lavender" actually contained a man-made facsimile. "But the judges will be able to tell the difference. Remember, your project is only to graduate. If you want to make it commercially, you can always go back to the synthetic."

A big smile brightened her face. "Eric, I think sometimes you are French."

In late summer, the Marché Notre Dame could be an enticing place, full of fruit and vegetables still dewy from the fields, fish caught that morning, artisanal cheeses, a kaleidoscope of temptations that excited the nose and inspired heavenly creations. But now, on a bleak afternoon in early April, the farmers market of Versailles looked dispirited. Only a handful of hardy souls manned the clothing stalls outside, and the food stalls inside—at least the vegetable stands—gave little promise of finding anything truly fresh.

Still, Eric figured he and Marie-Claire could lay their hands on a few things that would appeal to Diego. The guy, after all, was Spanish, a meat and seafood lover who would be happy with roasted potatoes and grilled onions on the side. But Eric couldn't help feeling awkward in the knowledge that, whatever they chose, the evening was going to turn out disappointing for Marie-Claire. Despite her pining for Diego, she came nowhere close to the kind of woman who lit Diego's fire.

On the other hand, none of this was Eric's business, and Diego had, in fact, accepted her invitation.

Turning to Marie-Claire, Eric asked, "What did you have in mind for the main course?"

"*Fruits de mer?*"

Fruit of the sea. A mélange of shellfish, mostly raw and including little sea snails that you dug out of their shells with a pin. Obviously she imagined a protracted meal. But raw seafood wasn't Diego's style.

"I think he'd prefer something cooked." Eric walked her to a fishmonger. "How about octopus sautéed in its own ink and served over rice? The Spanish call it *pulpo en su tinta.* You could do the rice in butter and saffron for a special touch."

"What is ink?"

"*Encre.*"

Marie-Claire's face twisted into a grimace. "He likes *encre?*"

"It's good. You get whole octopus and—"

"*Non!*"

Oh-kay. "Maybe poached sole in white wine, perhaps with chanterelles." He bent over some filets of sole on ice, sniffed, and detected no fishy odor. "These are fresh."

"Not sole, Eric It must be special."

"Flounder? That one looks good."

The fishmonger, a thickset man who apparently understood English, lifted the flounder by its tail and raised the head with his other hand.

"Not fish," she cried. "Special."

An hour later when they walked outside, Eric had a headache. Marie-Claire had a smile and a plastic bag filled with paper-wrapped portions of various shellfish for *fruits de mer.*

⌇

Marie-Claire hummed along as her home stereo belted out "La Marseillaise." At the chorus, she sang, "To arms, citizens. Form your battalions. Let's march, let's march." Unable to reach the high notes in the next line, she resorted to humming again. The national anthem always roused her, and she would play it tonight for Diego when she brought out the three-tiered presentation of pure, unadulterated fruit of the sea.

Carefully, she positioned two pearl-handled pins, gifts from her mother, in the crushed ice on the top tier where the raw periwinkles and whelks waited to be plucked from their shells. Fresh from French waters, untainted by foreign pollution.

Foreign pollution was the scourge of France. She glanced at her autographed photo of Jean-Marie Le Pen, the greatest man since Charles De Gaulle and the only political force who could save France from the toxic influx of her former colonies.

Of course, she wouldn't go quite so far as Le Pen, who advocated banishing all foreigners. Diego, after all, was Catholic and light-skinned and came from an old European family like her own. With her to guide him, he would fit right in.

A rush of heat suffused her cheeks. Would he kiss her tonight? She touched a paper towel to her mouth, in case she'd put on too much lip gloss. Her mother said men didn't like being smeared with lip gloss.

The clock showed only ten minutes remaining before Diego was supposed to arrive.

With nervous fingers, Marie-Claire quickly spooned crushed ice from the bag onto the second tier and spread it out evenly. Their first course, a Lyonnaise salad with bacon and poached egg, sat on her countertop ready for the eggs to be cooked. The crème brûlée, in large scallop shells, lay covered with cheesecloth and needed only a final application of sugar and browning with a torch to become the perfect dessert.

Three courses, delicious but not so filling that Diego would feel lethargic afterwards. The way to a man's heart.

But was that sufficient? He was used to sophisticated women, women with experience. Well, the new dress she wore was sophisticated enough to appear in *Vogue*. From the most stylish shop in Versailles, it flattered her nicely, not too tight in the wrong places, its décolletage daring but not lewd. As to experience, she'd read that all men wanted virgins. She could play on that, right up to their wedding night.

A drip of perspiration ran down her underarm. "Bad word!" she said, the foulest language she ever allowed herself. She snatched another paper towel from the roll and vigorously rubbed both armpits. *Please, God, do not let that happen when Diego is here.*

After crossing herself, she felt better and began arranging half-shell oysters on the second tier, leaving space for a ramekin of sauce mignonette made from vinegar, shallots, and cracked pepper. Simple and pure and as French as Le Pen.

Never mind that Diego was Spanish. Her parents would approve of him. What more could they ask for than another perfumer in the family? A daughter and son-in-law who would carry on the tradition, perpetuate the family's name and reputation. And preserve the financial health of the company.

God knew, the boutique fragrance business was difficult. Competition from the big houses left independent manufacturers only two roads to survival. Make cheap junk for the masses, including the sticky-sweet stuff those shifty Arabs seemed to love. She stabbed a knife into the second bag of ice. Or create perfumes so extraordinary that the world came to you.

Her family took the high road, and always had. For a hundred years, they had produced superior perfumes on the estate founded by her great-grandfather, an estate not unlike a winery and just as beautiful. Although they'd sold off most of their acreage to finance modernization of the laboratories and factory, the chateau in Grasse still commanded magnificent views of the flower fields and surrounding hills.

And her father had been inspired to carve out an even higher niche, custom perfumes for the wealthy. Actors and actresses, political figures, potentates she'd never heard of who spent half their time on yachts moored in Monaco—they came to him for personalized scents. At ten thousand euros apiece.

What if she asked Diego to create a perfume just for her? What would he come up with? Something with Bulgarian rose, ylang-ylang, possibly jasmine or lily of the valley. In the base note, he would definitely include oak moss and musk. Heavy on the musk. A little tingle thrilled her loins. Musk always got to her. Musk and castoreum. He'd use castoreum, also.

Perhaps tonight, if she had the nerve, she would ask him. But first, the delights of the palate, accompanied by her favorite recordings of Charles Aznavour. Nobody sang love songs the way he did. Then she and Diego would dance, slowly, their arms around each other.

Oh, my God, look at the time. He'd be here any second.

In a rush, she covered the bottom tier with crushed ice, then ringed it with a wreath of steamed crab claws that culminated in two boiled lobster tails.

All that remained was the shallow dish of mustard-mayonnaise she'd prepared for the lobster. She lifted it from the countertop, heard a knock, and jerked her head toward the door. As she did, the dish slipped from her fingers and crashed to the floor. Jumping back, she saw a long smear of mustard-mayonnaise running down the front of her brand-new dress.

"Bad word, BAD WORD!"

Electrified with panic, she dashed to the door, called out, "One minute," then ran into her bedroom to change clothes. *What to wear? What to wear?* She grabbed up her bedside statue of the Virgin. "Blessed Mother, please help me. In Christ's name, I beseech you."

Chapter 5

On Friday night, the first warm evening of the year, Eric stood with Abby and Marie-Claire at the edge of the crowd watching the glitterati of Paris file into the Panthéon.

It was like the Oscars meets the Grammys, denizens of the society pages in low-cut gowns and tuxedos mixing with anorexics of indeterminate gender in fishnet tops, silver jeans, and knee-high boots. All pretended not to pose as they paraded through a double phalanx of flashing cameras into the floodlit sepulcher.

In keeping with their bad-boy image, the gurus of couture at Styx had chosen France's grandest mausoleum as the venue for launching their latest perfume. Tomb and perfume, death and sex, a stroke of marketing genius Eric couldn't help but admire. On top of that lay the mystery of how they'd managed to rent the resting place of such national heroes as Voltaire, Victor Hugo, and Madame Curie. There were only two possible answers: someone high in the government got paid or laid. All told, it was a cocktail of decadence guaranteed to attract even the most jaded. And the jaded were Eric's target.

They were also his judge and jury. Their verdict—how they reacted to Balquees, if they reacted at all—would tell him whether he'd created a ticket to stardom or merely concocted a novelty. He swallowed to quell the nervousness in his stomach. He'd set his sights on a tough audience.

He could smell them individually as they emerged from their

limousines. Creed, Patou, some kind of Jordache shit. The few good ones he couldn't identify were almost certainly custom-made. A heady, almost dizzying array of—

Not almost. Eric's vision went watery. Whooshing sounds filled his ears. Suddenly unbalanced, as though he'd lost his footing on the cobblestones, he recognized the onset of the "storm."

Normally he could cope with the thousands of smells most people never noticed in their daily lives. But anxiety sometimes crashed his defenses, plunging him into a maelstrom of olfactory overload. Quickly he buried his nose in the crook of his elbow, trying to shut down the squall by inhaling only the clean, soft aroma of his cotton shirt.

It helped. After a few moments, he felt less disoriented. His vision cleared. The rushing wind in his ears settled down. Still, his hands felt clammy.

"Are you okay?" Abby asked.

Eric lowered his arm and took a cautious breath. Better. Myriad odors still came to him—a crusty baguette, spearmint toothpaste on somebody's breath, a new book, pavement still damp from the late-afternoon rain—but he could lump them together now and tune them out like so much background noise. "I'm fine."

"Bullshit. You're pale."

"Just nerves."

"Eric," Marie-Claire whined behind him, "we are not properly dressed. Look at those beautiful gowns."

Like Abby and himself, she wore black slacks and shirt, the "in" uniform of twenty-somethings in Paris and, by extension, of the students at ISIPCA. A faint scent of rust, her particular nuance of it, told him she had her period. It explained her lifeless hair and doughy complexion and made her an even better test of Balquees tonight than Eric had hoped.

"We'll be fine," he said, trying to assure himself as much as her. "Look, there's a girl in black leather pants and halter top." Eric glanced around. "Speaking of black leather, where's Diego?"

"Probably bonking some matron in a wheelchair." A thin smile punctuated the wisecrack Abby had obviously directed at Marie-Claire.

Marie-Claire glowered. "At least Satan did not make him a pervert."

Wishing they would just drop it, Eric stepped back from the sparring women. It was several months since Marie-Claire had given up bombarding Abby with tracts on sins of the flesh. But Abby still retaliated with occasional gibes, and no truce between them seemed to last long. The sooner Diego got here, the sooner they could all go inside and get on with the crucial test.

Eric peered down Rue Soufflot toward the distant Eiffel Tower, lit up like a Christmas tree against an indigo sky. Police barriers at the intersection with Rue Saint Jacques blocked all traffic, except limousines, from entering the Panthéon's square. But pedestrians could get through. He scanned those approaching from the intersection. No Diego. After all the help Eric had given him, late nights in the lab, adjustments to his perfume formulas, damn near writing some of the formulas for him, the least Diego might do was show up on time.

Eric gripped the vial of Balquees in his pocket. He and the two women had come in from Versailles by train this evening. But Diego had said he would already be in Paris and would meet up with them at the Panthéon. So where the hell was he?

"Diego," Marie-Claire gushed.

Eric whipped around to see the tall Spaniard grinning as though fresh from conquest. "You're late."

"Not so late." Diego cocked his head toward the beautiful people still promenading past shouting paparazzi.

No time to argue. Eric handed the vial to Abby and addressed them all. "This is water-based. So put a line of it down each side of your neck and wait a minute for it to dry."

While they applied his fragrance, Eric dealt out the engraved invitations Durand had given him.

"I don't know how you do it," Diego said. "Four invitations. You must be sleeping with the old man."

"I wish you do not talk like that," Marie-Claire scolded gently.

Abby waved the tip of her index finger under her nose. "I like it already. What's in it?"

"Is it one of your reconstructions?" Diego asked. "The fragrance Cleopatra put on her sails to meet Marcus Antonius?"

Eric's mind shot back to the evening of the organ concert. Had he forgotten to tell Diego what this was all about? He knew he'd told the women. "It's an aphrodisiac, I hope."

"*Afrodiasaco?*" Diego grabbed back the vial from Marie-Claire and drew a few more lines of the fragrance down either side of his neck. "Does it work?"

"Of course not," Marie-Claire snapped with a pout. "Why you would ask it?"

Apparently she and Diego held differing views of their relationship after the dinner she'd prepared for him three nights ago. To Eric, Diego had shrugged it off as a so-so evening from which he'd bailed when Marie-Claire wanted to dance. She, on the other hand, seemed to feel she had won Diego's heart. This would not end well. But it also, by God, would not come to a head tonight. Too much was at stake. Eric snatched back the vial and shoved it in his pocket.

"Aren't you going to wear any?" Abby asked.

"I need to observe."

"Ever the dispassionate scientist."

Ignoring her gibe, he looked back at the crowd. The last of the celebrities were climbing the steps. Within the Panthéon's chained forecourt, chauffeurs had parked their limos and were gathering in groups, lighting cigarettes. As police pulled back their barricades, the air filled with the acrid stink of diesel exhaust, the sound of accelerating engines, and the honks of drivers taking offense at one thing or another. April in Paris.

"Okay, let's go." Eric led his friends up the steps to the entrance where two buzz-cut bruisers stuffed into tuxedos scrutinized all four invitations before motioning them through.

Inside, the Panthéon glowed with palatial opulence, a surprising contrast to its blocky, almost windowless exterior. Feeling as jittery as an understudy about to finally go on stage, Eric paused to absorb the elegant setting. A forest of Corinthian columns supported elaborate cornices beneath neoclassical vaults and arches. Monumental statuary and brilliant mosaics of angels and shepherds hinted at the building's ecclesiastical role before becoming a tribute to intellectual reason. The floor, what he could see of it beneath the Prada and Bally heels, was a gleaming expanse of black and white marble in geometric patterns.

Even with his eyes closed, he would have known he was in France. The fragrance cloud bore all the floral notes characteristic of French preference. Except one. Eric sniffed again, confirmed the "fresh, clean" notes favored by Americans, and turned to his left where, a few people away, a tall, gray-haired man in tuxedo and cowboy boots stood with his arm around a Botox blonde.

Other odors swirled in thin currents through the cloud. Hairspray, self-tanning lotion, leather, mink overprinted with cedar wood from the storage closet, marijuana smoke.

From somewhere came techno music, tactfully turned down to about the same level as the hubbub of voices. Later on, after the early-to-bed folks had cashed out, the DJ, wherever he was, would probably crank up the volume to a level that damaged brain cells. Then things would get fun.

In the meantime, below the central rotunda where Foucault first demonstrated his famous pendulum, the marketers at Styx had arrayed six women in filmy negligees and six bare-chested Adonises, each with a spray bottle of Bête Noire, the star of tonight's show.

"What now?" Abby asked.

Eric refocused. "The last train to Versailles is at midnight. Until then, just circulate and enjoy yourselves."

As his three friends fanned out into the crowd, Eric waited a moment then headed after Diego and snatched him by the shoulder. "Do me a favor, would you? Stay out of Marie-Claire's sight."

"Amigo, you do not have to tell me."

Relieved, Eric plucked a glass of champagne from the tray of a passing waiter. Veuve Clicquot, his palate told him. The nutty undertone of black grapes sparkled in his mouth, and the fizz soothed his stomach.

After a second swallow, he worked his way closer to the negligees and Adonises until he could definitely pick out the Bête Noire they were spraying. His first impression was of acid bubbling on metal. It didn't quite sting the nose, but you wouldn't want to wear too much. In a way, Eric liked it, the way he might like the smell of an arc-welding shop. It could use some softening for this crowd, but the youth market would probably swarm all over it. He'd pick up a sample on his way out.

From another passing tray he snagged an apple slice topped with foie gras. As the buttery liver melted in his mouth, he munched the apple and retreated up a short flight of stairs at one side to search for his friends. In seconds, he spotted Diego surrounded by—*my God*—five women. With the dark eyes and erotic mystique of a matador, Diego hardly needed a fragrance to attract females. But five at once had to be a record. If Balquees was the reason, then it worked on women, as well as men. Or at least, as well as on himself. Eric felt his lips draw into a grin. What would Durand say to that?

Of course, Diego was only chatting so far. But not bad for starters.

So, where was the real test? Eric surveyed the assembly for Marie-Claire. If Balquees attracted men to *her*, especially men from this crowd, he'd have an honest-to-God triumph. And Marie-Claire might gain the self-confidence to become more outgoing. Something she'd surely need if she were going to find a soul mate truer than Diego.

There she was, below him to the right, not thirty feet away, talking with a man and woman of the society set. The guy wore a tuxedo with embroidered lapels, the woman a black gown that plunged to her navel. Marie-Claire, apparently no longer discomfited at being underdressed, held a half-empty champagne flute and seemed to be listening to the man. Suddenly she laughed.

Pleased she was enjoying herself, although less pleased than if she were hitting it off with an unattached fellow, Eric scanned the sea of people for Abby. Failing to spot her, he started over, searching sector by sector.

Not there. Not there. *Whoa, what was this?*

Below him, Marie-Claire backed up slowly, her wrist in the grasp of the woman with the plunging neckline. The woman wore a cajoling expression, as did her escort in the embroidered lapels. Were both of them after her?

An impulse to intervene tightened Eric's muscles. But this was too fascinating. Besides, Marie-Claire knew how to fend off unwanted advances. He'd once seen her wilt an Arab fellow with a few scathing words.

She backed into another man, this one dressed like Slash in concert, minus the funky top hat. The guy glanced over his shoulder, returned his attention to the people he'd been speaking with, then paused and broke off his conversation. After a nod to the couple pursuing her, he leaned close to Marie-Claire's ear. She stiffened, her mouth agape at whatever he'd said. Clutching the gold cross at her neck, she looked around like a trapped animal, then bolted toward the exit.

Damn. Eric rushed after her, sickened that her obvious discomfort was most likely his fault. He caught up to her in the foyer and grabbed her arm. "Marie-Claire, stop."

She spun around to face him, anger flaring in her eyes. "What is this? Why did you make it?"

"I just wanted to see if it would attract people. I didn't mean to embarrass you."

She rubbed her hands down the sides of her neck as though fire ants were attacking her. "It is of Satan."

"No, it's not. It comes from Solomon and Sheba. In the Bible."

"Blasphème!"

"Honestly. It's in the early Christian writings of Ethiopia. I can show you."

Marie-Claire gasped at something behind him.

Eric turned to see the couple who'd been pursuing her. The woman wore Angel, its saccharine sweetness somehow appropriate to the cloying way she'd hung onto Marie-Claire's wrist. Her escort, despite his suave demeanor, reeked like a goat of genital sweat.

"Excusez-moi," the man said, trying to shoulder Eric aside.

Eric blocked him. "You're excused."

The man stared blankly, evidently failing to translate "excused" as "dismissed."

To clarify for the boorish bastard, Eric put his hand in the small of Marie-Claire's back and steered her out into the cool night air.

Half of him felt as effervescent as the champagne. Balquees worked for his toughest subject. But the other half winced with guilt that its effects had backfired. Maybe he shouldn't have gambled on someone so conservative, especially when she was one of his very few friends.

He needed to make peace with her, and his experiment could wait until he did. From the top of the steps, he pointed at the cafés just the other side of Rue Saint Jacques. "Come on, I'll buy you some coffee."

"No. I am leaving."

"Please, can you just let me explain?"

"You explain nothing." She clutched his hands, her eyes fierce. "The only thing you do is make a promise. Before God."

"What promise?"

"This abomination. You destroy it."

Chapter 6

Eric slumped in his seat on the railcar's upper level, waiting for the train to depart. Alone up here, he felt like the only person left on earth. The car's bright lights hurt his eyes. His reflection, between finger and hair smudges on the window, looked worn-out. Odors from earlier travelers—Polish sausage, tired feet—fouled his nostrils. He felt terrible about Marie-Claire, and despite searching for an hour in the Panthéon after she left, he'd been unable to locate Abby or Diego before it was time to return to Versailles. Had the experiment cost him all his friends?

At the sound of footsteps behind him, he turned and saw Abby topping the stairs.

"There you are," she exclaimed, sounding out of breath. She crabbed past his knees and flopped down in the window seat next to him. "You've gotta give me more of that stuff. It's fantastic!"

Eric sat up straight. "Tell me."

Abby hugged herself.

"If you're going to relive it, relive it for me," he insisted, his heart suddenly pounding. "I need some good news."

She turned to face him. "I'll tell you only that you've seen her in films. She's married and has a young daughter. But childbearing hasn't hurt her figure. She's absolutely stunning."

"And …?"

Abby cracked a smile. "We desecrated that church next to the Panthéon."

St. Etienne-du-Mont, one of his favorites in the Latin Quarter. Eric couldn't help picturing them, Abby probably naked, the actress with the bodice and hem of her gown both bunched at her waist, the cold stone floor they lay on, the thrilling fear of getting caught. A tingle stirred him. Was it the sexual image or the Balquees still clinging to Abby?

"I was her first woman. But you never would have known it. And get this. Between orgasms, when we were kissing, she couldn't keep her nose out of my neck." Abby fixed him with her gaze. "Eric, that stuff is a goldmine."

A rush of triumph coursed through him, energizing his whole body. "Shall I take that as a reversal of your opinion about aphrodisiacs?"

"Oh, baby." She kissed him hard. "I am definitely reversed."

And he was definitely getting turned on.

With a jolt, the train pulled out of St. Michel-Notre Dame station.

Eric heard a hollow thunk and saw an empty Fanta can had rolled against a seat leg across the aisle. He concentrated on the orange-and-blue logo, trying to push thoughts of sex out of his head. As the train accelerated, the can rotated on the floor, elected which way to go, and rolled past.

Back to the experiment. "Any idea what became of Diego?"

"Are you kidding? I was in church." She closed her eyes. "Worshipping at the altar of a goddess."

That imagery again. Eric shoved it aside. "Marie-Claire's experience wasn't so religious." He related what happened.

"She's a virgin. By choice, for God's sake. What did you expect?"

"I feel like I used her."

"Eric, we're all grown-ups. We knew we were there to help you test a new formula."

A formula he was having real trouble ignoring. He crossed his legs to hide the evidence of his arousal. "All that lusty attention she got really bothered her."

"Give me a break. Perfume is about sex. It's always been about sex. You know that as well as I do. And so does she."

"Yeah, but this hits you pretty hard."

"Like a freight train," Abby said with a grin. "And maybe that's what a frustrated virgin needs. Hell, she bombed out with you, and from what Diego told me, she's bombing out with him. The poor girl needs to get laid. She should be thanking God you gave her this."

But she'd called it satanic. Satyric was a better word. That was certainly the way *he* was feeling with Abby sitting so close.

"What's in it, anyway?" She leaned back against the window, thankfully adding some distance between them.

"The main ingredient is oud from Socotra, that Yemeni island in the Gulf of Aden."

Her eyes popped. "They gave you some, after all?"

Eric shook his head, recalling the forearm-sized piece of wood in ISIPCA's collection of raw ingredients. The chairman of the school board had considered it too rare to allow Eric even a few shavings. "I found a dealer in Aden who had not only the wood, but also a few grams of steam extract. I bought the extract."

"Fabulous!" She sat up straighter and took hold of his arm. "You've got to get more."

Oh, man. Balquees had never affected him this strongly when he was building it. Was it the circumstances? A need to celebrate tonight's success? The fact that he and Abby were up here alone, in a place almost as taboo for lovemaking as a church?

The train, a subway in Paris, rose to ground level on the outskirts. It swayed into a curve, then righted, jostling him from carrying that lovemaking thought any further.

Inching back from her, he swallowed to moisten his throat. "I can't get more. I bought all the extract he had. And the area where the tree grows is now occupied by Somali pirates."

"Then buy up his supply of wood and extract it yourself. Believe me, go commercial with this and you can write your own ticket."

"I can't afford it at the moment. Besides, Balquees isn't ready. It still needs refinement." A longer lasting top note would add subtlety to the initial impression, the sort of romantic foreplay he considered a mark of all good fragrances. Marie-Claire's experience might have been more pleasant if her suitors hadn't come on to her like sex-starved teenagers.

"Balquees?"

"That's what I call the perfume. It was the name of the Queen of Sheba, and it's her perfume I've tried to recreate. The one she wore to seduce King Solomon."

Abby leaned closer, the fact that she wasn't wearing a bra now painfully obvious. "I thought all that Old Testament stuff was just a bunch of fairytales."

"Not for Ethiopians. They have a rich literature about her." Forcing his gaze back to Abby's face, he summarized the legend of Balquees, whose empire centered in southern Yemen and extended well into Ethiopia, how she anointed herself with the essence of Socotran oud on the night she enchanted the reluctant king and conceived their son, Menelik. According to the Song of Songs, Solomon burned with desire for this "black but comely" woman whom "the sun hath scorched" and who, in turn, had enflamed the wise man.

"It's a big deal for Ethiopians," Eric ended, "because Menelik became the first emperor of Ethiopia."

Abby rolled her eyes. "Yeah, well, I guess ancestry bullshit is important to some people. So what else is in it? That base note is deadly."

"You think so?"

"I smelled the civet, but there's something even more fecal than that."

Eric couldn't help grinning. "Actually, you helped me. Remember how you reacted to truffle when we were trying out scents from *Le Nez du Vin?*"

"Sweetheart, all I remember is what happened afterwards."

Struggling to keep his composure, he said, "You liked several things, but truffle got to you most. So I tried a whole variety of mushrooms and finally found one that's *really* down and dirty. Shiitake."

"I'll be damned. Well, you definitely made the right choice. When that note came out full strength, it was like my nose had just nuzzled in between her legs."

He crossed his legs the other direction. Was she bent on torturing him?

A few lights raced past behind her, pinpricks of civilization within the midnight blackness of French countryside.

"I'm telling you, Eric, this is great juice."

An "in" term for perfume, juice, to Eric, carried the shading of a work in progress. Which exactly described how he now felt about Balquees. "It'll be better after I fix it."

"Screw fixing it. It's perfect, as is."

"I can improve it."

Looking miffed, she sat back and folded her arms across her stomach. "It's your baby. But if you need an endorsement, I'm your girl."

To hell with endorsement. What he needed was her. To taste her skin, kiss every inch of her writhing body, feel her hands in his hair as he kissed inside her.

The train jerked then slowed to a crawl.

Eric blew out a breath and, with it, the candle of his reverie. Outside Abby's window, the station sign read "Versailles Rive Gauche." End of the line after a half-hour ride.

They descended to the platform where Eric searched both directions for Diego, in case he'd ridden in a different car. "I wonder what happened to our Spaniard."

"He's probably feasting at the altar of his own goddess," Abby said.

More like three or four, if what Eric had seen in the Panthéon was any indication.

The platform emptied quickly, leaving Abby and him standing alone—just them and the train, on a vacant platform in the middle of the night. From somewhere in the distance, crickets called. He and Abby stood there, a soft breeze lifting the fragrances of her body and swirling them around his face. Her skin, the musky richness of her hair, the marine scent of her recent lovemaking. All enhanced by Balquees, the way a fine wine enhanced *haute cuisine*.

As they walked slowly out of the station, Eric felt no embarrassment at his erection. In fact, he hoped she'd notice. But if she did, she gave no sign. "How about a glass of wine?" he suggested.

"The bars are closed."

"I have a good Margaux at my place."

She seemed to consider a moment. "Okay."

Encouraged but never certain with Abby, he tried to prepare for disappointment. Abby was probably satiated. They'd never made love twice in one week.

But, God, he wanted her.

By the time their trek up the narrow sidewalk of Rue du Parc de Cagny brought them to ISIPCA, he couldn't stand it any longer. He took her hand and stopped her. The light of a streetlamp picked out her high cheekbones, the curve of her jaw, her full lips. He drilled his eyes into hers. "Stay with me tonight."

With the faintest of smiles, she stepped closer and kissed him. Softly at first, then harder. Much harder, her fingernails digging into his shoulder blades, her mouth devouring his like a famished animal.

Chapter 7

One o'clock in the morning, and Diego was starting to feel primed again. That aphrodisiac of Eric's was amazing stuff.

Pushing himself up against the padded headboard, he gazed at the tangle of naked women sprawled around him. He had no idea which one had paid for this hotel suite, but he was glad it boasted a king-size bed that accommodated everybody.

His father would be proud. A champion stallion couldn't have done better. But the king of machismo would swallow his cigar if he knew his son truly craved only the eldest of these women, the widow.

Diego looked down at Arlette, comtesse of somewhere or other. Her skin glowed with the rich luster of burnished ivory. Her silvery hair, splayed across a pillow, reminded him of a Lipizzaner's mane at full gallop. And her fragrance. It was one of those older perfumes he could never keep straight, but it didn't matter.

He was about to rouse her when one of the younger women shrieked in French, "Oh, shit. Look at the time."

It was like tossing a cat in the chicken coop. Naked ladies scrambled off the bed and flapped around the floor, throwing one another's clothing to find their own. "That's mine." "Where are my shoes?" "My husband," one of them squawked, "what will I tell him?" "Who has cab fare?"

Diego felt sorry for them but couldn't help smiling, until Arlette sat up in bed next to him. "No," he said, placing his palm on her supple belly. "Please stay."

"Are you sure?" She pulled up the duvet to cover her chest in that delicious gesture of uncertainty so typical of women her age.

Just like Señora Davies, his English language tutor in secondary school, the first time they slept together. Outwardly prim, it was she who awakened him to the passions smoldering within women who'd borne and reared their children only to find themselves no longer appealing to their foolish husbands. My God, if there was something that lady would not do, he never discovered it.

Aglow with the memories, Diego kissed Arlette. "We have the room until morning. And soon we'll be alone."

The poultry were in full retreat, the raven-haired one already hopping toward the door, slipping into stiletto heels as she went. The blonde with the augmented breasts wriggled into her gown, while the other blonde, the screamer, stuffed her frilly panties into a pearl-studded handbag.

As Diego had suspected, not one of the fleeing women paused to glance at him, let alone say anything. Despite their breathless urgency at the Panthéon, he meant no more to them than the dildos in their nightstands. Which suited him fine, for the feeling was mutual. And utterly different from the way he felt about Arlette.

With peace finally settling over their suite, he thanked his stars this lovely aristocrat had stayed. Ladies in their autumnal years appreciated him, appreciated his heartfelt attention to those needs left cruelly neglected by a culture that despised wrinkles. But more than that, experience had taught him that women, like fine wines, required aging to reach their full potential. And their honest gratitude fulfilled him beyond imagining.

"What are you thinking?" Arlette asked.

Snuggling up to her, he whispered, "I'm thinking of you."

"Oh?" She nuzzled his neck. "I love that scent you're wearing. It makes me feel young."

"I like you the way you are."

"Liar."

"I am not," he said and meant it. Arlette, even more than other ladies of her vintage, embodied his ideals of grace and poise and classical beauty. If he had any skill with brushes, he would have loved to paint her portrait.

"What about those younger women?"

"I'm glad they left."

"But you enjoyed them." She pouted in that way only French women could do.

"In the frenzy, of course I did. But I wanted you most. Did you not see me always looking at you?"

Her pout turned into a little smile. "Not always."

"That's because ..." He kissed her earlobe. "... you were sometimes occupied with other things."

Arlette's eyes glittered with the coquettishness that came from experience—or desired experience—and that rewarded a lucky man with the joy of knowing he could make a parched garden bloom again.

"Other things?" Her hand slipped between his legs. "Like this?"

Hardening in her grasp, he pulled down the duvet and caressed her breasts, still luscious after so many years. Her dark nipples pointed provocatively toward the treasure of treasures, something a younger woman's nipples could never do. With practiced moves he straddled her, north to south, and kissed his way down. As he paused to thrust his tongue in her navel, he felt her warm mouth enclose him.

In whatever life she had lived previously, Arlette had been inhibited. He knew this from the tentative way she'd licked him earlier, before the others pushed her aside and swallowed him whole. Now he felt her trying to do what they had done.

He raised his hips, extracting himself. "You don't have to do that."

"I want to."

"Just enjoy." The heady aroma of her treasure drew him downward. He traced his tongue over her lower belly, into her pubic hair. Then he parted her and slowly licked her front to back.

Arlette's breath caught. She went perfectly still, as though he'd captured her.

He circled his tongue, sucked in the bud of her essence, and felt her belly quiver.

"Oui," she cried, her voice rising. *"Mon Dieu, oui!"*

Suddenly she stiffened, her body rigid beneath him.

He allowed her a few minutes to savor and settle down, then rotated his position and pleasured her again, the old-fashioned way.

Half an hour later, they stood on the balcony, naked in the night air, Diego behind her with his arms wrapped around her as they looked out at the Panthéon below and the lighted dome of Sacré Cœur in the distance.

Arlette turned slowly to face him. Peering into his eyes, she murmured words he had heard before but could never hear enough. "You have given me new life."

As dawn broke, Abby felt exhausted and invigorated at the same time, like she'd recently finished a hard aerobic workout. What a night, first with Audrey, then with Eric. Leaning over, she kissed Eric softly. "I'm going to take a shower."

"I'll help you," he said, pulling down the covers.

"Sssh." She put a finger to his lips. "I won't be long."

Liking to be watched and knowing Eric enjoyed looking at her, she left his bathroom door open and the shower curtain pulled back. Compared to her own shower, his blasted water with real force. The hot spray felt luxurious, like a massage on the back of her neck and a warm, liquid blanket over the rest of her body. His soap had almost no smell, but the bar glided over her like pure glycerine. Lathering herself, she glanced in his direction. And did a double-take.

Had she seen a movement beyond the window over his bed? In the house across the street—second floor, just like Eric's apartment—the draperies hung slightly parted. The room behind them was dark. As it would be if a voyeur were spying.

"Something wrong?" Eric asked, sitting up straighter.

"Just a shot of hot water. Someone in the building must have flushed a toilet."

As he settled back, she hoped the movement hadn't been her imagination. Maybe it was another student, preferably female, or perhaps an older man who'd lost his wife and kept her memory alive by watching other lovers.

Angling a bit more toward the window, Abby smiled, rinsed the suds from her breasts, and soaped herself again.

"I really think you need some help," Eric said.

For a second she felt tempted, but only because two of them in the shower would give the voyeur an even better eyeful. Instead, she squeezed out a dollop of Eric's unscented shampoo and scrubbed it into her hair.

He was sweet. And on those occasions when she needed a man, he served her nicely. But his obsession with fragrance and mania for perfection, got old after a while. On the other hand, that Balquees he'd created was truly breathtaking.

Breathtaking and a little scary. She hadn't intended to spend the night with him, had not even thought of it until the train started moving. She'd sat down beside him, totally sated from her conquest of Audrey, the star's whimpers and squeals still sounding in her ears. But once settled, she'd started feeling aroused again and realized the body heat from her rush to catch the train was wafting up Balquees from her own neck.

Never would she have imagined wanting a man after such a fabulous evening with a woman. But she'd wanted him so badly she nearly lost control. Fortunately, he lost control first, preserving her dominance in their relationship.

Bending her head under the spray, she rinsed her hair. As the shampoo swirled down the drain, she pictured the last of the Balquees swirling with it and felt a mixture of sadness and relief.

"I'll dry you," Eric said, sitting up again.

"Down, Fido." She shut off the shower and pulled a thick, fluffy towel from the rack. Whatever he had in mind, they'd been there and done that. Including things she normally didn't care for but had eagerly jumped at last night. Serious shit, that Balquees.

After toweling off, she used Eric's toothbrush, then ran his comb through her hair. On his sink stood a wooden shaving mug with a badger-hair brush, old-fashioned technology he'd picked up from his grandfather who was a Navy man or merchant marine or something. She couldn't quite remember but found it amusing.

Her own grandfathers dwelt only in stories she was supposed to revere but couldn't give a damn about. How could she care about an old iron monger, let alone some wizened idiot who hung from a rope to pluck bird's nests made of saliva off a cliff face just so they could be boiled into soup? Jesus. Give her shark's fin soup any day, but leave the bird spit in the kitchen.

Speaking of kitchen, she thought, coming out of the bathroom, "You want coffee?"

"If you're making it."

Still naked, she set a kettle to boil and measured three scoops of coffee into his French press. Then she struck a nonchalant pose for the voyeur across the street and cast her eyes around Eric's apartment. The antique perfumer's organ, with all his extracts and essential oils, held pride of place next to one of the windows. But for all the respect Eric seemed to have for his family, no photos of them hung on his walls. Instead, he'd adorned the place with old French circus posters. "Cirque d'Hivre" showed a man apparently falling from a hot-air balloon. "L'Homme Poisson" showed a clawed man, half skeleton, crawling across the sea floor. A more modern one, "Le Cirque des Vampires," showed a man with fangs, the same man with his arms around a naked woman, and a bat.

"Why no elephants or clowns?" she said, waving an arm to indicate the posters.

"You've been here I don't know how many times and you're just now asking?"

"Yeah. So, why?"

"Because elephants and clowns are boring."

No, there was more than that. With newfound clarity, she saw the posters as a reflection of Eric's self-image. He'd papered his walls with freaks, people separate from society who, like himself, had little or no community. Maybe that was the fate of geniuses, to live apart and only feel comfortable with others who also lived apart. Others like her, in a sense. A Chinese dyke who had exceptional taste buds and liked sex in public.

"Why are you grinning?" Eric asked.

"Because I love you. In my own way."

The kettle whistled. She poured the water, positioned the plunger, and waited the four minutes he'd told her were optimum before pushing down the plunger. After filling two mugs—black, no sugar—she carried them to the bed, handed one to Eric, and slipped in beside him. "You really should get a bigger bed."

"We spent most of the night on the floor."

"I mean the part where we slept."

"It's okay. I don't mind your snoring."

She elbowed him. "I don't snore."

"Just joking. But I'll make you a deal. Move in, and I'll get a bigger bed."

Not that again. Why did he have to ruin things? Abby lowered her eyes and took a sip of coffee.

"Sorry," he said.

After downing half her mug, she slid her feet out and stood. "I better get going."

"It's only seven-thirty."

"Exams in a couple weeks. You're probably already prepared, but I'm not." The disappointment in his eyes almost stopped her. Almost. To soothe things, she took her time getting dressed, the way he liked. "By the way, in case I haven't told you often enough, you hit a homerun with Balquees."

"There's more," he offered.

His face reminded her of the male lead in one of those romantic-comedy movies where the guy was making no headway with the girl—a spark of hope dimmed by wounded resignation. At times like this, she almost wished she could give more. More heart to go with her occasional body. But that wasn't in the cards.

She walked to the door, then turned and gave him a smile even she knew was wistful. "Don't tempt me."

Marie-Claire woke in a sweat, visions of debauchery swirling through her head. Unholy acts. Worse than anything in Sodom and Gomorrah. Acts presided over by a faceless man, hugely rampant in his trouserless tuxedo, who pinned her arms while his concubine and Diego did unspeakable things to every part of her body.

She jerked her hands from the shameful pleasure between her legs. "God, forgive me."

Still breathing hard, she hurried into her bathroom and turned the shower on cold. If she'd had a whip, she would have flagellated herself.

As the icy spray needled her skin, uncontrollable shivering tensed her muscles and shook away the images. How they'd enveloped her in the first place could only be explained by one thing—that horrid concoction of Eric's. Well, not actually horrid. In fact, it smelled quite good.

But that was the diabolical part. Satan worked through appealing to our senses, to the base instincts that all began with Adam and Eve. Odious to the core, the Prince of Darkness had recognized Eric's ambition as a mortal weakness and tried to exploit it in a nefarious attempt to reap chaste souls.

Teeth chattering, she turned her face directly into the spray. Thank God, Eric would destroy it. She'd seen the remorse in his eyes. He was a fine man, led temporarily astray. But through her, God's light had shone upon him, and he would now do what was right.

With that thought consoling her, she slowly adjusted the shower to a warmer temperature. Yet one thing still bothered her. Why did Diego appear in her nightmare? He would never participate in such depravity. The other two, the man in a tuxedo and his concubine with the groping hands, made sense in light of what had happened last night. Diego didn't. Not that she wouldn't do some of those things with him when they were married. Maybe even the sinful things. She'd have to do penance afterward. But penance would be worth it. And the Blessed Mother would forgive her, save her from Satan.

Satan! That was it. The third person was not Diego, at all, but another creature in black leather. The Panthéon had been full of them, and one had been Lucifer himself.

Either that, or Diego had simply become mixed up in her nightmare because she'd been dreaming of him before.

Oh, Diego. She turned the temperature up hotter. He had kissed her at last, just in the next room there. A short kiss before leaving after dinner, but soft and on her lips. Closing her eyes, she could feel it again, his mouth slightly open, pressed to hers so gently it sent shudders through her body. Little shudders, like right now.

Perhaps Eric shouldn't destroy all his perfume. He could save some for married couples only. Her mother had once let slip that passion drifted away over the years. It might not have to be so. Things could be different.

Reluctantly she shut off the shower and reached for a towel. How different things might have been last night if it were Diego, instead of Eric, who rescued her from that hideous couple chasing her around the Panthéon. They might have spent the night together. A chaste night, but one of kissing and touching and maybe just a little— No!

"Bad word."

Was Eric's perfume still affecting her? She scrubbed herself with the towel as if it were a scouring pad and she were a blackened pot. When she smelled it afterwards, she detected no remnant fragrance. At last cleansed, she tied the towel tightly around her chest.

Satan might walk among them, but he would not succeed. As a Christian, a soldier of God, she would make sure of that.

Chapter 8

Thanks to Diego, word of Balquees spread among the students. Soon everyone wanted it. By Tuesday morning, they were stopping Eric in the hall, pestering him in the lab, in the library. Girls he'd once coveted from afar stood close and touched his arm as they spoke. Guys who'd shot dirty looks every time an instructor praised him now practically dragged Eric for drinks at the Basque restaurant a few blocks away.

Wednesday evening, feet propped on the bed in his apartment, Eric sipped a glass of the Margaux he and Abby had forgotten about and reflected on his newfound popularity. It gave him butterflies.

He'd always been shy. In junior high, despite his winning times in the hundred-meter dash, the tough guys had ridiculed him as the "perfume pussy." In high school on Galveston Island, redneck bullies with lumps of chewing tobacco in their cheeks taunted him relentlessly, saying his father, an award-winning chef, was a faggot for doing woman's work. When he finally beat the shit out of one of them, Eric got suspended for a week, which landed him in huge trouble with his parents.

He hated conflict. And sudden celebrity made him almost as uncomfortable. Weird, since he craved nothing more strongly than recognition of his work.

He took another sip of wine, savoring the gravelly flavor of the soil it grew on and its undertones of chocolate and leather.

Good perfumers could work in seclusion, but great ones, like Jean-Claude Ellena, got thrust into the limelight. Replaying his favorite daydream, Eric pictured himself on a par with Ellena, being interviewed for glossy magazines, photographed with adoring actresses, wooed by the leading couturiers. He saw lunches at trendy eateries, travel on private jets. He'd have a place in Paris, or New York or Milan, a place with a killer view like Durand had. And he'd have a wife, not just a sometime-girlfriend who toyed with his emotions. She'd be supportive but independent, possibly an artist or musician, with long hair and a willowy figure and a mystique about her that inspired him to create masterpieces.

Unlike Balquees. When you came right down to it, Balquees was crude. Granted, he'd restricted himself to using only water-soluble ingredients, and within those limits he'd done pretty well. But this Margaux possessed more subtlety and finesse.

A knock at his door startled him. He stood and went to answer. "Diego. Come in."

Always a dresser, Diego had decked himself out in jeans, suede boots, a white shirt opened to mid-chest, and a vest of his signature black leather. He lifted Eric's hand and sniffed the wineglass. "Nice. You have more?"

Eric poured him some. "What's up?"

"Luc makes a party Friday night." Diego sampled the wine. "Very good. Can you come?"

"Sure." *Hell, yes.* At ISIPCA, Luc basked in a status equivalent to that of a star fullback. Like roughly a quarter of the perfume students, he was a native of Grasse, the historic seat of French perfumery. Those so blessed, except for Marie-Claire and one or two others, tended to consider themselves "chosen" by birthright. Their bearing broadcast to lesser mortals an attitude Eric dubbed, "*Grassoise*—and don't you forget it."

"Excellent." Diego turned around one of Eric's two wooden chairs, straddled it, and rested his arms on the back. "Your Balquees is miraculous."

So he'd said a few days ago. Four women, the eldest of which had stayed the night and most of Saturday.

"How do you make it?"

"Balquees?" For a friend, why not? Especially a friend who

needed all the inspiration possible if he were going to graduate.

Eric sat on the bed and propped a pillow behind his back against the wall. After reciting the list of ingredients, he said, "The only one I knew for sure was the oud. I read about it in an old text I found on the Internet, and all it said was a perfume made from 'oudh of Suqutra.' But that's the heart note, and perfumes always begin with the heart note. The difficult part was improvising the rest. Compatible top-note scents that would evolve gracefully into the oud, and base-note scents that would enhance the oud as body heat rises."

Actually, all of the notes—or accords—could be smelled on the first sniffing, as they could in any perfume. But like the classics Eric loved, the dominance of heavier components over lighter ones did increase with time.

"So few ingredients," Diego said.

"There don't have to be many. They just have to fit together. God's recipe for the oil of anointment contains only four, besides the olive oil."

Diego's eyebrows arched. "God gave a recipe?"

"Exodus Thirty, verses twenty-two through twenty-five." Eric couldn't help smiling. Here he was, quoting chapter and verse to a Catholic. But aside from the Solomon and Sheba passages, those bits of Exodus were practically all he knew about the Bible.

"If you want to smell it," he added, "I made some." He pointed toward the antique perfumer's organ. Its five tiers of crescent-shaped shelves, resembling the keyboards and stop ranks of a pipe organ, held his personal collection of some two hundred essences, tightly capped and alphabetically arranged around the small workspace in the center. "Third tier, right-hand side. But be prepared for an overwhelming rush of cinnamon. It totally knocks out the myrrh and calamus and cassia."

"No, thank you." Diego studied his wineglass a moment. "In Balquees, the oud is ordinary agarwood?"

"No. That's mostly used for incense. This is special." Eric explained the rarity of the wood, how the school board had denied him even a few slivers, and how he'd finally found a Yemeni dealer who sold him the extract. "Why do you ask?"

"I would like to make it. For myself."

"What?" Eric sat upright. "Diego, it's my perfume."

"But Abby said you are not happy with it. So I thought—"

"I can improve it, yes. But it's mine to improve."

Diego's dark eyes lowered. He shifted on his chair as though it were uncomfortable. "I'm sorry."

His contrite expression softened Eric's heart. He shouldn't snap like that at a friend, especially when he had so few. "Never mind. I apologize for the misunderstanding."

"So," Diego said, his tone brighter, "you will come to the party. And you will bring your Balquees?"

Of course that was the reason for the invitation. But it was also his *entrée*. After all, you could hardly expect to shine in the limelight if you were a social wallflower. "Sure," Eric replied, "I'll bring it."

Just after nine o'clock Friday night, Eric knocked on Luc's door. When no one answered, he chalked it up to the laughter inside and Nine Inch Nails wailing, "like an animal."

Eric wiped his palms on his slacks, found the door handle unlocked, and stepped inside. The revelers, like most of ISIPCA's pupils, were in their mid-twenties to early thirties. But this was *la crème,* the "in crowd." They filled two couches, several upholstered chairs, and most of the standing room.

After waiting a minute to be acknowledged, Eric gave up and made his way past some dancing couples to a table laden with wine bottles, hard liquor, and Pernod. A stiff Scotch would steel his nerves. He was about to pour one when a hand clamped his shoulder.

"Eric!" Luc grinned at him with teeth as white as a shark's. "You brought the juice? *Regardez,* everyone, Eric is here."

The laughter died down. All faces turned to Eric. Some people raised their glasses to him. Others nudged each other, and he heard a few giggles and titters.

Diego materialized from somewhere, possibly another room or from chatting up that girl now sulking in the corner. "You know everybody, yes?"

It was hard not to, after nearly two years of being together in such a small school. Eric raised a hand. "Hi."

Lame, but he felt too intimidated to say more. They stared at him expectantly, as though he were a dancing bear about to perform.

Giselle, whom he'd craved in his first months at ISIPCA, glided up with a gleam in her eyes. She wore a white silk blouse tied at the waist and a pair of low-cut jeans that dipped almost to her bikini line, with about a three-inch zipper below. "Your Balquees, can I try it?"

Loose as a courtesan, he'd later learned, she didn't need it any more than Diego did. But Eric handed her the vial, anyway.

She spotted a few drops on her wrist, rubbed them in, and sniffed the way a wine taster sniffs the glass. "Sandalwood, balsam, rose."

Wrong. She'd detected aspects of the oud but not its more complex essences.

She gave the vial to a guy behind her, who rubbed some into the back of his hand. "Lemon peel in the top note. Civet and something else in the base." He glanced at Eric as he passed along the vial. "Good base."

Eric watched his vial make the rounds, its contents applied to arms, wrists, throats, behind ears, between breasts. Jesus, they were using a lot, splashing it on as if it were some low-concentration product like *eau de cologne* or aftershave. Good thing he'd only brought half his supply.

"*Silage*," a redhead on one of the couches said, speaking the word in French.

The scent of rotting hay was another aspect of the oud. Eric was surprised she'd caught it and wondered briefly if she'd grown up on a farm.

A brunette in a leather miniskirt fanned herself with her hand. "That silage is semen."

People laughed.

"Not as good as mine," a fellow in the corner told her.

And it went downhill from there. Or uphill, Eric thought, depending on your point of view. The floor space filled with dancers, getting wilder with each song. Some people on couches and in the corners skipped the preliminaries. Hands slipped under blouses. Fingers tugged at zippers.

But was Balquees the real reason? It all happened so quickly Eric wondered if a placebo wouldn't have worked just as well, if the only thing these people needed was just anticipation and an excuse.

On the other hand, with so much Balquees in the air, it was also getting to him. That warm, light-headed sensation. The tingling in his dick. He wiped his brow with his sleeve and shifted his weight to the other foot. Man, there were some gorgeous breasts in this room. Puckered nipples he could almost feel in his mouth. But they were all "taken."

Frustrated, Eric poured himself an inch of Scotch and downed it in two gulps. It stung on the way down, leaving the characteristic aftertaste of iodine on his tongue. If Abby were here, maybe he wouldn't be the odd man out. He grew harder at the memory of their lovemaking a week ago, more passionate than any time before, more abandoned, as if both of them were supercharged and couldn't get enough of each other.

But not tonight. Tonight Abby was in Paris where she and her actress had a room at the George Cinq.

He blew out a breath His half-erection ached, bowed down inside his underpants. He should get out of here. But somehow he didn't want to. Instead, he knocked back another Scotch. When the burning subsided, he turned again to the crowd.

A couple on an overstuffed chair had abandoned all modesty, the guy sitting, the girl facing him astride his lap, her bare hips pumping. Same for another couple, half-clothed, who stood braced in a corner, her knee hooked over his arm. And another whose hips and legs, protruding from behind a couch, left no doubt he was bent over her from behind. The pungent odor of apocrine sweat roiled through an atmosphere permeated with Balquees.

Eric had been under the influence of Balquees before, but never this much. Not even with Abby. The lights seemed brighter, the music louder, colors more vivid. Too vivid, and changing. Almost like that time in college when he tried LSD. A fellow chemistry major had made it in the lab. Looking in a mirror, Eric had seen his face crack and crumble, like a slowly shattering bust of

Caesar.

He shoved aside the memory. Perspiration stuck his shirt to his body. He needed air. But his feet stayed planted as he swayed to the music.

A girl appeared in front of him. He couldn't remember her name, but she swayed with him, her eyes dreamily seductive. God, she was beautiful. Or maybe not. It was hard to tell. She grasped his hips and ground into him. He grasped hers and ground back. He felt sweat running down his face, smelled raw desire wafting up from between her legs.

Then she was gone, pushed aside by Giselle. Christ, this was bizarre.

Giselle vamped her arms around his neck. Her blouse, still tied at the waist, was unbuttoned down to the knot. He fumbled with the knot, got it loose, and cupped her breasts. She threw her head back, her mouth open, eyes closed. Then she whiplashed forward. With the fixed stare of a stalking tigress, she held his eyes, reached down the front of his pants, and pulled up his bent-over erection, gripping it at full staff inside his pants.

With her hand tight around him, she rasped, "I know you wanted me last year. And now?"

Her breath stank of semen. Not the hint of semen in Balquees, but the real thing. "No," Eric said, pulling away.

She stared at him in bewilderment, then pain. Then her eyes narrowed. As he retreated farther, her lips drew back in a rictus of hatred so vicious that Eric saw in her the eel-like face of the *Alien*.

He staggered between writhing couples and around Diego in a threesome to one of the two windows at the front of Luc's apartment. Throwing open the shutters, he stuck his head out and inhaled deeply of the cold, fresh air.

Slowly his brain cleared. What beast had he unleashed?

He shook his head. Whatever he'd done, he knew one thing for sure. If he ever again let anyone use Balquees, it had to be in moderation.

After a few minutes of air, he turned back to the room. It looked like a scene from *Caligula* or one of those '70s love-ins he'd read about. Fine, if that's what you wanted. But for the unwilling or unwitting, scary as hell.

Despite the body heat in the room, a cold shiver swept over him. Amid moans and cries of ecstasy, there was no sign of condoms, no evidence of restraint. Would they have acted the same without Balquees?

He saw his vial on the coffee table and snatched it.

"Hey!" A fellow with crazed eyes and a glistening, post-coital penis lurched toward him. "You can't take that. We're just getting started."

Eric pocketed the vial.

The guy tripped over his own feet and fell to the floor. Desperately he grabbed hold of Eric's ankles. "Give me that."

No way in hell. Eric high-stepped out of the fellow's hands, bolted for the door, and headed home.

Chapter 9

On Monday afternoon, Eric was cramming for final exams when his mentor, Jacques Durand, walked into the library. Eric leapt to his feet. "*Monsieur*, I thought you were hunting, in the Pyrenees."

With the bearing of a duke, wearing a chamois jacket and burgundy cravat, Durand positioned himself in front of Eric's table. "We have been summoned before the board."

"The board?" Near as Eric knew, the board never summoned anyone. Was this good news or bad? He couldn't tell from Durand's expression. "Why?"

"There has been … an irregularity."

So it was bad news. "What kind of irregularity?"

"Come with me."

Eric's brain launched into warp speed. Was this about the party at Luc's place? Had something happened he didn't know about?

On their way to the administrative chateau, they passed Durand's vintage Facel Vega, its top down, two rifle cases propped in the rear seat. He really had interrupted his hunting trip.

Climbing the stairs, Eric peppered him with questions but received only frosty silence. Half sick with apprehension, he stood back as Durand knocked on the boardroom door.

"*Entrez,*" came the response from within.

Durand gripped the door handle, then turned to Eric.

"Whatever happens, do not lie. Mistakes can be excused. But to lie is unforgivable."

Eric felt paralyzed, like a convict staring up at the gallows. "What is this about?"

"I will help you, if I can." Durand opened the door.

Heart pounding like a pile driver, Eric trudged in behind him.

In the oak-paneled boardroom, seven men sat somberly along one side of a polished wooden table. No chairs faced them. Eric and Durand had to stand.

"Mister Foster," the man in the center said. "Thank you for coming."

Like I had any choice. Eric held his hands at his sides, then clasped them in front of him, then held them at his sides again. The room smelled of beeswax and wool. Through the tall windows, cold light from an overcast sky shed vague rectangles on the parquet floor but left the board members' faces in shadow. As though they preferred it that way, no one had switched on the chandeliers. Why the hell was he here?

The man in the center—the chairman, Eric recognized from photographs—looked at him with the grim countenance of an undertaker. "Two months ago, you requested a sample of a rare wood in the institute's collection. You wished to recreate a perfume for which you believed this wood was essential. Your request was denied."

By you, personally, according to the letter. Eric shifted his feet. So this *was* about Balquees.

"By all accounts," the chairman continued, "you have made your perfume. Some sort of …" A derisive sneer twisted his lips. "… aphrodisiac."

"Sir, it's—"

"Do *not* interrupt me."

Eric took a step back, surprised at the man's harshness.

"Have you made the perfume? Yes or no."

"Yes. I bought—"

"Yes is enough, Mister Foster." The chairman glanced at the other board members, then leaned forward on his forearms, his eyes drilling into Eric's. "Your admission explains precisely why the wood in our collection, your essential ingredient, is now missing."

Eric's knees almost buckled. "I didn't take it. Honest to God, I did not." In his peripheral vision, he saw Durand wince.

Oh, shit. Eric shut his eyes, then trained them defiantly on the chairman.

"Sir, I am *not* lying. I bought the wood from a man in Yemen. Well, not the wood. The extract. A steam extract. That's what I used. The extract."

The chairman glared at him balefully.

But Eric couldn't stop. *Would* not stop. "I can get a receipt. If you just give me a few days, I can prove that I bought it."

Desperately he went on, pleading, begging, trying to reason. But he might as well have been shouting at statues.

Devastated, Eric waited outside the doors. He felt like he was going to throw up. His whole life lay in ruin, his dreams, everything he'd ever hoped for now rubble at his feet. The chairman's final words kept ringing in his ears. "You may leave now."

When Durand finally came out, Eric couldn't look him in the eye.

"I will do my best to find you a job somewhere," Durand said dully. Then he headed for the stairs.

Eric trailed behind him. There was nothing he could say that he hadn't already said inside, repeatedly and to no effect. It was almost as though the board had been looking for an excuse to expel him and wasn't about to let go of this one.

At the bottom of the stairs, Durand pushed open the door to the outside. "I am an old man, without children. I saw you as my legacy."

Tears welled in Eric's eyes. Through their watery blur, he followed Durand to his car, not knowing what else to do.

For a long moment, they stood there, facing each other. Then Durand got in his car, shut the door, and started the engine. "You have broken my heart."

Despite a threat of rain, Durand left the top down. A dark cloud had settled over him, thick as a fog on the Normandy coast. Neither the wind in his hair nor the throaty growl of the engine worked their magic on his mood. How could Eric have done this to him?

The boy should know when it's wisest to take a fall. You get knocked down, you get back up. When you become the champion, no one remembers you once stumbled. He, Jacques Durand, would have seen to that.

But now Eric had knocked both of them out of the ring. *"Merde!"*

At Rue Albert Joly, Durand braked to a stop, his hands strangling the wheel. Without thinking, he'd been heading for Paris. But there was nothing for him there. Dinner alone. A hotel room, alone.

Spotting a break in traffic, he turned right with a squeal of the tires. He took the next right, slipped into a parking space on the tree-lined street, and sat there in neutral, the engine idling. He did not deserve such misery.

The dragon in his gut bit hard. He clutched his stomach. Those money-grubbing Swiss. Treatments at the clinic in Crans-Montana cost more than a chalet in nearby Zermatt. And for what? They hadn't slain the dragon, or even wounded it, so far as he could tell. Sure they claimed progress. How else would they convince him to keep paying? Filthy trolls. Ten years they'd given him, if the injections worked. By then he'd be destitute.

With his thumbnail, he flicked the cap off a plastic bottle of antacid tablets. At two euros a bottle they did a lot more good than that serum the alchemists jabbed in his butt. He shook some tablets into his mouth and swallowed.

In a minute or so, the pain abated. But the dark cloud remained. First Alain, then Eric. Durand's throat tightened. He saw Alain, his only child, reckless with the immortality of youth, grinning astride his motorcycle. But despite closing his eyes, Durand could not shut out what always came next. The skid marks. On the Middle Corniche high above Monaco, less than a kilometer from where Princess Grace had gone over. They should dynamite that godforsaken road.

Durand took a deep breath that did nothing to assuage his loss.

And now there was Eric. Equally reckless, in his own way, and just as stubborn. Durand shook his head slowly. The things they could have done together.

A plop of water hit his forehead. He wiped it with a finger as more drops struck. Rain. He smelled it now. He should have smelled it before, and would have if it weren't for the havoc those injections wreaked on his nose. And palate. Damn every doctor in Switzerland, scallops should not taste like copper. Or Montrachet like piss.

With a crack of thunder, the fat drops turned into a downpour. He put the top up and slumped in his seat as waves of rain beat drum rolls on his canvas roof. It had been seven years since he'd created the crowning glory of his career. But although theoretically retired, he could not abide the thought of living the rest of his life with nothing more to show for it. The views from his villa had grown stale. The women, no matter their inventiveness, all merged into a blur. What other men might covet gave him little more than the briefest, most shallow satisfaction. Something inside him, his gift from God, still needed to create.

Yet perfumery offered few options to a man his age. He could craft new fragrances, but with his smell impaired, it would be a crapshoot that could fatally injure his hard-won reputation. He could nurture a new genius, someone to work with him. But geniuses were rarer than Facel Vegas still on the road, and his one hope had just shamed him so badly he could pound a spike through the boy's heart.

All for a caprice driven purely by hubris.

Aphrodisiac. He gnashed his teeth at the memory of being summoned like a servant by the chairman of ISIPCA's board, the man bleating about students distracted from their class work by rumors of a sexual frenzy attributed to one of Eric's creations. Durand, like the chairman, had dismissed this as hogwash. He'd been about to advise the old fop that he did not appreciate having his hunting trip interrupted, when the allegation of Eric's theft stopped him cold.

Damn you, Eric. Will you never listen?

Durand shifted his position in the seat. A true aphrodisiac would secure a man's reputation for centuries. But there was no such thing. He knew this because he, himself, had tried. He would never tell Eric, or anyone else. One didn't admit one's failures. But he'd devoted half a year to the effort before coming to his senses. And he'd done his best to save Eric a similar waste of time. He, Durand, did not have time. He needed the boy to focus on what made a great perfume so that, together, they could surpass the best so far created.

Now that would never happen.

Glancing at the windscreen, he realized the downpour had ceased. He rolled down his window, letting drips from the trees splash off the sill and ricochet into his lap. A typically brief spring shower, the kind he'd relished for the sweetness it brought forth from the earth. Before Arielle left him.

Arielle.

He put the car in gear, pulled out of the parking space, and headed into the heart of Versailles. Of course, she wouldn't see him. She wouldn't talk to him on the phone or even answer his letters. But he could look at her and imagine confiding—the way they used to do before her anguish over their son's death transformed into pounding fists and vitriolic tirades blaming *him* for the tragedy.

Twenty-one years had passed since she walked out, taking nothing with her, not even bothering to divorce him. But while she had abandoned him, he had not abandoned her. He'd tracked her down, kept a distant eye on her wellbeing. An unnecessary eye, it turned out, for she was a born survivor. But in truth, his motives weren't entirely altruistic. Every time he saw her, his heart lifted.

There, on the left, Arielle's shop glowed like a welcome-home light, its windows stocked with freshly baked pastries. He could park on this side, but there was a space directly in front.

Gunning the car, he made a right and three lefts and approached her patisserie from the other direction, only to find the space in front now occupied by one of those ridiculous Smart cars. With an oath, Durand double-parked behind it, willing the owner to come out and pedal the thing away.

As he thrummed the console, a familiar smell came through his open windows, the mouth-watering aroma of Arielle's hamantaschen. The thought of them, those triangular pastries with the prune and poppy-seed filling, brought back happy memories of sitting in the villa's huge kitchen while she filled the air with doughy sweet aromas from her native Warsaw. She'd come to his father's household as an escapee from the Nazis, the five-year-old daughter of a chambermaid. She and Durand had grown up together, fallen in love, and married a month after his father's death, the old bastard having told him flat-out that Jews were fine for practice but nothing more. *Burn in hell, you two-faced bigot.*

A young woman with short blond hair came out of Arielle's shop. Clutching a paper bag filled to bursting, she crossed the rain-glistened sidewalk and climbed into the silly half-car. A minute later, Durand had her vacated spot.

Arielle, statuesque and as beautiful as ever, stood behind the counter, her salt-and-pepper hair tied in a bun. He wondered if, untied, it would still cascade over her chest, its feral fragrance enhancing the buttery scent of her skin. He would never know, but just watching her eased the tension in his chest.

He shut off the engine, twisted in his seat to face her, and leaned back against his door. Would she notice him out here? Probably not. With darkness falling and the bright lights inside, her windows would act as mirrors.

"My love." Whether he spoke the words or merely thought them didn't matter. It only mattered that she heard them—or that he imagined she did. While customers came and went, Arielle smiling as she filled each order, he told her every detail of his miserable situation and started slowly to feel alive again. From time to time, when she glanced up, he fancied she was smiling at him.

He'd just finished unburdening himself when Arielle packaged two baguettes for a man with a briefcase and a furled umbrella. As the man left, she brushed a few strands of hair from her face.

Durand loved that gesture. In his mind, he saw her doing it in the villa's kitchen, swiping away hair and leaving a streak of flour on her forehead. If only he could turn back the clock. Or perform some grand act that would compel her to love him again.

With a sigh, he started the engine and revved it twice, feeling the car rock under the torque of its many horsepower.

Arielle looked up, but her expression was faraway.

He could tell she didn't see him. At all.

The fall from grace came so hard that, if told it had happened to someone else, Eric would not have believed it.

Mind in a haze, he packed his collection of essences until the perfumer's organ stood bare in the fading light of this, the gloomiest day of his life. Clothes, books, he'd have to find some place that sold used luggage. Or just throw them away.

His door burst open.

"Eric, what the hell happened?" Abby demanded. She looked frantic, perplexed. The way he'd felt four hours ago.

"They expelled me." He picked up his glass of Scotch—his third or fourth, or whatever—and pointed to the nearly empty bottle. "Have some."

"They can't do that. You're the best student they ever had. Durand said so."

"Ah, *Monsieur* Durand." Eric plopped onto the disheveled bed. "*Monsieur* Durand had the kindness to inform me that I'd broken his heart."

Abby closed her eyes a moment, then opened them. "Fuck him."

"He has mistresses for that," Eric said. "He rotates them through that villa of his overlooking the Med. You remember it, don't you? From the party he gave last summer. Big ancestral place with—"

"Stop it!" Abby wrangled the glass from Eric's hand. "This is no time to get drunk. We have to protest. There's got to be a higher authority."

"None higher than the board, it seems. Except the sponsors. And I'm fucked with them, too."

Abby furrowed her brow, then pulled up a wooden chair in front of him and sat. "What do you mean?"

"Haven't you heard?" Eric flopped back onto his bed. The cracks in his ceiling, divided into pairs, came back together, divided again. Damn, he *was* drunk. He took a deep breath and pushed himself up into a sitting position. "Where were we? Oh, yeah, the sponsors. Well, we can't allow someone as dishonorable as me to somehow gain employment with one of the great perfume houses, now can we?"

"Eric, what the hell are you talking about?"

The inquisitors. Confess, and we'll burn you at the stake. Deny, and we'll torture you until you confess.

"Eric?"

He felt moisture in his eyes and rubbed it away with his knuckles. "It's quite simple, really. For the theft I didn't commit, they expelled me. For the lie I didn't tell—that I hadn't committed the theft—they decided to inform all the sponsors of my expulsion and why they'd been *forced* to take such drastic action."

Abby's mouth fell open.

"Ah," he said, "I see you see."

"I don't fucking believe it."

"But it's true, my love. I've been blackballed."

They were lying in each other's arms, fully clothed, just hugging, when someone knocked. Eric ignored it. He was content to lie there. But Abby got up to answer.

Marie-Claire came in, followed by Diego.

Marie-Claire rushed up to Eric, sank to her knees on the floor as though his bed were an altar, and clutched his hand. "Eric, *je suis désolée*. Please, you must be strong. I will pray with you."

He smiled at her. "I think it's too late."

"It is never too late. God is punishing you, yes. But if you pray to Him and confess your sins, He will forgive you."

"Christ," Abby snarled, "would you stop it with this God shit?"

Marie-Claire shot her a poisonous glare. "*You* He will not redeem."

"Please, not now." Diego stepped between them and turned to Eric. "Don't worry. This is a temporary indignity. A fall from the horse. You will ride again in no time."

Eric wished that were true. At least his real friends were all here. The *Grassoise*, as if they truly did have a direct line to the gods, had sidestepped him on his way out of the school, some avoiding eye contact, Giselle bestowing her most vengeful sneer.

Marie-Claire lifted the gold cross from around her neck and pressed it into his hands. "Take this. It will help."

Eric saw Abby roll her eyes, but he took the cross, anyway. "Thank you."

"So we will drink," Diego said. "You have more of that Margaux?"

"Sorry." Eric's shelves were empty, as empty as he felt.

Chapter 10

Eleven months later, New York City

The 6:10 out of Penn Station rattled Eric's window, jarring him awake as it had done every weekday for nearly a year. He pulled the duvet to his neck, daunted from rising by the sight of his own breath and the thought of going to work.

He waited for the 6:23. When it clattered past, barely fifty feet away, he cast off the duvet, put on a terrycloth robe over his sweat suit, and shut the frost-etched window. Daisy, who couldn't get enough cold and panted all night if the window weren't open, lay asleep on her back, ears splayed, her three feet propped against the wall. *Glad one of us is comfy.*

In his "kitchenette," he brewed coffee then hefted an eighteen-pound bag of kibble out of the cupboard beneath the sink. The cupboard stank of mildew and of the Lysol and bleach that wouldn't get rid of it. As he poured food into her bowl, Daisy limped in, her nails clicking on the hardwood floor. The stub of her left front leg bobbed from muscle memory.

Her sad face, though typical of bloodhounds, never failed to pain him. He couldn't help thinking she missed her leg and her police master, both of which she'd lost to gunfire from a murderer she'd been tracking through Central Park. As she settled in front of her bowl, the radiators pinged, signaling the return of hot water.

Eric stepped over her and headed for his bathroom. The last thing he needed was a dog. But it gave him someone to come home to at night.

By the time the 7:15 rumbled past, audible even from the sidewalk, Eric was bundled and plodding up Tenth Avenue toward West 55th Street. March had arrived, yet patches of dirty ice still hid in doorways and between bulging trash bags. At least the near-freezing temperature subdued the usual odors of urine and rotting garbage. A street cleaner rumbled up the other side of the avenue, its sprayers and rotating brushes fighting a futile battle. Otherwise, few vehicles passed him, and no pedestrians. The city that never slept took its time getting started.

He detoured around a chain-link fence that blocked the sidewalk in front of a building under repair. The fence had been there since before he moved in, a seemingly permanent monument to work in progress and a trap for windblown trash. At the intersection, a frigid gust from the west stung his cheek. Ignoring the red light, he hustled across. The cold made his nose run. He wiped it with the sleeve of his overcoat.

In the next block, he stopped at a storefront post office and dropped a check in the mail to Abby's friend, the girl from whom he sub-let and who legally occupied his rent-stabilized apartment. God bless Abby. Without her help, he'd be living in a fifth-floor walk-up in the Bronx.

He wanted to call and thank her again, really just hear her voice. But their conversation would inevitably devolve into another pep talk. He couldn't stomach the embarrassment.

Less than a year out of ISIPCA, and Abby was already a rising star at the most prestigious flavoring manufacturer in New York. No "energy waters" or "hickory-smoked" potato chips for her. She flavored wines, specialty cooking oils, high-end coffees, products that demanded subtlety and finesse. And while she soared, he languished in the only job Durand had been able to get him—Quality Assurance Officer at a mid-rank compounder of chemical additives that made fabric softeners smell "soft" and new cars smell "new."

His mouth turned bitter. Assuring quality at Rheinhold-Laroche meant finding the cheapest way to evoke a scent of lilacs in room freshener or disguise the stink of cat piss in Frisky's litter box.

At 55th Street, he turned and trudged a hundred feet to the front entrance, portal to purgatory. What banalities awaited him today?

In his windowless office that afternoon, Eric waded through the lab's daily offering of "finished" scents. They came to him at 8:00 am and 1:00 pm in small, brown, screw-cap bottles, each with a lab sheet secured around it by a thick rubber band. Most were okay. Some needed minor adjustment. A few of them he rejected outright, with suggestions for how they could be fixed.

An electrostatic air-filtration system, which popped like a bug zapper, continuously cleared his office's atmosphere, preventing a build-up of disparate odors. In fact, the room was practically sterile. He had a built-in, L-shaped desk made of white laminate, an attached bookcase containing industry reference manuals and ring binders detailing company policies and procedures, a syringe-disposal-type plastic receptacle for used "smell strips," and nothing else. No personal items allowed. "This is a workplace," read signs posted in each corridor.

At four-fifteen, he had just blessed a "chocolaty" smell for a line of Japanese stuffed animals when his cell phone buzzed. Abby? No, the caller ID showed an unfamiliar number.

A woman identified herself as Sergeant Pérez of the 106th Precinct. "I got an abandoned baby here, and the captain thinks you might be able to help. He heard about some course you teach at John Jay."

Eric leaned back in his chair. In a sideline he called forensic perfumery, he'd made a small name for himself with the NYPD. Their appreciation of his talent was the one bright light in his life. But he was surprised his reputation extended to Queens. "How can I help?"

"The baby smells weird, like those telephone poles in Jersey. Does that mean anything to you?"

It meant creosol, and it was definitely strange for this country.

But not for Africa. "Is the baby black?"

"How'd you know?"

"Where did you find it?"

"In a fucking Dumpster."

"In this weather?"

"I'm gonna nail the bastard who did this."

Eric hoped so. His desk phone rang, its double jingles indicating an internal call. "Hang on a sec," he told Sergeant Pérez.

"You got that huggy-fuzzy yet?" someone asked without introduction.

Huggy-fuzzy? "That chocolate thing?"

"Yeah. Is it okay?"

"It'll do." Eric hung up and returned his attention to Sergeant Pérez. "Hundred and sixth Precinct. That's near JFK, right?"

"You think it's someone at the airport?"

"More likely a recent arrival." A dark suspicion lurked in Eric's mind, but he needed more information. "Is the baby healthy?"

"Screaming at the top of his lungs, until we stuck a bottle in his mouth. That's how a wino found him. The yelling. Wino flags down a patrol car and—"

"What was the baby wearing?" Eric interrupted.

"Nothing. Naked as the day he was born."

That pretty much confirmed it. "Okay, I'm extrapolating a bit, but here's what I think. The baby just arrived from West Africa."

"Africa?" Sergeant Pérez blurted.

For her sake, Eric backed up a step in his logic. "Most newborns smell like vanilla, honey, and almond. It's a combination everyone associates with 'soft and cuddly.' But after a month or two, they acquire the smell of household cleanser."

"You mean like Comet?"

"Not exactly." Butt-sprung from sitting all day, Eric stood and rubbed a hip with his free hand. "Makers of baby products— powders, soaps, and so on—scent them to convey the impression of cleanliness to the mothers. To do this, they mimic the fragrances added to cleaning products. Those fragrances vary in different parts of the world. Pine in Scandinavia, floral in the US, orange blossom in France and Spain. In West Africa, the most popular soaps contain an antimicrobial phenol called creosol. It's what you smell in the creosote used as a preservative in wooden telephone poles."

"You lost me with the antimicrobial whatever. But if the kid came in from Africa, I can circulate his picture to Customs at JFK. Someone'll remember a mother, or mother and father, coming in with a baby. That fails, we'll check the security cameras. We get the passport records, the bastard's good as caught."

"You can also tell Customs that the baby was probably crying and stank of excrement."

"How do you figure that?"

"The fact that you found him naked. I don't see a parent, or parents, traveling all this way just to abandon their baby. My guess is the kid was stolen in Africa and brought here as a mule."

"You mean like dope? How much dope can you hide on an infant?"

"I mean like diamonds. West Africa produces a lot of them. Stuff a couple handfuls in the boy's diaper before boarding, then don't change him for eight or ten hours, and you arrive at JFK with a screeching kid wearing a diaper full of baby shit and raw gemstones. If you were a Customs officer, would you search him?"

A long exhalation came over the phone. "Son of a bitch."

Eric smiled. From the NYPD, that reaction was the best pat on the back he could receive.

But Sergeant Pérez wasn't finished. "What you just said would explain the scratches on the baby's rump. Poor thing had to sit on diamonds for the whole goddamned trip. Foster, I owe you. You ever get collared for something in the hundred and sixth, you make your one call to me."

Bowled over, Eric stammered out a "Thank you" and wished her good luck. For that kind of praise he'd walk on fire.

He stretched, hearing his vertebrae pop as he worked them back into alignment. His wristwatch read twenty minutes to five. Maybe he'd knock off early. But there was still one bottle on his afternoon tray.

He sat and picked up the bottle. Unfolding the lab sheet wrapped around it, he read, "Mink, for artificial furs." Beneath that ran a numbered list of ingredients, their percentages, and unit cost. Forty-two ingredients. That told him the person who concocted this had struggled to build it and was probably lazy. Even great perfumes seldom contained more than thirty ingredients. Fragrances with more—in some cases, the total exceeded a hundred—suggested the creator had trouble "getting it right" and, in the end, didn't bother to remove those components that were ultimately superfluous. After all, it was easier to add things than to take them out.

Eric unscrewed the cap, dipped in a *mouillette*—called smell strips here—waved the thin slip of blotter paper in the air, then sniffed it. And recoiled. Had this really made it past a floor supervisor before coming to him?

Fixing it would be harder than just starting from scratch. But as he'd often been reminded, he was not a "creative." Creatives were authors. He was merely a copy editor, his job to correct the punctuation, perhaps suggest a different word.

Actually, Rheinhold-Laroche used the term incorrectly, although Eric had decided it would do him no good to point out their error. In the real perfume business, creatives weren't authors. They were the "idea men." Perfumers were the authors. Creatives proposed the concept, perfumers came up with the formula. One of the "big boys," a company such as International Flavors and Fragrances, made the perfume, and the "brand" sold it as their own, or as the creative's own if the creative were a movie star or celebrity designer. Many brands didn't even know the formulas of the perfumes they sold, and most creatives didn't care.

As to crap like this "Mink, for artificial furs," no amount of copyediting could fix it. It needed whole new chapters. Eric thought a moment, then scratched out four of the ingredients and jotted two replacements. But that wouldn't be enough. It needed one of the synthetic musks, or maybe—

His door burst open, banging against the wall. "Are you out of your damn mind?"

Eric cringed. If there was one guy he really hated in this company, one guy whose voice grated like a hacksaw cutting sheet metal, it was Charles Wigby. With a slow breath, Eric turned to face him. "What have I done now?"

"What have you *done?*" Wigby's Adam's apple jumped in his scrawny neck. His pencil-line moustache quivered. Clad in suit pants, white shirt, and a god-awful paisley tie, he flapped a lab sheet in the air, then threw it in Eric's lap. "This is what you've done. Where do you get off thinking our customers will accept something that adds eight dollars a pound to their product? Are you trying to put us out of business?"

God, he loathed this little Nazi. According to scuttlebutt, Wigby had come from the company's chemical plant in Georgia, where he'd caught management's eye for his ruthless cost cutting and for keeping out the unions. Now Assistant Comptroller, the bastard wielded corporate power. And Eric had more than once felt his wrath.

He shut his eyes against the queasy feeling that, this time, he might have gone too far. It had been a gamble, for sure, but one he'd thought justified. "People who buy cabin cruisers won't mind a few extra cents to have their phony wood paneling smell like Amazon hardwoods instead of pine."

"Fuck Amazon hardwoods." Wigby's voice leapt an octave. "They want it to smell like wood. They don't give a shit what kind of wood. Nobody gives a shit what kind of wood. Just wood. Got it?"

"Did you smell the stuff that came off the floor?" Eric asked, referring to the so-called fragrance he'd been sent to approve. "It smells like turpentine."

Wigby pulled the bottle from his pocket and thrust it at Eric. "It smells fine. Now you peel off your goddamned 'Ree-ject' sticker or start looking for another job."

Feeling dirty, in desperate need of fresh air and a shower, Eric pulled on his overcoat, rode the elevator down with two other employees who looked equally downtrodden, and walked out into freezing wind. A sandwich wrapper struck his ankle then blew past. Pastrami on rye, with mustard, "American" mustard. He knew a pastrami joint two blocks away that used French mustard with horseradish and decided to stop there and pick up a sandwich for dinner before heading home to Daisy. The horseradish would clear his nostrils.

Joining the flow of pedestrians, collars up, shoulders hunched, he'd made it halfway to Ninth Avenue when his cell phone buzzed in his pocket. He stepped into a doorway to shield himself from the wind.

"Eric, Fawcett. Where are you?"

Dear Detective Fawcett, layer-on of guilt trips. Fawcett, all innocence and compassion, had shown up at Eric's apartment three months previously with Daisy in tow and a sob story about her dead handler's not having any family, so the dog would go to a shelter and survive two weeks, tops, before they injected her— unless Eric took her in. They were, after all, both bloodhounds.

"You listening?" Fawcett said. "I'm at a crime scene. I don't have all night."

"I'm just leaving work."

"Stay where you are. I'll have a car there in ten minutes."

Two calls in one day. A record. But bad timing. "I have to go home and take Daisy out. She's been cooped up all day."

"Then your place in twenty minutes."

"It takes me twenty minutes to walk there."

"So run."

Thirty minutes later, Eric sat next to a "uniform" in a patrol car crawling up Eighth Avenue toward Columbus Circle. Their flashing misery lights and occasional bursts from the siren-squawker did little to part the sea of taillights in front of them. On the other hand, being in a police vehicle seemed to perk up Daisy, who had her nose pressed against the plastic-and-cage-wire barrier separating the front and rear seats.

Rather than short-change her on her evening walk, he'd clipped Daisy's badge to her collar and put her in the back seat. The badge was a souvenir, no longer valid. But it would get her in anywhere, and Eric figured she might enjoy being around cops again. If Fawcett chewed him out, then Fawcett could take her for a walk.

At Columbus Circle, the patrol car turned onto Central Park South, part of the ultra-high rent district. A block and a half later, it double-parked next to three other cruisers and the ME's van. Medical Examiner meant murder. Or suicide.

The uniform, Blazik according to his nametag, walked in with them. "They're with us," he told the deskman and said to Eric, "Eighth floor. You'll see the tape."

With Daisy on her lead, Eric took the elevator, all shiny brass and mirrors with a pink marble floor and lingering hints of roses and Panthere de Cartier. No trace of cigarette smoke. Fawcett must have crushed out his ever-present Marlboro Light before entering this bastion of the well-heeled. Or maybe he'd learned in Eric's class at John Jay not to pollute potentially telling odors at a crime scene.

A chime announced their arrival at the eighth floor. The doors opened to reveal another uniform. He looked them over then pointed. "Down there."

Yellow tape cordoned off the end apartment, one that, if Eric's orientation were correct, directly overlooked Central Park. He led Daisy down the blue-carpeted corridor. The closer he came to the open door, the more scents he encountered. Carnauba wax, feces, wool and leather, a plummy red wine that might be Malbec, and … Eric slowed. It couldn't be.

"What the hell is *she* doing here?" Detective Darrell Fawcett ducked under the yellow tape.

The man looked as haggard as ever, his bulky gray suit matching the color of his six o'clock stubble. The only thing about him that didn't look tired were his cold, blue eyes.

He trained them on Eric. "No dogs allowed."

"You're the one who conned me into taking her. Besides, I told you, she's been cooped up all day. And crime is her business."

"Not anymore." From his jacket pocket, Fawcett pulled a pair of latex gloves, like the ones he was wearing, and handed them to Eric. "Leave her out here. And take that shield off her collar. She's retired."

Prick. Eric gave Daisy the down-stay command, then bent over her. But instead of removing her badge, he rotated her collar so the badge wasn't visible from the apartment's doorway.

"I saw that," Fawcett grunted when Eric joined him. "Think you're a smartass, don't you?" He ducked back under the tape.

"Booties are in that box by the door."

Eric pulled on a pair of disposable blue booties, then stepped inside and surveyed the apartment. Mahogany floor, Persian carpets, Italian-modern furniture in white leather. A bottle of Argentine Malbec and two nearly empty wineglasses stood on a glass-topped coffee table. Abstract paintings, nice ones, adorned the walls. At the far end were sliding glass doors that presumably led to a terrace overlooking Central Park, although it was too dark outside to tell from this distance. Through an archway on the right, a stainless steel kitchen glinted in low light. Altogether, it was pretty close to the kind of place he'd once dreamed of.

A camera flash, then another, drew his attention. They came from a room at the far left, most likely the master bedroom, which would also overlook the park.

Fawcett led him toward the flashes. "Strangulation. White male, aged twenty-eight. Girlfriend, who owns this place, admits she did it. Claims she couldn't get enough of him. She needed more." Fawcett cast his eyes heavenward. "We've got her down at the precinct."

"So why am I here?" Eric asked. But he had a frightening suspicion he knew. That impossible smell. It grew stronger as they entered the bedroom. He stopped just inside the doorway, unable to move farther. Ripples of vertigo lapped the edge of his consciousness, the first sign of impending storm. *Please, not now.* If he buried his nose in the crook of his elbow, Fawcett would surely interpret it as wimpy queasiness. Instead, Eric held his breath. The ripples receded, leaving sweat running down his armpits.

"What's wrong with you?" Fawcett said. "It's just a body." Then he scowled. "If you puke in here, I'll haul your ass in for corrupting a crime scene."

Eric saw it now. On the bed, a black-haired guy with the chiseled physique and two-day beard of a fashion model lay sprawled on his back, his head hanging over the edge. Claw marks scored his face, neck, and chest. A long smear of dried excrement tailed from between his legs.

Three other men milled around the room, one taking pictures, one closing up a doctor's case, one laying out a black body bag.

"Did you hear me?" Fawcett said.

Eric looked away from the corpse to see Fawcett holding a plastic evidence bag with a dark, squarish object inside.

"We don't get a lot of murders in Midtown North. In a whole year, you can count 'em on one hand. Now we got three in two months. All of them the same. Lover kills lover, with his or her bare hands. Two male suspects, and now one female. All claim they couldn't help it. Only thing ties them together is this." He opened the bag and handed Eric a black bottle, a cube inscribed in gold with the letters, SF. "What is it?"

Eric shuddered. He didn't need to smell it. He'd smelled it halfway down the hall. With every step he'd taken, it grew stronger. In here, even mixed with the odors of death, it came at him like an avalanche through a snowstorm.

"Earth to Eric," Fawcett said, leaning his big-pored face to within a foot of Eric's nose. "You gonna jack off or smell it?"

Eric went through the motions of opening the bottle and taking a whiff. A shiver ran through him. Did he dare reveal what he knew? He had to. If he didn't, and the cops found out later, he'd be in the worst trouble of his life. He swallowed to moisten his throat. "It's Balquees."

"Balquees? What the fuck is that?"

Hand shaking, Eric gave him back the bottle. "A perfume. I created it."

"You?" Fawcett glared at him like he'd just slapped his mother.

Why did policemen always repeat what you'd just said? "It's … Well, I guess you'd say it's an aphrodisiac."

"Aphrodisiac?"

A zipping sound turned Eric's eyes to the bed as the dead man's face disappeared under the final tugs of a guy closing the body bag. "It has nothing to do with this fellow's death."

Fawcett lifted the lapels of his suit coat, straightening it on his shoulders in a gesture apparently intended to convey authority. "You and I are going down to the precinct for a little chat."

Chapter 11

By nine-thirty, Eric was exhausted. By ten, he could barely think straight. Detective Fawcett's face across the Formica-topped table was becoming a blur. Eric's butt ached from sitting on the hard steel chair. His stomach wouldn't stop growling.

"Can we call it quits?" he said. "I haven't had dinner, and neither has Daisy." She lay beside him on the linoleum floor of the interrogation room.

"She'll live. Be thankful I let her in here."

"Can you at least stop smoking?" Under the harsh lights, cigarette smoke hung in listless strata from ceiling to table. It fouled Eric's nose and stung his eyes. An old coffee can with water in the bottom sat on a corner of the table. For a while the water had hissed with every butt Fawcett dropped into it. Now the butts rose above the water, and each new one just lay there until it burned itself out, usually not before Fawcett lit up again. "Isn't it against the law in government buildings?"

"Call the cops." Fawcett flipped back a few pages on his yellow legal pad. "Let's talk more about Balquees."

"There's nothing more to tell." At least three times, he'd described every aspect of Balquees, from concept to creation to his experiment at the Panthéon and the party in Luc's apartment. Under Fawcett's relentless prodding, he'd even relived the bitter humiliation of his expulsion, ending with the crap job he now endured as a result.

But Fawcett had wanted more. Despite his note taking and a video camera mounted in one corner of the ceiling, he used an old-fashioned cassette player to record every sordid detail. He kept repeating questions, probing deeper, pausing only to change tapes.

They'd slogged all the way back to Eric's adolescence, when his parents moved "temporarily" from Chicago to Galveston Island to care for his grandmother, the sweetest woman on earth, reduced by a stroke to drooling in a wheelchair. Upon learning of his interest in fragrances, she'd slurred instructions to wheel her to her dressing table where, with a weak wave of her hand and "All yours," she'd given him his first great perfumes, precious classics like N° 5, Joy, Diorissimo, Youth Dew, Vent Vert.

Fawcett, playing him like a trout, even coaxed out of Eric the two defining incidents in his early life. First Melony Deason, the girlfriend of the most obnoxious bully in junior high, the Neanderthal who'd come up with the expression, "perfume pussy." Eric had gotten his revenge by stealing her away with a perfume he created and named in her honor. He didn't even like her very much, but he dated her for the rest of the year, immune from persecution thanks to Melony's telling the cretin she'd never speak to him again if he ever laid a hand on Eric.

Then there was Mary Jo Talbot. In high school, Mary Jo was the class bookworm, good-looking but disdainful of anyone who couldn't solve polynomial equations or discuss *Hamlet*. Eric, mediocre at math and lovesick to the point of pining, had spent two months crafting a perfume for her. End of story: she went with him to the prom and "parked" with him afterwards.

Those two successes had driven home to him forever the power of perfume.

And they seemed to grab Fawcett's attention. Eric had seen him scribble "Power of Perfume" and underline it three times, the way he'd previously underlined "Orgy" and "Theft."

Eric suppressed a groan. Why the hell had he agreed to come here? He'd bared his whole life, practically stood naked in front of Fawcett, and the bastard was singling out—

"Balquees," Fawcett repeated, lighting another cigarette. "Tell me about this oud shit you put in it."

"Again? What is this, the third degree?"

"We use rubber hoses for that. Talk about oud."

Eric sagged in his chair. Would he ever get out of here? Would there be anything left of him if he did? He took a long, slow breath and started at the top. "It's the Arabic word for wood. In the perfume business, it refers to—"

"Not that part. What's in it?"

"What do you mean?"

"Chemicals. You said you have a Master's degree in organic chemistry. So what's in it?"

"Probably hundreds of compounds. I never tried to analyze it." *Why bother?* "It's a resin, like frankincense or pine sap, and they're all complex as hell. This particular tree produces it to fight off fungal infection. So the chemical composition probably varies depending on environment. Different fungi in Indonesia versus Yemen versus wherever else the tree grows. In fact, I *know* it varies. No other oud has this same effect on people."

"The effect of driving them to commit murder?"

"For Christ's sake, would you get off that. I've told you a hundred times, Balquees is just an aphrodisiac. It doesn't make people kill each other. I don't know how someone else got my formula. I don't know what SF means or who's making it or where it's manufactured. And I don't think it has anything to do with the death of that man we saw tonight. Or anybody else."

"That makes one of us."

"Are you sure there were no drugs in the apartment? One of those date-rape things?"

"Not unless you can knock someone out with allergy meds or Naprosyn."

Eric slouched lower, almost slid off his chair, and struggled upright again. "I can't do this anymore."

"What? You got menstrual cramps?"

"Go fuck yourself."

"Nice talk." Fawcett flipped his notepad closed. "Okay, go home."

Thank God. Eric pushed himself to his feet, half expecting Fawcett to pull a Columbo on him—"Just one more thing." But Fawcett seemed preoccupied with writing something on the cassette he'd just extracted from the tape recorder.

Too stiff to bend at the waist, Eric knelt to pick up Daisy's lead. At the door, he paused. "Are you going to tell me not to leave town?"

"You planning to?"

"No."

"Then I don't have to tell you."

Eric waited for the 7:46 to rumble past, then phoned in sick. This being Friday morning, he now had three full days to concentrate entirely on SF and all its ramifications.

Barely able to sleep last night, he'd given up before daybreak and treated Daisy to a walk in Clinton Park. The exercise had helped him unravel the tangle of thoughts writhing in his head.

It didn't take a genius to figure out that, suspect or not, he was the only lead Fawcett had. Absent new evidence—maybe even *with* new evidence—the bastard would keep hounding him, grilling him like hamburger until he was burned to ash. That part was a given. What to do about it was not. But he now had some pretty good ideas.

At least, he thought they were good. In his addled state and with so little sleep, he could use another opinion, an independent perspective, someone to just talk to.

He looked at his watch, checking the seconds hand to make sure it was still running. Seven fifty-eight. He'd give her two more minutes. Next to the bed, his perfumer's organ now served as a filing cabinet for paperwork and as a nightstand for personal effects and the black, rotary telephone that had been here when he moved in.

At eight o'clock, he picked up the handset and dialed.

Abby answered on the fourth ring. "Hullo?"

"Sorry to wake you."

"I was awake. Sort of."

"I need to talk with you. Can we meet for breakfast?"

"I don't eat breakfast."

"This is important. There's been a string of murders. The police questioned me for three and a half hours last night."

"Murder?" Sounds of pushing up in bed came over the line. "Eric, what happened?"

"It's a long story. Can we talk?"

"Sure, of course." She paused. "Okay, there's a breakfast joint near NBC. On the south side—"

"I know the place." A dump, but who cared. "I'll be there in twenty minutes."

"I just woke up. Make it forty-five."

Braving the stink of cheap bacon, Eric shouldered his way into Mario's Diner. Along the right side ran a chest-high counter, behind which four guys and a woman scurried back and forth making breakfast for the patrons. An island in the middle held white plastic cutlery, paper napkins, four tall coffee dispensers, and carton after carton of little sealed tubs filled with the sorts of jammy stuff that Rheinhold-Laroche's "cuisine" division flavored and colored. Stand-up tables the size of manhole covers filled the remaining space, except by the front window where three similar tables had barstools around them.

Eric scanned the crowd for Abby. She wasn't there yet, but he did spot a man in a business suit who was maybe six mouthfuls away from leaving one of the window tables. Hoping to claim the vacancy, Eric hustled into line at the counter. The menu on the wall ran to forty or fifty choices, mostly variations on eggs, breakfast meats, and starches like toast, bagels and hash browns. The smell of burnt peanut oil put off any appetite he might have had. He ordered toast.

"Toast and what?" demanded a fat guy behind the counter. He wore a white T-shirt, stained yellow across the paunch, and an expression that said, *Don't screw with me.*

"Just toast."

The guy shot him a look and, less than a minute later, tossed a Styrofoam plate on the counter. Two limp pieces of white bread, barely browned. "Next!"

Down the line, juices swirled in five-gallon carboys. Eric stopped to consider them, then turned and saw the suit at the front table preparing to leave.

"Ya gonna park here all morning?" the woman behind Eric asked.

Eric skipped the juice, paid the cashier, and headed for the now-empty table. He was twelve feet away, threading through the crowd, when Miss Goodyear Blimp stepped in front of him. Like a bulldozer, she ploughed her way to the table. Shoving aside the abandoned remains of the suit's meal, she draped her bulk over a stool and settled in with a heaping plate of sausage, scrambled eggs, and four English muffins.

"Eric," Abby called. She stood just inside the doorway, radiant in this dreary dive.

He pushed through the crowd, protecting his plate of not-toast from the elbows in his path. "Hi. You look great."

She wore black with a single splash of color: black ankle-length coat, black business suit, black boots with two-inch heels, and a red silk blouse. In a symbol of unity with her current girlfriend, Kirin, she'd adopted the Southern Indian tradition of adorning herself with a tiny diamond stud in the side of her right nostril. The last time he and Abby had spent a night together, it was the only piercing she'd had. God only knew what would happen if she started dating a Goth.

"You look like hell." She glanced at his plate. "And so does that."

Eric dropped his plate in a trashcan and walked her outside. "Let's find somewhere else."

After two weeks of frigid overcast, the sky had cleared to pale, topaz blue. A bright sun, visible between buildings, offered the possibility of midday temperatures that would pass for balmy. Many of the pedestrians, apparently anticipating warmth, strode with their overcoats open. Eric followed suit, but Abby didn't.

Down a side street, away from most of the taxis and delivery trucks, they found a coffee shop that offered outdoor seating in a narrow area divided from the sidewalk by a row of four-foot-high, conically pruned junipers in redwood pots. He bought two lattes and carried them out to a table, where he withdrew for her the chair bathed in sunlight.

"Always the gentleman." With a smile, Abby unbuttoned her

overcoat and sat. "That's one of the reasons I love you."

Eric took the chair in shade. By New York standards, it was a secluded spot. Cars and trucks crammed the street eight feet away, advancing ten or twelve vehicles with each green light. But honking was minimal and foot traffic was thin. Fragrances of evergreen and juniper berries mingled with the aroma of coffee, reminding him of mornings in the woods during camping trips with his uncle.

Grateful for the relative peace and privacy, Eric related the grim events of the previous night. He left out nothing except the feces on the bed, which she didn't need to know about, and his childhood, which she knew as well as he knew hers.

"God, that must have been awful for you," Abby said when he'd finished. "But your cop friend's grasping at straws. You and I both know what Balquees does, and it doesn't make you strangle anyone."

"Precisely what I told him. That's why I think the copy has to be different."

"But you said it smelled the same."

"Initial impression, under stress. No counterfeit is the same as the original."

"So, what are you going to do?"

"First thing, I've got to get my own sample of SF. The bottle I saw had no maker's mark."

She considered a moment, her latte untouched although he'd consumed nearly all of his. "I could do a computer search for you. Your dial-up connection would take you weeks."

"I was hoping you'd offer." Abby's skills and equipment far outstripped his own.

"Then what?"

"Then find out who's making it, of course."

She pursed her lips. "I think you're overreacting. Who made it, where it's made, that's all police business. They asked you last night, so you know they're going to pursue it. Let them."

"And do nothing?"

"It's not your problem."

"It sure as hell feels like my problem."

"Because you've gotten too emotional about it." She reached her hand across the table and covered one of his. "You're angry that someone copied your creation. Who wouldn't be? But counterfeiting a perfume isn't illegal."

She was right about that. With perfume formulas, there was no such thing as protection of ownership. The European Union, in its pinheaded wisdom, had decided perfumery was a craft, not an art. And crafts were not patentable. Which was why the high end of the business, where Eric longed to be, relied on honor.

SF, however, went way beyond a breach of ethics or legality. "Illegal or not, whoever's doing this is getting me in big trouble with the cops."

"I think the most important thing for you to do is convince yourself that SF isn't Balquees."

He pulled his hand away. "It isn't. I know it isn't."

"Then instead of police work, that's what you should spend your time on. For two reasons. Most important, it'll allay your fears."

"What fears?"

She took hold of his hand again. "Sweetheart, we know each other inside out. Deep down, you're scared to death that your creation really is driving people crazy. I'm telling you it's not. And if you can prove the two are different, then you'll *know* it's not."

Had she detected something he refused to acknowledge? He didn't think so. But … Christ, he wouldn't be able to live with himself.

"The other reason," she said, "is because differences and similarities could help us figure out if someone made SF by analyzing Balquees, or if they stole your original formula."

Eric sat up straight. "The formula's in my notebook. No one could have taken it."

"Are you sure?"

Eric scaled the stairs two at a time, unlocked his apartment, then dashed into the bedroom. On hands and knees, he dragged out the cardboard boxes that held his collection of essences and, somewhere, his notebook. There it was, hardbound in black. He fanned the pages to his last entry. "BALQUEES," it read in his own hand, followed by two pages of trial and error before the page with his final formula. Thank God. No one had ripped it out.

With a rush of relief, he sat back on the floor. A perfumer's notebook was sacrosanct, the running record of a life's work, personal and absolutely confidential. Despite the honor of the brotherhood, most professionals kept theirs under lock and key.

Students learned this on day one—at the same time they learned that peering, uninvited, into a colleague's notebook was grounds for disciplinary action. Eric had shown his to no one. He'd kept it either in his possession or locked in his apartment.

Daisy limped in, toenails clicking on the floor, and stuck her prodigious nose in one of the boxes.

"Like those, do you, girl?" Because the bottles were tightly capped, Eric couldn't smell their contents. But Daisy obviously could. What a marvelous cloud of aromas they must be to her, strange scents she'd never encountered before and probably would never encounter anywhere else.

The phone rang.

Eric flinched. If it was Fawcett, he didn't want to talk to him. If it was Rheinhold-Laroche, they'd probably called before. He'd need an excuse for why he hadn't answered. Cough syrup. He had gone to the drugstore for cough syrup and decongestants. That'd work. In fact, the same excuse, that he was sick, would work for Fawcett, also. Practicing "hello" in a hoarse voice, he got to his feet and picked up the handset.

"Eric, it's Abby. What did you find?"

He sank onto the bed. "My notebook's intact."

No response.

"Abby?"

"Doesn't that tell you something?" she asked. "If no one took your formula, then it was copied by analysis."

He thought a moment. Whenever a new perfume was launched, the first buyers were the competitors. Overnight, they would analyze it by various techniques, most commonly by injecting it into a gas chromatograph that separated and identified the components. If any identifications were ambiguous, the separated components could be fed from the gas chromatograph into a mass spectrometer. By morning, your competition knew the ingredients, although the exact percentages often remained sketchy.

But if you had no product to analyze … "I never gave Balquees to anyone. I mean, I let people try it, but nobody ever got more than just enough to put on themselves."

"Are you sure?"

Oh, God. What if he was wrong? He dropped the phone and rummaged through his boxes. He found Balquees between Balsam of Peru and Bergamot. The bottle was half full, just as it should be. Picking up the phone again, he said, "I'm sure."

"Then it's definitely analysis."

Wasn't she listening? "I told you, no one ever got enough to analyze."

"Not machine analysis. Someone analyzed it by nose."

"Impossible."

"Not for a master."

"What master?"

"Isn't it obvious? Your mentor, Jacques Durand."

Chapter 12

Eric paced his apartment, from bedroom to living room and back. Sure, Durand knew the main ingredient. Eric had been expelled for it while Durand stood at his side. And any decent nose could identify the other components, even the shiitake. That was the beauty of analysis by smell versus machine; the nose would identify shiitake, while the machine—unless linked to a specialized database—would only recognize the chemical compounds *in* shiitake.

But Durand had no motive. He dwelled in the ranks of the gods, a master among masters, with more laurels than his silvery old head could hold. Besides, there was honor. To Durand, honor was everything. Stealing a perfume, especially a student's perfume, was simply out of the question. The idea would never cross his mind.

Even so, the counterfeiter had to be someone at ISIPCA, because no one else knew about Balquees. *Brilliant, Eric. That narrows it down.* The whole school knew about it, even the board of inquisitors. On the other hand, fewer than twenty-five people had ever smelled it, or at least worn it.

Diego. He was the only one to whom Eric had told the entire list of ingredients. Diego even admitted he wanted to make Balquees, supposedly for himself. And the poor guy carried some serious baggage. His father, a breeder of champion Andalusians, scorned perfumery as a limp-wristed pursuit for his only son.

Diego hoped success would restore him to favor. Unfortunately he had less talent than ambition.

Stopping at his living room window, Eric stared out at the Amtrak line and the litter of junk on either side of it. Balquees could solve both of Diego's problems. It could bring him financial success—assuming the copy was selling well—and the fact that it was an aphrodisiac could well appeal, at least in Diego's mind, to his father's view of manly cunning.

Now more than ever, Eric needed a sample of SF. There'd be subtle differences from Balquees, differences that might carry Diego's fingerprints. Perfumers had preferences, and often, especially with those who were less creative or less experienced, you could detect those penchants in the essences they'd chosen to build a perfume. Synthetic versus natural, for instance, or one variety of lemon or rose versus another.

Eric turned from the window and switched on his computer. Abby had said she'd run some Internet searches, but he could search, too. He connected his modem, which disconnected his phone line, then dialed up his ISP and waited for the awful, fax-squawk signal to stop. When his home page finally came up, he accessed Google, waited, typed in "SF perfume," and waited some more.

There it was, first hit. "SF, Guaranteed Aphrodesiac," the last word misspelled. Eric double-clicked on the link. As the blue "progress" bar crawled across the bottom of the page, he sat back and chewed his lip. Jesus, could it get any slower? He heard Daisy settle to the floor with an expulsion of breath that sounded like a sigh and mimicked his own frustration.

Having little need of a computer, except for occasional emails, he'd opted for a second-hand one advertised in the company rag at Rheinhold-Laroche. The seller, a mousy lady from Admin, had thrown in the modem for free. As Abby had said several times, he was probably the last person in New York with a dial-up connection.

The monitor started downloading a red background with "SF" in flaming gold letters at the top. Eric leaned forward. As the web page slowly expanded, he read the subtitle, "GUARANTEED APHRODESIAC," followed by "THE QUEEN OF SHEBA'S

SECRET FORMULA" and a series of links to other pages within the site. He clicked the "Buy Now" link and waited. No doubt anymore, he had to cough up the money for broadband.

A train rattled past. Robotically he checked his watch. The eleven-fifty, running five minutes late.

At last the order page came up, displaying a photograph of the same kind of black, cubical bottle Fawcett had handed him and a price of "USD 200/oz." Eric wouldn't have sold it that cheaply, if he were going to sell it at all. He typed "1" into the quantity box and clicked the link to "Checkout."

After a minute or so, a page appeared asking for name, address, and credit card details. Damn. He couldn't do that. His name would set off alarm bells, alert the seller that Eric was onto him.

So now what?

Staring at the page, he noticed that the first part of the web address ended with ".ch." Dot ch. The country code for Czech Republic? No, that was probably .cz. China, Chad? Chad made no sense. On the other hand, China had become notorious for its counterfeiting of consumer products. But how would Balquees have made it to China? There were no Chinese students at ISIPCA.

Except Abby.

Eric leapt from his chair. It couldn't be. She was ethnic Chinese but born here in New York City, daughter of an immigrant grocer who'd made her childhood miserable. When sober, he ignored her as though she didn't exist. When drunk, he screamed curses, blaming her for the loss of his wife who had died of complications arising from Abby's birth. Abby had grown up in constant fear of being carted off to Harlem and sold. Which accounted for how frightened she was of blacks.

At the same time, thanks to her father and his opium-smoking friends, she hated almost everything Chinese. No way would she have anything to do with the People's Republic.

Still … Eric squeezed his chin, trying to remember how much he'd told her about the ingredients of Balquees. The oud, of course, and the shiitake mushrooms. And she'd recognized civet on her own. But while her nose was good, he doubted she could identify all the components. Besides, her interest lay in flavorings, and she was doing damn well in that field.

Nevertheless, the China suffix on SF's web address had to mean something. And if not her, then who? Or what?

His cell phone buzzed. The screen showed "Unknown Caller." Rheinhold-Laroche didn't have this number, but Detective Fawcett did.

Again, Eric adopted a hoarse voice.

And again it was Abby. "Eric, I took off at lunchtime. I'm in my apartment. You better come here and look at this."

Eric rode the subway down to SoHo, where Abby had a converted loft in the Cast-Iron district near Washington Square. Climbing the stairs to the fourth floor of her building, he felt jittery at the prospect of confronting her with the China connection. Of course, she'd deny any connection existed. Could he read her well enough to tell whether she was lying?

She answered his knock wearing the same skirt and blouse she'd had on this morning. Her overcoat and suit jacket lay draped over the back of her couch, next to which she had shed her boots. Like her clothes, Abby's decorating ran to stylish and black, including the huge, framed prints on her walls of paintings by Mark Rothko. Even the hundred-gallon aquarium she'd bought, so Kirin could keep fish, rested on a fit-for-purpose stand of black acrylic.

"Grab a chair." She strode across an expanse of polished oak flooring to her array of computer gear in a corner by the front windows. "This is interesting."

"Hello, Eric." Kirin came out of the bedroom looking beautiful as ever, with her hair in a long braid down her back. She wore a pale green sari, wrapped low around her hips, and a traditional short-sleeved top that stopped just below her breasts to leave her stomach exposed. The sari swayed gracefully as she approached him, preceded by fragrances of cardamom and anise, with a hint of clove. She pecked him on the cheek. "How are you?"

"Fine. Well actually, I'm in a bit of a bind. Abby's trying to help me."

"She told me. There's no problem using my credit card."

Huh?

"Eric, you need to look at this," Abby said.

He excused himself from Kirin and pulled up a chair on rollers to sit next to Abby.

She pointed to the leftmost of her three flat-screen monitors, the one directly in front of him, which displayed the same red page with flaming letters that he had found. "This is where you buy SF. It's a place in Switzerland."

"Switzerland?" Fat chance. "Look at the dot ch in the URL."

She turned to him. "Dot ch *is* Switzerland."

How could that be? "I thought it was China."

"China, I think, is cn." She slid her mouse until its cursor appeared on the monitor in front of her, where she opened Google and speed-typed something into the search box. A Wikipedia page came up almost instantly. "Yeah, see? CN is the country code TLD for China."

"TLD?"

"Top-level domain." She clicked something farther down the page, and another page appeared. "Here. CH stands for Confoederatio Helvetica, the Latin name for Switzerland."

Eric tried to conceal a huge sense of relief. Thank God, he hadn't confronted her.

"Are you okay?" Abby asked.

"Better than I care to say."

She looked at him curiously, as if suddenly realizing he'd harbored suspicions about her. If so, she let it pass. Sliding her cursor back to the left-hand monitor, she clicked a link on the red page, and another one came up with several paragraphs in gold-colored lettering. "This is a bunch of that fairytale crap out of the Bible, the Solomon and Sheba stuff. And there's another page with testimonials, all signed with initials only, of course, and with 'addresses' like London, New York, Sydney."

Good Lord. "The stuff's being sold all over the world."

"The nature of the Internet," she said. "The testimonials are probably bogus. But I've checked, and I can't find anyplace to buy it except this site. In fact, this page." She clicked on another link, which brought up the same "Buy Now" page he'd seen on his own computer. "Two hundred bucks an ounce."

Same page and the same dead end he had run into before.

She turned to him. "I don't think you or I should order it, because whoever is selling it may have been at ISIPCA when we were. But Kirin can buy it, if you'll pay her back."

Eric straightened in his chair. "Of course. That's a great idea." Now he understood Kirin's comment about using her credit card. "Sure, I'll pay her. Let's buy it."

Abby picked up a silvery Visa card that had been lying next to the right-hand monitor, and a few minutes later their order was placed.

He looked around for Kirin, but didn't see her. The bedroom door was closed, and he now noticed the powdery, resinous fragrance of champa, a plumeria-based incense much favored in India for its sensuality. Perhaps he was overstaying his welcome.

"Please thank her for me," he said, rolling his chair back to rise.

"No problem. Now, there's something else I want you to see."

Well, if Abby weren't in a hurry, neither was he. He rolled himself forward again.

"You got me interested in who's behind this. So I ran a little hacker's program. It's better than Whois and its copycats at rooting out website owners." On the screen in front of him, Abby brought up a white page with half a dozen lines in plain, black typeface. "You can see here that the SF site is registered to someone called EDG, whose address is a post office box in Zurich."

"Who or what is EDG?"

"I'm not sure. I assumed it was a company, but I've searched the web, and all I can find are some design firms and a consulting agency. They all look legitimate."

"Damn."

"But it could be someone's initials," she offered. "Like in a partnership. And I'm wondering if the D might stand for—"

"Diego! Son of a bitch, I thought it might be him."

She screwed up her face. "You gotta be kidding. He doesn't have the brains. But there's someone else who does."

❧

Still annoyed at Abby's innuendo about Durand, Eric tromped up the stairs to his apartment. He felt like he was getting nowhere with this SF business. Yeah, he'd ordered a bottle of it, but who knew when it would arrive? Abby had pointed out that the shipping address would be on the package, but what if it was just the same post office box in Switzerland that she'd already found? When you stepped away and thought about it rationally, he was doing little more than treading water.

Maybe he should leave it to the cops, after all. If he mended his fences with Fawcett, the detective might keep him in the loop. Not much chance, but he could try.

Daisy greeted him at the door, her tail wagging. At least someone was glad to see him. He rubbed her ears. "You want an early walk?"

The word "walk" made her spin around happily, no small feat for a three-legged dog.

He looked for her lead, found it in the living room, and noticed his screen saver drawing phantasmagorical plumbing pipes. The monitor felt hot, probably on its last legs. Resolving to replace the whole system, as well as order broadband, he shut down his computer and disconnected the modem. "Okay, girl, let's go."

He'd just opened his door when the phone rang. Ignore it, or answer? Daisy looked up at him expectantly. But it might be Abby. He walked to his bedroom and picked it up.

"Who've you been talking to all day?" Fawcett demanded without so much as a hello.

"I was connected to my computer."

"Ever thought of moving into the twenty-first century?"

"Ever thought of trying my cell phone?"

"Rolls over to voicemail. You must have it turned off."

Eric pulled the cell phone from his pocket and saw the battery was dead. Make nice, he thought. "Sorry, I forgot to recharge it."

"Yeah, sure. Well, I've got good news and bad news. Bad news is, the tox screen shows no harmful chemicals in SF. More bad news is, that oud shit you put in it is too complex to analyze. Something about an 'unresolvable hump' in a gas chromatogram."

"I didn't make SF. Can you get off this 'you put in it' crap?"

"Someone did."

"Not me. What's the good news?"

"Did I say good news? I must be slipping. There's no good news. Not one damned bit of it."

Eric took the handset from his ear, exhaled, and put it back. "So, why are you calling me?"

"What do you know about a company or individual called EDG?"

Obviously NYPD had been doing their own computer search. "Never heard of them."

"No? Victims' computers show they bought the stuff off the Internet. Two of the suspects confirm it. The female claims she doesn't know where her boyfriend got it, but his computer shows the same thing. All from the same site. A drop box registered to someone called EDG. Doesn't ring a bell?"

Be nice, Eric reminded himself. "Sorry. I can't help you there."

"Doesn't stand for Eric something-or-other? Like Eric de Gaulle?"

"Fawcett, you're so full of shit your eyes are turning brown."

"Cute. You learn that in Texas?"

Eric slammed down the receiver. How far could the man's imagination stretch? About as far as Abby's, apparently, with her D for Durand. Except, Fawcett's implications were chillingly more dangerous. For a moment, Eric stood there, disgusted at both of them. Then his phone rang again. He snatched it up. "What?"

"Now I remember," Fawcett said. "Good news is, there's a pretty lady gonna show up at your class tonight at John Jay. She wants your Balquees. And you're gonna give it to her."

Chapter 13

The John Jay College of Criminal Justice occupied four buildings or parts of buildings, all within a few blocks of one another just north of Rheinhold-Laroche. The college's jewel, Haaren Hall, dated from 1903 and was a fine example of Flemish Baroque architecture in red brick and white limestone with spires, fluted columns, and grand archways. Also called the T Building for its location on Tenth Avenue, it was a thirty-minute walk from Eric's apartment when, as now, he had Daisy in tow.

The school didn't allow animals but had given Daisy a grudging exemption when Eric showed them her badge and fed them a crock about her being integral to a course on the forensic aspects of odors. Tonight, however, he would indeed focus on canine trailing of human scents. And when the "pretty lady" showed up for his Balquees, he'd tell her to take a hike.

As he and Daisy climbed the steps, he noticed three of his eight students drinking coffee and smoking at one side of the entry arch. They raised their cups to him, "Evening, Doc," then resumed their conversation.

Inside the front doors, Flemish Baroque gave way to institutional modern, the original courtyard having been redesigned in steel and glass to house conference rooms, a display area, and offices. Eric showed his ID and pointed out Daisy's badge to the man at the front desk, who scanned a page on a clipboard before waving them through.

Daisy headed automatically for the stairway to their right. Eric dropped the lead across her back and let her take the steps on her own. After reaching the second floor, he followed her to his classroom. But as Daisy limped inside, Eric stopped. He smelled hexane and toluene, two common solvents in organic chemistry labs. Interesting, since this wasn't a laboratory floor. He stepped to the doorway and saw, besides some of his regular students, a woman sitting by herself at the back of the room.

He wasn't sure he'd call her pretty. She wore her blond hair tied up in a bun on the crown of her head, which emphasized her high forehead and gave her a sort of Barbie look. On the other hand, her figure—as best he could tell through her gray turtleneck sweater and tight jeans—caught the eye nicely.

Like most classrooms at John Jay, this one was wide but not deep. At the front stood a long table with chairs around three sides. Behind that, another row of chairs lined a wall with windows at the back. A wall clock on the right, a coffee urn beneath it, and a blackboard in front completed the furnishings.

Eric walked to the long table, from the front of which he lectured and around which now sat his non-smokers, a woman and four men.

"Good evening, Mister Foster," said Lieutenant O'Keefe. A bulky, good-natured woman in uniform, she sat directly in front of him.

"Good evening, Lieutenant. Any news from the thirty-fourth?"

"Same ol' same ol', except for couples who seem to be beating each other up more often than usual. Cabin fever, I guess. Spring can't come too soon."

"Amen to that," said Sergeant Cohen of the 7th Precinct. He was the only cop Eric knew who wore a yarmulke.

The smokers filed in, spot on seven o'clock. Two of them, still holding take-out coffee cups, took their places at the big table. The third, Detective Jackson, a bearded black man in gangsta get-up, knelt to pet Daisy before pulling out his chair.

Daisy gazed after him then returned her chin to the floor, where she lay at Eric's feet.

When everyone was settled, Eric looked again at the woman in the back. "We seem to have a guest tonight."

Faces turned toward the blonde.

"And you are ..., " Eric said.

"Tanya Cole, NYPD."

"Everyone here is NYPD." He waved his hand to encompass the other students. "More specifically ... ?"

"Crime lab."

He'd thought so, from the smells of organic solvents clinging to her clothes. And while he had expected her to show up after class, he was glad he'd planned for the possibility that she might actually attend his lecture. "What brings you here, Ms. Cole?"

"I heard about the course and thought I'd sit in, to see if I want to take it next term."

"Well, we're happy to have you and hope you won't be disappointed." Until I tell you to take your request for Balquees and shove it.

As the others turned back to face him, Eric quickly reviewed his thoughts for this evening's lecture. If Fawcett hadn't reminded him of his regular Friday-night class, he probably would have forgotten until it was too late, a black mark he didn't need. As it was, the class gave him a chance not only to educate, but also to feel in control, to be the authority in front of a bunch of police officers.

"Human scent," he began. "It's as individual as fingerprints, and you can use it precisely the same way. Although its presence at a crime scene doesn't establish complicity, it does establish a relationship to the scene. If suspects have been identified, it can be used in what amounts to an olfactory lineup. If suspects *haven't* been identified, it can lead you in the right direction. But where does human scent come from?"

Students scribbled in their notebooks. In the chair at the back, Tanya Cole just watched.

"Three sources," Eric continued. "Breath, skin, and sweat. Among these, breath is the most transient. But skin cells are excellent carriers of human scent. On average, we shed almost seven hundred skin cells a second."

"The published figure is six hundred and sixty-seven," Tanya Cole interrupted.

Eric shot her a look. "As I said, *almost* seven hundred."

Receiving only a smirk from Ms. Cole, he went on. "The cells, once they are shed, are called rafts. Each raft contains minute quantities of both bodily secretions and the bacteria that act on those secretions to produce odors characteristic of the individual. Think of Tinkerbell and fairy dust. As she flees the scene, she leaves a trail of fairy-dust rafts in her wake. A bloodhound, like Daisy here, can detect that trail and track it."

Detective Jackson raised his hand. "If we're all shedding skin cells at the scene, how would she know which one is Tinkerbell's?"

"Excellent question. She'd do it by a process of subtraction. You let her smell the whole scene, then each officer individually, and a properly trained dog will know to seek the missing scent."

"Damn," Jackson said, "if she subtracts that well, I need her to balance my checkbook."

Several students nodded their heads in agreement.

"After she balances mine," Eric quipped before turning serious again. "Actually, however, skin cells aren't as useful as the bodily secretions themselves, things like perspiration and oils. Eighty percent of household dust is dead skin cells. So an apartment, for instance, could contain cells from any number of people who'd been there before the last thorough cleaning. But sweat and body oils can be sampled directly from articles associated with the crime, such as spent shell casings or letters sent through the mail. They've also been shown to survive explosions and fires, in case you're looking for a bomb maker or arsonist."

Everyone at the big table stopped writing and looked at him.

"It's true," he said. "An FBI study showed that bloodhounds can correctly identify the individuals who handled pipe bombs and gas canisters before the devices were ignited."

"Son of a bitch" Lieutenant O'Keefe murmured.

The words Eric lived for.

Then Ms. Cole chimed in. "With pipe bombs, the success rate was only sixty-six percent."

Eric dug his nails into his palm. Was she trying to undermine him? Well, let her try. "Sixty-six percent with no—that's zero—false identifications. The dogs made correct identifications two-thirds of the time and *no* identification the rest of the time. With arson debris, the success rate was seventy-eight percent. Also with zero false IDs."

That bitchy little smirk crossed her face again.

Eric paused to take a settling breath and re-gather his thoughts. He rarely bothered with statistics in this class. They tended to bore the students. He sprinkled in just enough numbers to make a point, and occasionally to impress. And he did not need this lab geek forcing him to regurgitate statistical facts simply to defend his credibility.

Okay, back to class. "I mentioned at the outset that body scent recovered from a crime scene can be used like fingerprints. To elaborate, a study funded by the Army showed that individuals can be uniquely identified by the patterns and ratios of certain organic compounds in their body oils." Training his eyes on Ms. Cole, he added, "Specifically, the patterns and ratios of forty-four particular compounds."

No snotty interruption.

Feeling he'd blocked her on that one, he went on with a caveat. "The identification technique is fairly sophisticated, and few labs have it, but—"

"Cryptofocused gas chromatography/mass spectrometry," she said. "We have it."

Eric clenched his fists. "Would you like to finish this lecture?"

"No." She smiled, all sweetness and modesty. "You're doing fine."

How generous.

The clock on the wall showed he still had half an hour to go.

Leaving aside other high-tech topics that might encourage her to pipe up, he described the best method for collecting scents at a crime scene—a commercially available, handheld vacuum cleaner equipped with sterile gauze pads that could be stored frozen for later use. He went through scent lineups as conducted in The Netherlands and a Chinese project that involved gathering and recording the body odors of known criminals for investigation of future crimes those criminals might commit. Knowing most cops favored "benign intrusion for the greater good" over individual rights to privacy, he noted a proposal to add scent patches to future U.S. passports.

As eight o'clock approached, he decided to come full-circle by bringing Daisy back into the picture. "Something you should be aware of is that bloodhounds can trail suspects who flee in cars, even if the getaway vehicle has its windows closed."

This raised about half the eyebrows at the front table.

"For several years now, cars have been equipped with positive-ventilation systems to prevent carbon monoxide build-up in the passenger compartment. The system runs all the time, even if the AC or heater is not on. It continually passes fresh air through the interior and out into the atmosphere, thus leaving a scent trail."

Note taking accelerated amid nods of comprehension.

Pleased to have concluded the formal part of his lecture without further disruption from the peanut gallery in back, Eric moved on to the snippets with which he usually ended class, the more-or-less useless tidbits that got laughs or expressions of surprise and closed the evening on a light note. "Skunk oil. A synthetic version of skunk oil has been used by police in Los Angeles to clear out crack houses and keep them clear for several weeks. But a little known fact is that skunk scent, in weak concentration, smells like freshly roasted coffee beans."

"At Starbucks," Cohen said, "it's just the opposite. The coffee smells like skunk."

"You got that right," one of the smokers said, raising his now-empty Starbucks cup in the gesture of a toast.

Glancing again at Ms. Cole, Eric decided it was time to get rude. The real cops could take it. But could she? From his pocket he pulled a clear, cylindrical vial with a spray top—the little surprise he'd brought in case the woman actually sat in. He handed it to Jackson. "Shoot a tiny bit on the back of your hand and pass it on."

Jackson did as told, then recoiled. "You gotta be kidding me. What is this shit?"

As the vial worked its way around the table, eliciting similar responses from each person in turn, Eric spoke of perfumes intended to shock. "In the Seventeenth Century, a man named Castellus advised men to rub civet into their pubic hair to, as he put it, 'make the uterus more greedy for semen.' Since then, a number of perfumes have been created to evoke the darker or rawer aspects of sex. Virgins and Toreador speaks for itself. Narcotic Venus is meant to convey a sort of whip-in-hand impression of female power."

Lieutenant O'Keefe raised her fist and shook it triumphantly.

"Go, girl," Jackson said. "I'll get you a bottle, right after class."

Eric let the chuckles subside. "On the flip side, there's a perfume specifically designed to conjure anal sex."

O'Keefe lowered her fist.

"Jasmine and Cigarette," Eric continued, "tries to create an image of the morning after an unfulfilling one-night stand. And another perfume, Magnificent Secretions, aims to mimic the smells of sweat, saliva, blood, and semen." He timed his discourse, waiting for the vial to make its rounds of the table. "Don't leave out our auditor."

Detective Marconi, a burly, silver-suited guy who looked the part of a *capo* in the *Godfather* movies, stood and gave the bottle to Ms. Cole. "I hope you're a dyke."

Eric suppressed a grin.

Tanya Cole eyed the bottle suspiciously, then sprayed a bit on her hand, raised hand to nose, and glared at him.

More gratified than he dared show, Eric said, "Strictly speaking, what you're smelling is not a perfume. At least it's not marketed that way. It's marketed merely as an odor. It's called Vulva."

Sergeant Cohen rubbed his hand furiously. "How am I supposed to go home and expect my wife to believe I've been working?"

Laughter erupted. Then another guy's face turned equally sour. "Yeah. How're we supposed to do that?"

"Soap and water," Eric told them. "There's a lavatory just down the hall. Or if you want, I've brought something from the opposite end of the spectrum, a fragrance called Virtue, full of fig and spikenard and other 'biblical' scents. No guarantees, but it might work as an antidote."

"Hell with that," Lieutenant O'Keefe said. "I'm not washing this off. It could be just the trigger my husband needs." She turned back to Eric. "Unless you've got some of those pherones."

She meant pheromones, and it was a good point. "Sorry to

say, no one so far has identified sex pheromones in humans. The closest thing is certain body odors. For women, it's the smell of male sweat. And for men, the smell of female urine."

"See?" Jackson said to Cohen. "I told you, you need to go down on your wife."

That brought another round of laughter and a perfect place for Eric to end class.

As the regular students filed out, Tanya Cole came up to him, her expression decidedly unamused. "I believe you have something for me."

"What might that be?"

"Don't play cute. You know why I'm here."

"To decide whether you want to take the course next term. Or so you said."

Her eyes narrowed. "I've wasted enough time on you already. Do you have it for me, or not?"

"It?" he replied innocently.

"The perfume you made, called Balquees."

"Sorry. I can't help you." Couldn't because he hadn't brought it. Wouldn't because there wasn't much of it, he couldn't replace it, and analyzing it wouldn't help the cops. Beyond all that, Balquees was his, a window into his creative processes that he didn't care to have scrutinized by total strangers.

"I can get a warrant."

"Worker bees in the crime lab can get warrants?"

She spun on her heel, retrieved her overcoat and purse, and fronted up to him again. "Just watch me."

Eric walked Daisy down the front steps of John Jay and turned south on Tenth Avenue. City lights sparkled in all directions. They gave an orange glow to the overcast, the cloud cover that held in radiant heat from a sunny day and made the morning's promise of spring feel like a pledge being honored. He left his overcoat unbuttoned. Since traffic was light, he also unhooked Daisy's lead. As a trained police dog, and in his own experience, she'd keep to the sidewalk, not even crossing an intersection without his okay.

Given her freedom, Daisy sniffed her way down the avenue, pausing every few steps to indulge an interest in one thing or another and generally slowing their progress. But a leisurely stroll suited Eric nicely.

All in all, he'd handled Ms. Cole pretty well. A warrant required probable cause, or something legalistic like that. Balquees wasn't involved in any crimes. And SF, no matter how closely it resembled Balquees, had passed the toxicology screen. So there could be no justification for a judge to force him into handing over Balquees.

He pictured Ms. Cole, sitting in the back, as the smell of Vulva wiped that smugness off her face. And again as her haughtiness changed to anger with his "worker bee" comment. Yeah, he'd handled her pretty well.

Daisy squatted to urinate.

That's it, girl. Piss on Fawcett's precinct.

Twenty minutes later, as they approached the entrance to Eric's apartment building, Detective Fawcett got out of an unmarked car at the curb and slammed the door. Eric stopped. Daisy kept limping along, right up to Fawcett, whom she sniffed in apparent anticipation of some head scratches or ear rubbing.

Fawcett didn't oblige. "What's this shit about you not giving your Balquees to Tanya Cole?"

"I never said I would." Still buoyed by his one-upsmanship this evening, Eric squared his shoulders and stood his ground.

"Don't fuck with me, Eric."

"I wouldn't dream of it. You're not my type."

Glowering, Fawcett planted himself well within Eric's personal space. "Give it to me, now."

Eric backed a pace.

Fawcett closed the gap.

"Look," Eric said in his most reasonable tone, "Balquees cost me a lot of time and a lot of money. I'm not going to hand it over just so she can inject it all into her gas chromatograph."

"What are you scared of?"

"Nothing. There's no reason for it. It's not SF. And even if it were, this whole notion of yours that SF somehow drives people to murder is a load of bull."

"You think so, huh?"

Eric backed again as Fawcett reached inside his suit coat. Was the guy going to pull a gun?

But Fawcett's hand came out with some letter-size sheets of paper folded in half lengthwise. He held them in front of Eric's face. "Read this and call me."

Eric laid the papers in his lap, realized his mouth was hanging open, and shut it. How could this be?

He got up to pour himself a glass of Pouilly-Fuissé then sat again in the wingback chair that had come with the apartment. Behind the chair, a 1940s-vintage floor lamp with a tasseled shade provided illumination, the bulb in his ceiling fixture having popped and gone dark when he'd flipped the switch. After a sip of wine to steady his hands, he reread the four pages of printout Fawcett had given him.

In addition to the three deaths in Midtown North, they briefly described five other murders and eleven cases of assault and grievous bodily harm in which lovers claimed to have been driven by uncontrollable lust, and SF had been found at the crime scene.

That was all in Manhattan. The final entry read, "Search continuing in outer boroughs. Notice sent to Interpol."

Interestingly, there was no reference to the FBI or an expanded search within the US. Eric attributed this to Fawcett's contempt for the bureau, which he called the Friggin' Bunch of Idiots. He wondered now if that was wise.

Intellectually, he was curious to know if nineteen cases was a large or small percentage of total SF users. After all, more than a million and a half people lived in Manhattan. Then Lieutenant O'Keefe's words came back to him. "Same ol' same ol', except for couples who seem to be beating each other up more often than usual." Jesus. Was the problem more prevalent, way more prevalent, than the cops yet appreciated? If an investigating officer weren't looking for SF, the connection would never be made.

Ultimately, however, total numbers mattered less than the fact that a copy of his perfume seemed irrefutably linked to at least some of these tragic acts of violence. It gave him a sick feeling in his stomach that the wine did little to soothe.

He stood and stared out the window, barely noticing the yellow rectangles of light in the apartment buildings across the tracks. No longer was SF merely an affront to his pride, and no longer could he limit his actions to purchasing a bottle from the website and waiting for it to arrive. He had to pursue SF to its source, kill production right there, and prove it was not the same as Balquees. To do that, he needed more information, which meant taking a more active role. It also meant he'd bang heads with Fawcett, even harder than he'd done so far. The guy was no fool. He could be dangerous and, right now, Eric Foster was not his favorite person.

With moist palms, Eric pulled out his cell phone and called. "She can have some Balquees."

"Thought you'd see it that way."

"But there's one proviso."

A moment of silence before, "What?"

"I want to help with the analysis and interpretation of the data."

"No way."

"This is my area of expertise."

"Forget it. It ain't gonna happen."

Eric steeled himself. "You want Balquees?"

"You wanna clear your name?"

Eric almost dropped the phone. Had he heard the man right? Very slowly he asked, "What are you saying?"

"Let me quote you from the crime scene on Central Park South. 'It's Balquees. I created it.' Does that ring a bell?"

"But I told you later, it's not Balquees. It can't be. I have all the Balquees ever made."

"Lawyer talk. You may have all the stuff you originally called Balquees. But after you changed its name to SF and started selling it out of Switzerland, which is right next door to France, which is where you made Bal—"

"God dammit!" Eric's blood pressure soared. "I didn't change its name. I never heard of SF before last night."

"So you say. But the facts say different."

Forcing himself to calm down, Eric sorted through the "facts." He had no legal training, but he'd seen enough television to know that the France-Switzerland connection was purely circumstantial. There'd been no tape recorder at the crime scene, so Eric's statement there was hearsay. To the contrary, he'd denied on tape in the interrogation room that Balquees and SF were the same. Add to that the negative toxicology results for SF, and Fawcett had no case.

Or did he?

"Look, I'm willing to help, but my conditions remain the same. I participate in the analysis and interpretation."

"I hear you're big on statistics, so here's a statistic for you. Nine out of ten arrests for major crimes in New York City result in conviction. And by the way, the crime is serial murder."

Chapter 14

Sarah took the bottle of champagne out of the fridge. Should she open it now or wait for Robert? He'd be here any minute. Unless his flight got delayed, or the traffic was bad. With her fingernail, she peeled up the end of the little red strip that was supposed to open the foil on the top of the bottle. Would it look spoiled if she did that? Quarter to ten. Traffic was always bad in Atlanta. But his plane should have landed forty-five minutes ago. She put the bottle back. Robert could open it. Men liked to do that sort of thing.

The candles were nice, real beeswax candles from the craft shop. They gave just the right glow to the dining room. She picked up one of the wine glasses and inspected it again for spots. That tip from her sister about using vinegar in the dishwasher had really worked. Sarah hoped the kids wouldn't be too much trouble for her. They liked their Aunt Ellen, especially her walnut-drop cookies, but a sleepover could be difficult to manage when you had an infant of your own to take care of.

Ten to ten. Sarah realized she was twisting the front of the pajama top. She smoothed it down. Too bad her old negligee smelled so musty. She should have checked it yesterday. Then there would have been time to wash it. But Doris Day had looked cute in men's pajama tops in that old movie. Of course, she wasn't Doris Day, not even close. Sarah undid the top button of three and spread the lapels. If she undid the middle button, her breasts would show. She might look too brazen. Oh, to heck with it. A little brazen might help. She looked around to be sure the curtains were drawn, then undid the middle button.

Lord in Heaven, she hoped this worked. What with Robert's business trips and sales conferences and him always being so tired, they hardly had intercourse even once a month anymore. And then it was … what? Perfunctory?

She sniffed her wrist. That SF stuff Ellen had lent her did smell good, like roses and vanilla and maybe wet soil. It gave her a tingle in just the right place. She felt her face flush at the memory of what she'd done to herself last night, after deciding to try out the perfume before Robert came back from St. Louis. Maybe she should put on some more. Ellen swore by it, said it made all the difference in the world.

She hurried into their bedroom. The clock read 10:01. With a quick prayer that Robert wouldn't be home for another minute or two, she went to her dressing table and unscrewed the cap from the black glass cube. She'd already put some on her wrists and behind her ears. Between her breasts would be good. And under them? Why not. After pouring some on a cotton ball, she undid the last button of the pajama top and rubbed in the perfume. Whew, it was getting warm in here. She flapped the sides of the pajama top to cool herself and help the perfume dry.

In her mirror, she looked pretty good. Her body seemed to sparkle with all the colors of the rainbow, and her nipples were getting hard all by themselves. She thrust out her chest. Look at 'em and weep, Doris Day.

But her panties were wrong. Prudish white cotton, like something a librarian would wear. Suddenly she felt herself grin. Did she dare greet Robert with no panties on? That *would* be brazen. Just for the hell of it, she inched them down. Sexy. So don't stop there. She slid them to her ankles and kicked them off. *Wowser. Now you're cookin'.*

Except for her pubic hair. Her panties had pressed it flat. Sarah fluffed the hair with her fingers, like a guitar player strumming chords. Much better. And the strumming felt good. Watching herself in the mirror, she did it some more, her body swaying the way Tina Turner's did when she sang a slow love song.

But if she kept this up, she'd be spent before Robert got home. On the other hand, she'd climaxed twice last night, the first time in her life.

No, wait for Robert. He'd do it to her, fuck her living brains out.

Oops. Sarah giggled. She and Robert were church people. They didn't use words like that.

But she was looking pretty hot. And feeling that way, too.

What if she put a few swipes of SF in her bush? In nine years of marriage, the only time Robert had done cunnilingus was on their honeymoon. The thought of it shot a thrill straight up her tummy. *Sarah Ann McColgin, what on earth has gotten into you?* All she'd wanted was some passion in bed. And now here she was, all enraptured in lustful fantasies, feeling like she'd drunk three martinis.

And loving every second of it.

Yes, SF on her pussy. She soaked the cotton ball and rubbed it in her pubic hair. And a dab or two on her thighs for good measure.

"What are you doing?" Robert asked behind her.

Sarah's breath caught. Embarrassment flooded over her. But it quickly faded. This was what she'd been waiting for. Dropping the cotton ball, she turned around. "I wanted to welcome you home."

"Dressed like that? You look like a harlot."

"I feel like your wife." She slid the pajama top from her shoulders and let it fall to the floor. "The woman who wants you."

"What's that smell?"

She sashayed toward him. "The smell of love. Do you like it?"

Robert took a step back, but she kept on advancing. He wiped his brow with the sleeve of his suit coat. "This isn't like you, Sarah."

"It is. If you want it to be." She draped her arms over his shoulders.

He shook his head. "I feel a little dizzy."

"Me, too." Rising on her tiptoes, she kissed him. When he tried to pull back, she held his head and kissed him harder, pushing her tongue into his mouth.

He resisted at first, then touched her tongue with his, then sucked her in. He sucked so hard it hurt. But Sarah didn't mind the pain. If he wanted to hurt her a little, that was okay. Anything was okay.

Tearing her wrists from around him, Robert held her at arm's length, fire burning in his eyes like she hadn't seen since their wedding night. He yanked off his suit coat and tie and started on the buttons of his shirt. But she couldn't wait. She ripped them open.

Sweat glazed his face. Beautiful, slippery sweat.

Then his hands were on her breasts, squeezing them, mauling them. "Harder," she breathed. She pressed into him, felt him pinch her nipples. "God, yes."

Frantically, she undid his belt. In seconds, she had his trousers open. When she reached inside, he let out an animal sound, like the growl of a bear. She took hold of him, his stiff cock, his swollen balls. She'd never sucked him before, but she wanted to now.

Kneeling, she peered at the pulsing head. She could feel its yearning. All up and down her belly, she could feel it. Praying she'd do this right, she plunged him into her mouth. She tried to push him deeper but couldn't. So she bobbed her head and sucked with all her might.

He came so fast she could barely believe it, filling her mouth, overflowing her, surprising her with its slightly salty flavor.

"Stop," he cried. "I can't stand it anymore."

But she kept on going, milking every last drop and wanting more, until he yanked himself out.

Panting, eyes wild, he looked down at her. "Sweet Jesus, Sarah, I can't believe this is you."

She wiped her mouth with the back of her wrist, then stood. She needed him. This very instant. Dragging him to the bed, she flopped back on it and spread her legs. "Do me with your tongue."

He dived in like a starving beast, head thrashing, mouth opening and closing, sending shockwaves of pleasure through her whole body. As though he couldn't get enough, he grasped her hips and spread her wide. Hungrily he lapped the entire length of her, his hard tongue probing front and back, his mouth sucking.

"Oh, yes. Yes!" She clutched his hair and thrust against him and exploded in a blinding flash that seared her from the inside out.

Lying there afterward, both of them panting, she savored the heavenly sensations still reverberating inside her.

Then Robert pulled himself up to lie on top of her. "I want you again," he rasped "Put me in."

When daylight brightened the curtains in their bedroom, Sarah stretched and thought she'd never felt better in her life. But when she turned to cuddle Robert, she found his side of the bed empty.

Trying to shake some sense into her groggy head, she pushed herself up and sat back against the headboard. She couldn't hear a sound, not a single sound, except her heart thumping in her ears. Had he left her? Oh, God, no. She wanted to call out for him but didn't dare. What if he didn't answer?

Suddenly cold, she pulled the covers up to her neck. It was her fault, all her fault. She'd acted like a godless whore, giving oral sex, demanding oral sex. She wanted to wash her mouth out. How could she have acted that way? Her Robert.

Tears welled.

Then something in the air changed. She heard nothing, saw nothing. But somehow she knew he was still here. She rubbed away her tears and sat up straighter.

A few moments later, he appeared in the doorway, naked and carrying a tray. With a smile, he said, "Good morning, sleepyhead."

As though her bones had dissolved, she slumped like a rag doll against the headboard.

"Are you okay?" he asked, a look of concern clouding his face.

"I'm fine. You?"

He winked and placed the tray on her lap. Scrambled eggs and cantaloupe.

"Robert, you've never brought me breakfast before." Not once in their married life.

"I should have." He gave her a soft kiss on the lips, then went around and got into bed beside her. As he sat there, his penis started rising. "When you're finished, I have an idea for dessert."

Chapter 15

After almost no sleep, Eric dragged himself out of bed at six-thirty. His teeth chattered from the frigid air, or maybe from Fawcett's last words.

All night, Eric's balance of confidence had teeter-tottered between faith in the judicial system and fear of the lengths someone like Fawcett might go to in order to maintain a ninety percent conviction rate. He'd drifted off only after convincing himself that no prosecutor could mount a credible case without a scientific analysis of Balquees, which meant he'd done exactly the right thing in sticking to his guns with Fawcett. Several scandals had plagued the crime lab, making it imperative that he, Eric, personally witness any analyses of Balquees, lest the scales of justice be tipped against him by pressure from an overzealous cop.

In fact, Eric wanted to do just that, prove conclusively that Balquees wasn't SF. But he'd leave the issue open before he'd rely on someone else's word.

Briefly he had considered using Rheinhold-Laroche's facilities to analyze Balquees. But Fawcett would never accept the results. Besides, that Nazi, Charles Wigby, had made it abundantly clear that staying out of the lab was a condition of Eric's employment. The company knew of his expulsion from ISIPCA and wanted no possibility of his "tainting the corporate reputation."

Energized by disgust for his employer, Eric pulled on his robe over his sweats and closed the window. The pinging radiator brought welcome confirmation that hot water, after being automatically shut off at midnight, would soon again be available in the shower.

Beneath the window, Daisy opened her eyes. Feet propped on the wall, head back, she watched him cinch his robe tighter. Her expectant gaze, though upside down, said, "I know it's Saturday and what that means."

It meant an extra-long, leash-free meander through Clinton Park. But not before coffee and a shower.

Eric and Daisy returned from their walk to find Tanya Cole, in overcoat and jeans, sitting on the stoop of his apartment building. His watch showed 8:05.

"You're up early," Eric said, hoping he concealed his surprise.

"The wicked, and all that."

Daisy climbed the steps, sniffed Ms. Cole's shoulder, then waited for Eric to open the door.

"Can she really track someone in a car, with the windows closed?"

That took Eric aback. He hadn't thought anything he said in class last night was news to the forensic chemist. "Trail. Tracking is following the path someone took by using smells of stepped-on vegetation and things like that. Trailing is following a specific person's scent. Yes, she can do it."

"How did you get her?"

"Why are you here?"

Ms. Cole stood, looking less pale in sunlight than she had under the classroom's fluorescent tubes. With her hair no longer tied in a bun but hanging several inches below her shoulders, she also looked less severe. She carried a gray leather purse on a short shoulder strap and smelled of vetiver-scented soap. Vetiver usually reminded him of old potatoes, but on her it smelled medicinal.

She brushed some strands of hair from her face. "Detective Fawcett called this morning. He said you were ready to let me analyze this aphrodisiac you made."

Oh? If Fawcett thought the cold light of dawn would make

Eric see things differently, he had another think coming. "Did he tell you my conditions?"

She cracked a smile, kind of a nice smile in spite of the tiny scar Eric now noticed on her upper lip. "He doesn't like the idea of you tramping around the crime lab, but I told him I'd keep a tight rein."

Well, how about that. Mister Hard-Nose had cratered. With a step lightened by victory, Eric ascended the short flight of stairs to his building's front door. "In that case, come on in."

When they'd entered his apartment, she looked around and pronounced it, "Not bad. And a whole bedroom. I have six hundred square feet in a converted hotel over on East Fifty-Second. With a curtained-off nook to sleep in and a smell of curry I can't get rid of."

He thought of letting her sniff the mold under his kitchen sink, but poor-me contests bored him, especially when the other person's woes seemed self-inflicted. "Why live in Midtown when the crime lab's in Jamaica? You could afford something a lot nicer out there."

"I moved to New York for New York. To me, that means Manhattan. The museums, the theater, the people." A passing train rattled his windows. "Even the noise."

With an inward smile, Eric bet himself fifty bucks she wouldn't last a week living next door to Amtrak.

"So, what's with the circus posters?" Walking over to one of them, the fish-man, she peered at it closely. "Looks genuine."

"They all are."

She moved to the "Le Cirque des Vampires," which showed a man with fangs wrapping his arms around a naked lady. "Does this express your attitude toward women?"

"Are you Doctor Phil?" When she answered with a smirk, he said, "I'll get the Balquees."

She followed him to the bedroom door, where she stopped. "How did you come up with that name?"

While he pulled out the cardboard boxes from his closet, Eric gave her a thirty-second discourse on the Queen of Sheba.

"Does it really work?"

"Yeah, it works." He stood with the bottle in hand. "But it's not the same as SF. I told Fawcett—"

"And he told me. Maybe it's true. But—"

"It *is* true. At least twenty people have tried Balquees, and no one ever got violent."

In a syrupy tone, she replied, "That you're aware of."

"It was a small school. If there were any problems, I would have heard."

On the other hand, there was a possibility that adverse reactions came only after multiple exposures. He recalled Abby's assertion that, deep down inside, he feared Balquees could actually cause this. But he had smelled it more often than anyone else and had never suffered a single ill effect. No, Balquees was benign. And he'd prove it.

Time to lay down the law. "Here's what's going to happen. You get one milliliter. You analyze it with me standing next to you, and the two of us interpret the results."

"A milliliter might not be enough."

"For a good chemist, it should be plenty."

She stiffened. "I'm a damned good chemist."

"What grade?"

"Criminalist Three."

The highest rank below manager. Okay, she probably *was* good. But he doubted she knew squat about perfumes. "When do you want to do it?"

She leveled her gaze. "Now."

A long subway ride and short walk brought them to the NYPD crime lab in the Jamaica district of Queens. Three miles to the south lay JFK airport, and Eric wondered if Sergeant Pérez had made any headway tracking down the people who'd abandoned the African baby in a Dumpster.

From her purse, Tanya removed a photo-ID card on a lanyard. She pressed the card to a proximity pad beside the crime lab's doors, and the electronic lock clicked open. Inside, they went through airport-type security. A heavyset officer double-checked Eric's ID then gave him a three-by-four-inch fluorescent orange visitor's sticker. "Make sure that's clearly visible at all times."

Eric waited until he was ten paces past the guard, then slapped the sticker onto a hip pocket of his jeans.

Down a corridor to the right, Ms. Cole opened the door to one of the chemistry labs. Stepping inside, Eric inhaled familiar smells of stainless steel and organic solvents, together with something like ozone which probably came from flame ionization detectors and electrostatic filters. The latter reminded him of the acid-on-metal scent of Bête Noire that night in the Panthéon—so long ago.

She donned a white lab coat and handed another to him. As he turned to hang his leather jacket on the coat rack, he felt something touch his butt and simultaneously heard the rasp of his visitor's sticker being peeled off. "Detective Fawcett said you were a wise-ass," She held out the sticker. "Put it on your lab coat."

He pressed it on at a haphazard angle and looked around.

The lab, windowless and spotlessly clean, contained an impressive array of bench-top and free-standing instruments, as well as a fume hood, two glove boxes, several wet-chemistry prep stations, cylinders of various gases, and exhaust lines running into the ceiling. Occasional clicking sounds punctuated the general low hum of vacuum pumps.

"We'll use this," she said, walking over to a footlocker-sized GC/MS connected to a desktop computer.

It was one of four gas chromatograph/mass spectrometers he'd noticed. "What kind of column are you using?"

"Fifty-meter capillary, coated with methyl silicone." She raised the lid on the oven section of the GC to reveal an inch-thick coil, about a hand span in diameter, of hair-thin glass tubing—the guts of the gas chromatograph.

An injected sample, propelled by a carrier gas, would travel slowly through the tubing as the oven temperature rose. Inside the tubing, a microscopic layer of some polymer, in this case methyl silicone, allowed lighter components of the sample to travel faster than heavier components. This separated the components, which then passed through a detector that recorded their time of passage and relative concentration.

Just ahead of the detector, a splitter diverted part of the flow stream to the mass spectrometer, which measured the mass, or molecular weight, of each constituent. A computer compared the mass data to a library of known compounds to identify the molecules in the original sample.

"Of course, I need to extract the sample first." She extended her hand, palm up. "Let's have it."

"Not so fast. What method of extraction?"

"Are you always this full of questions?"

"If you feed the GC an incompletely extracted sample, you'll get incomplete results."

"Who's the chemist here?"

He smelled a burst of vetiver, the scent of her body soap. Although her face betrayed nothing, experience told him the burst came from a slight jump in skin temperature, signaling a flash of anger. "I just want to know what method."

"Speemee," she said, using the jargon term for SPME. "Solid phase—"

"Micro-extraction. I'm familiar with it, and that'll be fine for the volatiles, the components that readily evaporate. But what about the non-volatile chemicals that remain in the liquid? Right now, we don't know if the violence-inducing compound, our Agent X, is something inhaled or a non-volatile ingredient absorbed through the skin. I suspect the latter."

"Based on …?"

"The fact that I couldn't smell a difference," although he hadn't smelled SF carefully.

A glance at the ceiling conveyed her opinion of the nose as an analytical instrument. "We'll use Speemee to extract the liquid, as well."

"What?" So far as he knew, that was never done.

"Isn't your perfume water-based? SF is."

"Yes," he said, wondering why that was important.

"Then no problem. If it were an alcoholic solution, I'd use pulse-and-trap. But with aqueous solutions, Speemee works fine."

That was news, although he tried not to show it. But he still had reservations. "If SF is like Balquees, all of its ingredients are natural. Which means they contain hundreds of organic compounds, some of them highly complex, some present in only trace amounts. I'm not convinced SPME"—he purposely avoided the jargon—"can get all those compounds out of the liquid."

"It got more than a hundred out of SF."

"Which means it probably missed at least half. Including, if I'm not mistaken, the elusive Agent X."

He caught another burst of vetiver. She really should buy a different soap.

"Okay, wise guy, what would *you* suggest?"

"Freeze-drying."

"Old school. Besides, you lose volatiles when you do that."

"But we'll get them with SPME of the headspace."

Backing up a step, she planted her hands on her hips. "We need to get one thing straight. This is my lab, and we'll do it my way."

With an effort to appear indifferent, he shrugged and started unbuttoning his lab coat. "Then the deal's off."

In silence, she stood her ground.

He headed for the door, peeling off the lab coat as he went. Would the bluff work? He sorely wanted to prove the two perfumes were different. In fact, he had to, if he were going to clear himself from Fawcett's one-name list of suspects. But she needed this also, for the sake of pride, if not credibility.

At the door, he hung up the lab coat, took his jacket from the rack, and reached for the doorknob. *Come on, dammit.* If she didn't buckle, he would have blown this opportunity.

"If we freeze-dry, I'll need more than one milliliter."

That hadn't occurred to him. On the other hand, winning the bluff, which he seemed to have done, was worth an extra mil. "Two, then."

"Four. One to freeze-dry, one for Speemee, and two in reserve for any additional analyses I may need to do."

Eric gritted his teeth, pissed that logically she was right.

She held out her hand again.

He walked up to her, took the bottle from his pocket, then hesitated, thumbing the label.

"I'm waiting, Mr. Foster."

Eric slapped it into her hand. "Four mils."

"Put your lab coat back on. I don't need extraneous fibers or other trace floating around in here."

"Anyone ever tell you you're a control freak?"

"Anyone ever tell you about the pot calling the kettle black?"

He tramped back to the door, pulled on his lab coat, and turned to see her sniffing the bottle. "Aren't you afraid it'll turn you into a lust-crazed maniac?"

"I doubt one whiff will do that. Besides, you said Balquees never hurt anyone. Are you retracting that statement?"

Eric swallowed a retort. The sooner they finished with this, the better. "Don't forget, we'll need a freeze-dried sample of SF, also. That is, if you want to compare apples to apples."

With less of a smirk this time than a sneer, she walked to a bench-top safe and reached to punch the combination. When he followed, she pulled her hand away. "Excuse me. Do you mind not peering over my shoulder?"

He retreated several paces and watched her open the safe and retrieve a small black cube that he recognized as a bottle of SF. Staying two steps behind, he trailed her to a prep station and stood to her left, ready to pounce on any mistake she might make. But as she pipetted one-milliliter aliquots of SF and Balquees into separate freeze-drying vessels and set about preparing the SPME analysis of Balquees, he saw nothing to criticize. Her technique was good, the procedures fairly routine.

Increasingly he felt useless, in need of something to do. "Have you got a printout of your earlier results on SF?"

"Just a minute." She clamped the SPME apparatus, a "wand" the size of a policeman's flashlight, into a ring stand and lowered the wand's syringe through the septum-topped vial containing Balquees. The vial rested in an aluminum-block heater. After extending the fiber, she switched on the heater then dropped onto a swivel chair in front of the GC/MS she'd said they would use. She typed something on the computer's keyboard, and a few seconds later a GC trace slid out of the printer, followed by three pages of mass spec data.

"SF," she said, handing him the papers. With mockery clothed in sweetness, she added, "Let me know if there's anything you don't understand."

Eric ignored the slight. But in fact, the mass spec data listed dozens of compounds he'd never heard of before, things like 1,8-cineole and cis-3-hexanol. "Where's the summary?"

"What summary?"

"The summary of ingredients."

"You're looking at it."

"You've got to be kidding. No one can reconstruct a perfume from a list like this. You need a fragrance library, a database program that will put all this stuff together and tell you what ingredients the perfumer used."

"I have the best forensic databases in existence."

"But obviously not the right ones." He held the pages so she could read them and placed a finger on limomene. "This comes from zest of lemon." He moved his finger down the page. "This one, cis-9-cycloheptadecen-1-one, is civetone, the prime ingredient of civet. I just happen to know that. But a perfumers' library would have told you. These other things, most of them? I have no idea. Some are probably from shiitake mushroom. Others will be components of the oud. But for you and I to try and deduce those ingredients from this list would be like trying to reconstruct the first act of *Macbeth* from a list of its words."

For a moment, she looked deflated. Then she stood resolutely. "It doesn't matter. Comparable analyses will give comparable results. And that's all we have to do. Compare the two."

"What about identifying Agent X?"

"Would you stop using that stupid term? And stop being such an ass. I know how to do my job."

"Then do it."

"I am. In case you haven't noticed, the Speemee is extracting, and the freeze-driers are freezing. They'll both take about thirty minutes." She glanced at her watch. "I'm going to lunch. You can do whatever you want, as long as it's outside the building."

Chapter 16

Bright sunlight tempered the chill outside, and Eric's lab coat provided adequate warmth as he and Ms. Cole crossed Jamaica Avenue at 150th Street. After weighing the prospects of half an hour wandering the streets versus suffering through a meal with Her Imperial Highness, he'd asked to join her and received a charming, "If you must."

Now that she was using techniques he trusted, maybe it was time to attempt a ceasefire. God knew, he'd always hated conflict, and this constant sparring with Tanya Cole—Tanya, he'd try—twisted his gut more than he'd ever let show. He snuck a look at her profile. Kind of pretty, despite the jaw muscles working. Yeah, a truce might be worth the effort.

From the intersection, they walked past a shored-up building under renovation and a joint selling mattresses for $99, before she stopped in front of a Mexican restaurant. As she pulled open the door, Eric spotted another Mexican restaurant a few doors down.

Evidently following his eyes, she said, "Forty-seven violation points on their last health inspection. Including mouse droppings. But you're welcome to go there if you want."

"I'll stick with you."

She preceded him into an interior straight out of the seventies: red walls, heavy wood, paintings on black velvet of matadors and voluptuous women, dusty piñatas hanging overhead. Mariachi music blared from shoe-box-size speakers, and Tex-Mex aromas of grilled onion, red salsa, and tortillas suffused the air. As his eyes adjusted to the dark, he saw the only other customers were two construction workers in a corner at the back, their hardhats on the floor by their feet.

He and Tanya took a booth by the front window.

A skinny man with slicked-back hair set down menus, a basket of tortilla chips, and a bowl of salsa. "You want something to drink?"

Tanya ordered Diet Coke.

Eric asked for Dos Equis. When she squinted at him, he said, "It's a Mexican beer."

She changed her order to a margarita on the rocks.

Either she was loosening up a bit or going him one better. Eric wasn't sure.

When the waiter returned with their drinks, she ordered beef tacos, which she pronounced "tack-ohs," and Eric chose cheese enchiladas with charro beans, instead of refried.

While they waited, he unfolded the SF data she'd printed out. As he'd expected, the GC trace looked like a spiny-backed brontosaur. A spectrum of sharp, vertical peaks rose atop a hump that ran from the dinosaur's tail at the left, up over its back, and down again to its lowered head on the right. While the peaks corresponded to identifiable compounds, the hump beneath them represented materials the gas chromatograph hadn't been able to separate. If the GC couldn't separate them, the mass spectrometer couldn't identify them, and neither could Tanya's toxicology screen. Since toxicology had found nothing, he suspected Agent X lay hidden in the hump. If they couldn't tease it out, he'd have no scientific proof of a difference between SF and Balquees.

Holding up the trace, he pointed at the hump. "Can we can do better than this?"

She stopped munching a mouthful of chips and frowned.

Before she could swallow, he tried to soften his words by adding, "I mean, maybe we should try a different column in the GC."

"Like what?"

"Maybe something more polar."

She glanced toward the ceiling. "If you want to know what *I* think, that hump is your oud."

"The counterfeiter's oud," he corrected. "And a lot more than that, judging from how broad it is. Which only makes sense. Natural ingredients are full of compounds you can never identify, even with the most sophisticated techniques. But if we're going to stand any chance of uncovering Agent ... the violence-inducing chemical, then I think we need to concentrate on this hump, since all the identified compounds passed your tox screen. That's why I'm wondering about a different column."

In a sarcastic tone, she informed him, "When we get back, you can look through the suppliers' catalogues."

Eric balled his fist under the table. If forging a truce with this woman meant accepting her unwillingness to consider technical alternatives, then screw the truce. But unfortunately, he couldn't afford that indulgence. Distasteful as it might be, he had to keep trying. His proof of innocence depended on it.

A few minutes later, the waiter cautioned, "Careful, very hot," as he used hand towels to set down their plates. "Another margarita?" he asked Tanya.

"Yes, please."

Eric, whose beer bottle was still half full, hadn't realized she'd finished her first drink, and his surprise evidently showed.

"Don't worry," she told him. "Alcohol doesn't affect me very much. My uncle taught me to drink."

For the sake of their work this afternoon, he hoped her uncle was a good teacher—whatever that entailed.

Tanya angled the end of a taco into her mouth and crunched down, dribbling beef juice over her chin, which she dabbed daintily with her napkin. "How are the enchiladas?"

He tried one. Filled with melted Velveeta, it took him straight back to a dive he'd frequented on his way home from high school in Galveston. The memory brought him a mental smile. If his father had ever found out he liked this "junk" almost as much as he liked a classic fondue, the *cordon bleu* chef would have choked.

"True Tex-Mex," Eric said, forking off another bite.

Her smile suggested a lightening of her mood, as if his approval were an olive branch she accepted. "So tell me. When you create a perfume, what do you do? Sit down and mix ingredients until you get something you like?"

"Just the opposite. You create it in your mind. You start with an impression you want to convey. A garden in Kashmir, for instance, or a starry night at an oasis in the Sahara."

"You know what those places smell like?" Her second margarita arrived, and she sucked in a mouthful through the plastic straw.

After a silent prayer that this hole in the wall served weak drinks, he said, "You aren't trying to duplicate the smell. You're trying to create a fragrance that evokes the imagery and erotic sensuality."

"Is it always about sex?"

"Pretty much." He tried the charro beans and found them good, with just the right amount of smoked ham. "Except with children's perfumes. They're more about freshness and sweetness."

"They make perfume for children?"

"They have beauty pageants for children, complete with gowns and skimpy swimsuits. Grotesque, in my opinion, but no one's asking me."

"Me either," Tanya said, then crunched another bite of taco. "So you're trying to evoke this sensual image. And you mix together ingredients until you get it?"

"No. That's what I meant by creating it in your head. You don't mix anything. Based on your knowledge of hundreds of essences, oils, and extracts, you write down the ingredients in the exact percentages you want. Actually, you usually write down three or four variations on the melody. Then you give the formulas to a lab tech or assistant, and the next morning, your creations are waiting for you." He chuckled. "Unless, of course, you're a student. Then you do mix them yourself."

"You're joking." Tanya set down the remaining half of her taco. "You don't smell anything until it comes back from the lab?"

"Not if you're a real perfumer. You smell what they've prepared, write down any changes, and send it back. The better you are, the fewer iterations it takes to get what you want."

She shook her head slowly. "How do you keep all those hundreds of smells in your head?"

"Training and practice," he said, warming to the fact that she seemed impressed. "In the school I went to, you have to be able to identify at least a hundred scents and combinations of scents just to get in. To get out, among other requirements, you have to identify at least three hundred."

"Wow."

Eric couldn't help grinning. Now maybe he'd get some respect. And maybe the truce that had almost forged itself would hold up in the lab.

"So, what's the most expensive ingredient?" she asked.

He thought a moment. "Probably *Iris naturelle*. Last time I checked, it was almost thirty thousand dollars a pound."

"Thirty grand?" Her taco stopped halfway to her mouth. "The drug cartels should switch to perfumes."

"I hope not. Already, half of the perfume sold is black market. Stuff originally sent to Third World countries that gets 'diverted' back at dirt-cheap prices to Europe and the US and Japan. The legitimate business is already tough. We don't need more undercutting."

She crunched off a bite of taco. After swallowing and dabbing her lips, she said, "Then let's switch gears. What about the most common ingredient?"

"That's easy. Water."

"Huh?"

"Even the best perfumes are about seventy percent water. Colognes are at least ninety-five percent. Without it, the fragrance would evaporate too rapidly."

"We spend a hundred bucks for something that's three quarters water?"

"Eight hundred for an ounce of Joy."

She shook her head disbelievingly. "Not for me."

"Who knows?" he said with a smile. "Maybe one day."

"In my dreams."

And there he detected an opening. "Speaking of you, where are you from? You don't have a New York accent."

Between more mouthfuls of taco and draining her margarita, she told him she had grown up in Wichita and gone to the University of Missouri, where she majored in chemistry and minored in theater arts. She'd been overseas twice, Rio two years

ago and Monaco last year. Both trips had been to attend
conferences on forensic chemistry, although she'd missed half of
the Rio conference due to "traveler's tummy." Her favorite dishes
were cheese casserole and scalloped potatoes, which made him
wonder how she stayed so slim, until she said she loved kayaking
and aerobics.

When the bill came, Tanya insisted on paying. He started to
protest but decided a battle over twenty-five dollars would be a
step backward. Instead, he paid the tip.

As she slid from the booth, she smiled again, which drew his
attention to the scar on her upper lip. Touching the same spot on
himself, he said, "Mind if I ask how you got that?"

Her smile disappeared. For a moment she just looked at him.
Then she shouldered her purse. "Asshole in college. I seem to
attract them."

Hitting a woman was among the basest acts of cowardice Eric
could imagine, right down there with beating a child, kicking a dog,
or smacking an elderly person. As he and Tanya walked back to the
crime lab, he wanted to say he was sorry it happened. But she'd
sought no sympathy and would probably greet an apology from
him with another roll of those eyes that seemed born to mock.

One thing he *could* do was show more respect. As a first step,
he peeled the crooked visitor's sticker off his lab coat and re-
affixed it horizontally.

During the forty-odd minutes they'd been gone, freeze-drying
had reduced the samples of Balquees and SF to brownish stains in
the conical bottoms of their glass vessels. Something about them
caught Eric's attention. Looking more closely, he realized, "The
Balquees residue is thicker. That means the counterfeiter is selling a
more dilute product. No wonder he only charges two hundred an
ounce."

After dissolving each residue in a hundred microliters of ethyl
acetate, she took up one microliter of Balquees and injected it into
the GC/MS. "We should have the results in thirty minutes. Then
thirty minutes to run the SF sample and thirty more for the

Balquees extracted by Speemee. Or, we can use three machines and do them simultaneously."

An hour and a half. Plus something she'd neglected to mention but undoubtedly assumed he knew—an additional ten to fifteen minutes between runs to bake off the GC column and clear it of any remains from the previous run. So, two hours versus half an hour, the guaranteed reproducibility of using the same column for all three samples versus the risk that identical but different columns could yield somewhat different results. She was challenging his confidence in her obvious belief that any differences would be trivial.

Eric's gut told him not to take that risk. But the scar on her lip reminded him, *show more respect.* "If you're happy with three machines, then I am, too."

She cocked her head. "You feeling okay?"

"Better capitalize quick," he said with a grin, "before I regain my senses."

Including prep time, it took about forty-five minutes before they had all the data. While Tanya ran her toxicology programs on the mass spec results, Eric used an adjacent computer to overlay the GC traces.

"Look at this," he said. Although the identified peaks were nearly identical, the unresolved hump for SF displayed a slight shoulder that wasn't present in Balquees. When she rose from her chair and stood behind him, he pointed to it on the screen. "They're different."

"Not enough to count."

"What?" He swiveled to face her, incredulous that she could say that.

"Statistical error. If we ran both samples multiple times and averaged the results, they'd look the same."

"Bull. The shoulder's real, and that's where the culprit is."

"Prove it."

"That's *your* job. You're the forensic chemist."

Her icy glare dropped the temperature of the whole room, although another rush of vetiver revealed she was boiling inside.

"Show me the—" He checked himself and replaced his almost-demand with a request. "Let's look at the mass spec data."

She stomped back to the computer she'd been using and printed the results. "Negative toxicology."

No surprise. Agent X remained hidden in the unresolved hump, specifically in that shoulder he'd spotted. He felt vindicated, to a degree, to see five pages of mass spec data for each of the freeze-dried samples as compared to three pages for the same samples extracted by SPME. But he could make no more sense out of one set than the other.

Returning to his chair, he gave up hope that technology could prove his contention. A whole day wasted, which left him back at square one. The proof lay only one place. In his nose.

He had an idea. She definitely wouldn't like it, but maybe if he buttered her up and acted casual. "I'm sorry I yelled at you."

No response.

He rose from his chair. "This isn't getting us where we want to be."

"I know that." In a gesture that raised Eric's hopes, she rubbed her temples with her thumbs. "This is so damn frustrating. It's in there. I know it is. But I can't get it out."

"So you agree it's in the shoulder?"

"No." She pursed her lips. "But it's in the hump."

Good enough. He strolled a few steps to the nearest prep station, where he hoisted himself up to sit on the edge of the sink, feet dangling. "If you don't mind, I'd like to try an experiment of my own."

"What kind of experiment?"

"I'd like to try to smell the difference."

She got up and handed him the bottle of SF. "Go ahead."

"Not here. My nose is shot from all the solvents in this lab. I'd like to take it home, give my nose a rest, and then take my time comparing."

"No way." She snatched back the bottle. "This is evidence."

"But you must have four or five bottles of it by now. No one will miss a few milliliters."

She speared him with her eyes. "It's illegal."

"Strictly speaking."

"They'd fire me."

"Who's to know? Let's say you had to go to the bathroom."

Eric pulled a disposable pipette from a box of them on the prep station counter and fitted a rubber squeeze-bulb to the end. "You're gone no more than a minute."

"Women can't pee that fast in an institutional restroom."

"Two minutes, then. You tell me to wait outside the lab, and when you get back, I'm still standing there."

"Why don't you just go out and buy some?"

"I did. But you can only get it mail-order from Switzerland. It could take a week or more to get here."

"Is that the end of the world?"

"Tanya, people are dying. I'm a suspect."

She looked aside, then back at him. "Let's say you *can* smell a difference, or think you can. What does it matter? It's your word against anyone else's."

"It matters to me."

"That's not enough. If you're right, that they're different, then the only valid non-chemical test is to try them both in real-life situations."

"Us?"

She stiffened. "No, you idiot. Not us."

"Well, I'm not rubbing that crap into my skin. And you're out of your mind if you do."

She seemed to ponder that, but didn't reply.

"Think of it this way." He slipped off the sink and stepped closer to her. "You're right about trying them both. But it's a whole lot safer for me to try smelling the difference, alone in my own apartment, than for anyone to try using it with a partner."

She said nothing, which he took as a more positive sign than calling him an idiot.

"I promise, I'll call you the second I detect a difference." He searched his mind for some carrot he could dangle, something *she* would get out of it. "I can identify a lot of chemical classes by smell. Aldehydes, ketones, amines, even if they're complexed with other things. If I can tell the class of compound, we can design a procedure specifically to extract that class and isolate all the chemicals in it."

That raised her eyebrows, but just for a second. She looked despondent, like a doctor burdened with deciding which patient would receive the only available kidney.

"Tanya, please. Two milliliters is all I ask."

She lowered her head. After a long moment, she set the bottle of SF on the counter beside him and walked to the door. "I can't believe I'm doing this."

On the subway ride back to Manhattan, they sat in adjacent seats in a car with only one other passenger. Apparently four o'clock on a Saturday afternoon was too late for day-trippers to the city and too early for the evening crowd. As the train jostled and clattered over aging rails, Eric clutched the screw-capped vial of SF in his jacket pocket, while Tanya seemed to gaze down at nothing.

"I really appreciate this," he said for about the fifth time.

She looked up. "Is your nose really so much better than anyone else's?"

As a matter of fact, he'd smelled something when they took their seats that might impress her. Something truly unusual. He leaned toward her and inhaled again to confirm the combination of scents. "Try this. The last person to sit where you are was an old Jewish woman from Syria."

Tanya laughed out loud, prompting a sidelong glance from the Hispanic youth who sat sullenly at the far end of the car. "Is this a joke?"

"Dead serious."

"I don't believe you."

"Close your eyes and inhale fast through your nose. What do you smell?"

After a doubtful look, she closed her eyes and sniffed. "Dirt. Shoe polish, I think."

"What else? Something acidic?"

She shook her head. "Nothing. Just New York subway."

"You don't smell tamarind?"

"What's that?" she asked, opening her eyes.

"A fruit. The main ingredient in the tart red sauce you get in Indian restaurants."

"I've never eaten Indian food."

The train stopped at a station, but no one else got on their car. As the doors hissed closed, Eric said "How about artichoke?"

"I hate artichokes."

Why wasn't he surprised? "But do you smell them?"

"No."

"Well, I smell both. And so far as I know, it's a definitive combination, unique to certain Jewish groups in Syria who boil artichokes in a tamarind-flavored broth."

She stared at him derisively, as though he were making it all up. "I'm supposed to buy this line of bull?"

"My father's a chef. He likes to experiment with obscure ethnic dishes. He made it for us once." Eric smiled. "Only once, since no one in the family liked it."

"Gee, I can't imagine why not."

"I admit the old-woman part is a guess. But it's based on the scent of L'Origan by Coty, which is both an older woman's perfume and a common fragrance in face powders." As in the face powder he clearly remembered on his grandmother.

Tanya leaned forward and made an exaggerated charade of looking around the car. "An old Jewish woman from Syria, who just happens not to be here. Unless that's her down there, dressed up as a guy going in for a night of trolling in Times Square." She settled back in her seat. "You'll have to give me something more provable than that."

Provable left him not many options. In fact, only two he could think of. He chose the less intimate. "You bathed this morning with vetiver-scented soap."

Her eyes widened, shining mahogany-brown in the carriage's lights. Then she shook her head. "Too easy. Especially for a guy in the perfume business. If that's the best you can do, I'm not bowled over."

Of course he could do better, but he wasn't sure it was such a great idea. There was intimate, and there was invasively intimate.

Seeming to interpret his silence as an admission of failure, she goaded, "Come on, dazzle me."

Still he hesitated, wondering how she'd react. She could slap him in the face. Or as a scientist, she could be rational enough to finally accept the analytical power of the nose.

With a smirk, she said, "Can't do it?"

That tipped the balance. "Okay. You're ovulating."

She jerked back as though he'd spit on her.

Oh, great. Nothing like throwing a boomerang. "Look, I'm not prying." When her expression turned incredulous, he felt compelled to explain. "I wasn't certain until you took off your lab coat. And of course the tight jeans, you know, being absorbent."

Quickly crossing her legs, she snarled, "Who the hell do you think…?" But instead of finishing, she just shook her head.

"Hey, you're the one who threw down the challenge."

Her eyes flared.

"Look," he said, "I can't help it if there's a distinctive way women smell at that time of month."

"By God, if you say anything about fish, I'll knock your goddamned lights out."

"A boorish joke, and wrong. What's true, though, is everyone has a unique olfactory signature. If I were blindfolded, and you walked into my room—"

"That's never going to happen."

"I'm just saying, I'd know it was you."

"Which it won't be."

"But I'd also know, just as I know now, that your fertility is peaking. There's a change in scent." In hopes of smoothing her feathers, he added, "In fact, it's rather pleasant. A friend of mine …" He didn't say Abby's name. "… likens it to the aroma of a roux. But I'd say it's closer to a mixture of mink and saddle leather with a hint of bitter chocolate."

"I don't fucking believe you." Glowering, she folded her arms across her stomach. "And for the record, I am not ovulating."

That did it. He had no more time for a "scientist" who denied the truth because it embarrassed her. With a shrug, Eric leaned back in his seat. "Sorry I said anything. But for the record? You are."

Chapter 17

At the Fifth Avenue station in upper Midtown, Eric parted company with Tanya Cole, their leave-taking wordless, the atmosphere between them more glacial than the frigid air of late afternoon. On the plus side, she hadn't moved to another seat after the ovulation fiasco. Maybe there was some scientist in her, after all. Maybe he should have minimized his own experience and cited studies she could look up, like the reason strippers made bigger tips at that time of month. But, dammit, it was *his* nose she was questioning.

On the minus side, any thoughts he might have entertained about getting to know her better now swirled down the toilet. Never mind. She probably wasn't worth the effort. Macaroni and cheese, her starry-eyed view of this filthy city. He kicked an empty Sprite can off the sidewalk as he walked along 51st Street.

Would Abby have plans for tonight? Kirin worked weekends at a high-class Indian restaurant in SoHo—a place that served tamarind sauce, at which Ms. Cole undoubtedly would turn up her pert little nose. Occasionally, when Kirin wasn't home, he and Abby spent a fiery evening in each other's arms.

Granted, he sometimes felt guilty for "cheating" Kirin. But he wasn't really an interloper. He and Abby had been lovers since long before Kirin ever met her. Besides, the deception never seemed to bother Abby.

Sidestepping a couple walking glove-in-glove, he pulled out his cell phone and punched her number.

"Eric, good thing you called. There's been a change on the SF website."

He stopped walking. "What change?"

"It has your name on it."

"What?" Eric's mind spun like a hurricane. Out of the tempest came a theater marquee flashing "Eric Foster, Final Performance." Who the hell could be doing this? Were they actually trying to frame him? What had he done to piss off someone so badly that they wanted to pin a murder rap on him?

"There's more," Abby said, yanking him back to 51st Street and the parking meter he'd grabbed hold of to steady himself.

He released the meter, but couldn't stop looking at its red "Expired" flag. "Tell me."

"A quote, so-called. It says you made SF from the purest ingredients and tested it on perfume sophisticates with stunning results."

"Son of a bitch." He slammed the heel of his hand into the parking meter. If Fawcett saw that quote, he, Eric, would spend the rest of his life in a cold cell trying to fight off genetic throwbacks from *Deliverance.* Wait a minute. "Can you kill it?"

"Kill what?"

"Hack the website. Shut it down." Why hadn't he thought of this before?

"I don't know. I can try."

"Do it now. I'll be there as fast as I can." He flipped his cell phone closed, turned back toward the subway station he'd just left, and halted. Damn. He'd forgotten about Daisy. She'd be uncomfortable as hell by now, after being cooped up since 8:30 this morning. Five blocks to his apartment. Eric took off in a jog.

Screw the law. On the sidewalk out front, Daisy's eager face after she'd finished her business by the big tree pierced Eric's heart and hardened his resolve. She wanted exercise, he needed to get to Abby's, and if he had to break the law to accomplish both goals at once, then let them try to catch him.

Back in the apartment, he poured three cups of kibble in her bowl and went into the bedroom. He pulled on his thickest sweatshirt, donned a black baseball cap, and clipped Daisy's badge to his belt, tugging the sweatshirt down to cover it. Now for the *pièce de résistance.*

In a rare gesture of compassion, Fawcett had given him the black NYPD windbreaker Daisy's handler was wearing the night he was killed in Central Park. Fawcett suggested the dog might like to sleep next to it, a sort of Linus blanket, while she adjusted to her new owner and surroundings. Eric knew better. Daisy would adjust much faster without a constant reminder of that traumatic night. He'd taken the jacket to be dry-cleaned and hung it at the back of his closet. But tonight he would put it to good use.

Daisy perked up the second she saw it, then looked confused when he shoved it into a shoulder bag.

"Come on, girl. We're going out."

She spun in a circle, dashed for the door, and waited with wagging tail for him to hook on her lead. At the bottom of the front steps, they turned right and headed down Tenth Avenue.

Shivering inside the sweatshirt, he tried to concentrate on the ramifications of his decision. Number one: He'd get to Abby's a little later than planned. But in truth, he possessed no hacking talent that could possibly help her. Number two: Abby, the clean freak, wasn't fond of dogs but had at least tolerated Daisy in her apartment once before. Number three, the big one: Dogs weren't allowed on subways. But cops with dogs could probably get away with it.

Probably.

At 42nd, they turned left toward Times Square, where the lights of the Great White Way shone like a city within a city beneath the darkening sky. Unfortunately, NYPD had a storefront station in Times Square, right next to the subway stairs. Eric approached it slowly, looking for cops on patrol. Maybe he was being paranoid, but his palms moistened nevertheless.

At the station, he picked up his pace, averting his face from the big glass windows. Around the corner, he stopped at the stairs leading down to the subway and saw two cops strolling up Broadway. Eric tried to look natural, praying they'd walk on past, instead of descending the stairs.

"Good looking dog," one of them said. The man's breath stank of smoked sausage and cabbage, washed down with beer. "What happened to his leg?"

"Car accident," Eric lied.

"Yeah, he looks sad."

She, Eric thought, but said nothing.

"You're carrying a poop bag, right?" the other one asked.

"Yes, sir." Another lie. He didn't need one. She'd already gone. But no way would these guys buy that as an excuse. Eric patted his shoulder bag. "Right in here."

"See that you use it."

When they'd disappeared into the station, Eric blew out a long breath. He scanned quickly for other cops, saw none, and hustled Daisy down the stairs. Just before the bottom, he looked back and unzipped his shoulder bag. His heart beat faster. Trying to take a dog on the subway would only get him a tongue-lashing. Impersonating a cop would land him in jail.

After another look up the stairs, he slipped on the NYPD windbreaker and walked Daisy to the turnstile, where his monthly pass let them through. On the platform, he heard the rumble of an arriving train and felt the whoosh of air being pushed ahead of it. The air carried that typical odor of Midtown subways, like the smell of wet ashes from burned trash.

"Hey!" A white guy in Transit Authority uniform pointed at him from thirty feet away. "You wit' da dog."

Trying to calm his heart, Eric turned away from the man to display the big "NYPD" emblazoned across the back of the windbreaker. Then he turned again to face him. As the guy swaggered up, Eric raised the bottom of his sweatshirt to reveal his—Daisy's—badge.

The train pulling into the station was the one he wanted. "I gotta get to Houston, fast." Eric spoke the street name as New Yorkers did, Howston, which always sounded wrong to anyone from Texas.

"Sorry, I didn't know you was a cop." With a look of surprise, the man pointed to the chest of Eric's windbreaker. "Is that a bullet hole?"

"Yeah. Almost killed me. I'd show you, but this is my train."

"Oh. Okay. Good luck."

With a tug on her lead, Eric took Daisy onboard. As the train jerked forward, he tossed off a quick salute to the Transit guy then grabbed hold of a strap, willing his knees to stop shaking.

At Abby's door, Eric told Daisy, "Best behavior, girl," then knocked.

When Abby opened it, her smile turned into a frown. "Did you have to bring *her*?"

"Come on, you like her." Not really. "At least she likes you."

"Kirin's here."

Uh-oh. Having grown up in a lower-class New Delhi suburb where dogs ran wild and were presumed rabid, Kirin suffered an ingrained fear of all things canine. "I thought she was working tonight."

"She's packing. She leaves tomorrow for her annual trip home."

"I wish you'd told me." He couldn't leave Daisy out here on the landing. "How 'bout if I have her lie down next to my feet?"

"Kirin?"

"No, silly. Daisy."

Abby stepped back to let them enter. "If she slobbers on anything, you clean it up."

"Kirin?"

"Touché. But I'm serious about the slobbering."

"Daisy doesn't slobber," he said, closing the door behind them.

"Go take a look at the computer screens while I warn Kirin."

But at that moment, Kirin backed out of the bedroom dragging a huge, soft-sided suitcase. When she straightened and saw Daisy, she froze.

Abby strode up to her. "Just for a little while, love. Sorry, I didn't know." She pecked Kirin on the mouth, which Kirin seemed not to notice as she disappeared back into the bedroom. To Eric, Abby said, "You can make amends by carrying this thing to the door."

Eric hoisted the suitcase. "Jesus, what's in here?"

"Gifts. There's another one just like it that she's still trying to cram stuff into. We'll have to pay a stevedore to get them down the stairs." Abby's tone turned syrupy. "Unless you want to come by around one tomorrow afternoon."

He set down the suitcase by the front door. Hauling two of these down four flights of stairs didn't hold much appeal.

Hips swaying, Abby came to stand in front of him. "We'd have the rest of the day to do … whatever."

Oh? Suddenly, four flights seemed entirely manageable.

She kissed him lightly on the lips, then walked to her computer desk by the front windows. "In the meantime, take a look at this. Unfortunately, I can't shut down the SF website. There's a guy at work who knows this stuff better than I do and may be able to help. But for now I can at least alter it."

Eric sat in the chair next to her, told Daisy "Down," and looked at the rightmost of her three screens. A flashing yellow banner across the website's home page read, "Danger! Do not buy this product."

"What do you think?" Abby asked.

"You inserted this?"

"No, the tooth fairy did."

"Can we modify it? The text, I mean."

Abby looked crestfallen. "You don't like it?"

"No, I think it's great." Damn, how many times in one day could he stick his foot in his mouth? "But what if we added something like, SF has been implicated in several murders? Or, SF has driven several people to kill their lovers?"

She pinched her lips then nodded. "The second one is good. Say it again."

As he did, she typed. Seconds later, the banner displayed his words. Eric sat back. "I think that's perfect."

"Oh, I also killed that 'quote' from you." She pulled up the site's second page, where a line of black squares spread across the top like freight cars behind a stalled locomotive. "I couldn't delete the quote, but I could cover up the words."

"Excellent. Abby, you're really good."

She gave him one of those smiles that always turned him to putty. "You can thank me tomorrow afternoon." Then her expression sobered. "There's something else. Two things, actually. One is that I found several blogs dedicated to SF. Everyone seems to rave about it."

"Are you defending this stuff? I have four pages of print-out from the police that show how bad it can be."

"Relax. I'm just saying there's information out there you might want to read."

"What's the other thing?"

She hesitated a moment. "I've also done some checking on Durand. He's no longer listed on ISIPCA's site."

Durand? Was she still beating that drum? Eric wanted to say "So what?" but toned it down to, "Which tells you …?"

"That he no longer needs the money."

"He's never needed money. He has a villa on the Mediterranean, a classic luxury sports car, a ton of income from forty-odd years in the perfume business."

Abby stood from her chair. "I think we need to talk."

"About what?"

She walked to the kitchen alcove. From an overhead cupboard, she withdrew a bottle of Lagavulin, his favorite Scotch. After pouring two brandy snifters half-full, she returned to the main room, where she sat on the black leather couch and held out a glass to him. "I never told you this before."

Warily he accepted the offering and sat next to her. It wasn't just her words that bothered him. It was also the fact that the only hard liquor he'd ever seen her drink was vodka. Having such a sensitive palate, she preferred foods and beverages with only the subtlest of flavors.

After taking a sip, she turned her back to the armrest to face him. "You remember the party he threw for senior students that weekend."

Eric remembered it vividly. Brilliant July sun, the deep blue Med, exquisite food and wine, Giselle backstroking naked through Durand's pool, the heady aromas of hot female skin as Abby and many of the other women—although not Marie-Claire—sunbathed topless on chaise lounges.

"Well, Durand invited me back," Abby said, instantly dispelling Eric's vision. "It was in the late fall. He said he could help my career. Of course, I jumped at the chance."

Eric sat up straighter. "You never told me that."

"I told you I never told you." She took another sip of her whiskey.

He took a sip also, savoring the rich, smoky flavor and the thought that Durand had taken another deserving student under his wing. Maybe that was how Abby got the great job she had now.

"Long story short, he could help me if I fucked him."

Eric almost blew out the Scotch still in his mouth. With an effort, he swallowed. "No way."

"Sorry to burst your bubble." She held his eyes a moment, then tilted her snifter from side to side as she ticked off possibilities. "I don't know if it was because he wanted to conquer a lesbian, or he knew you and I slept together and wanted to prove he could do it if you could, or what. But it doesn't matter anymore. The important thing is what I saw."

So stunned he barely speak, Eric simply stared at her.

"What I saw was blank spaces on his walls. You remember those paintings he had? Not the ancestor things in that room with all the swords and armor. The valuable ones in the entry hall. Picasso, Chagall, Miro. Well, they aren't there anymore."

"You mean missing, or he hung them somewhere else?"

"I mean gone. He sold them."

Eric clutched his snifter so tightly he feared he might break the glass. Slackening his grip, he said, "I don't believe you. He must have sent them out for cleaning. Or loaned them to a museum." But for some reason, he did believe her.

"All you can see are the spaces on the walls where they used to be." Abby's pained expression told him she knew how much this hurt. "And the pool is empty. Well, not completely. But the water in the bottom looks like pea soup."

Eric closed his eyes. How could this be?

"I'm sorry," she said, touching his hand. "But I had to tell you. The man is broke. Or at least he was. Now, with the news that he no longer supplements his income by teaching at ISIPCA, I have to wonder—*we* have to wonder—if he hasn't found another source of income."

"No." Now he saw what she was getting at. "Not SF."

"Motive and means, Eric. Regaining his regal lifestyle and, yes, SF."

Standing, he glared down at her. "I don't buy it. Maybe he's had to sell some things to make ends meet. A few paintings he's gotten tired of. But he would never steal someone else's formula. Hell, look at me. I went from being a star to being nobody. But *I'd* never do such a thing. And I don't have half the obsession with honor that Durand has."

"Okay, maybe I'm wrong."

"You are."

Although her eyes clearly said he was deluding himself, she pushed up from the couch and went to her computer. "So let's run a search on Diego. He's still top of your list, right?"

He hated it when she humored him. He hated this whole damned business with Durand. How could such a wealthy man fall on such hard times? How could the idea of theft even tempt him? Selling influence for sexual favors. Durand had mistresses most men would kill for. Eric felt crushed, his heart stepped on and squashed underfoot.

"Are we going to do this or not?" Abby asked.

"Later maybe. I'm going home. Daisy, come."

Dragging her lead, Daisy limped up to him, her sad face a mirror of his own desolation.

Eric knocked down the remainder of his Scotch, barely tasting it but welcoming the fire in his throat. He wanted another, to help burn out all the things Abby had told him. But it would have to wait until he got home. Right now, he just had to get out of here.

At the door, he stopped but didn't turn. Among all his questions lurked one too difficult to ask face-to-face. "Did you sleep with him?"

After a moment of silence, her voice came softly. "Good night, Eric."

Chapter 18

Outside Abby's building, Eric started to take off the NYPD windbreaker. He was in no mood to try to bluff his way onto the subway again. But an icy wind made him refasten the snaps and turn up the flimsy collar. Briskly, he walked Daisy to Broadway, passing warmly bundled couples who hastened toward Saturday-night venues undoubtedly more cheerful than his own destination.

On Broadway, after hailing two cabbies who slowed but wouldn't stop for someone with a dog—never mind his cop jacket—he finally flagged down a more civic-minded driver. The woman, bulky and Slavic-looking, kept up a monologue about "help police" and "green card soon" and "goddamn Communist drivers."

When they got home, he and Daisy walked into an apartment the temperature of a meat locker. Daisy headed straight for her water bowl, lapping noisily while he closed the window over her sleeping spot, twisted squeaky radiator knobs to full-on, and poured two fingers of Scotch into a tumbler.

Propping his butt against the kitchen counter, he glanced around the shabby apartment he shared with no one but a dog. He felt alone, abandoned, as if the two people who mattered most in his adult life had both deserted him, and he'd never seen them leaving.

Had money truly trumped Durand's most fervently held principle? Or had he never believed in honor, but only professed it? Eric pictured the curtain pulling back to expose the Wizard of Oz as nothing more than a charlatan.

But Durand wasn't a charlatan. He'd created exquisite fragrances that became classics. Unless underlings created them for him.

Eric refused to believe that. Yet he couldn't quell the cockfight in the pit of his stomach where his disbelief was losing the battle against a fierce sense of betrayal.

He downed a gulp of whiskey. No help.

On the other hand, his distress sprang entirely from Abby's suspicions. And how much could he trust a woman who waited more than a year to tell him Durand had offered her career advancement for sex?

Eric pushed off the kitchen counter, went into the main room, and plopped down in the wingback chair. Had she accepted the offer? The thought hurt. It didn't bother him one bit that she liked women. But where men were concerned, he'd come to think of himself as special to her, their relationship essentially committed.

"Oh, knock it off," he said out loud. He had no rights to her. She gave him leftovers, when she felt like tossing them to him. And whether she'd slept with Durand was none of his business.

So why did he feel jealous? No, betrayed. Betrayed by her, as well as by Durand. Eric slouched lower in the musty-smelling chair. Was he the only person without a secret life, ulterior motives, hidden agendas? All he wanted was to create perfumes and be recognized for his talent.

The phone rang. He tried to ignore it, but it wouldn't stop. Exasperated, he got up and answered it.

"Stunning results, huh?" Detective Fawcett said, reciting part of the quote attributed to Eric on the SF website. "What kind of asshole are you?"

Eric shut his eyes. This was the last thing he needed. "I didn't write that."

"And I suppose you didn't blank it out afterwards?"

"A friend of mine did."

"Oh?"

Damn. How had he let that slip?

"And this friend's name would be ...?"

Eric hung up.

Almost immediately, the phone rang again. Eric picked it up, depressed the cradle button to disconnect, and left the handset off-hook. He needed peace and quiet and almost certainly a few more whiskeys.

Fifteen minutes later, three loud raps on the door startled him.

Fawcett's voice bellowed, "Open up, Foster."

Christ. Eric set his glass on the kitchen counter and opened the door.

Through a cloud of cigarette smoke, Fawcett glared at him. "Don't ever hang up on me. And what the hell are you doing with that jacket on?"

The windbreaker. Eric tried to shut the door, but Fawcett blocked it with his foot.

Shouldering his way in, Fawcett said, "Take it off now. And give it to me."

"It's cold in here."

"Take it off."

From her Sphinx position by the water bowl, Daisy merely looked up at the intruder.

Great guard dog. Eric popped open the jacket's snaps. "Would you get rid of that cigarette?"

"When I'm done with it."

"Now."

With a sneer, Fawcett glanced around the room, apparently looking for an ashtray.

"Just give it to me," Eric said. He took the stub, doused it under the kitchen faucet, and dropped it in the garbage bin under his sink.

"The jacket, asshole."

"Daisy likes it." Eric tossed the windbreaker onto his chair. "What do you want?"

"The name of your friend."

"Forget it. Anything else?"

"You're pissing me off."

"Then leave." Eric walked to the kitchen and picked up his glass from the counter.

"I'll take one of those."

Was the man off-duty? No, not Fawcett. It had to be a ploy to make him, Eric, drop his guard. Just two pals tipping a wee dram at the end of the day. Playing along, he poured a finger's worth into a second glass and held it out.

Fawcett sampled the drink. "Pretty good. Expensive?"

"Not if you sip it a little at a time."

"Either it's expensive or it's not."

"Are we going to spar here all night?"

Fawcett unbuttoned his overcoat. "Cute trick you pulled with the flashing notice about SF killing people. Your friend do that, too?"

Vintage Fawcett—circle around, then home back in on the main question. But it wasn't going to work. "No comment."

"No comment," Fawcett mimicked. "My, aren't we the big shot?" He took another sip, then eyed his glass. "What is this stuff?"

"Lagavulin."

"Laga …"

"It's getting late. How 'bout you drink up and go?"

Fawcett's gaze turned frosty. "How 'bout you come clean with me, dickhead? There's no slack in the noose anymore. Lab tests confirm SF is Balquees. Your name's on the—"

"Bullshit!" Eric smacked his tumbler down on the countertop. "Lab tests showed they're different."

"Not according to Miss Cole."

"Miss Cole's biased. I was standing right there when we analyzed the samples."

"Hey, asshole. You're talking about a damn good forensic scientist who volunteered to do this and gave up half her weekend to prove you right. But you're wrong. So if you got a beef with anyone, it's with me."

"Prove me right? That's a load of crap. She raked me over the coals."

Fawcett shrugged. "Maybe she loves you."

"Maybe you're as full of shit as she is. Did she tell you about the shoulder on the hump?"

"Shoulder, schmoulder. She says it's nothing, and I believe her."

"On the grounds that you're a great chemist?"

"Remind me again what your friend's name is."

Eric's blood pressure shot off the chart. On the verge of bursting, he stomped to the door and jerked it open. "Get out!"

"I haven't finished my drink. Hate to waste it. It's expensive, remember?"

"*Out*, dammit."

"So your ... friend ... blocks out your name and puts up a warning about SF being dangerous to your health. What are you, the Surgeon General?"

"Wait a minute." Eric's mind flashed to something that made no sense. "Why haven't you put a notice in the *Times*? Same thing. SF can kill you?"

"Oh, you *are* cute."

"Huh? What are you talking about?"

"Well, let me see." Fawcett touched a fingertip to his temple. "Could it be lawyers? Could it be the fact that without proof of a causal relationship, we could be prosecuted for libel? Yes, I believe that's it. But you knew that, didn't you? And no causal relationship is the *same* fucking reason why your fucking service provider won't shut down your *fucking* website."

Eric stared at him, speechless at the man's sudden outburst. Fawcett the unflappable. Then the real reason for his frustration dawned. Causal relationship. Fawcett might *think* Balquees and SF were the same, but he still had no proof that SF could induce murderous violence. Which meant that, despite his "noose" comment, he still had no defensible basis for arresting Eric. He was badgering, bullying, groping for straws. And hoping for a slip-up.

Eric felt sorry for him, but not enough to divulge any of his own suspicions. He wasn't about to subject his friends from Versailles to police interrogation until he, himself, had winnowed the potential traitors down to one. All he could do at this stage was say, "Look, man, I honest-to-God have nothing to do with this."

Fawcett slowly tipped his glass, spilling the remainder of his Scotch on the floor. With venom in his eyes, he tossed the glass to Eric and tramped out.

❧

Eric punched up his pillows and closed his eyes again, but his brain kept churning. Why couldn't Fawcett get it through his thick skull that the two of them were on the same side? Deep down, Eric actually liked the guy. And if Fawcett, from the start, had treated him less like a suspect and more like an asset, Eric might feel more inclined to share information. But vitriolic outbursts, like the one tonight, only made him want to upstage the great detective by solving this on his own.

The problem was lack of information, like trying to solve a mathematical equation with too many unknowns. *Hang on.* "There's information out there," Abby had said, referring to the blogs.

He tossed off the covers, went into the living room, and booted his computer. When the fax-squawk of his dial-up connection ceased, he typed "SF blog" into Google's search window and found—among websites for San Francisco and science fiction—three sites dedicated to SF, the perfume.

The enthusiasm of the bloggers was just as Abby had said. But the comments posted by readers chilled him. All over the country, people swore by the bogus perfume. New Agers called it the "soma of our time." Aromatherapy buffs hailed it as the solution to "tired sex." People Eric couldn't type by their on-line monikers or style of comment waxed ecstatic.

What really bothered him was that high school kids were also raving about it. They talked as though it were a date-rape drug. "If you wanna get laid ..." "She'll take it in the ass if ..." "She scratched the fuck out of me. Best sex EVER!!!" "Dude this shit is way cool. My girlfriend gave it to me and we both freaked out."

Among a hundred or so comments, he found six that reported bad experiences. Things like, "I almost killed my wife" and "Flush it down the toilet." Each of these brought a string of invectives in the vein of "You're full of shit," "Get the hell out of here," and "Faggot!!!!!!"

Eric sat back in dismay. Like dissenters at a hot-blooded rally, people warning about the dangerous side effects of SF were being shouted down and told to go to hell.

Maybe a more factual warning would help. He typed a Word document giving the statistics of SF-related murders and assaults in Manhattan. Then it occurred to him that details of what had happened during the bad experiences might give some clues about the nature of Agent X. He appended a request for details plus his email address, then copied the document and pasted it into the "Add a Comment" box on the three blog sites.

The whole effort was probably a long shot, but he had to try.

Chapter 19

Using a knot one of the women had shown her, Laura Ferguson tied a one-pull bow in the ribbon that bound the front of her negligee. "Care to try it?"

Her husband, Mark, who'd just slipped into a black see-through jock strap, came up to her with a smile and gave the ribbon a tug. The negligee fell open, revealing her midline from neck to pubic hair. "Very nice. Whoever tugs it tonight is going to drool like a baby."

She kissed him and felt his fingers slip between her legs. With a little shudder, she imagined Vicki doing that. But the shudder quickly passed, chased away by uncertainty.

"What's wrong?" Mark asked.

Laura bit her lip. The moment had arrived, the moment she'd never imagined a few months ago when Mark first mentioned the "lifestyle."

He'd broached the subject one evening after dinner, holding her hands and speaking of the spiritual enrichment they could find in sharing their love with others. She'd felt crushed, like all this time she'd been a failure in bed. But he hugged her tightly and assured her their sex life was perfect and he would never want to do anything that made her uncomfortable. In the following days, he was even kinder and more attentive than usual. Then he brought it up again. He quoted from the sermons he'd recently preached about modern interpretation of scriptural taboos. Things like Lot and his daughters, Deuteronomy's verses on pretty women among the captives, Paul's teachings about the "natural use" of women. He spoke of like-minded people and dismissed as superficial any comparison to the wife swapping of the seventies.

Certain Mark's motives weren't purely spiritual, but wanting to please him—and frankly growing curious—she'd finally agreed to just go and look.

What a night. They'd walked around and watched and gotten so feverishly aroused that they took the plunge and had sex in the spa, with each other. One of the strongest orgasms of her life.

The next time, encouraged by the club's code of etiquette, they'd ventured out to try other partners. After a bout of jealousy watching a busty blonde swallow Mark completely, she'd accepted three men in succession, two mediocre, one so skillful she could hardly breathe afterwards.

But in the interludes, she had also found herself strangely attracted to Vicki Simpson, a lively aerobics instructor who "went both ways." What Vicki did with men was nothing special. What she did with women ignited Laura like she'd never felt before. Not so much the scissoring as the way Vicki savored a woman between the legs. And even more, the way she responded ecstatically to a woman doing the same to her. Laura wanted to be that woman.

In the month since then, fantasies of sex with Vicki had slithered through her daydreams like the serpent offering forbidden fruit. The problem was how Mark would react.

She looked into his eyes, choosing her words carefully. "I've come to terms with what we're doing. You know, in regard to the Bible and all. And I love what it does for the passion in our marriage."

With a concerned look, he took hold of her hands. "But you're having second thoughts?"

"No, nothing like that. I'm looking forward to tonight." She rolled her lips in, gathering strength. "I'm just wondering how you'd feel if I ... tried something different."

"Different how?"

Please, God, help me to just say it. She took a fortifying breath. "What if I kissed another woman?"

Mark broke into a huge grin. "Vicki Simpson?"

Laura stepped back, shocked that he could have known. Had she been that obvious?

"My love," he said, eyes sparkling, "I think you and Vicki would have a marvelous time together."

"You wouldn't feel … you know, inadequate?"

"Am I inadequate?"

"Lord, no." Since the first night they'd spent together, he a missionary, she a nurse at a bush hospital in jungles of Gabon, she'd felt the two of them were destined for each other. "You're the light of my life. I just want you to know that, whatever happens, you're the only person I could ever love."

"Which is exactly how I feel about you." He wrapped his arms around her, gave her a kiss, then held her at arm's length. "Now finish getting ready. And remember, no perfume. The card says the theme for this month's meeting is perfume, and our hosts will provide it."

The "book club" met at nine in the evening on the second Saturday of each month, always at the home of Jeff and Jenny Blanchard whose house, a sprawling ranch-style in the foothills of Mission Viejo, boasted an inspirational view overlooking Laguna Beach and the Pacific Ocean.

As Mark parked their Toyota in the curbside lineup of much fancier cars, Laura spotted Tom Dorcet and his wife walking toward the house. Tom was the parishioner who'd approached her husband after the series of sermons on scriptural taboos. Like the other men, Tom always wore trousers until he got inside. But since bare legs were acceptable for women in public, most of the ladies wore next to nothing beneath their Burberry coats and mink jackets. For appearances' sake, one member of each couple, Tom's wife in this case, carried a book. A quirk of the club was that you left with a different book from the one you'd brought.

Getting out of the car, Laura inhaled the smells of sagebrush and newly cut lawns, a combination she'd come to associate with these once-a-month gatherings and which sent a thrill up her thighs. Would she connect, as they said, with Vicki tonight? She clutched Mark's hand and felt a reassuring squeeze.

Jenny Blanchard greeted them at the door. After kisses on the cheek and the usual, "Books and coats down the hall, second door on the left," she added, "Drinks and perfume are on the patio. We'll serve Vietnamese food at midnight, if you're interested. And please stay out of the water until then. We don't want the perfume to wash off."

Was this mystery perfume that special? Well, if so, Laura was game. She undid the belt of her trench coat and let Mark take it off her shoulders. Dressed now in nothing but the diaphanous negligee, she felt exposed, a little insecure. And excited.

"Meet you on the patio," Mark said and headed down the hall.

Laura walked through the living room, giving a wide berth to the Persian cat enthroned in one of the armchairs. Tonight of all nights, she did not need an allergy attack. Fortunately, the cat stayed put as she opened a sliding glass door to the patio.

Besides the view, the Blanchards' backyard sported an infinity pool, a Jacuzzi spa, a built-in barbecue, and a thatch-roofed bar. About twenty of the club members were already here. In various degrees of undress, they chatted in groups or danced to the sounds of soft rock under Japanese lanterns strung across the patio. Among the dancers, Vicki Simpson shimmied and swayed with Moby, a black man who'd played tight end—didn't that fit?—for some football team. True to stereotype, Moby was big. Moby Dick, members called him.

Although club meetings, in Laura's limited experience, took an hour or so to get "heated up," Moby was already hot. And Vicki, wearing only a string-tied bikini bottom, used her fingertips to make sure he stayed that way.

The girl wasn't gorgeous but, God, she was sexy. Long brunette hair, a trim body toned by hours in the gym, a provocative smile that practically moaned "I want you." Laura felt dumpy in comparison. Her breasts were still firm, but her hips were larger than she'd like, and two years of subsisting mainly on root vegetables in the Gabonese jungle had given her some padding in the tummy that she couldn't get rid of. What about her could a goddess like Vicki find attractive?

"Laura," Jeff called from behind the bar. "Come hither and let me anoint thee."

Tearing her eyes from Vicki, Laura crossed the flagstone patio and greeted their host, a jovial man known as Scarecrow Tim to the children in his TV audience. Laura shuddered at what the kids would think if they could see him now, decked out in absolutely nothing, half-erect, and grinning as he stepped out from behind the bar.

With a glance over her shoulder, he asked. "Where's Pastor Mark?"

"Taking off his coat." In club speak, leaving your "coat" in the bedroom included leaving any other garments you cared to shed.

"Good news for the ladies, bad news for me. They sure do flock to him. Get it?" Jeff winked. "Pastor, flock?"

"You're a card."

"That's me." He thrust his arms out to the sides and hung his head in a naked imitation of his TV persona. Then he held up a small spray bottle. "You're going to love this stuff." With three quick squirts, he "anointed" her chest and arms. "And a little down below?"

The perfume smelled delightful, roses and sandalwood and something earthy she really liked. In response to Jeff's question, she spread the lower part of her negligee. "Just a little. What's it called?"

"SF." He knelt and gave her pubic hair a shot. "You're beautiful. May I touch?"

She'd never been attracted to Jeff. He was kind of doughy and always grinning. But as she inhaled the perfume rising from her chest, she thought a touch would be nice. She widened her stance.

Jeff slid his hands up her thighs, brought his fingers together at the top, and spread her labia. "Beautiful."

When he probed inside, a shiver of pleasure coursed through her. He used his fingers and thumbs with staggering skill.

"Good evening, Jeff," Mark said, wrapping strong arms around her waist.

"Pastor Mark." Jeff rose to his feet, jolting her from her trance and leaving nothing inside her but unfulfilled craving. "Good to see you again."

Mark nuzzled her neck. "Mmm, that's a lovely fragrance. What is it?"

"Guaranteed aphrodisiac." Jeff held out the bottle. "Here, give yourself a few spritzes."

In her ear, Mark whispered, "Why don't you cut in on Moby."

Her body still throbbed, hungering for Jeff to finish what he'd started. But she knew Mark was rescuing her from a man she didn't much care for. Bless his heart, she could not ask for a better husband. She turned and kissed him. "I love you," she whispered back and reached inside his jockstrap. "I want this, later. Every inch of it."

"It's yours, honey. Now go get her."

With a smile, she squeezed him, then made her way toward the dancers.

In the few minutes she'd spent getting anointed and fingered by their host, more people had arrived, while those already here were approaching the boiling point in record time. Kissing and fondling in twos and threes, lots of manual stimulation, one guy dancing with a woman from behind with his erection between her legs. At the sight of it all, Laura felt dizzy with desire.

Then a loud groan in a male voice yanked her eyes to an air mattress at the side of the pool. Moby's wife, a full-figured beauty with a reputation for being voracious, lay sandwiched between two men while a third pounded into her mouth. The man on top, the one in missionary position, threw his head back and groaned again. Laura cupped herself to stave off a climax. God, she'd love to try three men at once.

But not tonight.

Suddenly afraid that someone else might have gotten to Vicki first, Laura searched the crowd. There she was, on the far side, still dancing with Moby. Only dancing, thank goodness, although Vicki was now totally naked. Naked and as radiant as a heavenly vision.

A man put his hand on Laura's shoulder, protocol for "I'd like to bed you." She brushed it away, realizing in some corner of her mind that it was the first time she'd ever denied a club member's advance. But she had courage now. More than courage. She had the self-assurance to take the lead and go after what she wanted.

As she walked toward Vicki, the music seemed to fade, the crowd to dissolve. Vicki glowed under the changing colors of the

Japanese lanterns. Her bronzed skin glistened. Her pussy—Laura didn't like that word, but all the club members used it—was shaved or waxed, so deliciously smooth that Laura could already feel herself kissing it, licking it. She could feel herself nibbling the folds between Vicki's labia, scratching gently with her teeth, burying her face and sucking Vicki's clitoris the way she'd suck a shrimp from its shell.

Then suddenly Vicki rose. Moby had lifted her. Vicki wrapped her legs around his waist. He was going to impale her, right there where they stood.

No! She wanted to taste Vicki. Pure Vicki. Not Vicki polluted with semen. Laura dashed forward and ripped them apart.

"What the fuck are you doing?" Moby snarled.

Laura pulled Vicki away. "I want you. Now."

"Girl, you're on fire." Vicki slid her hand between Laura's legs. "And wet? Jesus, you're wetter than me."

Moby clamped a hand on Laura's arm. "Hey, bitch, she's mine."

"Moby, get lost," Vicki told him as she clasped Laura's hips.

Laura drew her a few steps away, then yanked the bow and tore the negligee off her own shoulders. With both hands, she crushed Vicki's breasts. "Here and now."

"On the stone patio? There are air mattresses."

"Right here." Laura dragged her down, pushed her back, and spread her legs. The most beautiful pussy she'd ever seen. Pulsing, yearning, just like hers. She dived in.

"Ouch! Take it easy. You're biting too hard."

Laura needed this. Needed all of it. Every fold and furrow.

"God dammit! You're hurting me." Vicki clutched Laura's hair and tried to pull her away.

Vicki tasted so good. Her love juices were intoxicating. The feel of her pussy lips as Laura burrowed between them drove her mad. *Come on, baby, cum in my mouth.*

"Help me," Vicki screamed, twisting her body. "Get her off me."

Laura launched up from between Vicki's legs and kissed her hard, sharing the lovely pussy juice.

Thrashing beneath her, Vicki clawed at Laura's face.

It hurt. But it hurt good. So Vicki liked a little pain? *Darling, we can share that, too.* Laura grasped handfuls of her lover's hair and pulled.

Vicki cried out, her face the very picture of ecstasy.

Yes! Laura shook Vicki's head, banging it on the patio. Even greater ecstasy on Vicki's face. Was that what Vicki needed? Laura banged the girl's head again and heard a cracking sound. She felt hands grappling with her shoulders, but she wouldn't let go. Vicki was almost there. Her eyes were closed now as she rocketed toward the pinnacle. She'd climax any second.

"Come on, baby. Come on."

Chapter 20

First thing Sunday morning, Eric booted his computer and checked for replies to his postings on the SF blogs. He found four short notes of the "Fuck you" variety, none of them signed with the online monikers of the people who'd reported bad experiences. Nor had anyone sent him an email. Patience, he told himself, as though that were a virtue he'd ever possessed.

On Sundays, he usually treated himself to pancakes and bacon with a side of scrambled eggs that he shared with Daisy. But he'd forgotten to buy bacon, found only one egg in the refrigerator, and discovered the instant he opened the bottle that the milk had gone sour.

He soft-boiled the egg for Daisy, then poured a bowl of Wheat Chex and added water. Munching quickly, before the cereal became too soggy, he rationalized that the odor of bacon in his apartment would have distracted him anyway. Today of all days, he needed to apply his olfactory senses with maximum concentration.

From his bedroom closet, he dug out some *mouillettes* and a thick reference text on perfumery. Using an eyedropper, he transferred a milliliter of Balquees into a standard 5/8-dram, screw-capped vial of the kind used for fragrance samples. With these and the vial of SF, he sat down cross-legged on the cheap Chinese carpet at the foot of his bed. He dipped a *mouillette* in Balquees with his left hand, another in SF with his right, and closed his eyes, holding his arms out in the position of the crucified.

First, the SF. He brought the smell strip to his nose, inhaled rapidly, and extended his arm again. The top-note ingredients registered immediately, each in correct proportion. He knew Balquees so well that he didn't need to compare with it. But he did anyway and detected no difference.

Okay, that was the easy part. Any half-good student at ISIPCA could identify those components by smell and get the proportions by trial and error. Eric waved both strips in the air to hasten evaporation and let the heart note bloom. Then he inserted the undipped ends between the pages on opposite sides of the closed reference book, leaving the dipped ends exposed to dry further.

Waiting, he chewed his cuticles, certain the difference lay in the oud but half-sick with worry that the dissimilarity would be too subtle to smell. Even the GC had found only a shoulder on a hump, and a pretty good chemist thought the shoulder fell within statistical error. Or so she'd said.

After five minutes, he sniffed the SF strip again. The heart note definitely was oud of Socotra. No other oud smelled quite that way, the fragrances of sandalwood, balsam, and rose overlying a scent of composted grass that people at Luc's party had likened to silage and semen. But was there something else? Something vaguely putrid? Maybe with a faint acidic sting, like chlorine. For some reason, he pictured the garden shed at his grandmother's house.

He waited a moment to clear his nose, then squeezed his eyes shut and smelled the SF strip again. He couldn't be sure, not in the presence of the civet and shiitake, both of which possessed strong fecal tones that competed with the putrid ghost note.

Annoyed at himself, Eric stalked into the bathroom to wash out his nostrils. As he resumed his lotus position on the Chinese carpet, the tip of his dick started tingling. *Interesting.* SF worked pretty fast, considering that the freeze-drying results indicated it was more dilute than Balquees. On the other hand, he'd decided after the Panthéon that Balquees needed dilution. So speed probably meant nothing.

Still, the ghost note bothered him. Was it real? For reference, he smelled the Balquees strip. Nothing acidic, except a hint of lemon zest left over after dry-down. And nothing he'd call putrid.

For the next quarter hour, he alternated between the two *mouillettes* until his head reeled and his confined erection strained painfully for release. Damn. This was getting him nowhere. Time for a break.

Without donning a jacket, he took Daisy out for a mid-morning pee. A cold wind clattered the skeletal branches of her favorite tree and thankfully wilted his erection. He faced into the wind, inhaling deeply to purge the remnant fragrances from his nostrils. So far, he'd struck out. But perhaps Agent X, loathe though Ms. Cole was to call it that, lurked in the base note.

Back inside, he laid the two *mouillettes* on a radiator for sixty seconds to drive off as much of the oud as possible. When he smelled them again, he wanted to scream. The base note of Balquees contained only civet and shiitake, and that's exactly what he smelled in SF. Nothing more, nothing less.

He shoved the *mouillettes* between the pages at opposite ends of his book, leaned back against his bed, and stared at the ceiling. If the ghost note was real, it was elusive as hell. To stand any chance of confirming it, he'd have to clear his nose completely and start all over again.

At the sound of clicking toenails, he shifted his gaze from the ceiling to Daisy. She limped in, sniffed one strip then the other, then settled herself on the carpet by his knee.

He wondered briefly whether the fragrances would affect animals. And in that moment, inspiration struck. He jumped up, grabbed the two strips, and rushed into the living room, where he stuck the SF sample under his armchair and placed the Balquees sample in the far corner of the kitchen. Returning to the bedroom, he passed the vial of SF under Daisy's nose and said, "Seek."

As she got to her feet, Eric held his breath. But all she did was look up at him, nose his right hand, and sit.

Crap. "Alerting" on his hand was no good. In fact, the whole apartment probably reeked of both smells by now. He washed his hands, changed clothes, and took the strips outside. He dropped the Balquees strip under a bush and the SF strip near the sidewalk, then went back to get Daisy and the two vials. At the top of the stoop, he gave her another sniff from the vial of SF. "Seek."

When he released her, she trailed the route he'd taken, pausing at the Balquees strip then continuing to the sidewalk, where she nosed the SF strip and sat.

Eric's heart leapt. Suddenly the frigid air felt refreshing.

"Good girl," he told her, then, "Stay." He gathered the two strips, held them in different hands, and walked south, halfway down the street. He slipped the Balquees strip under one side of a bulging garbage bag and the SF strip under the opposite side. This time, the two trails lay on top of one another until the very end. And this time, he passed the bottle of Balquees under her nose. When he told her to "Seek," Daisy trotted off and sat next to the Balquees.

Eric could hardly contain himself. He jogged down to her, told her, "Good girl," and rubbed his knuckles under her earflaps the way she liked best.

In his final test, he decided to rule out any possibility that Daisy could have seen which smell strip went where. He walked north to the corner of 52nd Street and turned left out of her sight. He dropped the Balquees strip in the gutter between two parked cars. Now where to put the SF? He stepped between the cars and looked up and down the street. Thirty feet to his left, a guy climbed into a delivery van, tossed a Coke can out the window, and pulled into light traffic. Perfect.

After the van passed by, Eric dashed to the Coke can, slipped the SF strip inside it, and kicked the can to the curb. Now the SF strip was not only hidden, it was also contaminated by the strong smell of Coca Cola. Plus, the drink was acidic—acidic enough that a human tooth placed in a glass of it would dissolve in a matter of days. So residual liquid in the can might even degrade the SF a little before Daisy reached it.

Tough test.

Stuffing his hands in his jeans pockets against the cold, he returned to Daisy. He gave her a sniff from the vial of SF, told her "Seek," and let her get twenty feet ahead of him before following. When he rounded the corner, his heart sank. Daisy was sitting at the curb where he'd dropped the Balquees.

For half a minute, he stood and watched her. She looked back at him but didn't move. She was waiting for her reward.

Then it dawned on him. Daisy was trained not to step off the curb unless given permission. He checked both directions, saw no oncoming traffic, and called out, "Okay."

Daisy limp-trotted between the two parked cars and headed left out of his sight. He followed up the sidewalk and, sure enough, she was sitting next to the Coke can.

Eric punched his fist skyward. "Yes!"

An approaching woman gaped at him and quickly crossed the street.

All the way back to the apartment he told Daisy what a good girl she was. Inside, he poured her two cups of kibble, then called Fawcett. When it rolled over to voicemail, he said, "Read 'em and weep, Sherlock. I've got proof positive that Balquees and SF are different. And you'll never guess how I did it."

Chapter 21

Eric climbed the stairs to Abby's apartment. After Daisy's verification that morning of a difference between Balquees and SF, he was more than ready to celebrate. And Abby's promise of an afternoon together, once Kirin left, was the best kind of celebration he could imagine. But as he reached her floor, the fear of rejection gripped him. Had the strained circumstances of his departure last night soured Abby's mood? Would he find himself, twenty minutes from now, kicking pebbles down the street?

Pasting a smile on his face, he knocked.

Abby opened the door, shot a glance back into her apartment, then stepped out and gave him a hug. "Whoa. I haven't smelled *that* in a long time."

He'd showered and shaved and thought he got rid of any lingering hints of Balquees and SF. But evidently the air in his bedroom was so saturated with the odors that they'd seeped into the clothes in his closet. And his nose, after so much exposure, had become temporarily desensitized.

"Did you bring some for me?" she murmured in his ear.

Thinking fast, he replied, "Maybe this hint of it will inspire us both."

"Mmm. Come on in."

His burden of doubt lifted. Standing taller, he stepped inside, where two large, soft-sided suitcases stood like sentinels guarding the door.

"Hello, Eric." Kirin came out of the kitchen wearing a navy ankle-length skirt and white long-sleeved blouse. "Thank you for helping with my luggage. Last year, I had to pay fifty dollars for the cab driver to take them down. From only a second-floor flat."

One of his guilt pangs bit hard. Here he was, just waiting for her to leave so he could hop into bed with her lover. But Abby was *his* lover, too. Since long before Kirin ever met her. Okay, maybe he was rationalizing. But he wanted Abby, and judging from her welcome on the landing, she wanted him.

The three of them chatted for a few minutes before Eric hoisted the suitcases and left the women to say their goodbyes. Struggling under the load of what had to be home appliances and auto parts, he half-carried, half-dragged Kirin's bags down the stairs and out to the sidewalk.

There he waited. Bundled pedestrians hurried past, hands thrust in their overcoat pockets. But the cold felt good to him. His muscles slowly unwound, leaving that sense of natural strength that comes after a strenuous workout.

Despite being overcast, the gray sky seemed bright. He caught a whiff of garlic bread from the Italian place at the corner. Italians. He was willing to bet they purposely vented their kitchens to the street. And it sure did work. His mouth salivated. Maybe he and Abby would grab a meal there this evening.

A few minutes later, she came out of the apartment building with Kirin. "No cab?"

"Not yet," he said, his eyes feasting on the seductive way Abby carried herself.

"There." Kirin pointed toward Broadway where a Yellow Cab was rounding the corner onto their street.

Eric loaded her bags into the trunk, then opened the rear door and waited while the women hugged. When Kirin finally climbed in, he mustered a warm smile, wished her, "Safe journey," and shut the door. As the cab turned right at the end of the street, he took hold of Abby's hand.

Her grip tightened on his. "Come on."

❧

Exhausted, drained, and totally happy, Eric settled back against the headboard, Abby's cheek on his chest, his fingers teasing the fine hairs at the base of her spine. Shallow, rhythmic breathing suggested she might doze off, which was fine with him. Lying with her like this, immersed in their aromas, gave him a feeling of peace he hadn't known for a long time. The warmth of her body. The weight of her leg on his. The marine flavor of her lingering on his tongue.

His gaze drifted over her pale, flawless skin, half-entwined with the black sheets of her black lacquered bed. From the foot of the bed, five red toenails peeked out at him.

Dreamily he looked around the room. Two mirrors and a dresser, also in black lacquer. Two large charcoal sketches of nude women. No change from the last time he'd been here. It was signature Abby, except for two saris hanging in the open closet.

He noticed through her undraped window that lights had come on in apartments across the street. Yet despite encroaching dusk, a pinprick sparkle glinted off the tiny diamond stud in Abby's nose. He kind of liked the stud. Like nature's earring, the birthmark below her ear, it added an exotic complement to her natural beauty.

When she woke, they'd go to dinner. After nothing to eat last night and only Wheat Chex in water this morning, he could plow his way through half the menu in that Italian place down the street. A table for two, bathed in the flickering glow of a candle in an old Chianti bottle.

Abby stirred. With the languid fluidity of a stretching cat, she turned her face to him and cooed, "That was nice."

No sweeter words could she ever speak. And from the painful nail scratches in his back, he knew she meant it.

"But your stomach's rumbling." In a rustle of sheets, she pushed herself up to sit beside him. "If you're going to spend the night, we should get some food in you."

Spend the night? God, would he love that. They hadn't watched daybreak in each other's arms since Versailles.

But he'd have to take care of Daisy first. Or bring her here, if Abby would allow it. Then he remembered. Turning to face her, he said, "I forgot to tell you. Daisy can smell the difference between

Balquees and SF."

Abby arched her eyebrows. "Are you sure?"

"Absolutely positive."

"But where'd you find the SF? We only ordered it last night."

"The crime lab." He summarized his day with Tanya and his experiments that morning with Daisy. "I thought I could smell something different, but I wasn't certain. Now that Daisy confirms it, I'm going to try harder."

"Different in what way?" she asked, pulling the sheets up over her breasts.

"I got an image of something in the garden shed at my grandmother's place on Galveston Island. But not dirt or fertilizer. More like a chemical of some kind."

"A cleanser?"

"I don't know. But I will. I just need to concentrate more."

"Well, that's great news." She tugged up a pillow and positioned it behind her head. "And I have news, too. Marie-Claire and Diego are in town."

"*What?*" Eric sat bolt upright. "How do you know?"

"I check my office voicemail. Which you obviously don't. She says her family is opening a boutique here. The launch is tomorrow at five o'clock, and we're invited. They'd also like to have dinner with us afterwards."

"You spoke to her?"

"No, that was all in the voicemail."

"How did she get your number?"

"Durand, I imagine. There should be a similar message on *your* office phone. By the way, *T Magazine* in this morning's paper confirms the opening. Your favorite perfume critic promises an interview with Marie-Claire. Apparently she's the queen bee."

Eric thought a moment. On the surface, it all sounded reasonable enough. Or would have, except for one thing. "Why Diego?"

"That's the question. She didn't leave a phone number or say where they're staying, so we'll have to wait to find out. But it's strange, don't you think? Marie-Claire and Diego?"

"It sure as hell is." Eric got out of bed. Naked, he paced the room, his mind churning. In Versailles, Diego had wanted nothing to do with her. Yet now they were together—Diego, to whom Eric had given a complete list of Balquees's ingredients, and Marie-Claire, whose family's company made specialty perfumes. He clamped his jaw, his vision filling with Marie-Claire's cherubic face. She'd declared Balquees satanic. She'd begged him to destroy it, asked him to pray with her. Of course, he'd done neither. And eleven months later, here he was, under investigation for a deadly knock-off. In his mind's eye, Marie-Claire's pouty little mouth warped into a vengeful sneer.

"God *damn*." Two of the only three friends he'd ever had at Versailles. Either this was a vicious act of duplicity or one hell of a coincidence. He scanned the floor, spotted his jeans, and pulled them on. "We'll have to skip dinner. I need to go think about this."

As soon as the door closed behind him, Abby threw off the sheets, opened the cylindrical safe built into her closet floor, and pulled out a dime bag of hydro. She groomed out the sticks and seeds, rolled a joint, and lit up. Then she stretched out naked on the living room couch, hoping the rich smoke would calm her nerves. How in hell could SF and Balquees be different? She'd copied Eric's formula exactly.

Fortunately, she had covered her shock at his announcement, his proof. And just as fortunately, bless her luck, she'd been able to get rid of him with the news about Marie-Claire and Diego, because she, too, needed to think.

She took a deep drag, held it just a second, and blew it out slowly, pleased she could afford to smoke a joint the way others smoked cigarettes, rather than having to hold in lungfuls like a junkie. With another drag, she pictured Eric's apartment in Versailles, a piece of cake to open with her Swiss Army knife, as she'd shown him once when he locked himself out. And opening it was just as easy on the night of Luc's party, the night she'd told Eric she couldn't go with him because she was meeting Audrey, her actress, at the George Cinq in Paris. Within sixty seconds, she was inside and removing Eric's notebook from the middle drawer on the right-hand side of his perfumer's organ. On the last page, in penmanship a mapmaker would envy, he'd printed his final formula.

Through the plume of an exhalation, she gazed at the lighted windows across the street. Reflected glow from a streetlamp below Eric's apartment had given her more than enough light to copy the formula word for word, number for number.

With a mellow buzz on, she snuffed out the last inch of the joint and went to the kitchen to pour herself a tall glass of vodka. Balquees and SF had to be the same. The only "mystery" ingredient was the oud, and she *knew* that was the same. She'd swiped ISIPCA's sample, extracted it herself, and blended it precisely with the other ingredients to make her very first batch—the batch that later drove Audrey and her to even greater heights of pleasure than on that night in the church. Abby tingled at the recollection, then felt a twinge of guilt.

She'd never imagined Eric would be accused of the theft, let alone get expelled for it. But that was Durand's fault. If the mighty master had done his job instead of wimping out, poor Eric would have gotten off scot-free.

Durand. There was no trusting that arrogant snob with his nose in the air and his medieval view of women as a collection of holes. Abby swallowed a mouthful of vodka and topped up the glass.

Finding Eric an affordable apartment in Midtown—no small feat—had done little to assuage her feelings of guilt. But if he'd had any gumption, he could have rebounded. Balquees had given him the ticket. Yet he'd thrown it away. No one could blame *her* for that. All she did was pick up his castoff, like a prudent buyer at a secondhand shop.

He was wrong about the formula. It needed no adjustment, at all. She'd told him that on the train. But would he listen? Of course not. She took another long swallow.

He was wrong, too, about there not being enough oud to go commercial. For a boutique fragrance there was plenty. Finding in his notebook the contact information for the dealer in Yemen had been all the encouragement she needed. When Eric was expelled and simply gave up, she'd used part of her nest egg—pilfered coin-by-coin over the years from her father's cash register—to buy the dealer's entire supply of the wood, including the low-grade stuff. The quantity of extract, when cut back to seventy-five percent of the concentration Eric had used, turned out to be enough for eleven thousand bottles of SF. Eleven thousand. If that wasn't commercial, nothing was. And new shipments arrived almost every month, as the dealer received them from Socotra.

After expenses, she would net more than two million dollars. In fact, she'd already made nearly half of that. One person's trash was another's treasure.

Drink in hand, Abby walked the length of her living room, smiling at the proceeds of SF—this apartment, her designer clothes, her whole lifestyle. No way would she give those up. Not after a childhood spent cowering behind the produce crates in her corner of the storeroom, trembling at the fear of being sold into slavery by that monster who'd supposedly sired her. Worst of all, as a little girl in rags, being pulled out by the ear late at night and forced to stand half-naked in front of the bastard's "friends" while they smoked opium and nodded stupidly at his re-telling of how she'd killed his beloved wife by simply being born.

"Fuck you!" Abby wanted to throw her glass at the wall but settled for splashing its contents into the aquarium. "And fuck every scraggly-bearded shit who ever pulled up a chair in the back room of your goddamned store."

She strode naked to the front of her apartment and stood at one of the windows, daring anyone to look at her, wanting them to look at her on her own terms now. No longer powerless. But nobody on the street glanced her way, and even the old dependable lech on the fifth floor across the street wasn't currently manning his telescope.

Needing something to perk her up, she logged onto the SF website as "Administrator" and checked the stats for recent sales. Very good. With a smile, she transferred $19,000 to her numbered account at New China Bank, directly across the street from her father's store. How beautifully poetic. In her mind's eye, she saw the bastard ringing up a sale of bok choy while utterly oblivious to the fact that the bank holding his mortgage also held the account whose access code, 16-1-25-2-1-3-11, was a simple numerical substitution for P-A-Y-B-A-C-K.

Chapter 22

Diego and Marie-Claire. Burning up inside at his friends' treachery, Eric barely noticed the walk from Abby's apartment or the subway ride north. At least he retained the presence of mind to get off at his stop. From Times Square, he trekked homeward through the blustery evening, not even bothering to turn up his collar against the cold.

From the beginning, he had suspected Diego. The talentless leech practically drooled over Balquees. He'd admitted wanting to make it for himself. He had to be the motivating force. In fact, it was probably Diego's blundering screw-up of the formula that somehow gave SF its violence-inducing property.

Eric crossed an intersection against the red light. When an approaching car honked, he flipped the bird and kept walking.

Diego didn't surprise him. But the idea of Marie-Claire as an accomplice raised a lump of sadness in Eric's throat. He'd had it wrong at Abby's place. Religious zealotry, the idea of punishing him for doing the Devil's work, had played no part in her production of SF. Poor Marie-Claire, homely and pitifully lovelorn, had simply succumbed to the wiles of her dashing young Zorro.

The soap-opera scene played out in Eric's mind. Diego oozing up to her door, professing to have been blind to his true feelings, declaring his newly realized love for her the way a sinner claims he's found Jesus. Marie-Claire swooning into his arms. Diego choking back his revulsion as he takes her virginity, then later fishing out his grimy version of the formula for Balquees and telling her that, if she loved him as much as he loved her, she would help him make and market this fragrance.

Then a more heartbreaking realization struck. The theft. No doubt about it, SF contained genuine oud of Socotra. But he'd never told anyone how to contact his dealer in Yemen. Which could only mean that the counterfeiter had used ISIPCA's sample of the wood. The counterfeiter was the thief.

"You son of a bitch!" Diego hadn't just stolen his perfume, he'd wrecked Eric's whole damned life.

Hardly able to contain his fury, Eric looked around for something to hit, spotted a bulging trash bag and kicked the shit out of it, spewing garbage and papers all over the sidewalk.

Tomorrow night at the boutique opening, he'd do the same to that backstabbing Spaniard.

Then he'd call Fawcett.

But a minute later, as if summoned by the thought, Fawcett called Eric's cell phone.

"Okay, dazzle me," the detective said.

"Dazzle you?" Oh, Daisy. He stepped into a doorway, struggling to change mental gears. "Daisy can smell the difference. I put her through three tests this morning, and she alerted to SF every time."

After a moment of silence, "You got this SF where?"

Uh-oh. He scrambled for an answer that didn't implicate Tanya. "I ordered it off the website, for comparative purposes. The point is, the difference is real, and I can prove it."

"So you say."

"And so does Daisy." *You idiot.* "A bloodhound's testimony is legal in court."

"So you're a lawyer again."

Eric clenched his cell phone to the point of almost crushing it. "Are you interested in the truth, or only in pinning a bogus rap on someone who's trying to help?"

"Dog versus science. Which one would you go with?"

"Your so-called science is bullshit."

"Your so-called proof comes from your very own dog."

Damn this guy. "You've got other bloodhounds. Bring any of

them. Bring them all, and we'll run the tests again. With someone from the DA's office to witness."

"Careful what you wish for."

"Don't have the balls?"

Another silence, then, "You watch, asshole. You're gonna find out what kind of balls I have." With a bang of his handset, Fawcett disconnected.

Eric flipped his cell phone closed. What was it with that man? Overwork, stress, some demented hard-on for closing a case regardless of the facts? The fact was that Diego and Marie-Claire were the ones who needed interrogating. And after tomorrow night, Fawcett could have them. *Unless I kill Diego first.*

Eric stepped back into the frigid wind scouring Tenth Avenue. He turned up his collar, lowered his head, and stomped on. At the entrance to his apartment building, the eternally unrepaired lock offered no resistance when he turned the handle. Who cared? He had nothing worth stealing.

Climbing the stairs inside, he smelled SF, or Balquees, more strongly than he would have expected. It had been hours since he carried the smell strips down this morning. Must be the cold air in the stairwell, hindering evaporation, or—

What the hell? He halted, eyes fixed on a huddled creature sitting in the corner of his landing.

"Eric?"

A woman's voice. But she cowered there like a frightened hobo, a big sweatshirt enclosing her body and drawn-up knees. He approached cautiously. In the dim light of the forty-watt ceiling bulb, he saw a face purple with bruises, one eye swollen half-shut. She reeked of SF. *Oh, Jesus, no.*

"Tanya!" Eric leapt out of paralysis. Dropping to one knee, he wrapped an arm around her trembling shoulders. "What happened to you?"

"Help me."

Half-panicked at how badly she might be hurt, he unlocked his door, sidestepped Daisy rushing out, and bent to lift Tanya to her feet. Beneath the Red Sox sweatshirt, her legs and feet were bare. He noticed on her shins some tiny red spots that looked like bedbug bites, which made him wonder what kind of dump this seemingly fastidious woman must live in.

Never mind. Steadying her, he asked, "Can you walk?"

She tried but faltered.

He swept her up and cradled her in his arms. *Christ, no panties.* How in the world had she gotten here wearing nothing but a sweatshirt? He carried her inside and kicked the door closed behind him. Her skin felt frozen. She needed a hot shower.

Unless …

"Tanya, were you raped?"

Through chattering teeth she stammered, "C-c-cold."

Not an answer, so no shower. He carried her to the bedroom, laid her on the bed, and pulled over the blankets from the other side to cover her. "I'm calling an ambulance."

"No!"

"You have to see a doctor."

"No. Please." She pulled up the blankets. "I'm so c-cold."

He'd left the heat off for Daisy and now noticed he could see his own breath. He twisted the knob of the radiator next to his bed. "I'll make you some hot soup."

In the kitchen, he opened a can of chicken broth and dumped it in a saucepan. As he adjusted the flame, he heard Daisy whining. He must have left her outside.

Opening the front door, he found her sitting there, looking pitiful and anxious. But instead of coming in, she went to the head of the stairs and looked back. Not *now.* Then he remembered that she'd been cooped up since noon. He glanced at the stove. Okay, the broth would take a few minutes to heat. He rushed her down for a quick pee and poop. "Come on, girl, out with it. I don't have time to stand around here."

When she'd done her business, she practically raced him back upstairs. On the landing, she sat in the corner where Tanya had been.

"What's wrong with you?" Then Eric saw something on the floor. Tanya's handbag. He snatched it up. "Good girl."

The broth was steaming, just this side of a rolling boil. Eric poured a large mug three-quarters full and took it in to Tanya. All he could see was her face. Her eyes were closed, and she was still shivering. God *damn* the bastard who'd done this.

"I've brought you some soup. Can you sit up?"

"No handcuffs. No pantyhose."

"Tanya?"

"So good last night."

Gently he shook her shoulder. "Tanya, wake up."

"No," she screeched, cringing away from him. Terror contorted her face.

"Tanya, it's me. Eric." He backed off to show he meant her no harm. "You're safe. We're in my apartment."

She closed her eyes and settled again on his pillow. "I'm cold."

Was it just that, or had she gone into shock? Either way, he had to warm her up fast. He set down the mug and tried to think.

Mountain climbers warmed an exposure victim through full-body contact, but she'd probably freak out. He didn't have a hot water bottle. What else? Heat from the radiator would take forever to get through the blankets he'd pulled over her.

Of course. Blankets and radiators. "Hang on, Tanya."

Working fast, he pulled an extra blanket from the top shelf in his closet and wrapped it around the bedroom radiator. And clothing. He found the pants from his black sweat suit, dug out a pair of woolen hiking socks, and draped these over a radiator in the living room.

When he returned to check the blanket, Tanya had curled into a fetal position. Daisy stood at the bed with her chin on the mattress, just inches from Tanya's face. Eric felt the blanket. Warm enough. He yanked it from the radiator and pushed part of it under her covers. "Wrap this around you. Stuff some of it under your sweatshirt."

In fits and starts, the blanket disappeared under the covers.

Heartened that she was at least lucid enough to care for herself, he headed into the living room to check the sweatpants and socks. Almost too hot. Bundling them into a ball, he rushed back to Tanya. He shoved the sweatpants under her blankets. "Give me a minute to put some socks on your feet, then pull these on."

"No, I'll do it." She stuck her hand out.

A complete sentence. Maybe the crisis was over. As he stood back from giving her the socks, he felt the tension in his shoulders slowly loosen.

The bedding bobbed and undulated with her efforts to clothe herself. Then for ten minutes or maybe a quarter of an hour, she lay motionless, completely covered except for some wisps of blond hair splayed across a pillow.

Eric could think of nothing more to do but watch over her.

Finally, her face emerged.

"Better?" he asked cautiously.

"A little." She yanked her head back, her good eye wide. "What's *she* doing here?"

Obviously Tanya meant Daisy, who hadn't moved—her chin still on the mattress—since taking up her vigil. "She's worried about you. So am I."

The tiniest of smiles curled Tanya's lips. Another good sign.

"Ready for that soup?" he asked.

"Okay."

The mug had gone tepid. "I'll warm it for you."

In the kitchen, while waiting for the broth to re-heat, Eric felt a tingling in his dick. Damned SF. Tanya must have bathed in the stuff. He tried willing away the effect. When that didn't work, he hung his head over the saucepan and inhaled repeatedly.

Success at last.

And the soup was hot again.

Eric refilled Tanya's mug and took it back to her. She'd slipped between the sheets, propped his pillows behind her, and pulled the covers up to her neck, leaving her arms exposed. Daisy now lay on the floor in her Sphinx position, apparently less worried but still watching Tanya with unwavering eyes.

"Does she really know I'm hurt," Tanya asked, "or is she always this attentive to women in your bed?"

He held out the mug. "Drink."

"You didn't answer my question."

"Soup first, then talk." Eric felt encouraged to see the old, combative Tanya coming back.

She took a sip, declared it "good," and downed half the mug.

"Finish it. Then I'll get you some more."

After draining the mug, she handed it back. "That's enough. I feel better."

He believed her. She'd stopped shivering. Around the bruises on her face, her natural color was returning, although her swollen left eye looked painful as hell. Gingerly, he sat on the edge of the bed. "Tell me what happened."

She clutched the covers to her neck, but said nothing.

"Tanya, someone beat the crap out of you." He'd concluded that it had to be someone she already knew, since Tanya didn't seem reckless or stupid enough to put on a dangerous aphrodisiac and go barhopping. "Was it a boyfriend?"

She winced as though the memory slapped her.

Eric touched her arm, but she jerked away. He felt heartless pressing her, but couldn't help it. "Why did you use that stuff? You know what it can do."

She sniffed and rubbed her nose. "How bad do I look?"

"You won't be going to work tomorrow."

Suddenly the dam broke. Her shoulders heaved. Through sobs and sniffles, she blurted, "It wasn't his fault."

"Bull. I smelled that stuff all morning, and it didn't make me want to beat up anyone." Instantly ashamed at the harshness of his tone, he asked more sympathetically, "Has he ever been violent before?"

She looked away before answering. "Not really."

"Not *really?* Oh, Tanya." Her words in the Mexican restaurant came back to him. *Assholes, I seem to attract them.* Compared to what this asshole had done to her, the scar on her lip looked trivial. Her swollen eye, the ugly bruises on her cheekbones. This once-pretty woman, beaten to a pulp.

His temper flared. Whoever the son-of-a-bitch was, Eric wanted him behind bars. He rose from the bed. "I'm calling Fawcett."

"No!"

"Tanya, 'not his fault' is bullshit."

"Please, you can't."

"The bastard's going to jail."

She stared at him miserably, her chin quivering. "He's a cop."

Chapter 23

Eric woke with a headache, a dull pain centered above his left eyebrow. As he squirmed to find a more comfortable position in the wingback chair, the 6:10 out of Penn Station rumbled past.

Man, it was cold. The radiators wouldn't come on for another twenty minutes. With a groan, he pushed himself up from the chair, letting his blanket slide to the floor. He stretched to relieve the kinks in his back, but it didn't do much good.

On frozen feet, he padded to the bedroom door and peered in at Tanya. She lay curled in a ball, Daisy next to her on the floor, just as they'd been the three or four times he'd checked during the night.

All his efforts to convince Tanya that they should call Fawcett had proved futile. Even when he'd brought her a mirror—under the guise of allowing her to clean herself up with alcohol and peroxide—she'd begged him not to call. Obviously, she was either scared to death of her so-called boyfriend, or scared of what Fawcett would do to a fellow policeman.

After a few minutes of just watching her, Eric walked to the kitchen and started brewing coffee. As he waited to plunge the French press, the radiators pinged. Oh, crap, it was Monday, and he'd totally forgotten about work.

No way could he go in today. As soon as Tanya took a shower and got dressed, he was taking her to the hospital.

He plunged the coffee, then picked up his cell phone from the counter. Feigning sniffles and coughs, he told the departmental secretary's voicemail that he still had the flu.

He'd just hung up when Tanya called his name. Hustling in, he found her sitting in bed, her back propped against two pillows. "How are you doing?" he asked.

"Better. Thank you for taking care of me." She looked down at Daisy, who'd resumed her vigil from the Sphinx position. "You and Daisy, both."

"Forget it."

"I feel terrible putting you out like—"

"I just brewed coffee. Would you like some?"

Tanya screwed up her face. "Do you have any tea?"

"Sorry."

"Well, maybe if you put a lot of sugar in it. And milk."

He still hadn't gone to the store. "I'm out of milk. But the sugar hasn't gone bad."

"Sugar goes bad?"

So much for trying to make her smile. "Be right back."

Before he got halfway to the kitchen, she cried out, "Oh, no. Eric, I think I left my purse outside."

"Don't worry, I have it." He detoured to the armchair to retrieve her handbag. But as he snagged it by the shoulder strap, it slipped off his finger and tumbled to the hardwood floor, spilling contents everywhere.

On hands and knees, he scooped up her stuff. A lipstick and something else had rolled under the chair. Bending low, he swept his arm in an arc and recovered them.

What? The "something else" was a brown glass sample vial labeled "Balquees." Damn her. She'd said she wanted it for other analyses. A sudden chill raised goose bumps on his arms. It couldn't have been Balquees that got her beaten up, could it?

Horrified at the possibility, he tore through her purse, tossing its contents onto the chair cushion. Wallet, keys, ID badge, a bottle of aspirin, wadded-up Kleenex, a calculator. At the bottom, among pens and loose change, he found another brown vial. Its label read "SF."

Thank God.

He pocketed the two vials. While dumping her other detritus

back into the handbag, he recalled her comment in the lab that the only real proof of a difference between Balquees and SF would be trying them both. *Tanya, you never should have taken that risk.*

But of course, *he* had. On the other hand, he hadn't chanced doing it with another person, unless it was SF and not Balquees that Abby had smelled on his clothing. He shook his head. No way to tell. In fact, now that he thought about it, Tanya's experiment—assuming she'd tried both—was the only true test he actually knew of, except for his own attempt to smell a difference yesterday morning.

"Eric?"

Coffee. Quickly he poured two cups, dosed hers with three spoonfuls of sugar, and carried them into the bedroom. "You're a brave"—*and foolish*—"woman."

"Brave?"

He handed over her cup, then fished out the two vials from his jeans pocket. Praying for a positive answer, he asked, "Did you try both of these?"

"You went through my *purse?*"

"It tipped over. All I did was pick up the stuff that fell out."

With a soft exhalation, she lowered her eyes. "You think I deserve what I got, don't you?"

"Of course not," he said, perching tentatively on the edge of the bed. "I just can't believe you gambled your own safety. That guy could have killed you."

"I had to know."

And he'd accused her of not being scientific. Eric felt like slime. But he needed to confirm, "You were wearing SF last night, right?"

"I don't want to talk about it." She turned away.

Eric swallowed his frustration but apparently didn't swallow hard enough, because when she turned back to him, her good eye narrowed. "So now you're angry at me?"

"No."

"You look angry."

He should guard against being so transparent. Besides, his questions could wait. They had all day. "If I'm angry at anyone, it's myself. We can talk when you feel like it."

She studied his face, then took another sip of coffee. "Last night was SF. Saturday night was Balquees."

Relief coursed through him like an infusion of new blood. In her delirium, she'd said, "So good last night," meaning Saturday night.

Obviously, telling him even that much had been tough for her. Yet tell him she had. And with Balquees cleared, there was other information he needed. "Tanya, you're the only person I know who's survived a bad experience with SF. I'm not trying to be voyeuristic, but would you mind describing what actually happened?"

Her fingers tightened around the mug.

"Okay, not now," he said. "Maybe later."

"No. It's better I get it over with. But can I take a shower first? I feel so dirty."

"Whatever you want." He retrieved the mug from her hands. "Fresh towels are in the cupboard, and I'll lay out another sweat suit."

After helping Tanya to her feet and walking her to the bathroom, Eric took Daisy downstairs. A Vietnamese family ran a tiny all-night grocery three blocks away where he bought milk and jasmine tea. By the time he returned, Tanya had changed into his clean, gray sweat suit and was sitting in the wingback chair, her knees tucked against her chest, a towel wrapped in a turban around her head.

"I got some tea and milk," he announced, thinking this would be the third hot drink he'd made for her in the past twelve hours. Eric the nursemaid. Not a role he cared to continue, although he felt some pride that his ministrations seemed to be helping her recover. If only he could overcome her resistance to getting medical attention. Maybe reverse psychology would work. "By the way, you look a lot better."

"I look terrible."

Jackpot. He squatted in front of her. "You really need to go to the hospital. You could have a concussion or a damaged eye."

"No!"

"Tanya."

"I can't. They'll ask questions. If I say I was mugged, they'll call the police. If I say my boyfriend did it, they'll call Special Victims."

"Then a private doctor."

"I don't know one."

Neither did he, but he'd find one. Maybe Abby could help. Deciding to ease off the subject for now, he stood and said, "We'll think of something."

"Thank you for understanding." She glanced down, then peered up at him earnestly, her face round and solemn and surprisingly young. "Eric. I hate to ask, but would you mind if I stayed here for a day or two? It's okay if you say no."

Turn her out? Like hell. "Stay as long as you like."

As Daisy chowed down a double ration of kibble, Eric busied himself making tea, which suffused the room with the sweet scent of jasmine and a soothing undertone of sandalwood. When he returned, Tanya had changed positions to sitting cross-legged in the chair, a more open posture that he hoped reflected growing ease with the prospect of speaking about her ordeal. He handed her a mug, then pulled up his desk chair, placing it not directly in front of her but a little to one side so this wouldn't seem like an interrogation.

"Feel like talking?"

She lowered her head, avoiding eye contact. "Patrick, that's his name, he's a really nice guy. Fun and funny. And he knows all these Irish pubs where musicians just come in and start playing. It's kind of like bluegrass, like at the Winfield festival." She looked up at him. "That's in Kansas."

"I've heard of it. So you've had some good times with Patrick."

"Great times. That's why I'm sure he didn't mean to …" She touched her cheek and again averted her eyes. "I mean, he kind of likes bondage stuff. It was a little scary at first. But I've gotten used to it, and it can even be … well, you know. The thing is, it's all about trust. You never go too far because there's always a safe word. And he always honored that. Which is why I can't believe he really meant to hurt me."

Eric had guessed the bondage bit from her delirious statements about handcuffs and pantyhose. He'd once known a girl who liked being tied up spread-eagle with pantyhose.

"Anyway," she said, "Patrick and I really liked your Balquees. We never even got to the bondage thing. It was wonderful." She gazed off at something only she could see. Then her face darkened.

Turning away, she grasped a handful the sweatpants' fabric, as though squeezing the life out of it. "SF was different."

"Tanya, you don't have to—"

"It started the same as Balquees. Tingly all over, and the intense colors. And that burning desire. The craving. Like there's nothing else in your whole life but that you have to have this man. You need him. You …" She paused, her breath coming in short gasps. "And then he chokes you."

"Tanya."

"And you think maybe it's nothing. But he shakes you and slaps your face. He needs more, he says. Why can't I give him more? Why aren't I trying? But I *am* trying." Her mug tilted, spilling a splash of tea in her lap as she pressed her hands to her face. "And then he hits you, and hits you again and keeps hitting and—"

"Please stop." Eric sprang from his chair and gripped her shoulders.

She froze in his hands, then collapsed in sobs. "How could he do that?"

At a loss for what to say, Eric sat on an arm of the wingchair and put his hand on her back.

When she finally looked up at him, Tanya's expression was as hard as flint. "I jammed my thumbs in his eyes. He howled, and I broke away and grabbed his sweatshirt off the floor and my purse and ran out. But I couldn't go home. He'd find me there. So I flagged down a cab. The driver thought I was a nutcase. But I gave him all the money in my wallet if he'd bring me here, because you're the only person I felt I could trust."

"You *can* trust me," Eric said quickly, hoping the rush of her last words didn't portend another breakdown.

She searched his face, apparently found some sign that he spoke the truth, and said, "Thank you." Then suddenly she sat upright. "Oh, my God. I've made a terrible mess."

Obviously she meant the tea in her lap. "I'll take care of it. Go change into the sweatpants I gave you last night."

She'd left them in the bathroom, and after closing the door, she called out, "Do you have any hydrocortisone?"

"I think so. Look in the medicine cabinet."

When she came out, she brought the tube of hydrocortisone, squeezed flat. "Sorry, I used it up. I'll get you another one." She pulled up one of the sweatpants legs and rubbed her shin. "Damn bedbugs."

"You could get your apartment sprayed."

"Not my place. Patrick's. He's deathly allergic to pesticides."

"Serves him right. I hope he's bitten all over."

She looked at Eric a moment, then gave him a sheepish smile. "Thanks for not saying I've reaped what I sowed."

"Tanya, it's *not* your fault."

The reassurance seemed to relax her a little, maybe even give her some strength. She looked toward the wingchair, then back at him. "Could I ask you a favor?"

"Of course."

"If you're sure it's okay for me to stay here, would you mind going to my apartment and getting some of my things?"

The phone rang.

Who would be calling at eight fifteen in the morning? He walked into the bedroom and picked it up.

"Eric, this is Margaret at Rheinhold-Laroche. I'm sorry you're still sick. When Mr. Wigby asked where you were, I told him about your phone message."

"Thank you." For effect, Eric coughed and sniffed his nose. "This flu's hanging on longer than I expected."

"I know what you mean. My grandson has it also." She paused. "But Mr. Wigby wanted me to remind you about our corporate policy."

"What policy?" Eric pictured the ring binders on the shelf in his office, the tomes of policies and procedures he'd never bothered opening.

"For any absence due to illness, more than one day away from work requires a note from your doctor."

Wigby, that bureaucratic prick. "Look, Margaret, I just need bed rest. And liquids." Eric sniffled again.

"I understand. Believe me, I do. But Mr. Wigby … I hate to tell you this, but he says, if you don't come in today, you better get a note from a doctor. Or you'll be fired."

Chapter 24

Pissed off that a big corporation would treat its employees like school kids, Eric shoved open the door of his surgically sterile office at Rheinhold-Laroche. Three trays of the company's cheap fragrance additives awaited his approval—this morning's tray plus the morning and afternoon trays from Friday. All told, there were about sixty product samples. A lot of work, if he were conscientious. Or he could plow through them quickly and get back to helping Tanya. It all hinged on the company's silly rules.

He gazed at the daunting library of policy and procedures manuals on his shelf and decided to call Margaret, the departmental secretary. After greetings that he punctuated with a cough and a sniffle, he asked, "Does half a day here qualify as a return to work?"

"Oh my, I'm not sure. Let me check." Sounds of pages turning came over the line as he mentally crossed his fingers. Finally, she came back with, "The policy isn't really specific. How are you feeling, Eric? You sound awful."

"I should be in bed."

"Poor dear. I wish I knew what to tell you."

"That's okay. Thanks for trying." He rang off and gave himself a thumbs-up. "Not specific" was good enough.

That settled, he sat in his chair and psyched himself up for a descent into olfactory hell. Two of the fragrances, one for camping tents and one for automotive upholstery, were reformulations in accordance with his recommendations and actually smelled pretty good. Most of the others, for things like toilet paper, roach spray, and tire cleaner, were okay. The remainder needed work, and one of those should have been poured down the sink. But he passed them all.

And why not? It seemed that no one else in this company could tell the difference between pretty good and complete crap. So to hell with his self-respect. Let them go to market with the junk okayed by the lab supervisors.

At eleven o'clock, having cleared a day and a half's work in two hours, he pulled on his overcoat and was about to leave when his door banged open to reveal Charles Wigby.

"Where do you think *you're* going?" Wigby demanded, his Adam's apple bouncing like a frog lodged in a chicken's throat.

Eric coughed as hard as he could, not covering his mouth. When Wigby recoiled, Eric said, "Sorry. I didn't mean to—" He coughed again, this time turning his head away. "I finished the samples. I've got to go home."

"Finished?" Wigby straightened himself and smoothed his tie, a knitted thing in burnt orange that his mother had probably given him. "Let's take a look, shall we?"

Standing aside to let Wigby enter his office, Eric suppressed an urge to click his heels and give a *Sieg Heil* salute.

Grumbling under his breath, Wigby pawed through the bottles on the three trays, then whirled on him. "You passed everything? You never pass everything."

"I can hardly breathe." Eric sniffled dramatically. "But they seemed okay."

Wigby peered at him. Then, for the first time since Eric had known him, the guy actually looked sympathetic. "I need better than 'seemed okay.' Go home and go to bed. But I want you back in here the minute you're well." And with that, Wigby walked out.

In utter disbelief, Eric stared at the open door. Obviously, pragmatism had driven the man's decision, but Eric had definitely seen a spark of compassion in his eyes. Suddenly he felt petty for his childish act of approving the bad with the good. He had a job. And lousy as that job might be, his employer depended on him to do it.

Turning to the sample trays on the right side of his desk, Eric picked out all of the fragrances that needed work. After peeling off his green "Approved" stickers, he placed the bottles on the left side of his desk. In a day or two, when Tanya was out of the woods and he'd wrung the truth out of Diego and Marie-Claire, he would come back and give these samples his full attention.

Half an hour later, Eric stepped out of the elevator on the fifth floor of Tanya's building. She was right, the hallway stank of stale curry. And of bleach and cigarette smoke and carpeting not cleaned this decade. Apartment 506, which presumably had been Room 506 when this was a hotel, was halfway down the hall on the left.

Although she'd asked him pick up some clothing and toiletries for her, he hesitated at the threshold, feeling uncomfortable about intruding on her personal space. She'd left here with no idea that he would be the next person to enter, no thought of straightening up the place, washing dirty dishes, putting away things she'd rather he didn't see. In giving him the key, she was exposing her private life to the eyes of a near-stranger. The very act implied an unspoken trust. He had every intention of honoring that trust, but it didn't diminish the awkwardness he felt as he stepped inside.

The first thing he noticed was a jukebox, a real one in chrome and gaudy plastic with what looked like two tail fins from his grandfather's '59 DeSoto. Sure enough, the index tabs on the front displayed late-fifties titles like "Smoke Gets In Your Eyes," "Stagger Lee," and "Splish Splash."

These were all songs his mother had loved. Eric shut his eyes a moment. He could hear them coming from his mom's room, where pancreatic cancer took her life only four short weeks after diagnosis. For a ten-year-old, death was something that happened in the movies or on TV. It didn't happen to your mother. She was invincible.

After the funeral, his father had thrown out her LPs with the re-mastered oldies, unable to bear the thought of hearing them again. But Eric still remembered the songs.

On a shelf of the wall unit next to the jukebox stood a cut-glass fingerbowl filled with nickels, dimes, and quarters. The last time he'd seen a fingerbowl was when his grandmother gave him a tour through her Lenox tableware and silver-plate cutlery—service for twelve. He smiled at the thought that Tanya might have a similarly "proper" grandmother and the prospect of light-heartedly comparing one *grande dame* with the other.

Of course, Tanya could simply have found the bowl in a flea market.

He plucked a nickel from the bowl, dropped it into the jukebox's coin slot, and pushed the G and 7 buttons for "Quiet Village." The robotic arm removed a 45-rpm disk from the horizontal stack and placed it on the turntable. A few seconds later, the piano, conga beat, and bird whistles of Martin Denny filled the room at a volume unlikely to bother the neighbors.

With a mental image of his mother and father dancing to the tune, back in the good times, Eric got to work gathering the things Tanya had asked for.

He pushed aside the batik curtain that separated her sleeping nook from the rest of the place and saw a single bed neatly made up and covered with an honest-to-God patchwork quilt. The quilt imparted a homey aroma of cotton and old wool to the small room, an aroma that reminded him again of his grandmother's house. If Tanya missed Kansas, sleeping here probably brought her pleasant dreams.

At the foot of the bed stood a simple pine dresser that faced a rack of hanging clothes and left barely three feet of space in which to stand while selecting what to wear. No wonder she envied his "real" bedroom.

The first item on her verbal list was underwear. Pulling open the top drawer of the dresser, he found bras and thong panties lined up in a rainbow of colors. He stuffed a handful of each into his shoulder bag, closed that drawer, and opened the second one down. T-shirts. The top one, maroon and oversized for her, read "Kansas Cook-Off" in a semi-circle across the top and, in a semi-circle below, "Battle of the BBQs." Well, that was a plus, a shared taste in food, at last. In addition to that T-shirt, he chose a "Greenpeace" and a "Broadway or Bust" and called it good.

From the bottom drawer he extracted a white turtleneck sweater and some sweat socks. He stuffed these into his shoulder bag, then added a pair of jeans from the clothes rack and a pair of running shoes from the row of footwear lined up below.

With a nearly full bag, he headed for her bathroom but stopped when he noticed Martin Denny had finished. Eric quickly searched for his mother's all-time favorite song, "The Wayward Wind." Not finding it, he dropped in another nickel and picked his own favorite from that era, Crazy Cole's "Topsy Part 2."

To the beat of tom toms, he continued into Tanya's bathroom. Probably a standard bathroom in the building's hotel days, it was now about the size of an airplane lavatory, the remainder having been converted to a kitchen. With only an under-sink cabinet and barely enough room to turn around, she'd hung multi-pocketed fishnet organizers on the back of the door and the wall behind it.

In the confined space, a cloud of aromas enveloped him. Together, they revealed the woman at her most private level. He faced the mirror, closed his eyes, and stood perfectly still. From the shower stall behind him came strong scents of chamomile shampoo and her vetiver soap. From the sink in front, a hand soap, probably Dove, plus the chalky spearmint of toothpaste and the tangier mint of mouthwash. Concentrating harder, he detected in his right nostril the powdery, waxy scents of makeup in the fishnet organizers, while his left nostril picked up the fainter smell of her skin on a cotton bath towel.

He opened his eyes. Everything he'd inhaled spoke of an all-American girl. Smiling at the thought, Eric set about collecting the few cosmetics she'd asked for. He was about to leave the bathroom when he noticed two bottles of cologne in one of the organizer pockets, Eau Sauvage and Diorella. That figured. Natural blondes—and his inadvertent glimpse of her pubic hair when he carried her into his apartment confirmed she was natural—preferred fresh, light scents. And athletic women tended to favor citrus notes. Both of Tanya's fragrance choices fit this bill. But to his way of thinking, an even better perfume in that same general family was Thé Pour un Été by L'Artisan. Maybe he'd get her a bottle after she recovered.

Back in the main room, he paused to look around. The jukebox had occupied his attention before, but as "Topsy" ended in a flourish of drums and cymbals, he took the time to give Tanya's living area more careful scrutiny.

Although small, it felt much less cramped than her sleeping nook. Most of the furnishings came from some place like Ikea, practical pieces in pale tones with clean lines and efficient functionality. Opposite the jukebox, a hide-a-bed loveseat and wood-veneer coffee table faced the wall unit that held a TV and several rows of novels separated by framed photographs. He looked more closely at the photos: parents, he presumed; Tanya in maybe the fifth grade; grown-up Tanya smiling in a kayak on a river; an 8x10 group photo of thirty or so people on the steps of— *What the hell?*

Snatching up the group photo, he felt as if the floor were shifting under him. In the front row, second from the left, stood Jacques Durand.

Eric dropped his shoulder bag and sat on the loveseat. His hands shook so badly he had to lay the photo on the coffee table to study it. Tanya stood in the second row, behind Durand and only two people away from him. This must have been taken at the conference she attended in Monaco last year, a forensic chemistry conference, she'd told him. But Durand wasn't into forensics.

Okay, think. Eric studied the others in the photo. Nobody he knew. Just a typical group of conference types, mostly men, but two other women besides Tanya, all dressed in what corporate jargon called business-casual. Except for Durand who, as usual, wore an impeccably tailored suit.

Durand must have been an invited speaker. Normally, he would have declined. From Eric's knowledge of the man, such a conference was beneath him. But if Durand needed money, as Abby claimed, the honorarium might have come in handy. Or maybe he agreed to speak as a favor to a friend on the organizing committee. He could easily concoct a suitable lecture, and he lived only a couple of miles from Monte Carlo.

Eric sat back, relieved. That had to be what happened. It was a coincidence, pure and simple.

But another thought nagged at him, like a beggar tugging his sleeve. Tanya had never mentioned Durand. How commonplace could it be to have heard a legendary perfumer at a forensics conference and, a few months later, be involved in analyzing a potentially deadly perfume? Especially since Tanya knew Eric had studied in France. No, that stretched credibility too far.

He ground his teeth as a more sinister scenario played out in his mind. She'd met Durand. Either they'd met by prior intent, or he'd approached her. Durand, jealous of Balquees, had created SF. But he knew there was something wrong with his counterfeit formulation. Tanya, with her high-tech lab and proximity to Eric and his Balquees, was uniquely positioned to decipher the problem and help fix it. In a searing flash, Eric saw it all. Durand would have wooed her with visions of wealth. And Tanya, at the top of her pay grade but stuck in this converted hotel room in a city that offered so much more, had succumbed to the wiles of that silver-haired fox.

No wonder that, according to Fawcett, Tanya had *volunteered* to analyze Balquees. Volunteered to work on a weekend. Eric had told her Balquees and SF were different, and although she pretended not to believe him, she knew it also. Her mission was to discover the difference.

But could it really be? Leaning back in the loveseat, he rubbed his eyes. Maybe he was seeing demons where none existed. The conspiracy scenario was pretty far-fetched and relied at least as much on coincidence as the idea that Tanya and Durand merely chanced to attend the same conference. On the other hand, he already had Marie-Claire and Diego just happening to show up at this time of crisis. Another coincidence on top of that was just too many.

Only one way to find out—confront her with the evidence. He jammed the photograph into his shoulder bag. After a final glance around, he opened the front door and came face-to-face with a huge, uniformed cop.

"Who the hell are you?" the cop demanded, his hand going to his pistol.

Shocked at first, in fact damned lucky not to have pissed his pants, Eric quickly recovered his composure. So, this was the boyfriend, fresh out of Gorilla Land at the zoo. Besides the NYPD bomber jacket that enhanced his size, he wore mirrored aviator sunglasses, no doubt to hide the damage Tanya had done to his eyes.

With a surprising sense of calm, smugness even, since he held the keys to the gorilla's cage, Eric said, "Nice job you did on her, Patrick."

The cop lunged and shoved him in the chest, knocking him backward onto the floor.

Before Eric knew what was happening, rough hands flipped him over, face-down, and wrenched his left arm into a hammerlock behind his back. Blinding pain shot up Eric's shoulder.

"I said, who are you, fuckwad? And what are you doing here?"

Through clamped teeth, Eric gasped, "Eric Foster. I'm here to pick up some of Tanya's things. She asked me to."

"Yeah, sure." The ape planted a heavy knee in the small of Eric's back and wrenched the arm higher.

"Stop," Eric cried out in agony. "Check my bag. You'll see."

"Move one inch and I'll cripple you for life." Without releasing his grip on Eric's wrist, the cop frisked him quickly, then shook out the contents of the bag. He fingered the clothing, then picked up the photo. "Why this?"

"I don't know. She just asked me to bring it," he lied.

"Where is she?"

"Safe. Recovering from what you did to her."

"Where!" A twist of Eric's wrist almost tore his arm out of the socket.

"My place. Please let go of me."

"Why a scumbag like you?"

Scumbag? Look who's talking. "I met her a few days ago. I guess she thought she could trust me."

"Met her how?"

"In my course at John Jay. Then we—"

"John Jay?" Patrick's grip relaxed just slightly. "You in law enforcement?"

"No, but I know a lot of cops."

The grip tightened again. "So do I. How'd you get in here?"

"She gave me her key."

"Bullshit. She won't even give *me* a key."

"It's in my front pocket."

"Show me." The cop released Eric's arm and stood. "On your back. Try to sit up and I'll knock your fucking head off."

Wincing with pain, Eric rolled onto his back, fished the key from his jeans pocket, and dropped it on the floor.

The guy picked it up, peered at it with a pained expression, then pulled out his handcuffs. "You're under arrest. Criminal trespass and burglary."

"Better think twice." Rubbing his shoulder, Eric felt a trickle of confidence returning, along with his circulation. "You arrest me, and the first call I make is to Detective Darrell Fawcett at Midtown North."

"Fawcett?"

"Know him, do you?" Having apparently struck bone, Eric raised himself onto his elbows. "Mean son-of-a-bitch, goes through three packs of Marlboro Lights in one shift. And it so happens he thinks the world of Tanya."

Arctic silence.

Encouraged, Eric sat up tentatively, saw no move to stop him, and got to his feet. "In fact, Fawcett's the guy who sent Tanya to my class at John Jay. If I tell him what you did to her and where he can find her, he'll have your ass in a sling you'll never get out of."

When the ape still said nothing, Eric felt a rush of power he could hardly believe. Maybe confrontation wasn't so bad, after all. Provided you held the right cards. He glanced at King Kong's nametag. Flynn, it read. But Eric had no intention of using the surname. "So go ahead and arrest me … Patrick."

If looks could kill, Patrick's would have ripped Eric to shreds. Even the guy's sunglasses couldn't conceal his hatred.

But Eric was no longer scared. "Give me back the key. It's time for me to lock up here. And for you to leave."

Patrick Flynn dropped the key, then straightened his cop jacket. "You're dead meat, motherfucker. Got that? Dead. Meat."

Chapter 25

Emboldened at having faced down Patrick, Eric unlocked his apartment door and extracted the photo of Tanya and Durand from his shoulder bag. He needed to hear her explanation.

Unfortunately, she lay asleep in his bedroom, looking as angelic as anyone could with a face full of bruises. He wanted to wake her, get this over with one way or the other, but he didn't have the heart.

On the floor by the bed, Daisy turned her head to him, then got to her feet. He took her downstairs for a pee, brought her back up, and poured a cup of kibble into her bowl. But she ignored her lunch and limped back into the bedroom to resume her vigil.

So now what? He felt too antsy to just sit around and wait for Tanya to wake up on her own. Maybe the sound of the toilet would rouse her. He went in and flushed it.

"Eric?" Tanya called, her voice apprehensive.

"Yeah, it's me." He washed his hands, partly for the sound effect and partly because they felt grimy. As he hung up the hand towel, someone knocked at the front door. *Uh-oh.* Only two people ever came here, Abby once in a while and, lately, Fawcett. But Abby wouldn't show up without calling first. Quickly he poked his head into the bedroom. "Quiet. I think it's Fawcett."

She gaped. "Detective Fawcett?"

No. Dripping Faucet. Jesus. Eric shut the bedroom door as the person outside knocked louder.

"Coming!" He shoved the photo back into his bag, zipped the bag closed, and set it on the floor next to the wingchair. Halfway to the front door, he halted. What if it was Patrick? If Patrick had followed him here, this could get really ugly. Eric pulled out his cell phone, punched 9-1-1, and left his thumb on the Send button. Wishing he had a peephole, he said, "Who is it?"

"Your fairy godmother," Fawcett growled.

Eric let out a long exhalation, pocketed his phone, and opened the door.

"Where've you been?" Fawcett said, eyeing him suspiciously.

"I was at work, but I had to come home." He faked a coughing spasm without covering his mouth. "I've got the flu."

"Uh-huh." Fawcett tried to step inside and, when Eric blocked him, responded with a leery squint. "Hiding something?"

Just your forensic chemist. Although tempted to remind the great sleuth that he needed a search warrant to enter private premises, Eric decided that any attempt to exercise his rights would only boomerang on him. He stood back. "To what do I owe this pleasure?"

Fawcett looked around, then pointed his chin at the bulging shoulder bag beside the wingchair. "Going somewhere?"

"If you're worried I'm skipping the country, don't be." Eric shut the front door. "That's some stuff for a friend of mine."

"The friend who does your website?"

"I told you, I don't have a website."

"Would that friend happen to be the Chinese girl you spent time with yesterday? After her girlfriend left?"

Eric felt his jaw drop. "You've been following me? Where the hell do you get off with shit like that? I haven't done anything wrong, and you know it."

"Struck a nerve, did I?"

"Blow it out your ass."

"Your mother should have potty-trained your mouth."

"Why did you follow me?"

"I didn't."

"Then you had one of your goons do it for you." And suddenly a horrifying thought knocked everything else out of his mind. If he'd been trailed to Abby's, had he also been trailed to

Tanya's? He shot a quick look toward the bedroom, and instantly regretted it.

"Now we're getting somewhere," Fawcett said, a predator's gleam in his ice-blue eyes. "Why's that door closed? It's never been closed before."

Scrambling for an excuse, Eric came up with, "Daisy's in there. She's been sick, and I don't want her throwing up all over the place."

"So you're sick, and your dog's sick." With a look that said, *Next you'll try selling me the Brooklyn Bridge*, Fawcett unbuttoned his overcoat.

"Don't get comfortable. I need—" Eric feigned another coughing spasm. "I need to get some rest."

"Interesting how that cough of yours comes up whenever you want it to. Seen the newspapers? Seems your hero in L.A. has been a bad boy."

"What hero?"

"Isn't Scarecrow Tim one of your idols?"

"Never heard of him."

Fawcett handed Eric some photocopies of what looked like faxed newspaper stories. He'd circled headlines and certain sentences in red pencil.

Among the headlines, Eric read, "Murder at Celeb's Wife-Swapping Party," "Scarecrow Tim and the Deadly Love Potion," and "Children's TV Hero Hosts Orgy Gone Bad." Among the circled sentences were "Police are holding a pastor's wife in connection with the death of her lesbian lover at the home of children's TV star Scarecrow Tim," and "Hollywood is buzzing about SF, a new perfume guaranteed to skyrocket your sex drive—if it doesn't kill you." SF was triple-underlined in red.

"This is terrible," Eric said.

"Which part? The dead woman or poor Timmy?"

"The death is bad enough, but I'm talking about the publicity. This 'Hollywood is buzzing' thing could start an epidemic."

"Dipshit, you've already got an epidemic." Fawcett took a threatening step forward. "I have Interpol reports from Germany, Japan, and England. In France, they just arrested a government minister for strangling his mistress, and guess what perfume the gendarmes found in the love nest."

Eric sank into the wingback chair. The arrest of a government minister meant even more publicity. Against all the media hype, his efforts on the SF blogs were a total waste of time. But there was a real chance he had one of the culprits right there in his bedroom. He fought an impulse to look again at the door.

"What, no coughing?" Fawcett said. "You must be getting better. Maybe Daisy is, too. Let's go check on her."

In a single motion, Eric leapt from the chair and planted himself between Fawcett and the bedroom. "She's sleeping. I don't want her disturbed."

"You lying sack of shit."

"You've overstayed your welcome. Goodbye, Detective."

Fawcett glared at him, then walked to the front door. "I'll be back with a warrant."

Peering at the bottle of Lagavulin in his kitchen cabinet, Eric debated whether a shot of Scotch would soothe his nerves or be nothing more than a tangible sign that Fawcett's constant harassment truly was getting to him. Although the man was gone, his olfactory presence still lurked like a menacing specter. Stale cigarette smoke, something Hungarian the guy had eaten for lunch, the myriad street odors his overcoat seemed to trap like a woolen filter. Eric closed the cabinet. No way could he enjoy the smokiness of Lagavulin while the ashtray stink of Fawcett polluted the air. Maybe later, after he'd thrashed things out with Tanya.

In the living room, he opened both windows to clear the atmosphere and pulled the photograph from his shoulder bag. He knocked on the bedroom door, then opened it. No Tanya. She had spread up the bed and … Ah, the closet. "You can come out now."

She cracked open the closet door. "He's gone?"

"I wouldn't say to come out if he weren't."

With a perturbed frown, she sat on the edge of the bed. "I was listening at the door. Until he asked if he could come in here."

"Fawcett's not your biggest worry. Not yet." Eric handed her the photograph. "What do you have to say about this?"

She glanced at it, then squinched up her face. "Nothing. Why did you bring it? I asked you to get me some clothes."

Studying her carefully, Eric detected no shock, no smell of rising body temperature. Was she that cool in the hot seat? "I find it particularly interesting. You and Jacques Durand."

"Who?"

"The man you're standing next to." Eric stabbed his finger at Durand's image. "Him."

"I don't know what you're talking about. This was taken at a conference in Monaco. There were lots of people. I don't know this particular— Wait. He gave a talk on perfumes, I think." She looked up at Eric. "So what?"

"That's what I'm asking *you*."

"You've lost me," she said, shaking her head.

"Have I?"

"I don't care for your attitude. Or your tone of voice." She set down the photo and braced her palms on the bed, either side of her thighs. "If you have something to say, then say it."

Forcing him to lay it out, was she? Well, fine. "Durand was my mentor in Versailles. He's one of the few people in the world who could reproduce Balquees. Or a version of it, like SF. And here you are, standing next to him, just a few months before you *volunteered* to analyze Balquees and compare it to SF."

Tanya glared at him. "Are you trying to implicate me in SF?"

"Interesting you should come to that conclusion."

"Eric, what's gotten into you? This photo was taken …" She looked up for a second, apparently trying to recall. "… seven months ago. I never talked to this guy. I only attended his lecture because it was part of a plenary session."

"So it's all coming back to you, huh? And do you also remember that the job he gave you was to find out what he got wrong when he created SF?"

"Oh, for God's sake." She rose from the bed. "Did you bring my clothes?"

"I want an answer."

"The answer is, you're out of your mind." She snatched her purse from the closet and walked around him into the living room where she picked up the shoulder bag. "Here I thought you were a smart guy. But you're an asshole, like all the others. And a paranoid asshole, to boot." She stamped to the front door and opened it. "Detective Fawcett's wrong about you. You're too damn dumb to be the mastermind behind SF."

When Tanya slammed the door, Daisy barked.

Eric looked down, surprised the dog was beside him and even more surprised that she'd barked. Daisy almost never barked. But now she raised her stump, trying to paw the door, and barked again.

Then she turned her eyes on him, and whined.

Chapter 26

Eric stopped short of Abby's building to look around for unmarked cars. Nothing he could spot—like he was a big expert on such things. In fact, parked vehicles lined both sides of the street, although none he could see into had two guys in the front seat trying to look casual. Of course, Fawcett's boys could be hiding anywhere. Maybe in one of the apartments across the street. Or more likely in a trash can, where they'd feel at home.

Screw them.

And screw me for blowing it with Tanya. Replaying the scene in his mind, for about the twentieth time, he had to concede that she'd shown no alarm at seeing the photograph, no apprehension at being "found out." All she'd really shown was disdain and the kind of pity you'd have for a slobbering idiot. He could chalk it up to good acting. She'd minored in theater arts, after all. But the kicker was the fact he hadn't appreciated until after she left—seven months had elapsed between the conference in Monaco and her volunteering to analyze Balquees. That was a long time, long enough to demolish any chance that the two events were related.

Eric dug his fingernails into his palms. Almost certainly he'd accused an innocent woman, driven her out when all she'd done was come to him for help. She had every reason in the world to hate his guts. Which no doubt accounted for why he felt like crap.

And why he hoped against hope to find Abby at home. With another glance up and down the street, he closed the distance to her building. In case Fawcett's goons knew only her address and not her apartment number, he stepped to within a few inches of the doorbell pad so no one could observe which button he pushed.

Of course, she didn't answer. It was six in the evening, an hour after Marie-Claire's opening was scheduled to start, and Abby was the impatient sort. He'd been foolish to think she might wait for him, although it would have been nice to walk with her.

A shift of breeze brought the garlic-bread aroma from that Italian place down at the corner. It made his mouth water and reminded him of how little he'd eaten these past ... however many days. He really could use some food in his stomach, something to get rid of the burning sensation. Not an ulcer, he hoped. Could an ulcer develop in just five days? Hard to believe this whole damned mess only began, at least for him, last Thursday. Reaching between the buttons of his overcoat, he pressed on his abdomen, just below the ribcage. The pain felt no worse. Seemed like an ulcer should feel worse if you pressed on it, but he wasn't sure.

And it didn't matter. All that mattered was how he handled the next few hours. He had one shot to nail the bastards who'd rained down hell on his life.

With a vow to himself not to blow it this time, he pulled the crumpled paper from his jeans pocket, rotated it to orient Abby's scrawl, and reread the address. About eight blocks from here.

He tracked back to Broadway, then turned south into a crush of pedestrian traffic. Trendy as SoHo was, window shopping at this time of day was a nonstarter. You needed all your concentration just to navigate the sidewalk, lest you accidentally bump into a native and incur the kind of snide upbraiding New Yorkers claimed as a birthright.

Several blocks south, progress slowed to a crawl, the flow constricted by street vendors whose makeshift carts and tables lined the curbside. His mother would have loved it. Latter-day hippies hawking paintings, books, scarves, soaps with obnoxious mixtures of "natural" essences like banana and sage. Unbidden, his nose told him the banana was nothing more than synthetic amyl acetate, the sort of additive Rheinhold-Laroche would mix into a product that was supposed to smell tropical.

Eric angled toward the storefronts, slipped in behind a fat guy with a briefcase, and let him run interference. After a few blocks in the guy's wake, he ducked out and turned right onto a quieter side street. Ahead, art galleries and "fusion" restaurants lined the street, interspersed with the occasional jeweler and high-fashion ladies' store. Eric sidestepped a pile of dog shit, then stopped to check Abby's scribble again. Was that first number a four or a nine? He decided to go with four.

In the next block he found it, all curved glass windows and bright lights and gleaming brass. And one hell of a crowd. No tuxedos or evening gowns at this hour, but the clientele held champagne flutes as though they were second nature to silver spoons.

Envy bit the pit of his stomach. Or maybe it was just the ulcer he hoped he didn't have. Never mind. He had fish to fry. And appearances to keep up.

He checked his reflection in a window of the shop next door. Jesus, he looked like Death. His face was pale and drawn. Dark crescents underlined his eyes. With a few brisk strokes, he clawed his hair into place, more or less. Then he stepped back, unbuttoned his overcoat, and took a reinforcing breath.

Inside, among the beautiful people, Eric paused to appraise. The place smelled good. Really good. Obviously they'd sprayed a lot of sample in the course of the evening. And just as obviously, Marie-Claire, or her family's perfumery, had come up with some truly fine products—subtle, refined variations on the traditional themes of jasmine, mimosa, and orange blossom so typical of Grasse.

True to their roots. He admired that. But he wasn't here to admire. He was here to extract confessions.

"Eric!" Diego emerged from the crowd, clad in black leather and grinning like a half-wit. "Amigo. Long time, don't see. *Comment ça va?*"

With as much calm as he could marshal, Eric shook the proffered hand of his former friend. "I'm fine. And you?"

"Marvelous! *Regardez ceci.*" Diego swept an arm through the air, indicating the throng. "Is this not wonderful?"

"We need to talk."

"Of course. We will dine soon. But let me take you to Marie-

Claire." Diego's face clouded. "She was ... how you say? ... *désolée* that you do not come here before now."

Not half as desolated as she'd be when he got through grilling her. Both her and this Spanish slime ball.

Diego touched Eric's elbow. "Come, amigo."

Toward the rear of the boutique, a horseshoe-shaped glass counter displayed the products on offer, ten or twelve of them, none of which was a black cube with "SF" in gold script. Two sales women who were probably "actresses between jobs" wrote up receipts and placed gold-and-white striped boxes into small, gold-and-white striped sacks.

At the focal point enclosed by the horseshoe, Marie-Claire held court. She looked radiant, barely recognizable as the shy Catholic virgin he'd known in Versailles. She'd cut her hair in a bob that flattered her round cheeks. But what struck him most was her clothing. She wore a low-cut, miniskirted dress in a pattern of colors that might have been inspired by Jackson Pollock, and black tights that showed off better-looking legs than Eric remembered.

Recalling his reflection in the window outside, Eric pictured himself as the dark-hooded intruder, come to the banquet to reap souls. He smiled as he approached her. "Marie-Claire."

"Eric!" she cried, throwing her arms around his neck. "I am so happy to see you."

"You look ravishing."

With the adoring eyes of a puppy, she threaded her arm through Diego's. "It is because I am in love."

"Congratulations." So he'd been right. Diego had traded love, or at least sex, for the opportunity to manufacture and market his version of Balquees. The criminal version that clearly was making them rich. Like mobsters, they'd established a legitimate business in New York, a front for sales of their real cash cow.

Abby materialized at Eric's side. "You're late."

"Busier day than I expected." And nice to see you, too.

Grasping Eric's hand, Marie-Claire said, "You must tell me what you think of our creations. Come, please. I will take you to the room behind here, where there is not so much busy."

Time alone with her? You bet. Eric followed her to the back, into a small room with packaged product arranged on metal shelving and, on the opposite wall, a narrow door that presumably led to the toilet. For the next fifteen minutes, he did his best to put her at ease by smelling each product and declaring it wonderful.

"Thank you, Eric," she said at last. "A newspaper reporter came before. He said I will like what he writes. But your opinion is more important. For me."

As though a veil had lifted from her face, Eric saw clearly the insecure cherub who'd felt they were underdressed at the Panthéon. And who, later that evening, had declared Balquees the work of the Devil.

Time to reap a soul. "Tell me," he said, "do you know what SF is doing to people?"

"SF?" She scrunched up her face, just as Tanya had. "I do not understand."

"Your counterfeit of Balquees."

With a puzzled expression, she shook her head. "Balquees was your experiment. You are making it?"

"I'm not, but you are."

"*Mais non.* It is yours. I would not make it."

"Wouldn't you?"

"*Jamais!*" She frowned. "I told you, Balquees makes people act … against God."

"If anything makes people act against God, it's SF."

"What is SF?"

Damn, she was good. He perceived none of the classic signals. No sheen of perspiration, no touching of the face or long pauses or glancing away. Only a burst of the fragrance she wore hinted that he was making progress.

He moved in closer, purposely intruding on her personal space. "Diego gave you my formula, didn't he? You made it and called it SF. Come on, you can tell me."

"Eric." Her hand went to her chest and pinched closed her neckline. "*Tu me fais peur.*"

Frightening her? Well, maybe that was good. Clearly cajoling wasn't getting anywhere. Then inspiration struck. They were in the back room, the very place from which SF would be sold—"under the counter." Nothing she'd given him to smell was SF, so she must have held it back. He scanned the shelves, searching for product boxes the right size, and came up blank

"Where is it?" he growled.

No answer.

The bathroom? He yanked open the door but saw only a toilet and tiny sink.

"Eric, what are you doing?" She looked horrified. "You are acting ... *dérangé*."

"I'm not the one who's deranged. I'm the one who—"

"There you are," Diego said, poking his head in the door. "We are closing. We must say *adieu*."

Marie-Claire peered at Eric, her expression expertly retouched from shock to concern. She started to reach out a hand but apparently thought better of it and left with Diego.

Damn. Eric gripped a chest-high shelf with both hands. Was this another case of screwing up, like he'd just done with Tanya? Could he no longer trust his own judgment? Marie-Claire had always worn her emotions in plain sight. Perhaps he'd seen no deceit because she really didn't know what was going on. Maybe Diego was using her parents' perfumery to make SF without Marie-Claire's knowledge.

That had to be it. Just as he'd thought at the start, Diego, in all his sucking-up charm, was the real Benedict Arnold. Eric pushed back from the shelf. He had to stop Marie-Claire from saying anything that could possibly alert the bastard.

Rushing out of the stockroom, he found hands being shaken and cheeks being kissed as Diego and Marie-Claire bid good evening to their customers. Abby, elegant in black business attire, stood to one side. Rather tactlessly, the two sales women were already collecting champagne flutes from the countertops and side tables before all the guests had left. Eric snagged a glass that looked untouched, chugged its contents, and winced when the effervescence tried to come back up.

He refilled it from a half-empty bottle and sipped more slowly as he sidled up to Abby. "It's Diego."

"She told you that?"

"Not in so many words, but I know it." Now all he had to do was get the creep in a relaxed setting and unguarded mood.

When the last customers had departed and Diego closed the

door, Eric declared himself famished. "Where do you want to go for dinner?"

"Tapas," Diego said. "There is a tapas restaurant in the next street."

Throughout the locking up and their subsequent stroll to the restaurant, Eric made a point of sticking close to Diego, denying Marie-Claire any private access to her boyfriend. Fortunately, her concern for Eric seemed to have faded, replaced by the gleeful chatter of an entrepreneur who had successfully launched a new business in the Big Apple.

Whoop-de-doo.

At the restaurant, they secured a table by the window, and everyone agreed to let Diego do the ordering. He selected four cold dishes to start: roasted red peppers, spinach with pine nuts and currants, mushrooms in truffle oil, and the traditional Serrano ham with Manchego cheese. To compliment these, he ordered chilled amontillado sherry all around.

As soon as the sherry came, he lifted his glass. "To a debut *perfecto*."

They all clinked glasses, Eric wondering when he should spring his trap, and whether Marie-Claire would ever stop bathing the guy in that stupid, soppy gaze.

When their cold dishes arrived on four small plates, the start of a meal that would consist entirely of *hors d'œuvre*-size portions, Diego forked a mushroom into his mouth. "Excellent."

Abby sampled one, then exhaled through her nose. "Too bad about the truffle oil."

"What do you mean?" Marie-Claire asked. "What is too bad?"

"The truffle oil is fake."

"No." Diego banged his fork down. "They give us fake truffle oil? I protest!"

Eric couldn't help grinning. Abby's palate was second to none, and everyone at the table knew it.

"Don't bother," she said. "Most chefs can't tell the difference, let alone most people. But ninety percent of all the truffle oil is olive oil with a flavoring chemical."

Their waiter fronted up to see if everything was all right. Diego told him to take back the mushrooms. Eric asked for another round of sherry, an unspoken salutation to how artfully Abby had gelded this son of a Spanish horse breeder.

When the waiter brought four fresh sherries, compliments of the house, Diego ordered their first round of hot dishes and a bottle of Rioja. "You will like the *Merquez*," he told them. "It is sausage in the style of Morocco. And the *pulpo* ... uh..."

"Octopus," Eric said, relishing the opportunity to translate something Diego couldn't. There were advantages to an adolescence in Texas. And now that he'd delivered his own small bit of one-upsmanship, he ached to capitalize on it.

"Yes, octopus. With garlic and onion. It is very typical." Then Diego rose from the table. "Excuse me. I must go to the *aseo*."

The men's room. Perfect. After giving Diego a minute's head start, Eric polished off his sherry. "Excuse me, also."

He wove his way through the tables and past the kitchen to a short hallway lined with replicas of bullfight posters. There were three doors: Private, Damas, and Caballeros. He pushed open the one marked Caballeros and saw Diego standing at one of the two urinals.

Having no need to pee, Eric stepped to the sink and started washing his hands. "I've been meaning to ask you. Have you ever tried SF?"

"SF? *Es fantástico.* Everybody loves it. I congratulate you, amigo." There was a zipping sound, then without flushing, Diego joined him at the sinks. "Of course, I cannot use it with Marie-Claire. She is very ... conservative."

"But other women?"

"I will not tell." Diego feigned a frown, then winked. "Unless we finish the night in a good bar. You and me."

Shutting off the taps, Eric pulled some paper towels from the dispenser. He had no intention of waiting for later. "Does Marie-Claire know you make it?"

"Perdóneme?"

"Don't play dumb with me." Eric crushed the paper towels and threw them on the floor. "Not only did you steal my goddamned formula, but you fucked it up. As usual. Do you have any idea how many people have been killed because of you?"

Diego stared at him. "I don't understand."

"Dead, asshole. *Muerto!* What don't you understand?"

"Someone dies from perfume?" He appeared to consider this a moment, a bit of acting that could have gotten him an audition on Broadway. "They must have an allergy."

Yeah, sure. Or was the bastard so dense that he didn't even realize what his filthy counterfeit was doing? Eric grabbed him by the lapels of his leather sport coat. "It's not the perfume that kills them, you stupid ass. The perfume drives them wild. It makes them crazy, and they beat the hell out of their lovers."

"No." Diego shook his head emphatically. "If your lover is not strong, you must control the passion."

"Blame the user. That's just like you." With a shove to the chest, Eric released Diego's lapels. He'd had it with this charlatan. "Listen up, pal, 'cause here's what's gonna happen. I'm turning you in to the cops. Got that? And Marie-Claire as a material witness."

Diego's eyes flared. "You accuse *me?* For what?"

"For killing people, you incompetent shit."

"No." Diego stabbed a forefinger in Eric's chest. "I kill nobody. If people die from SF, it is you who kills them. SF is Balquees." Another stab of the finger. "You made it. I do not."

Eric slapped away Diego's hand. "Don't touch me. I had you pegged from the start. And now you're gonna pay."

Flipping up his palms, Diego said, "Where is my friend? What has happened to him?"

"You wrecked his life when you stole Balquees."

Diego shook his head sadly. "You are wrong. He wrecks himself. In *la cabeza.*" With a tap to his temple, Diego walked out.

Eric slammed his hand against the paper towel dispenser. Why couldn't he break these people? Hoping for more help from Abby, he went back into the restaurant, only to see Diego dragging Marie-Claire out the front door.

"What the hell happened?" Abby demanded.

Eric plopped himself in the chair Diego had vacated. "I couldn't make him confess."

"That figures." Abby speared a chunk of sausage, chewed, and swallowed. "Not true Moroccan. The lemon in it is fresh, not pickled."

"Fuck the sausage. Are you listening to me?"

"Don't get pissy. I'm listening. And I think both of them are innocent."

"Bullshit."

"Would you like to swear," she said in that paternalistic tone of hers, "or hear me out?"

Eric gnashed his teeth, then reached for his wineglass and gulped a mouthful of Rioja.

Apparently appeased, Abby crossed her forearms on the table and leaned forward. "While you and Diego were blowing each other in the men's room, I had a chat with our no-longer-virgin friend. Best thing that could have happened to her, by the way. Anyhow, it seems Diego's father disowned him. Something about no faggot perfumer getting anything from *him*. So Diego has an epiphany. He's been wandering in the wilderness but finally sees the light. He comes to Marie-Claire on bended knee, confessing the error of his ways and his belated realization that she has always been his one and only."

"I figured the bended-knee part a long time ago."

"Makes you want to gag, I know. But did you figure this? It turns out Diego's good at marketing."

"Marketing?"

"The boutique tonight was his idea. And judging from all the product going out the door, the idea was pretty good."

"Not as good as SF."

"She says you badgered her about that. Scared her, actually. She's worried about you."

"She should worry about herself." He drained his wineglass and poured another.

"Eric, I'm pretty good at reading people, and I think she's clueless about SF."

"Diego isn't. He admits using it. Not with her, but when the 'wilderness' calls him back. I think he produces it on the sly at her parent's perfumery."

"Think again. Marie-Claire, besides working as a perfumer, is in charge of quality control. She smells every batch of product before it goes to packaging. There's no way a flask full of SF would get past her."

"There has to be." Eric racked his brain. If he couldn't get it out of them, maybe Fawcett could. "Where are they staying?"

"No idea. You scared them off before I thought to ask."

"Shit."

Abby reached her hand across the table and covered one of his. "I honestly don't think they're involved."

Not involved? What the hell was going on here? Suddenly on alert, Eric peered into Abby's eyes. His ally, his only ally, was trying to exonerate the obvious culprits, or at least culprit—with a story so neat and tidy there could be no arguing against it. Except for one thing. He had only Abby's word for it, just the way he had only her word for Durand's financial condition.

"Well?" she said.

Had he been blind from the beginning? "Why exactly are you defending them?"

"I'm not defending them. I'm just telling you what—"

"You sure-as-hell are." He yanked his hand from under hers, knocked back his wine in two gulps, and sloshed some more into the glass.

"Maybe you should lay off that stuff."

"Maybe you should come clean." Fresh out of Versailles, and she was already a star? If it sounded too good to be true, it *was* too good to be true. "Start by telling me how you can afford that fancy apartment of yours."

"My apartment?" Then his real question apparently struck home. "Good Lord. You don't think—"

"Tell me!"

"Bonuses," she spat. "And an uncle who owns the building." She leaned closer across the table. "Eric, you're going off the deep end."

Always the quick answer. The helping hand. Like when she conned him into thinking she was helping with the website. "How come you could alter the SF website, but you couldn't kill it?"

She sat up straight. "You ungrateful sonofabitch."

Like he should be grateful for deception? Not any longer. He saw her now as one of those demons in a horror movie, a beautiful woman whose façade falls for a split second to reveal the underlying creature from Hell. "You're one of them!"

"You're pathetic." Abby pushed back her chair and stood.

"You know what your problem is? You're jealous. Your friends from Versailles are all doing well, and you're stuck in a dead-end job you'll never get out of because you don't have the balls to pull yourself up and put this behind you and strike out on your own. You just sit there in that dingy apartment of yours and wallow in self-pity. 'Woe is me.' And in the meantime, your talent is totally fucking wasted."

She threw some money on the table. "I hate to tell you this, Eric, but you're a loser."

Chapter 27

Gnawing her lip, Abby strode away from the restaurant. She shouldn't have lost her self-control, let her temper burst out like that. But she'd felt backed into a corner, and even now, as she put distance between Eric and herself, her muscles still felt coiled to strike.

He was getting too damned close to the truth. Her expensive apartment, her "help" with the SF website. Her knowledge of the ingredients in Balquees, even if he thought she didn't know them all. If he remained suspicious after sobering up, things could get bad. She turned up the collar of her overcoat.

The weakest part of her cover was the apartment. Anyone could check property records and find out who owned her building, which most certainly was not her uncle. She didn't even have an uncle that she knew of. And the police, if Eric went to them, could question her employer and discover in five minutes that she'd never received a bonus. No two ways about it, she had to sidetrack Eric's suspicions.

At the intersection, she flagged down a cab, then realized she had no particular destination in mind. After a moment, she decided on, "Chinatown. Bayard and Elizabeth streets."

She needed to re-center, replace all this negative energy with positive thoughts. And nothing did that better than spying on her father and visualizing payback.

The cab's rear seat sagged on both sides from too many lardassed fares. She sank into the right-side depression, from which she could barely see out the windshield, and cracked open the window for some air.

She'd probably made a mistake trying to exonerate Diego and Marie-Claire so that Eric would focus on Durand. But Durand was the perfect fall guy. He had means, and she'd done her best to give him motive. Of course, the old fart was not in need of money. He'd never invited her privately to his villa or tried to seduce her. But Eric didn't know that. And framing the great perfume god gave her almost as much satisfaction as contemplating what she'd do to her father.

As the lights of Canal Street sped past, she pictured Durand's smug face. Until he came along, she'd had Eric to herself, at her beck and call whenever she needed help in her studies, or a sounding board, or a man in her bed. But in their second year at ISIPCA, Durand had materialized, wooing Eric with visions of glory. She'd cranked up the heat with Eric, and sometimes it worked. But most of the time, Durand won.

If anyone got in shit for SF, she wanted it to be him. And like her father, Durand would never see it coming.

Unless Eric fucked things up. Damn, she shouldn't have called him a loser. The grain of truth made it crueler than she'd intended.

The cab pulled to a stop.

Peering through the window, she felt the old tightness in her stomach. So many nightmarish memories. She hesitated, then paid the driver and got out.

Less touristy than most of Chinatown, the area around Bayard and Elizabeth was a place people lived, not only above the shops, but at street level, as well. Aside from the restaurant she happened to be standing next to, with its disgusting odors of chop suey and egg fu yung and its window displays showing stock photos of menu items to attract foreigners, most of the shops catered to locals. Meat market, video store, clothing store, electronics repair, pharmacy. No flashing neon or blaring music or scumbags hustling passersby into sleazy clubs. In fact, at this time of night, passersby were few, mainly middle-aged, and all Chinese.

Above the shops on Bayard Street, fire escapes zigzagged down the buildings past backlit window shades. Abby pictured the families behind those shades, the father waiting to be served, his mother scolding the wife, the sons playing video games while the daughters did their homework in desperate hope that an education would be their ticket to escape.

Run, little girls. You can do it.

With a determined step, Abby marched down Bayard Street to New China Bank, home of her wealth and her payback account. She leaned back against the night-deposit box. Across the street stood Han Yong Grocery, its name proclaimed in red Chinese characters five times the size of the English translation below. And there he was, elbows on the counter as he read what appeared to be one of Chinatown's ethnic newspapers. She could almost smell the bastard's breath, the foul stink that came from bad teeth and a weakness for dried fish eaten bones and all.

Boxes of produce on cheap wooden stands lined the sidewalk on either side of the glass door. In the windows, hand-written signs proclaimed bargains she knew were false. His apartment, directly above the lighted storefront, was dark behind drawn shades. As dark as his motherfucking heart.

Abby drifted a hand over the granite wall of the bank behind her. Soon she would buy out the lease on Han Yong Grocery. She'd evict the bastard. Deprived of income, he'd have to leave his apartment and move to some place cheaper. But she'd buy up the lease on that place, too. And she'd keep doing it until Mister Han Bao Yong had no place to go. He'd end up huddled beside a Dumpster in some fetid alley, just the way she'd huddled in her corner of the storeroom at the back of that goddamned store.

Suppressing an urge to walk in right now and tell him his fortune, she fast-forwarded to the climax of his payback. She would pretend to accidentally find him. Dressed to the hilt, she would grasp his hand and raise him to his feet. He'd gaze at her in wonder, tears of gratitude overflowing his eyes. She would take him to the most expensive restaurant in Chinatown, order a twenty-course feast of the most exotic delights, thank him effusively for his love and the wonderful childhood he'd given her. At the end, she'd walk out and leave him with the bill. The cops would come. He'd go to jail and come out a degraded wreck, universally despised, spat on by young boys as he crouched in the gutter and begged for coins.

A thrill coursed through her, like an orgasm that lasted a lifetime. She could hardly wait.

And she was on the cusp. If Eric didn't ruin everything.

As her father folded his newspaper, Abby pushed herself off the wall of the bank and headed back down Bayard Street. Eric, once a good friend, had become a serious problem she needed to solve. And in a stroke of clarity, it came to her.

Unlike the few other men she'd slept with, Eric liked her—even loved her—for herself, rather than for the novelty of bedding a lesbian. So that was the solution. Cuddle up to him, flatter him, give him sex any way he wanted. Win him back. Steer him to suspecting Durand, and let him point the police in Durand's direction.

And if that didn't work?

Abby slowed her pace. If that didn't work, there was only one alternative.

∿

"How did this happen?" Sitting on the floor, his back against the wingchair, Eric searched Daisy's eyes for wisdom. Light from the floor lamp behind him lit her face and showed her concern. Of course she couldn't talk, but she did understand.

He slugged another mouthful of Lagavulin. "They were my friends. Well, not Tanya. But I was beginning to like her."

At the mention of Tanya's name, Daisy perked up.

"Yeah, I know. You liked her, too. I can't believe I made such an ass of myself." When Daisy's ears drooped, he knew she felt his sadness. He knocked back the remainder of his Scotch. "Hang on a sec."

Listing a little, he navigated to the kitchen, refilled his glass, and plopped back down against the chair. Daisy hadn't moved. Stalwart friend. He leaned forward and scratched the furrow between her eyes. "You're the only one I can truly trust."

Everyone from Versailles had turned Judas on him, selling him out for a quick buck without the slightest misgiving, the tiniest speck of regret.

"You know what hurts most?" He opened his mouth to say Abby's name but choked up. What an idiot he'd been. He took a breath and wiped some moisture from his eyes. IDIOT. All this time, he'd believed in her, counted on her. The biggest Judas of all, the one who actually kissed him.

Hell, they'd made love just yesterday. Yesterday, right? Yeah, Sunday afternoon, and this was Monday night. He raised his wrist and tried to bring his watch into focus. Almost midnight, it looked like. Only eighteen, no, thirty hours ago—whatever—Abby had lain in his arms. "Like fucking Mata Hari!"

Daisy's head popped up at his outburst.

"That's right, girl. I'm surprised you didn't see it." The room swayed. No big deal. He was sitting down. "Where were we? Oh, yeah, Abby. That swanky apartment and all? And remember when I told her you could smell a difference between Balquees and SF? First thing she said was Diego and Marie-Claire were coming to town. Why do you suppose she did that?"

When Daisy fixed her eyes on him, he felt like a prosecutor about to surprise the jury. "I'll tell you why. Because … Uh, hang on. I had it a second ago." At least he thought he did. He rubbed his face with his free hand, trying to clear the fog. "I tell her about you. She tells me about them. Because … because … Shit."

Some Scotch might help. Eric swallowed a mouthful, then closed his eyes and took another run at his reasoning. But it was like trying to climb up a waterslide. And at the top, Abby starts pouring down truffle oil. By the bucketful. And his feet are slipping all over the place and his legs are getting tired. And she's grinning because, no matter how hard he tries, he just slides back down until he collapses in a heap at the bottom.

A low rumble shook his window. At midnight? Eric forced his eyes open.

Cold gray light filled the room, along with ice-cold air. His head throbbed. His mouth tasted like he'd been licking out latrines.

Beside him, his glass from last night had tipped over, spilling whiskey across the floorboards. It stank like Bourbon Street in the morning, before they hose down the sidewalks.

Eric's gut wrenched. Doubling over, he swallowed repeatedly against the threatening eruption and managed, barely, to keep it down.

Thank God for that. But, man, did he have to piss.

Slowly he inched up into a seated position, praying Daisy wouldn't waken. She lay asleep at his feet, oblivious to his misery. Let sleeping dogs lie. He was nowhere near ready to take her downstairs.

As he struggled to his feet, the radiators started pinging. Daisy didn't move. Good dog. He trudged into the bathroom, then, too wobbly to stand, sat on the toilet. Macho man, peeing like a girl.

After brushing his teeth, he downed four ibuprofen and three glasses of water. In the mirror, he looked as good as he felt—like he'd been run over by a garbage truck.

Eggs. That's what he needed. Three or four soft-boiled eggs on a couple slices of toast. With a little salt and a lot of pepper.

In the kitchen, he pulled open his refrigerator. No eggs, no bread. When did he last go to a grocery? Tea and milk for Tanya. Her face came to him, battered, bruised, incredulous at the accusations he'd hurled like a psychotic off his meds.

Resolved: I will apologize. Whether she accepted it or not, he owed it to her. And the sooner, the better. Like now.

Eric chugged half the quart of milk, then took a cold shower and lathered his face to shave. On an upstroke from his chin, he felt the blade catch at the same instant he felt the sting in his lower lip. "Damn." He blotted the nick with toilet paper and continued shaving as blood dripped into the sink. This one wasn't going to stop any time soon.

He toweled his face dry and went into the bedroom. While dressing, he used up three or four more wads of Kleenex until the flow diminished to a slow ooze and the wastebasket looked like a place where he'd slaughtered chickens. Someday he had to figure out a way to break in new blades without carving his face to shreds.

After tending to Daisy's needs, he was about to leave the apartment when it occurred to him that she hadn't had a long walk since Saturday. More important, she liked Tanya, and Tanya's heart might soften a bit if Daisy were there. He clipped on Daisy's lead and pocketed her badge in case someone in Tanya's building raised a stink. "Come on, girl. We're going to see a friend of yours. I hope."

Chapter 28

Clear skies, crisp air, and nearly deserted streets at this early hour made for an invigorating walk, marred only by Eric's fear that Tanya wouldn't even open her door. On the off chance a peace offering might help, he detoured up and down several side streets in search of an open flower shop. No luck. But he did come across a bakery that smelled like heaven and, five minutes later, walked out with a bag of fresh croissants. Who could resist croissants?

At Second Avenue, he stopped for a red light and noticed a squad car parked half a block beyond, directly in front of Tanya's building. Suddenly the car's tires squealed, spinning off a cloud of white smoke as the big engine roared away. Eric tensed, no doubt in his mind it was Patrick behind the wheel.

Fearing the butthead's encounter with Tanya would have left her in a rotten mood, Eric screwed up his courage and pressed on anyway. The elevator car in her building stank of star lilies, a cloying odor he'd always found repulsive, but a sure sign that someone this morning had had better luck finding a florist than he did. On the fifth floor, as he walked Daisy down the hall, the smell persisted. Must have been Patrick who brought the flowers.

When Eric knocked, Tanya hollered from inside, "God dammit, what do you want now?"

"It's me. Eric."

Her peephole darkened. "What do you want?"

"I want to apologize."

"Go away."

"Can we just talk for a minute?"

A door opened behind him, releasing a flood of curry odors. "Stop yelling or I call the super," a female voice shrieked.

He turned to see a shrew-faced woman wearing a wrinkled punjabi, her hair disheveled, her eyes frazzled with the exhaustion of someone who's gotten no sleep. Inside her apartment, a baby screamed so loudly Eric grimaced, which popped open the cut on his lip.

Suddenly the woman shrank back, her face petrified. "No dogs! I call the police."

As Eric reached for Daisy's badge, Tanya charged out in jeans and sweatshirt snarling, "Get back in your hole, you bitch. And stop spying on me."

"I call the super. I call the police."

"And I'll call fucking Immigration." Tanya grabbed Eric's arm and yanked him into her apartment, Daisy's lead dragging her in with them. A swift kick from Tanya slammed the door. "I swear to God that woman's a health hazard to the whole damn building. And her screeching brat is a demon from Hell." Then she narrowed her eyes. "Why are you bleeding?"

"Cut myself shaving." Still amazed—and amused—at Tanya's foul language, he fished out a wad of Kleenex and dabbed his lip.

"It's running down your chin. Come in here and let me put some peroxide on it." She pulled him toward her bathroom. "What's in the bag? A bomb?"

"Croissants."

"Sack lunch?"

"Actually, they're for you."

"Me?" She drew a brown bottle of hydrogen peroxide from one of the fishnet organizers hanging on the bathroom wall. "So they're laced with arsenic?"

Every statement a question. She'd been hanging out with cops too long. "I'll eat one first, if you like."

She soaked a cotton ball and pressed it to his lip, standing close enough that he found the smell of her a little disarming—the toasty aroma of her skin, the sweet tang of recently applied nail polish.

After about fifteen seconds, she replaced the cotton ball with a little square of styptic tape. "Been shaving long?"

"New blade. I hate new blades."

Tanya arched her eyebrows. "Only you would say something like that. Is it just to be contrary?"

"I shave very close. When you push hard with a new blade …" Why was he telling her this? "Never mind."

Holding up the package of styptic tape, she said, "Want some of this to take with you?"

No, thanks, Nurse Nightingale. "All I want is to apologize."

"In the bathroom?"

"Would you stop it with the questions?"

"Who's asking questions now?"

Obviously she wasn't going to make this easy. "Look. I admit I was a jerk yesterday."

"Unlike previous days?"

"Dammit, just let me finish. Then I'm outta here."

"Before we eat the croissants?" She snatched the bag from his hand and strode out of the bathroom. "We'll have them with orange juice."

We will? Staring at the empty doorway, Eric wondered if they'd reached a truce or if she was just prolonging his discomfort, toying with him like a cat with an injured mouse. Warily, he walked into the living room. The funereal stench of star lilies permeated the place like a miasma. But he saw no flowers. Nor any sign of Daisy, until Tanya emerged from the kitchen nook carrying two large glasses of orange juice with Daisy limping behind her.

"Do you like oldies?" Tanya asked.

"Yeah."

"The jukebox works. There're some coins in the fingerbowl next to it."

Still wary of what she might be up to, he decided not to reveal that he already knew about the jukebox and coins. Instead, he played neutral. "What songs do you like?"

"All of them." She set the glasses on her coffee table in front of the loveseat. "Should I warm the croissants in the microwave?"

"No more than twenty seconds, or you'll ruin them," he said

and instantly regretted how pedantic that might sound.

Tanya confirmed his fear with a sidelong glance that could have meant, I know that or, Who cares?

Maybe he should just cut his losses and bail. Only problem was, he didn't want to. For some perverse reason, he felt compelled to ride this out. Stepping over Daisy, who'd settled into her Sphinx position in front of the jukebox, he scanned the titles, then dropped a nickel in the slot and punched "Mack The Knife."

"Here we are," Tanya announced, bringing in a plate stacked with croissants. As she set them on the table, Bobby Darin snapped his fingers and opened with the classic lines about the shark and its teeth.

When she settled into the loveseat, Eric scanned the room for some other place to sit. He spotted a chair in the corner, a dining-height director's chair made of ash-colored wood and white canvas, and pulled it to the end of the coffee table.

As though responding to the song, Tanya said, "I'm done biting." Then she gnawed off an end of croissant, chewed it slowly, and smiled. "Not ruined."

Let's change subjects. "I saw Patrick leaving outside. Mind if I ask what happened?"

"He came to apologize. Same as you."

"How'd it go?"

"He brought flowers, which I'm sure you can tell." Tanya took a swallow of juice and leaned back in the loveseat. "They're in the trash."

Good news. But too bad she hadn't thrown the trash out. The dense, syrupy stink of Patrick's offering was beginning to give him a headache. Still, since he was here and ape-man wasn't, he felt like he and Tanya had, in fact, struck a truce.

"What I'd really like to know," she said, "is how you became such an arrogant snob."

"What?" He sat up straighter. "I'm not a snob."

"What else do you call somebody who thinks he knows more than anyone else? Who thinks he's more cultivated, more gifted?"

Eric bristled. "You mean, compared to a hayseed from Kansas?"

"Says a shit-kicker from Texas." She tore off a small piece of croissant and placed it daintily in her mouth, her little finger pointed skyward in a gesture mocking aristocratic etiquette. "But I wasn't comparing your majesty to my humble self. I was wondering where you got the conceit to imagine you're a better cop than one of the shrewdest detectives in New York City."

"Fawcett? If he's shrewd, New York's in trouble." Eric took a slug of orange juice. "A shrewd cop would have figured out a long time ago that I'm not the guy behind SF."

"He doesn't think you are."

Eric almost laughed, but it was no laughing matter.

"At least," Tanya added, "I don't believe he does."

"You haven't been grilled in an interrogation room until ten at night. You haven't had him show up at your apartment, repeatedly, ranting on until he's red in the face about *my* website and people dying because of *me*."

"So why hasn't he arrested you?"

"Because he can't prove it."

"Spoken just like a snob." She got up and dropped another coin in the jukebox. A few moments later, Ricky Nelson's voice came out singing "Poor Little Fool."

"What's that supposed to mean?"

"You haven't touched the croissants."

"I'm not hungry." In fact he was starving, but he wasn't about to sit here "breaking bread" while she played games.

Sitting down again, she said, "Have you ever considered the possibility that Detective Fawcett might be smarter than you think?"

"Not once."

"Of course not." She gave him a snotty little smile. "Which is why you're strung out like a crack whore and so paranoid you're digging yourself into an early grave."

"I don't know what you're talking about."

"In a nutshell …" She leaned forward, elbows on knees. "… I think he's using you."

"Bull. Did he tell you that?"

"No. But I've seen him with suspects a couple of times, and he's a cunning actor."

Whoa. Was the guy really that diabolical? Eric slowly scanned the room, barely registering the now-familiar furnishings, as a newsreel of his encounters with Fawcett cycled through his brain. The imagery kept pausing at one particular place, the website.

Refocusing on Tanya, he said, "NYPD has a computer fraud division, right? With hackers and all?"

"Some of the best hackers in the world, I hear."

"Then why couldn't Fawcett kill the SF website?"

"I didn't know there *was* a website."

"In Switzerland. It's the only place you can buy SF. Fawcett said the service provider wouldn't shut it down. But why didn't he just have his hackers bomb it out of existence?"

"I don't know." Tanya scooted to the end of the loveseat, her knees almost touching Eric's. "I'm sure they could have done it, if he wanted them to."

"So for some reason, he wants the site to stay up."

She slapped her palm on Eric's thigh. "Now you're thinking like a detective. Instead of a know-it-all."

Trying to ignore the warm spot her slap left on his leg, he said, "But nothing about the website amounts to 'using' me."

"Maybe we just can't see it yet. Let's keep going." She leaned forward and flipped a fall of hair out of her face. "Why would he want to leave the website running? Especially if it's the only place you can buy SF."

The only reason Eric could think of was, "It's a lead to the real criminal."

"Okay."

"A dead-end lead, according to Fawcett. But I suppose leaving it up is kind of like keeping a line open in hostage negotiations. Or maybe more like lulling the perpetrator into a sense of security. Keeps him from disappearing completely." Abby's face popped into his mind. "Him or her."

"Her? Are you being politically correct, or do you still think I'm involved?"

"No, not you," he said quickly. "There's another woman. Well, two maybe. And a guy. Plus a very slim chance of another man. Jacques Durand, the man in your photo. But I don't really believe it."

"Eric, if you have all these other suspects, how in the world did you think I fit into—"

"I was dumb. I'm sorry. I told you that."

She sat back in the loveseat. "I hope your evidence against these other people is stronger than your so-called evidence against me."

"It is."

"And you've told Detective Fawcett?"

"Well, it's not that strong. Not yet." The second he said it, Eric winced inside, fully expecting her to rip him a new one at this admission—suspecting a whole list of people, all on grounds too flimsy to disclose to Fawcett.

But instead, she spread out her arms along the back of the loveseat, crossed an ankle on her knee, and said, "Maybe you should tell me what you've got."

Maybe he should. She seemed ready to help, and a fresh mind might see something he'd missed. Besides, it was kind of nice just sitting here and talking with her.

If only his sinuses weren't clogged from the odor of those damned flowers. Not to mention a residual headache from his hangover. "Mind if I open a window?"

"Go ahead."

The two wooden casements would only open about six inches, pegged there by bolts presumably intended to prevent potential suicides from nose-diving into the alley below. Still, the rush of cool air helped clear his head. Returning to his chair, he noticed Daisy look up, then lower her chin onto her forepaw, her nose reoriented toward the windows. *That makes two of us, girl.*

Over the course of the remaining juice and croissants, he told Tanya about Diego, Marie-Claire, and Abby. Not everything, of course—certainly not with Abby—but the parts that seemed germane. At the end, he felt a surprising sense of relief, the way Catholics must feel after unburdening themselves in the confessional. Or perhaps it was just the relief of having solid food in his belly.

"It's Diego," Tanya concluded. "Plus or minus Marie-Claire."

"Not Abby?"

"All you've got on her is a big apartment and the fact that she knows some of the ingredients."

"And her ability to alter the website," he reminded her.

"Why mess up your own website, especially if it's your source of income? It doesn't make sense. Besides, where's her access to manufacturing, packaging, distribution?"

He hadn't thought of that.

"Actually, Durand seems as likely as Diego," Tanya added. "But you say he has no motive."

"And it goes absolutely against his code of honor."

"Codes of honor can be broken. But never mind. We now know why Detective Fawcett has been hounding you."

"We do?"

"Seems obvious to me. He has no idea who the real suspects are, but he knows you do. He's trying to goad you into finding them for him." Tanya leaned forward again, her mahogany eyes glittering. "Eric, he's counting on *you* to build his case."

Chapter 29

As the United Nations tower came into sight, Eric finally settled the debate in his head. He glanced at Tanya, who had mercifully tolerated his silence during their stroll down First Avenue. The thick makeup she'd applied to cover her bruises gave off the powdery, waxy aromas of a backstage dressing room, a major improvement over star lilies.

Lucking into a green light at 49th Street, he gave Daisy's lead a tug and said, "I'll build the case. But it won't be for Fawcett."

"I don't understand."

They shouldered through the flood of lunchtime pedestrians coming from the other side of the street, Eric drawing Daisy closer to him until they gained the far sidewalk. "I always intended to positively identify the culprit before telling Fawcett. But now that I realize he's been conning me, making my life hell for his own selfish reasons, he can go screw himself."

Tanya frowned. "His reasons aren't selfish."

"Think again. He could have asked for my help. But no, he wanted the glory and was perfectly willing to sacrifice *me* to get it. Collateral damage, that's all I was."

"You're being too hard on him."

"Beware of hero worship."

When they reached 47th Street, she pointed to the far side. "Ever been there? It's a park dedicated to Katharine Hepburn."

The Katharine Hepburn Garden, which he'd never heard of

before, turned out to be a sliver of land about forty feet wide that ran along the south side of 47th Street between First and Second avenues. It was bounded on one side by wrought-iron fencing and on the other by a wall decorated with red-stenciled notices to "Post No Bills."

"It's nicer in the springtime," Tanya said, as she led him along the winding, stepping-stone path.

"I imagine so." Now, however, in early March, the skinny birch trees looked like sticks, and most of the shrubbery either drooped sadly or lay brown on the ground. Still, they had the place to themselves, except for a man eating a hotdog up near the Second Avenue end.

At a polished steppingstone engraved with Miss Hepburn's photograph, Tanya halted. "Wasn't she beautiful."

"You a fan of hers?"

"Who couldn't admire a woman who protected her lover's reputation for all those years? To the point of not even attending his funeral."

So, hard-nosed Tanya was a romantic at heart. Eric liked that.

"You're being pig-headed," she said as they continued walking. "You should tell Detective Fawcett what you know."

"Even if I agreed with you, there's nothing he could do. France is outside his jurisdiction, and I don't see him handing over his case to the Sûreté or Interpol."

"He'd think of something."

They paused at a bronze statue of a stag, only four feet high. Farther up the path, the man with the hotdog popped the last of it in his mouth as he strolled casually their way. Something about his gait seemed vaguely familiar, or maybe Eric just noticed because it resembled a Texas amble more than the resolute stride of most New Yorkers.

"If you don't tell him," Tanya persisted, "there's nothing he can do. Except keep hounding you."

"Look, this isn't just a crime against innocent users of a fragrance. It's a crime against me. Why doesn't anybody get that? It's a counterfeit of *my* creation. I mean, scent-wise, it's not even a great perfume. But it got me kicked out of Versailles on trumped-up charges, and now it's wrecking my life again." He felt Daisy tug on her lead but ignored it. "In my own defense, and for my own self-respect—what little I have left—I need to solve this thing myself."

"Solve what thing?" Fawcett said.

Eric almost choked. Tanya spun around. Daisy tugged again on her lead, apparently anxious to greet the man.

Wiping his fingers on a paper napkin, Fawcett closed the short distance between them. "They make better hotdogs on the west side. I recommend the Hungarian guy over at Forty-third and Broadway. Assuming you're both well enough to make the pilgrimage."

With a supreme effort, Eric tried to hide the anger welling inside him. "So your goons have nothing better to do than follow me around? No murders to investigate, no—"

"Shut up." Fawcett peered closely at Tanya, then glared at Eric before turning back to her. "What happened to you?"

"What do you mean?"

"If you tell me you fell down the stairs, I'm gonna arrest this prick right now."

"He didn't do it."

"Do what?"

Eric put an arm around Tanya's shoulder. So much for his belief that, with a bit of makeup, she could return to work, no questions asked. Time to right an injustice, and simultaneously turn the tables on Fawcett. "One of your boys in blue beat her up."

"Bullshit."

In a shaky voice, Tanya said, "Eric's wrong. All that happened was I got mugged Sunday night."

"I'm not wrong, dammit. Come on, tell him the truth. He should know what kind of animals are supposedly protecting us."

Fawcett shoved Eric aside and faced Tanya. "Level with me."

"Flynn," Eric said. "Patrick Flynn."

Fawcett whirled on him. "If you open your mouth one more time, I'll haul your ass in for interfering with an investigation." Taking Tanya's elbow, he ushered her up the path to a spot out of Eric's earshot.

But not out of Eric's sight. Stewing, he watched Tanya's face change from denial to rationalization under Fawcett's inaudible probing. Then her expression turned miserable, and when she wiped her eyes, Eric suddenly felt like spit.

It wasn't supposed to happen like this. He didn't want to hurt her. He wanted to help. With the truth out in the open, she was supposed to gain strength, stop protecting Patrick like a battered wife. But as he watched her face become more and more wretched, his good intentions withered like the wilted shrubs in this miserable garden.

Finally Fawcett turned and shot him a look. "I'll deal with you later." Then he took Tanya's arm again and walked her away toward Second Avenue.

They'd gone only a few paces when Tanya glanced back and mouthed, "You son of a bitch."

At a loss for anything better to do, Eric dropped off Daisy at his apartment and headed for Rheinhold-Laroche to clear his backlog. Once again, he'd blown it with Tanya. But she had no right to be angry. Patrick was a bad apple who needed to be taken off the streets, and that would only happen if she pressed charges. Eric kicked a cigar butt into the gutter. Okay, he could have been more diplomatic, tried to persuade her once more to level with Fawcett. But he'd let his temper get the better of him. Just the way he did with Abby. And with Marie-Claire and Diego.

At the front doors of Rheinhold-Laroche, he felt for the first time glad to be going inside. The routine, he hoped, would give his subconscious a chance to mull things over and point him in a productive direction.

Expecting a pile of sample trays, he opened his office door to find a stranger sitting at the desk. The man, thin and probably in his sixties, gave him a quizzical look, then said, "Oh. Are you Mister Foster?"

"Yeah," Eric replied cautiously.

"Aaron Braithwaite." Braithwaite smiled, stood, and extended his hand. "So you're the young man who took over when I retired. Pleased to meet you."

Eric shook his hand, which was soft as a surgeon's. Based on the accent, he said, "I take it you're English?"

"Not for the past thirty years. But once a Tyke, always a Tyke, I suppose."

"Tyke?"

"Yorkshireman." Braithwaite smiled broadly. "And I suppose you're here to collect your things."

My things? Eric unbuttoned his overcoat. "I'm here to finish the backlog I left when I got sick."

"Oh, there's no need. I'm getting through it pretty quickly." Braithwaite gestured at two trays on the right-hand side of the desk. All of the sample bottles, except two, bore green "Passed" stickers on their lids. "It's good to be back at work. To use the vernacular, retirement sucked."

So did the ominous sensation now souring Eric's gut. "Uh, I'm not sure I understand what—"

"Foster," Wigby exclaimed behind him. "It's about time. I see you've met our Mister Braithwaite. Now say good-bye and give me your card-key. Security is here to escort you out."

Eric couldn't believe it. "You're firing me?"

"You're already fired." A tiny smirk twisted his lips.

"But just yesterday you told me to come back when I got over the flu. I'm over it now."

"Oh, dear," Braithwaite cut in, his face a mixture of surprise and concern. "I had no idea you were coming back, Mister Foster."

"And it's none of your business," Wigby told him. Turning to Eric, he flipped up his palm. "Your card-key."

With growing indignation, Eric stood his ground. "What's changed since yesterday?"

"What's changed, if you must know, is that executive management has finally gotten fed up with all your high-handed rejections and the time and money they've cost us. Not to mention our customer relations when we have to explain why deadlines are slipping. You can't seem to get it through your thick skull that good enough is good enough."

"So your promise means nothing?"

"Alas," Wigby replied with a phony smile, "I'm but a small cog in the executive wheel."

You're a two-faced liar, Eric wanted to say. But he held his tongue and handed over the card-key.

Braithwaite touched Eric's arm. "There are some voicemail messages for you." He pointed to the pulsing light on the phone. "Perhaps you should listen to them before you leave."

Wigby rolled his eyes, then turned to the security guard standing just outside the door. "Give him five minutes, then escort him out."

As Wigby disappeared, Braithwaite said softly, "I'm so sorry. I had no idea."

"Forget it. It's not your fault." Eric glanced around the office, a workplace totally devoid of anything personal, except the black seat cushion he'd bought for the chair. The job stank, literally. He'd hated it, often cringed at the thought of coming here. But it was *his* job, and he'd tried to make a difference. Now it was gone, and he felt like the cast-off skin of some molting insect.

He'd wake up tomorrow with nowhere to go, nothing to do, no one who needed him or wanted what he could offer. Another faceless statistic in the unemployment line.

"Mister Foster, are you okay?"

The sadness in Braithwaite's eyes made Eric feel even worse. Too distressed to reply, he picked up the handset and punched the flashing light.

"You have nine new messages," a female voice informed him.

The first came from Lieutenant O'Keefe, the big jovial woman in his class at John Jay. "Remember last week you asked me how things were going in the thirty-fourth, and I said nothing new except a lot more cases of domestic violence? I think I called it cabin fever. Well, we followed up on a notice from Midtown North, and turns out about a third of those cases are linked to a perfume called SF that makes people aggressive. Can you help me out on this? Citywide, it looks like we've got a plague."

Eric hit the Erase button and went on to the second message.

"This is Sergeant Cohen from the Seventh Precinct. I'm in your class at John Jay. I may have something that's right up your alley. "We've got this perfume—"

Eric hit Erase.

Next came Detective Jackson, the black man from the Gang Unit who always gave Daisy a few head scratches before taking his place at the classroom table. Then Detective Marconi and, one-by-one, all of Eric's other students.

"Time's up," the security guard announced.

Eric felt numb. Lieutenant O'Keefe was right—they had a plague on their hands.

"Hey, pal." With a firm set to his jaw, the guard stepped into the office. "I said it's time to go."

"Hey, pal," Eric mimicked. "You can take my job, but you can't take my personal messages."

The man glanced at the open door, then turned back to Eric. "Look, I'm sorry you got the boot. But Mr. Wigby gave me a direct order, and if he comes back and finds you still here, he'll fire me."

The poor guy was probably right. "One minute?"

"Okay. But hurry."

The last message was from Sergeant Pérez of the 106th Precinct, out near JFK, saying they'd caught the diamond smugglers. She thanked him again, then ended with, "By the way, we got some weird perfume implicated in one homicide and several IPVs. That's intimate partner violence. The name of the perfume is SF, as in Sierra Foxtrot. No maker on the bottle. You ever heard of this stuff? Gimme a call."

After leaving the seat cushion as a gesture of gratitude for Braithwaite's sympathy, Eric plodded down Tenth Avenue toward his apartment.

Could things get any worse? He had no job. No one who mattered would speak to him anymore. Violence tied to SF was spreading like wildfire, and he had no clue how to clear his name, let alone avenge himself against the demon who stole his formula, stole the wood from ISIPCA, and was destroying his life.

As he approached his apartment building, the monetary realities of being unemployed deepened his misery. He had bills coming up. He had to eat. Daisy had to eat. To pay his rent and just survive, he would need to dip into the inheritance from his grandmother. It might last him six months in this city. Then he'd be a man with a nose and nothing else.

Eric climbed the steps to his building, opened the door, and stepped into the gloomy foyer. From out of the dark, a fist smashed into his face. He stumbled to the floor, pain spearing through his whole head as blood gushed out his nose.

"Dead meat," Patrick growled and kicked him in the balls.

Chapter 30

Having faded in and out of consciousness, Eric could muster only patchy recollections of the neighbor lady who came down the stairs to find him crumpled in a pool of blood, the subsequent ambulance ride with an ice pack on his face, and being lifted onto a table in a hospital examination room. But he sprang to full alert at the sight of two men in scrubs staring down at him. A nurse with short brown hair stood behind them, her back against the wall, her face dispassionate.

One of the men, gray-haired and fatherly-looking, shined a penlight in each of Eric's eyes, then held up an index finger. "How many fingers do you see?"

"One."

"Now?"

"Three." Eric ached everywhere. His balls, his ribs, but especially his face. When he reached to feel his nose, the man stopped him.

"Don't touch. We just swabbed you."

Dried blood encrusted Eric's hand, and he suddenly realized he was breathing through his mouth. He tried to inhale through his nose but couldn't. *Oh, Jesus Christ.* "Is my nose broken?"

"We're going to fix it. Just relax."

In a burst of panic, Eric tried to sit up. He had to get out of here. Get to a specialist.

The man pressed him back, pushing more forcefully when

Eric tried again. "Settle down. This won't take long."

"I need a specialist."

"I *am* a specialist. I set bones for a living."

"No, you don't understand." Eric's head swirled from the exertion to sit. But he had to explain. "I'm a perfumer. My nose is my life."

"Then relax and let me fix it."

"You can't just fix it." A cold sweat broke out over Eric's chest and arms. Bones weren't the only thing. "If you damage the olfactory tissue—"

"I won't," the man said with a note of annoyance. "But I *will* tell you, the longer we wait, the harder it'll be."

Eric shivered. What would he do if he couldn't smell? He'd be nothing. His talent worthless, his training wasted. His whole life, everything that mattered, shot to hell.

"This is going to sting a little." The second man, younger and wearing an earring, held up a hypodermic syringe with a short needle.

"What's *that* for?"

"We're going to numb your nose."

"It won't damage—"

"No, it will not."

Oh, God, please let that be true. Eric clenched his eyes and clamped his jaw. He felt a hand brace gently on his chin, then the jab of a needle in the soft tissue halfway up the inside of his right nostril. *Chee-rist!* Then came another jab in the same nostril, and another. A ring of them, each one stinging like the bite of a fire ant.

"You're doing fine," the man said. "Now the other side."

Again the pinpricks. Four or five, he couldn't tell. But he could take the pain a lot better than the sense of being pinned down helplessly while total strangers messed with his future.

Or so he thought until he opened his eyes and saw the same man bending forward with a syringe that had a much longer needle. "Oh, no. You're not going to stick that—"

"Lie still. We need to do this."

Eric's vision funneled down to that one, long needle, its beveled tip impossibly sharp. Coming closer, disappearing into his nose. He squeezed his eyes shut.

The jab came like a jolt of electricity straight to the brain. Sparklers flashed behind his lids.

"Hold still," the doctor ordered. "John?"

Gloved hands held Eric's head firmly down on the pillow as the man with the syringe again shot multiple injections inside each nostril, these so far up that Eric felt them between his eyes.

Then the pain subsided.

With a finger, the gray-haired doctor, apparently named John, tapped Eric's nose in several places. "Do you feel that?"

"No."

"Okay, we're ready to realign." He picked up what looked like a pair of curved, needle-nosed pliers. "This part won't hurt."

True enough, Eric didn't feel the pliers go in. But through the bones in his skull he heard a sickening crunch like someone treading on broken glass. Then another, less loud this time, more like the sound of breaking up crispy toast.

After a few more crunches, the man stood back. "What do you think?"

His colleague peered at Eric. "Difficult to tell with so much swelling. But I think a little more to the left."

Holding the bridge of Eric's nose in the fingers of one hand, the first man again inserted the pliers deep into Eric's nose.

The sounds seemed muted, more like clicks than crunches.

"That's good," the younger one said.

"Okay, let's pack it." Using forceps and a sort of speculum, the man pushed about twenty feet, it seemed, of thin gauze up inside each of Eric's nostrils. Fortunately, Eric felt almost nothing except a profound sense of relief that this was nearly over.

"Okay, tape him up. Jenny, you can assist." With that, the older man wrote out a prescription and handed it to Eric. "This is for pain. You could feel groggy for an hour or two while the injections wear off. So be careful when you stand up."

"Are you sure my sense of smell won't be impaired?"

"No reason why it should be."

Eric mentally crossed his fingers—like that would do any good.

As the first doctor left, the younger one laid a plastic splint down the length of Eric's nose. He molded the splint to fit the nose's contours, then fixed it in place with strips of adhesive tape cut by the nurse. When they finished, the doctor pulled off his latex gloves. "You can have the gauze out in two or three days. But we'll leave the splint on for a week."

"I'll get a wheelchair," the nurse said.

Alone now, Eric sat up on the table. He felt a head rush and closed his eyes, waiting for it to pass. The soreness in his groin had abated somewhat. His ribs on one side still hurt, but when he took a deep breath and felt no sharp pain, he figured the ribs weren't broken. Small comfort. That sonofabitch Patrick would pay for this. Maybe Tanya wouldn't press charges, but Eric sure as hell would.

Oh, no. Tanya. What if Patrick had gone after her, too?

Eric fumbled in his pants pocket for his cell phone and punched her number. It rolled to voicemail, and he punched the number again.

Finally she answered. "What do you want?"

"Are you okay? Has Patrick been there?"

"No. Why would he?"

Eric blew out a breath of relief and winced at the pain in his ribs. A dull pain, thank God.

"Eric, are you there?"

"Yeah. Just licking my wounds. Patrick beat the hell out of me, and I was afraid he might come after you."

"Good God. Are you okay? You sound strange."

"He broke my nose."

Tanya gasped. "Eric, I'm so sorry. How bad is it?"

The nurse came back with a wheelchair.

"Hang on a minute," Eric told Tanya. He slid off the table and braced himself as another wave of dizziness made him falter. When the nurse took his arm, he rotated into the wheelchair, grateful for her support. In a moment, the dizziness cleared. "Tanya?"

"I'm here."

"Look, you should get out of your apartment. In case. Go someplace he can't find you."

"Like where?"

The nurse wheeled him through the door, out into a hallway

with gurneys lined up along one wall and people in scrubs striding purposefully in both directions. The bright lights stabbed into his eyes.

Squinting, he put the phone back to his ear and tried to recall what Tanya had last said. Oh, yeah. *Like where?* Well, certainly not his place. It would be far too obvious if Patrick didn't find her in her own apartment. "Maybe a hotel. No, cops can find people in hotels. How about a friend?"

"I don't really have any friends here. Except ... well, you, I suppose."

Eric cheered up a little. He was pondering how to respond to that when the hallway ended in a waiting room full of people holding bloody handkerchiefs and towels and whining kids. Huddled masses, if he'd ever seen them.

The wheelchair stopped, and the nurse said from behind him, "Are any of these people waiting for you?"

"Waiting?"

"To take you home."

Eric hadn't thought about getting home. Here he was, in a city of eight million people, and there was no one to pick him up. Unless perhaps ... "Tanya, is there any chance you could come get me at—" He craned his neck to look at the nurse. "Where am I?"

"Twenty-Four Emergency. Ninth Avenue and Thirty-fourth."

He relayed the address, Tanya said she'd come, and the nurse wheeled him up to a cashier.

"Tanya, hang on again. I gotta pay." Eric fished out his wallet and laid his insurance card on the counter.

A plus-sized woman with dreadlocks and a bored expression drew it toward her.

"Okay, where to go," he said into his cell phone. "You know, there's one place. Remember that girl I mentioned? Abby? Maybe you could stay with her for a few days."

"She doesn't even know me."

"But she'd do me a favor." *If she doesn't slam the door in my face.*

"Mister Foster." The lady with dreadlocks slid his card back across the countertop. "Your insurance has been cancelled."

❧

Feeling sorry for Eric but irritated at his request, Abby stood on the sidewalk in front of her apartment building as he and the girl, Tanya, said their good-byes. Poor Eric looked like he'd been trounced by a prizefighter. Uncertain he could climb the four flights to Abby's apartment, he had gotten out of the cab just long enough to thank her and make introductions. Now back in the rear seat, he accepted a twenty-dollar bill from Tanya, swore to repay it, and squeezed her hand. Tanya gazed at him soulfully, straight out of a daytime soap, then closed the door.

When the cab pulled away into evening traffic, Abby glanced at Tanya's factory-outlet overnight bag and said, "Let's get you settled."

"I can't thank you enough."

She had that right. Abby opened the door to her building and started up the stairs. Despite Eric's call and her happy surprise that it was he, rather than she, who first apologized, the idea of housing a stranger held about as much appeal as finding out she had a tumor. Only her need to keep up appearances with Eric had made her acquiesce.

Inside the apartment, Abby said, "I hope the couch is okay. There's a half-bath next to the laundry room."

"The couch is fine." Tanya set her bag on the floor and looked around. "Your place is beautiful. Oh, you have an aquarium. I love fish. But it looks like one of them is sick."

"Sick?" Abby trailed her to the aquarium where Kirin's favorite fish, a blue diamond discus she'd named Rani, swam slowly near the surface, its body listing to one side. Suddenly she remembered dumping a glass of vodka into the aquarium a few nights ago. Damn. Now she'd have to replace the fish before Kirin returned from India. "Never mind. I'll get another."

Tanya frowned.

It's a fucking fish, Abby almost said before deciding it would do her no good to get the girl worked up. "Or maybe there's some medicine I can put in the tank." When Tanya nodded her approval, Abby forced a smile. "Want a drink?"

"A beer would be great. Today's been a killer."

"Sorry, no beer." But that definitely fit the image, now that

Abby could get a good look at her in decent light. Dishwater blonde with a button nose and corn-fed cheeks, one of which was swollen and plastered over in a shade of makeup that didn't suit her. A recent immigrant from one of the red states, no doubt. "How about a vodka and tonic?"

"I've never had vodka before."

Of course, she hadn't. Ripple, sloe gin, possibly Southern Comfort if a guy really wanted to wow her at the local park-and-fuck. What did Eric see in this girl? Probably a damsel in distress. He always did have a soft spot for the less fortunate. But this infantile puppy love between them raised Abby's hackles. Eric was hers—when and how she wanted him. And with SF getting all this attention from the police, he was also her conduit to inside information.

Abby walked to the kitchen and pulled down a bottle of Stolichnaya Elit. The quality would be as lost on Tanya as the subtleties of Montrachet on a wino. But Elit could coldcock the uninitiated, which would bring a quick and welcome end to their banal conversation.

She mixed two stiff drinks, adding a generous squeeze of lemon to Tanya's to conceal the alcoholic punch. "Here you go."

Tanya took a tentative sip, then a larger one. "It's good. Reminds me of the lemonade zingers my uncle used to make when I was a kid. They always put me in a happy mood."

"Glad you like it. Sit down. Make yourself comfortable." Abby chose the leather chair, leaving Tanya the couch, where she could pass out and not have to be moved. "So, how is it you came to know Eric?"

In his call, Eric had mentioned that a rogue cop, Tanya's former lover—didn't *that* fit the picture—had assaulted first her, then him. He'd also mentioned that Tanya was the forensic chemist who gave him the sample of SF. But he'd left out the details, and Abby figured that filling them in would kill time while Tanya got snockered.

After two more vodka-tonics each, Abby had the whole grisly story. In essence, a bad scene supposedly caused by SF. Noble Eric rats out the beef-boy, beef-boy clobbers him, and now Eric vows to press charges, which rests uneasily with Our Lady of the Single

Brain Cell. Abby would have ripped the guy's nuts off and had him thrown in jail before he could pull up his pants. She stood, took the girl's glass, and went to the kitchen to refill it.

As to SF making the man violent, maybe it did. According to Eric, the police had a number of similar cases. But if that happened, it was just bad luck and certainly not her fault. Even prescription medications had adverse side effects on a small percentage of users. That didn't stop the pharmaceutical companies from selling their drugs, and it certainly wouldn't stop her from selling SF.

"I think he likes me," Tanya burbled from the couch.

"Who?"

"Eric."

Abby's hand tightened on the girl's glass. She splashed in an extra shot of Elit and an extra squeeze of lemon juice. "What makes you think so?"

"The way he looks at me sometimes."

With slightly unsteady steps, Abby carried out the drinks. What were these, their fourth? Maybe she should have eaten something beforehand.

Tanya, looking bright-eyed and bushy-tailed, accepted her glass and raised it in a toast. "To a friend in need. I can see why Eric is fond of you."

"Actually," Abby said, plopping heavily into the chair, "Eric and I are lovers."

"What?" Tanya sat bolt upright. "He never told me." Then her face clouded. "Maybe I should leave."

"Nonsense. I like you." *The way I'd like a good case of genital herpes.* "So, tell me about this SF. Eric said you gave him some."

Looking deflated, Tanya settled back on the couch and gulped a swig of her drink. "I really am sorry."

"Forget it." Abby waved her hand dismissively, which sloshed some of her drink down her arm. She should quit now but was determined to match the girl glass for glass. "What about the SF you gave Eric?"

"Not exactly gave. He wormed it out of me. In the lab. The GC-MS showed no difference between it and Balquees, but he thought he might be able to smell a difference." She paused. "You know about Balquees?"

"I tested it for him in Paris."

That stopped her, but just for a moment. "Have you tried SF?"

"Never heard of it until a week ago."

"Well, Eric was right. They *are* different. They start out the same but ..." She touched her cheek. "It was really frightening."

"Poor thing." Couldn't have happened to a nicer girl.

Tanya held up an empty glass. "Another?"

Holy crap. Did that woman have charcoal filters in her stomach? Unwilling to fall behind, Abby knocked back the rest of her drink. But when she tried to stand, the room seemed blurry. "Uh, how 'bout you make 'em?"

"Sure. What proportions?"

"Fifty-fifty." If that didn't knock the bitch on her ass, Abby didn't know what would. "With a squeeze of lemon."

"Coming right up." Tanya took both glasses and headed into the kitchen. "You know, Eric can't get his mind off SF. It's been eating him up inside. But on our way here tonight, he said he had a new idea."

Tanya's voice sounded like it was coming down a long tunnel.

"He said," she continued, "that whoever was making SF had to be getting the oud, the wood, from the same place he got it. A man in Yemen. He's going to email the man and find out who's been buying it."

Abby's vision cleared instantly. Her heart hammered. "Uh ... look," she said, pushing up from the chair. "I hate to be a party pooper, but I'm suddenly very sleepy. I better get to bed."

"Are you sure? It's only nine o'clock."

"I'm sure." On unsteady legs, she made it to the desk, where she scooped up her laptop. "I'll see you in the morning."

"Okay. And thanks again for letting me stay here."

Abby staggered to the bedroom and closed the door. Drunk or not, she had to kill the Yemeni's email account. Right now.

Chapter 31

The pain pills came with a standard printout that warned against alcohol use while taking the medication. Eric figured he was at home and not about to operate heavy equipment or a motor vehicle. So a wee dram couldn't hurt. Still, to be on the safe side, he filled a glass with only club soda and ice. A bad drug reaction was all he needed to cap off this supremely lousy day. On top of losing his job and getting his face smashed, he now had a monstrous credit-card charge for the ER.

But he also had a breakthrough on SF, or at least the idea for one. Carrying the drink to his computer, he did some quick mental math. If Yemen was two hours ahead of France, then it was eight hours ahead of New York. Which meant it was a little after five in the morning there, and the dealer wouldn't see his email for another three or four hours. Eric hated having to wait for a response, but the information would be worth it.

He dialed up his Internet connection and had just started searching through his email contacts when the knock came. About time.

"Fawcett?" he asked through the closed door.

"Who else?"

Eric opened it to one sour-faced detective. "I hate to say this, but I'm glad to see you."

"The feeling isn't mutual." Fawcett studied Eric's face. "Officer Flynn did that?"

"Like I told you," Eric said, referring to the phone call he'd made during the cab ride home from Abby's. "And I'm going to press charges."

Fawcett stepped inside, shut the door behind him, and glanced toward the bedroom. "Where's Tanya?"

"Not here. Are you ready to take my statement?"

"Don't fuck with me. Where is she?"

"Safe." But since Fawcett was no threat to Tanya, Eric added, "With a friend."

"Abigail Han?"

Eric started, then realized it would have taken no time at all to identify the Chinese woman living in Abby's building, especially since she had an Indian girlfriend.

Fawcett pulled out his cell phone.

"What are you doing?" Eric asked.

After punching a number, Fawcett spoke Abby's address and said, "Stakeouts front and back. If you see him, bring him in. In cuffs." He paused. "No. Maintain surveillance at Cole's apartment. And his."

Oh, Christ. Fawcett had no idea where Flynn was. With a cold sense of foreboding, Eric also realized something he should have figured out when Patrick pounded him. "You never jailed that guy after talking to Tanya this morning?"

"Don't tell me my job." Fawcett walked to the computer desk, sniffed Eric's drink, and set the glass back down. Facing away, he said sullenly, "I took his badge and gun and put him on administrative leave, pending an IA investigation."

Obviously that hadn't been enough. But Eric said nothing because, just as obviously, the detective knew it.

Fawcett bent down to scratch Daisy's head. After a moment, he straightened and finally met Eric's eyes again. "I checked out the doctor who worked on you. He's good. And that insurance thing? It's bullshit. The labor laws say you're still covered by your employer—former employer—for thirty days. I'll straighten them out tomorrow."

Eric felt dumbstruck. Fawcett had done all that? Maybe a human heart did beat beneath that smelly overcoat. "Thank you. And I truly mean it."

Fawcett shrugged, then reached into his pocket and pulled out a business card, which he handed to Eric. "Lieutenant Sarah Bridges. Go to the precinct tomorrow, and she'll take your statement about Flynn."

"I thought *you* were going to take it."

"That's IA's responsibility." Then Fawcett leaned forward and poked a finger into Eric's chest. "None of this would have happened without your goddamned SF."

When the 6:10 out of Penn Station woke Eric, his first thought was of the Yemeni dealer. The minute Fawcett left last night, Eric had sent the dealer an email asking who had been purchasing oud of Socotra. The answer should be waiting for him.

As he got to his feet, a rush of pain flooded his face. He sat again, then stood more slowly and made his way to the bathroom. His face in the mirror looked as bad as it felt, two black eyes set within a sunburst of white adhesive tape. He touched the nose splint and winced, then downed two pain pills.

After booting the computer, he pulled up his email. No response from the dealer.

Was it a holiday? He googled "Muslim holidays" and found nothing in early March. Ditto for "Yemen holidays." Frustrated, he re-sent his message from last night, then went into the kitchen to make coffee.

Daisy padded up to him, toenails tapping on the wooden floor.

"Just a second, girl." He waited for the water to almost boil, poured it into his French press, and set the plunger. After taking Daisy downstairs, he returned to find a response on his computer. "Delivery Status—Failed. No account by that name." Had the dealer changed his email address? Eric checked the message he'd sent last night. No failed delivery notice, so it must have gone through.

He sent the message a third time and went in to plunge the coffee and feed Daisy. At the sound of a "ding," he rushed back to find another "Failed" message.

Now what?

The answer came with his first sip of coffee: If anyone could help, it was Abby.

Nursing the worst hangover ever, Abby broke her no-breakfast habit and downed two slices of dry toast with a glass of cranberry juice. Four ibuprofen hadn't yet stemmed her headache, but at least Tanya wasn't here. She'd gone out to find a place that served bacon and eggs. The thought of grease at this hour made Abby want to puke. She poured another glass of juice, called her office to say she'd be late because of a doctor's appointment, then braced herself for Eric's arrival. Dealing with him today was infinitely more important than anything at work.

When he showed up, twenty minutes later, Tanya was with him. Abby gnashed her teeth. Why couldn't that woman just fall under a bus?

"We ran into each other outside," he said in a pathetically nasal tone. The strips of tape radiating from his nose gave the impression that a white starfish had glommed onto his face.

Tanya, looking as robustly healthy as the Queen of the Corn Parade, held out a white paper bag as she stepped inside. "I brought you some glazed doughnuts. Eric said you wouldn't eat them. But you looked pale this morning, and I thought some sugar might help."

Abby took the bag with thumb and forefinger and handed it to Eric. "So, what's this failed email address you called about?"

"The dealer in Yemen where I bought the extract. I'm getting a message this morning that says, 'no account by that name.' But I didn't get that message when I emailed him last night."

"You got a reply from him last night?" she asked cautiously.

"No. But I didn't get the 'no account' message, either."

Evidently she'd killed the account before the dealer could reply. And dead it would remain. "Well, let's give it a try."

For a quarter of an hour, while Eric ate those disgusting doughnuts, Abby ran diagnostic programs that, in fact, had nothing to do with penetrating or unblocking email accounts. Finally she shook her head. "No luck. He must have changed accounts. Or maybe his service provider dropped him."

"If he's still in business," Tanya offered, "we could just google his shop. There should be some contact info."

"Good idea." Having thought of it last night, Abby smiled inwardly and looked at Eric. "The name of the shop?"

"Al Rawd." He spelled it. "It means the garden."

She typed in the name, received 136,000 hits, and narrowed the search by adding terms like "Yemen perfumer" and "Aden perfume shop." All to no avail, of course.

"Search his name," Tanya suggested.

Shit. Abby had forgotten about that. She could choke this bitch.

Eric beamed at the Corn Queen, then said, "His name is Faraj 'Abd al-Bakr" and spelled it.

She could choke Eric, too. She might be able to control him most of the time, but there was no controlling his memory for every single fact he'd ever learned about anything related to perfumery. Wishing she'd taken more ibuprofen to quell her headache, she slowly typed in the dealer's name while scrambling mentally for a course of action if a positive hit came up. To stall, she mistyped the name.

"Not Abdul." Eric spelled it again. "With an apostrophe in front of Abd."

As she made the corrections, nothing came to her. No way out. Biting her lip, Abby hit the return key.

Eight hundred thousand hits.

How the hell could that be? But when she scanned the first page, she saw that all of the hits were partial—matching only Faraj or Al-Bakr or 'Abd al-. None matched the full name. With silent thanks for the luck she'd worked so hard to amass, Abby sat back in her chair. "Sorry."

"Scroll down," Eric said, leaning in closer.

Knowing the full name would have come up within the first ten hits if it were going to come up at all, she scrolled, clicked "Next" at the bottom of the page, and went through six more pages of Google results before he finally straightened and leaned back.

"Put quotes around it," Tanya said. "Then it'll only find the exact name."

Sweetheart, you're out of your depth. Since the name wasn't on the first page, there was almost no chance it would come up with quotes. Happily she added double quotation marks.

Presto amazo. The page came up with "No results found."

Tanya lowered her head and let out a dismayed sigh.

Music to Abby's ears. But unwilling to push her luck, she shut down the computer and stood. "Maybe you'll think of something else. But I have to go. I'm late for work. Tanya, I assume you're moving back to your own place today?"

"Wait a second." Eric held up a hand in a "Stop" gesture and closed his eyes. "The extract came by DHL. There was a return address. It was ... wait a sec. Not a numbered address. 'Between' something. Two hotels. Yes!" He opened his eyes. "'Between the Rock and Grand Hotels.'"

Tanya squinched up her face. "That's an address?"

"For him it is. And it's not the first time I've seen this kind of thing for businesses in the Third World. 'Behind such-and-such supermarket' or 'Next to such-and-such bank' or some other landmark. It makes sense in places that don't have numbered addresses, or sometimes even street names."

"But can you send a letter to an address like that?"

Abby watched all this with a sense of amusement that was making the whole morning worthwhile. She knew exactly where it was going and exactly how it would end.

In response to Tanya's question, Eric shook his head. "Government postal services in countries like Yemen are almost nonexistent. But I could use DHL. Just the way he did."

Faking a concerned frown, Abby said, "But courier services like DHL and FedEx require the recipient's phone number, don't they?"

Eric's shoulders dropped.

Checkmate. She allowed herself a few precious moments to savor the dejection on Eric's and Tanya's faces, then took a not-too-subtle step toward the door. "Look, folks, I really would like to help. But I've got to get to work."

Eric glanced around the living room, as though something in

it might give him a new idea. Apparently coming up blank, he said, "Thanks for trying. Oh, by the way, there are cops watching your apartment, in case Tanya's ex-boyfriend shows up. They'll probably leave when we do."

A shiver swept over Abby. She didn't need any attention from the police. She fired a look at Tanya.

"I'm sorry," Tanya said. "I didn't know about the police." She turned away and collected her overnight bag from the floor by the couch. "But I do appreciate you putting me up for the night."

"Of course!" Eric suddenly beamed like he'd just struck gold. "I know the address. I can just go there."

Abby stared at him in disbelief. "Are you out of your mind?"

"What other choice do I have? We've exhausted everything else."

"Do you read the newspapers? Yemen's a hotbed of terrorism. They blew up the Cole. They kidnap people."

He seemed to mull this. "I'd only be there for a few hours."

Tanya opened her mouth as if to speak, but before she could, Abby grabbed Eric's arm. "This is just a perfume. Let the police handle it."

"No. SF isn't just killing other people. It's killing *me*. I don't even have my job anymore. Not to mention that my one real asset is now broken, and I'm scared shitless it'll never be as good as it used to be. I want revenge." Face red with fury, he ticked off on his fingers, "Visa. Tickets. Hotel reservation. Cash."

"Stop it!" Abby grabbed hold of his hands. "Look, you're overwrought. You need to calm down. How about you take Tanya home, then come back and we'll talk this through. I won't go to work. We'll relax a little."

Tanya's eyes turned venomous.

Fuck you, bitch. Moving to within kissing distance of Eric, so close she could smell the adhesive tape, Abby pressed one of his hands to her thigh. "You need to clear your mind."

"My mind is clear as crystal." He pulled his hands free. "I'm going to Yemen."

⁂

Ten minutes later, Eric and the Corn Queen had left, and Abby was seething. If Eric got to the dealer, he'd learn everything. She'd be destroyed.

She paced her living room, summoning options. There were damn few, none of them good. Not one offered any assurance of success. Except … She blew out a very long breath. Could she actually do that?

Her pacing brought her to the fish tank. The blue diamond discus, Kirin's favorite, lolled at a kilter, its fins barely moving. Worthless creature. Abby scooped it out with the fish net. She started to take it to the bathroom to flush down the toilet, then changed her mind and carried it into the kitchen. She dropped it into the garbage disposal, flipped the switch, and listened with satisfaction as the whirling blades ground the fish into nothingness.

Yes, I can do it.

Chapter 32

"The problem is the visa," Eric said in a cab headed up Broadway. "Even with an expediting service, it could take a week or more."

"Maybe not." Tanya twisted to lean back against her door. "There's an Egyptian girl in the crime lab. Zahra, a tech in Ballistics. She's dating a Yemeni fellow at the consulate. At least she was a few months ago."

Eric sat up straight. "Can you call her?"

By the time the cab reached his apartment, they had an appointment for 1:30 that afternoon at the consulate and the information that "we" would need to present confirmed, round-trip air tickets.

The "we" was a glitch Eric hadn't anticipated. Not wanting to raise a scene in the cab, he waited until they were standing on the sidewalk in front of his building. "*We* aren't going. I'm going."

"That's the thanks I get for helping you? The International Man of Mystery dashes off to solve the crime, while the hayseed from Kansas clutches her hands to her heart as his jet becomes a distant speck in the sky?"

"You're being a little dramatic, don't you think?"

"What I think is that you'd still be at square one without me." She shifted her bag to her other shoulder. "Besides, you know damn well two heads are better than one."

"Look, I don't have a lot of time. I have to get to the bank, then to a travel agent, then to the consulate."

"Actually, you don't have to go to the consulate." She pulled out her cell phone.

"Who are you calling?"

"Zahra. To cancel the appointment."

"You wouldn't."

She started punching numbers. "If you don't need my help, then it's a simple matter to let you make all the arrangements on your own."

He grabbed her hand, squeezing her fingers around the phone.

"Change of heart?" she asked, with a grin that said, *Gotcha*.

At 2:30 that afternoon, Eric shared a sausage and pepperoni pizza with Tanya in a small joint just a block from the Yemeni consulate. With his sense of smell totally blocked, he could barely taste anything except salt. But sitting here while she powered down slice after slice was the least he could do to thank her for getting their visas in record time.

Zahra's boyfriend, a handsome young man wearing a business suit and an impeccably trimmed beard, had issued the visas with an engaging smile and a recommendation that they stay at the Gold Mohur Hotel, on the beach.

"Very romantic," he assured them. "But you must, of course, book separate rooms, as you have different surnames."

No problem. Romance was the last thing on Eric's mind. And they weren't going to stay at the Gold Mohur, anyway.

Tanya picked up the last piece, a narrow wedge that drooped in her hand and from which a chunk of sausage dangled precariously on a thread of cheese. With a deft flick of her wrist, she flipped the hanging sausage back into place. Three mouthfuls later, the slice was gone.

"So, are you happy now?" she asked, wiping a paper napkin across her lips.

"Except for the flights. I wish there was something that didn't take twenty-four hours and two intermediate stops."

"We could have gotten the midnight flight. Only nineteen

hours, if you were willing to fly first class."

"At three times the price?"

"Just saying."

As it was, his own ticket had required a trip to the bank to tap into the inheritance from his grandmother. He wanted to save his credit card for other expenses, and it was already dinged by the ER charges that hadn't yet been re-credited.

Tanya poked around through the pieces of crust he'd discarded, the thick outer rims that lay like severed fingers on their serving plate. She selected a piece with some tomato sauce on it, bit off the end, and dropped the remainder back on the plate. "One thing bothers me. This hotel you want, The Rock. Why do you think the travel agent couldn't get confirmation from them?"

"I'm not sure."

"So, we arrive at five-thirty in the morning. What if we show up and it's out of business?"

"Another hotel, the Grand, is supposed to be two doors down."

"Supposed to be."

"Look. If you're worried, you don't have to come." Once again, he tried to dissuade her with, "Think about it. Muslim country, State Department warning to travelers."

"And …" She looked at her watch. "… less than four hours before we have to catch a cab to the airport."

Abby kissed the visa in her passport. Ten months ago, she'd decided to obtain a business visa for her only trip to Yemen. The visit was, after all, for business—establishing a rapport with the dealer, arranging for a continuous supply of oud, exchanging confidential bank details. The benefit now was that, being a twelve-month visa, it still had two months of validity. If Eric's pig-headedness persisted and he really did go to Yemen, he'd need at least a week to obtain a tourist visa, which would give her plenty of time to get there first. Most likely, he'd regain his senses. Eric was the most rational person she knew. Still, fortune favored the well-prepared and was smiling on her now.

As she replaced her passport in the floor safe, her palate proposed a celebratory drink. She rarely drank during the day, but a glass of cold fire would ready her tongue for a nice dinner at her favorite sushi bar.

In the kitchen, she poured three fingers of vodka, took a sip, and contemplated the kinds of sashimi she'd order. Which suddenly reminded her of Kirin's fish—and the drastic measures she'd steeled herself for when she ground the stupid thing into pulp. Those measures probably wouldn't be necessary now. She glanced at the mouth of the garbage disposal and flicked on the switch. Not the same satisfying sound. She considered dropping in another fish.

Then her cell phone sounded the opening notes of "La Marseillaise," the ring tone she used for Eric. She turned off the disposal and answered.

"I need a favor," Eric said. "Can you take Daisy for a few days? I got a flight to Aden tonight, and I need a place for her to stay."

A black curtain fell over Abby, like the shroud of Death.

"Are you there?" he asked.

"Yeah, I'm here. Just surprised. How did you get a visa so fast?"

"Miracle of miracles. Turns out Tanya has a colleague who has a boyfriend at the consulate."

That filthy bitch. Abby looked again at the garbage disposal and pictured shoving Tanya's hand into it and watching as the machine sucked her down, munching her flesh and bones into a bloody soup.

"We leave tonight at ten-thirty," Eric said, "which means we have to be at the airport by seven-thirty. There's no time to find a kennel."

This was bad. She had to think. "What flight are you on? When do you get there?"

"Delta to Cairo, then Saudi Airlines to Jeddah and Yemeni Airways to Aden. We get in at five-thirty Friday morning."

Five-thirty. Was there any way she could get there sooner?

"So, will you take Daisy?" Eric asked. "Please. I promise I'll make it up to you."

"Yeah, sure." Just get off the fucking phone. I've got calls to make.

"You're a treasure. I'll be there in an hour."

Abby pushed the "End" button and threw her glass at the wall. "Fuck, fuck, FUCK."

No way could she risk being on the same plane as Eric. Typing at light speed she found one set of flights that left JFK later than Eric's but got into Aden two and a half hours earlier. Why hadn't he taken this one? Then she saw it. The originating flight was fully booked, except for first class.

She blessed her luck, the luck she'd stolen bit by bit during all those years in her father's back room. He and his filthy friends, obsessed with luck, never realizing that she pilfered it from them like the coins from her father's cash register, pick pocketing it with the power of her hatred. Abby punched the keys harder. Her power had been confirmed every time one of them moaned about a wager he'd lost, a business heading for shipwreck, a wife who mocked his prowess in bed. So sweet, and her *only* form of revenge until the accumulated luck landed Eric's formula in her lap, paving the road to her greatest revenge of all.

With a few final keystrokes, she printed out a first class ticket and boarding pass. She still had to pack, figure out what to do with the damn dog, and … Shit. She knew there was something else. The dealer.

How could she have forgotten that? It was the whole reason for going. She booted one of her special programs, reactivated the man's email account, and sent him a message saying she had to see him at four o'clock Friday morning—a critical issue that couldn't wait.

Satisfied with that, she cleaned up the mess from her thrown-glass tantrum, using the time on her hands and knees to plot a way of dealing with Eric's lousy dog. She wished she'd fended him off with an excuse, like she had an out-of-town conference to attend. But by the time he buzzed her apartment from the sidewalk—a courtesy, since he knew the code—she had a solution even more gratifying than her disposal of Kirin's fish.

When his knock came, a minute later, she opened the door to see him clutching a bag of dog food, two nested bowls, and the end of Daisy's leash. The animal sat at his side, looking up at her with the sad eyes of the doomed.

You know, don't you. "Come in," Abby said.

Eric stepped inside, but Daisy stayed planted.

"Come on, girl." He tugged her leash. "What's wrong with you? You've been here before."

Daisy whined.

Eric dragged her inside and pushed the door closed with his foot. "I think she knows I'm going away."

"She'll get over it. Put her stuff in the back bathroom."

"She always eats in the kitchen."

"Okay, put it in there."

Eric propped the bag in a corner of the kitchen. "Four cups a day. I sometimes give her a cup at lunch. But she'll be fine on one in the morning and three at night." He filled one of Daisy's bowls from the faucet. "It's really important that she has plenty of water." After placing the bowl on the floor, he added, "She's good at holding it during the day, but she needs a poop-and-pee walk in the morning and at least once at night. When you get home and before you go to bed."

"Got it." Not that it mattered.

"And don't worry about the neighbors. Daisy never barks."

"Never?"

"Hardly ever. She's trained not to."

The seed of a new plan sprouted in Abby's head, a plan even more delicious than her original idea of removing the animal's collar and turning it loose on the streets to get run over or picked up and taken to the pound. "Plenty of water, you say."

"A full bowl every day. Is that a problem?"

"No, no. I just wanted to be sure."

"Dogs need water more than anything else. They can't survive more than two or three days without it."

Oh, this was good.

"Abby, I can't thank you enough. You're the best friend I ever had."

"No problem. Daisy and I will get along fine." The animal under discussion stood at the front door, its nose practically touching the wood.

"She's a great dog. I can't believe how attached I've become."

Be still, my beating heart.

Eric looked at his watch. "I'd better get going."

When he opened the door to leave, the dog tried to leave with him. He had to use his leg to keep her inside until, amid whines of desperation, he finally closed the door.

Still whining, the creature rose on its rear legs and clawed the door with its one front paw. Then it lay down and whimpered.

After waiting five minutes to be sure Eric wouldn't come back with some forgotten instruction, Abby picked up the loop end of the leather leash. "Come on, you're going out on the fire escape."

But it was like pulling a dead weight. The despicable thing braced itself, refusing to budge on its own. Fortunately the oak floors weren't carpeted. After dragging it all the way to the back door, Abby pushed it out onto the iron grillwork. "Welcome to your last resting place."

She gripped Daisy's collar while she unhooked the leash, wrapped it around an upright bar on the landing, passed the hook end through the loop end, and re-hooked the leash to the collar. The beast was now firmly anchored to the fire escape. Minus food and minus water.

Abby stood back to admire the beauty of the moment.

"See you in a few days."

Chapter 33

Friday morning at 3:45, Aden time, Abby got out of her cab at the Rock Hotel. She had no intention of staying here, or any place else that would leave a record of her presence. In fact, she didn't even want to show her face where it wasn't necessary.

To avoid going inside, yet appear normal to the driver, she stood on the sidewalk and feigned searching for her reservation while the cab made a U-turn. When it disappeared around the corner, leaving a cloud of diesel exhaust in the muggy air, she carried her canvas suitcase fifty paces up the street to the dealer's shop.

The shop looked just as she remembered it—a two-story, colonial-era, stone-block building that housed his business at street level and his residence above. In front of her, a pair of arched windows with iron grillwork flanked a similarly arched doorway protected by a wrought-iron gate. The gate stood slightly ajar.

So he *had* received her email.

She set down her suitcase and gathered herself mentally. Now that she was alone, after all those hours in airplanes and airports, her anger rose again. It hadn't been so bad until her plane took off from JFK and she finally had time to settle back with a stiff drink and think about what this old bastard was forcing her to do. Bribery, her only alternative, had been a non-starter; if he was crooked enough to take it, which she doubted, then he'd be crooked enough to turn on her for a larger bribe from someone else. Which left her no choice but to get on a plane, fly nineteen goddamned hours to fucking Yemen—steaming asshole of the universe—and solve the problem in person. By God, he would suffer for this.

She scanned the sidewalk in both directions, then stooped to open her suitcase. It still had its checked-luggage tags, which she ripped off and shoved into a rear pocket of her loose-fitting trousers. Normally, she never checked anything. But this time, the contents required it. She unzipped the suitcase and removed her Swiss Army knife, a white plastic bag with a drawstring, and her stun gun. The stun gun, about the size of a cigarette pack, delivered a hundred thousand volts of electricity. Although she'd tested the batteries before leaving New York, she now tested them again, pushing the button and hearing a satisfying buzz as a blue arc jumped between the two metal electrodes.

She distributed the three articles among the pockets of her trousers. Since the gate was open, she wouldn't need the knife for lock picking. But it might still come in handy.

A light shone in the back room he used as his office. She rapped on the front door and, a few seconds later, saw his silhouette come out of the office and toddle toward her. She'd guessed his age to be somewhere in the seventies and now judged from his gait that the past ten months hadn't been his best. The door opened with a tinkling of the overhead bell.

"Miss Han, I am honored to see you again. Please come in. May I take your bag?"

"No. I'll just set it inside. Thank you for meeting with me so early." She stepped past him into a heady atmosphere of pungent fragrances. They came from row upon row of wooden bins filled with roots, woods, dried blossoms, chunks of resin, gnarly mushrooms, bundles of twigs. Behind the long counter at the back ran several shelves of thick glass bottles filled with liquids the color of amber and gold and that vile liqueur, Chartreuse.

At the sound of the door closing behind her, she put her suitcase down and pasted on a smile. He was a fine-looking man, as old men went. Tall and thin with an elegance about him, an easy grace clad casually in brown slacks and a thin white shirt. In the dim light, his weathered face seemed the very picture of desert nobility and grandfatherly kindness.

She felt her resolve wavering. This was a whole different level, way above grinding up a fish or leaving a dog to die on her fire escape. But unlike those acts, this one was necessary. Steeling herself, she said, "I'm sure we can finish our business quickly."

"But first we will have tea, yes?"

"That would be wonderful. It's been a long flight."

"Please follow me." He led her into his office, a largish room crowded with wooden crates on the floor, shelves of ledger books on the walls, an old desk that held his equally old computer, and a side table with stacks of papers at one end and an electric tea kettle at the other. He switched on the kettle, then slid open the lid of a wooden box about a foot long and five inches square. "Orange pekoe? I just received it from Ceylon. Pardon me, Sri Lanka. It is the first picking, truly one of the world's finest."

"I'd love some."

Get ready. There's no backing down now. She'd be cutting off her supply of oud, but one shipment had arrived in Marseilles a few months ago, and another had been scheduled to go out yesterday. The two would keep her in business for at least a year, more than long enough to set her up for life. And who knew? Maybe his half-witted son would continue the family trade.

But all that rationale did nothing to steady her trembling hands. Her heart pounded so loudly she feared he could hear it. *You have to do this.*

As he bent to scoop a measure of chopped tea leaves from the box, Abby withdrew her stun gun.

"Your latest shipment," he said. "I must apologize. It is—"

She shoved the stun gun into his back and pushed the button.

The dealer flailed like a dancing marionette, but she managed to keep the gun in place until he fell to the floor, still twitching. She yanked out her plastic bag, slipped it over his head, and cinched the drawstring tight.

The bag inflated and deflated, first slowly, then faster. His hands groped for his neck.

Abby zapped him again, holding the button down and feeling a godlike power course through her own body as the dealer convulsed, then finally lay still. The bag had stopped moving, too.

Silence filled the room like a physical presence.

Wiping spittle from her lips with one hand, she reached out with the other and felt for a pulse. Nothing in the neck. She pressed her fingertips to his wrist. She'd done it.

As the adrenalin subsided, a rush of new emotions swept over her, the same emotions an artist must feel upon finishing an exceptionally difficult sculpture. Astonishment, relief, pride. She sank to the floor and sat there, staring at the lifeless form. *I created this.*

To be certain, she felt once more for a pulse. Was he turning cold already, or was it just her imagination? She dropped his hand and wiped her own on her trouser leg. The tea scoop lay a foot or so from his head, surrounded by chopped leaves that would never become tea. Too bad. She could use some.

In fact, she could use a hearty meal right now. Which seemed strange, considering the butterflies in her stomach just a short time ago. But that was before she'd discovered the latent strength within her. Smiling, she got to her feet. It had been so easy. One minute she had a problem, the next minute she didn't. Taking care of business had acquired a whole new meaning. And given her an appetite.

Which unfortunately would have to wait. There was still his computer. Abby switched it on and pulled up the dealer's email program. She checked the Sent, Received, and Saved folders, trashed everything pertaining to her, and deleted the Trash. "Damn." If she hadn't left New York in such a rush, she would have thought to bring a program that would delete the Trash beyond even NSA recovery. But did it really matter? This was the Third World, where computer skills ranked on a par with respect for women.

For her final touch, she opened the email from Eric requesting information on who had been buying oud of Socotra and left it on the screen for the authorities to find.

"Explain that, lover boy."

No sooner had she said it than an even sweeter deterrent to Eric's meddling slinked into her mind. What if the police were to receive an anonymous call, just about the time Eric found the body? The cops wouldn't hurt him—she didn't want that—but they'd surely threaten and yell and scare the bejesus out of him before finally letting him go. That kind of encounter would be the perfect thing to convince him, once and for all, that he should drop the whole question of who was making SF.

Abby glanced at her watch. Eric would be landing in fifteen minutes.

She knelt and removed the plastic bag from the dealer's head. His wrinkled face had already turned pallid. Suddenly it morphed into her father's face. She did a double-take, and the image vanished. But an unexpected thrill lingered in her belly.

Savoring it, she pocketed the plastic bag and checked to be sure she'd left no evidence of herself. *Good to go.* She picked up her suitcase and slipped out of the shop, leaving the door and gate slightly ajar, for Eric. With a lightness in her step, she strode past the Rock Hotel to the main street, where she flagged down a taxi and told the driver, "Airport."

The first leg of her return flight was scheduled to depart in six hours. She'd spend her waiting time in the first-class lounge, drinking a well-earned vodka or two, finding out the phone number of the local police, and calling them to report a suspicious death.

Chapter 34

Eric and Tanya walked out the doors of Aden airport into a sauna. Beggar kids swarmed them, eyes pleading, cupped hands tapping their mouths with studied practice. "Please, Mister. One dollar." Men in long-sleeved shirts and either western trousers or plaid sarongs plowed through the kids shouting, "Taxi?" "I know good hotel, very cheap." "You want nightclub?"

A nightclub in Yemen? Yeah, just what Eric wanted. The sun couldn't have been up more than ten minutes, and already he was sweating. Spotting a line of taxis, he told Tanya, "This way."

Hands groped his arms and tugged at his pockets as a clump of kids moved with them toward the cabs like fish in a feeding frenzy. Not until the driver at the front of the queue yelled in Arabic and shook his fist did the urchins turn back for easier prey.

"You have hotel?" the driver asked, hoisting Tanya's suitcase into the trunk. A portly, white-bearded fellow, he looked about sixty and wore a tan turban with his rumpled gray suit coat and white sarong.

"The Rock." Eric had brought only a shoulder bag and kept it with him. Two fresh shirts, some underwear and toiletries, and a book on Arab perfumes that he'd reread on the seemingly endless flight. He felt grimy, his cheeks as raspy as sandpaper, his clothes sticking to his body. His mouth tasted like something you should flush.

But his sense of smell was super-sharp. After a TSA screener in New York had insisted on running her magnetometer wand over his nose splint, Eric figured a taped-up face could get him delayed, and possibly detained, in Egypt or Saudi or Yemen. So before landing in Cairo, he'd gone into the aircraft lavatory and violated doctor's orders by removing the splint and pulling out yard after yard of gauze from each nostril. The gauze had been pushed up so high into his head that it felt like he was pulling out his brain. And when he finished, his first inhalation stung so badly and felt so cold that tears came to his eyes.

Since then, he'd had to mentally block out most of the smells assaulting him, or risk suffering that disorienting olfactory overload he called "the storm."

But as he sank back next to Tanya in the taxi's plastic-covered rear seat, he dared to test the air. Cigarette smoke from a strong Turkish tobacco. Sweat, not his or Tanya's, laced with coffee and garlic. Newsprint from the paper in the front passenger seat, dirt in the rubber floor mats, varnished wood from the beaded cover draped over the driver's seat.

"What are you doing?" Tanya asked. "You look like you're in a cloud."

"Trying out my nose." Which worked great. The only problem was, with the bones still unhealed and lacking protection, he had to be careful that no one touched it.

The cab driver slid into his seat, slammed his door, then hooked a bungee cord around it and the window post.

"The Rock," he said and lurched off.

Eric rolled down his window. The divided highway, flanked here and there by trees and dust-covered shrubs, cut a straight swath across the jetty of land to the city itself. Beyond the highway, jagged peaks jutted into the morning sky like broken teeth. He'd read that the Aden peninsula was dominantly volcanic, and ahead of them loomed a genuine volcanic cone, the core around which the city had evolved as a trading port since the first century B.C.

"Where you are from?" the driver asked, his eyes looking at Eric in the rearview mirror.

"New York."

"I love New York. Kojak. You know Kojak?"

Good Lord. That took Eric back. The series had ended before he was born, but he'd seen reruns in his youth, Telly Savalas as the bald, wisecracking detective.

"Kojak is best," the driver said. "You have meet him?"

"Not really. I think he died."

"No!" The driver turned to face Eric. "I do not believe. I see him in television, before only two nights."

"Watch where you're going," Eric said as Tanya gripped his wrist.

After a glance forward, the driver turned back to Eric. "You do not tell my son. He is police leftenant. He loves Kojak. He makes his head … with no hair. And he eats, how you say, pops?"

"Lollipops."

"Look out!" Tanya shouted, her nails digging into Eric's arm.

The driver made a mid-course correction that brought him back into his own lane. "Yes, lollipops. You must not tell him Kojak is dead."

"I promise. Just watch the road."

"Not to worry. I am best driver in Yemen." He opened the glove compartment, rummaged around, and came out with a business card, which he handed back over his shoulder. "I take you for sightseeing, yes?"

His card read, "Hassan Salah, Expert Taxi Driver and Tour Guide," followed by a phone number. "Thanks," Eric said, "but we're not going sightseeing."

"You must. There are many things to see. Very interesting. Cisterns, Old City. Many things."

"Cisterns?"

"Is not English? Other name is Tanks. You know, for catch water. Very old. Make by Queen of Sheba."

To mollify him, Eric said, "We'll see."

"Yes, you will see."

Entering the city proper, Hassan Salah plunged into early morning traffic, weaving around delivery trucks, pick-ups loaded with men in the back, mini-van buses, and vintage Land Rovers. All the pedestrians Eric saw were men, and among them it seemed the sarong was more popular than trousers. Although there was little trash on the streets, more or less everything looked covered in dust.

Eric was just beginning to get comfortable with Mr. Salah's driving when the man abruptly swerved across oncoming traffic. Tanya's nails gouged so deeply that Eric was sure she'd drawn blood.

Forty feet up a diagonal street, Salah stopped in front of a multi-story building with prominent balconies wrapping around the curved front. "Rock Hotel."

From street level it looked fine, a lot better than many of the buildings they'd passed. After paying Salah and promising he'd call, Eric tugged on the hotel's front doors. He pushed, then tugged again. "They're locked."

Tanya glanced skyward. "Did I tell you this might happen?"

"Problem?" Salah, who'd turned the cab around, climbed out and came up to them. He tried the doors himself, then rapped on the glass, shouting in Arabic.

From somewhere inside, a bleary-eyed man shambled toward the doors and admitted them.

"You see?" Salah said proudly. "I am expert. What time we go for sightseeing?"

Taking a shine to the fellow, Eric told him, "This afternoon maybe. I'll call you."

With a big smile, Salah waved and left.

The hotel clerk, who stank of fish and cardamom and cotton unlaundered for at least a month, made his way to a spot behind the check-in counter. "Reservation?"

After giving him their names, Eric watched the man's hand pass tentatively over the computer keyboard as though feeling for heat above an electric stovetop. The computer's screen was dark.

Apparently outwitted, the fellow bent down behind the counter, burped, and came up with a pair of printed forms. "Passports."

"No way I'm giving this guy my passport," Tanya muttered.

Eric wasn't crazy about the idea, either. "When does the manager come?"

A blank stare.

"Manager," Eric repeated, turning his watch toward the man. "What time?"

"Eight o'clock."

"Okay, we give passports at eight o'clock. But we need our room keys now." Eric held up his apartment key, then pointed to the keys hanging on a rack of old-fashioned wooden mailboxes on the wall behind the counter. "Keys now."

Scratching his stubbly cheek, the fellow seemed to ponder this irregular request.

To help him make up his mind, Eric laid a twenty-dollar bill on the countertop.

The man stared at it for barely a second before his hand flew out like a striking cobra, and the bill disappeared. Turning to the mailboxes and selected a key.

"Two keys," Tanya told him.

Eric walked her to the elevator, pushed the button, and heard the clerk call out, "Not work."

"Lovely place." Tanya rolled her suitcase to the foot of the stone stairs. "So what's the plan?"

"Meet you back here in ten minutes, and we'll go see the dealer."

"It's only six forty-five."

"Morning prayers were more than an hour ago. He'll be up."

"I could use a shower first."

So could Eric, but, "I want to catch him before he gets busy."

The shop called Al Rawd, The Garden, gave Eric a good feeling. Made of hand-cut stone with fancy grillwork decorating its arched windows, it spoke of strength and respectability. "Look," he said, pointing to the wrought-iron gate across the doorway. "It's open. I told you he was up."

Eric swung the gate outward, opened the door, and stepped inside to the tinkling sound of an old-fashioned overhead bell. A second later, he felt like he'd entered Ali Baba's cave, except the treasure was entirely olfactory. Superb aromas filled the air, hundreds of them. Aromas of frankincense and myrrh, cassia and calamus, balsam of Mecca, oil of ben, ladanon, costus, storax, ambergris, even hyraceum from the petrified excrement of the Cape hyrax, which he'd only smelled once before. Better still, there

were things he could not identify, things that filled him with the
thrill of discovery.

Sensing the warning vertigo of the storm, Eric quickly buried
his nose in the crook of his elbow.

"My sentiments exactly," Tanya said behind him. "This place
stinks."

It smelled heavenly. But it was almost too much. If his nose
weren't so sensitive from having the packing removed a few hours
ago, he could surely have handled this much better. Resolved:
they'd stay another day in Aden. Tanya could hole up in her room
if she wanted, but he would spend the day right here, going
through every one of these fascinating bins.

She came to stand beside him. "So where is he?"

Eric looked around. Behind a counter at the back of the shop,
there was a room with the light on. The dealer must not have heard
the tinkling bell. Eric called out, "Mr. Faraj?"

"Maybe he's hard of hearing," Tanya offered.

Eric walked to the back and poked his head in through the
door. *Holy Christ.* An old man lay on the floor, not moving. Like a
shot, Eric was at his side. He felt the man's wrist. No pulse, and
the skin was cool. "Oh, no." Gently he raised one of the eyelids.
The pupil stared past him, at the ceiling.

Tanya, who'd materialized at his side, pressed her fingers to
the carotid artery, then raised the lid again and touched the eyeball.

Eric started chest compressions, one hand over the other on
the man's sternum. Pump, pump, pump, pump. He pinched the
nose, pulled the chin down, and blew two breaths into the man's
mouth.

"Eric, it's too late."

"Maybe not." He positioned his hands to resume pumping.

"There's no corneal reflex. No blink when I touch the eyeball.
He's dead."

Eric stared at her a moment, not wanting to believe her but
knowing she was right. Reluctantly he sat back on the floor. It was
bad enough the poor fellow had passed away. But along with his
passing had gone any hope of finding out who was buying the oud.

"We have to call the police," Tanya said. "This guy was
murdered."

"Murdered? That's crazy. He probably had a heart attack."

"Look at the ligature marks." She pointed to a red line around the man's neck.

It didn't seem possible. Who would do such a thing? Why?

"And not very long ago." she added.

"How can you know that? You're a chemist."

"You don't specialize in forensic chemistry without taking courses in general forensics." She lifted the man's arm, flexed it twice at the elbow, and laid it back down. "No rigor mortis. That means less than three hours."

"Oh, man." The killer had been here just before them. Eric got to his feet, trying to make sense of the bad news that kept getting worse. For a moment, he was sidetracked by a smell that seemed out of place, like it shouldn't be here. Not the urine staining the dealer's trousers or the tea on the floor. Something creamier. But this was no time to veer off on tangents.

Okay, the dealer was dead—fact one. Heartless though it might seem, there was nothing they could do for him now. Fact two: he'd been killed only a few hours ago. Fact three: they were first on the scene, a murder scene in a Third World country. Conclusion: they were potentially in very deep shit if they didn't get out of here fast.

"Are you daydreaming? We have to call the police." Tanya stood and moved to the dealer's desk, where she reached for the telephone.

"Don't touch that!"

She turned and stared at him. "What's wrong with you? We have a responsib—"

"Tanya, shut up and think about our situation, will you? We're foreigners. Just arrived. And here we are with a man who's just been killed. Who do you think the cops will arrest?"

"We had nothing to do with this." Then a shadow of horror darkened her face. "Do you really think …"

"I think we should get out of here."

"Oh, Jesus."

"Just wait a second." He looked around, trying to remember if either of them had touched anything that might preserve fingerprints. "Can they lift prints from a body, from the skin?"

"A good lab can. Here? I doubt it."

Okay, anything else? Not the desk. Or the phone. None of these crates. "What the hell?" The crate next to the table with the dealer's tea kettle had a shipping label made out to "Encens du Globe." Bending closer, he read an address in Marseilles.

"I found it!"

"Found what?" she asked.

He jabbed his finger at the label "Encens du Globe. EDG. EDG is the registered owner of the website that sells SF."

"Who cares? We have to leave."

"Look for a crowbar."

"Are you out of your mind?"

"It'll just take a minute." If there was one thing he could salvage out of this tragedy—the one thing he'd actually come for—he had to have it. Not just the shipping address, but also proof that the crate contained oud of Socotra. "Look, just sit there at his desk while I open this. Then we'll go. I promise."

"Customers could start arriving any minute." She looked at her watch. "It's a quarter to eight."

Moving fast, Eric searched the office for anything he could use to pry open the crate. Beneath some shelving on one wall, he found a cloth satchel containing hammer, nails, pliers, and screwdrivers. He grabbed the largest screwdriver.

"Uh-oh," Tanya said.

He turned to see her hand on the dealer's computer mouse. "Dammit, you're leaving prints."

"I'll wipe them in a minute. But first, you better look at this."

He stepped around the dealer's body, giving only half a thought to the morbid fact that it had somehow become just a fixture of the office. Over Tanya's shoulder, he saw an email displayed on the screen. He read less than a line before the bottom fell out of his gut. "Is someone trying to frame me?"

"I don't know. But I do know one thing." Tanya dragged the email to Trash and deleted it. "It's better gone than sitting there staring the police in the face."

Eric braced himself against the desk. This was surreal. "I'm at a dead end in New York. There's only one guy who can help me. I email him. No answer. I come here to see him, and he's just been killed. And my email is on his computer screen." He looked at Tanya. "Am I being paranoid, or …?"

"Keep going." Her expression had changed from anxiety to the intense concentration of a predator that smelled blood. "Don't stop now."

"If I keep going, there's only one conclusion I can come to." A lump swelled in his throat. He tried to swallow but couldn't.

"You're thinking Abby, aren't you?"

"It's not possible." Abby was the best friend he had.

"Who else knew we were coming here?"

"It could have been anyone," he said, not really believing it. "Maybe the bad guys were bugging my apartment. Or hers. Or listening in on my cell phone."

"And they somehow got here before us?"

His mind raced. "Maybe they were already here. Or in Switzerland, where the website's located. Hell, maybe it's got nothing to do with SF. Some guy comes strolling down the street, sees the door open, figures he can steal something before any customers arrive—"

"Eric! Look around you. Does it look like anything's been stolen?" She grabbed his hand. "And what about the email?"

"Maybe it was up there because it was the last email he received."

"Stop being blind. It has to be Abby."

He jerked his hand away. "Abby's in New York."

"How can you be sure?"

"I'll call her. It's what?" He checked his watch and subtracted eight hours. "Midnight."

"Her cell phone will ring anywhere."

"Dammit! What do you have against her?"

"Nothing. She took me in when I needed a place to stay. But I honestly can't think of anyone else."

"Well, think harder. You said the dealer died less than three hours ago. If it was Abby, she'd have to be *here*. In this city as we speak." Then he remembered. "She has a land line. If she's here, she can't answer it."

Tanya stood from the dealer's chair. "So call it. But do it in the hotel. We need to get out of this place."

Eric barely registered her warning as he dredged up the number from the recesses of his memory. He'd never called it before. But like the old rotary phone in his apartment, hers had the number printed in the center of the dial. He punched it into his cell phone.

"Eric, I'm leaving."

After a series of clicks and pauses, it rang. Two, three, four times. Five, six, seven, eight. Eric closed his eyes in dismay.

"Hullo," Abby's groggy voice answered.

"Abby, it's Eric. Where are you?"

"Where do you think I am? In the living room. With a stubbed toe from just kicking the foot of my damn sofa. Why are you calling this number?"

He looked at Tanya, who'd been heading out the office door but had stopped. With the joy of the vindicated, he mouthed, "She's home."

"Is something wrong?" Abby asked.

Tanya came back and whispered in his ear, "Make her prove it."

How could he do that?

A long exhalation came over the line, then, "Eric, it's midnight. I was asleep. I'm exhausted. Daisy's been pining for you ever since you left. She hardly eats any of her food. I've been worried sick. And now you get me out of bed for no reason?" A pause. "Are you drunk?"

"I'm not drunk. Put her on." That would be proof.

"You want to talk to your dog?"

Okay, that did sound kind of dumb. "Where is she?"

"In my bedroom. Asleep under the wind— Oh, shit."

"What?"

After a few seconds of silence, she came back with, "Kirin's fish is dead. Her favorite. The Blue ... whatever. What do you do with a dead fish? Flush it down the toilet?"

"I guess so."

"And now I've got to go get a new one before she comes back. God, my toe hurts. Eric, if you ever call this number again in the middle of the night ..."

Vintage pissed-off Abby. Hugely relieved, he told her, "The

reason I called is I'm in the dealer's shop in Yemen, and someone just killed him."

"What?" she exclaimed. "That's impossible. What are you going to do?"

"Get out of here fast and catch the first plane to France. You'll never guess what we found."

Tanya yanked his arm and shook her head vehemently.

"Just a second, Abby." He pressed the cell phone to his chest and asked Tanya, "What?"

"Don't say anymore."

"I have to tell her."

"Not yet."

Perplexed but thinking Tanya must have a reason, he chose a compromise and put the phone to his ear again. "I think we're close to nailing the person who's making SF. But I'll tell you more later. We've got to go."

He'd just flipped his cell phone shut when a thunder of boot thumps came charging through the shop. Eric whipped around as four men in olive-drab uniforms and dark blue berets burst into the office. The two in front drew pistols.

With a shriek, Tanya scuttled behind Eric.

The men started shouting like a SWAT team on attack, waving their pistols, motioning Eric and Tanya to get down on the floor. When Eric didn't move, one of the men hauled back with his gun as though about to strike him. But another stopped him. As the first man lowered his hand, the one who'd intervened, a rat-faced fellow thin as Death, aimed his pistol at Eric. "On your knees. Or I shoot."

"I told you this would happen, Eric. I told you." Tanya's voice quavered close behind his ear. "Why couldn't you call from the hotel?"

"Don't worry. We just have to explain." Brave words that he wasn't sure he believed. But he *was* sure they needed to buy time. To the man aiming the pistol, he said, "We had nothing to do with this. We only—"

"Knees!"

Jesus, would he really pull the trigger? Reason said no, but the man's hooded eyes said *you better believe it*. Trembling, Eric took

Tanya's hand and drew her down with him into a kneeling position.

"Pray to God," the man said and pressed the barrel of his pistol squarely in the center of Eric's forehead.

Chapter 35

Abby wanted to punch someone. Had the cops ignored her call? Were they too stupid to understand simple English? They should have been at the dealer's shop by now. And what had Eric found that made him think he was close to identifying the person behind SF? She lifted her glass of vodka, then set it down and pushed it away. She needed to think clearly.

Butt-sore from sitting so long in the same leather armchair, she stood and looked around. The first-class lounge had been empty when she got here. Since then, several other passengers had arrived. Two men in dark business suits, five others in white Arab garb. There was only one woman, a pretty thing in black robes, sipping orange juice next to a fat guy who seemed to be speaking to her while looking straight ahead, as though she was expected to listen regardless of whether he gave her the courtesy of eye contact. That was a guy worth punching.

Disgusted, Abby walked to the bank of windows and gazed out at a jet being fueled. Eric's call had shocked her. Not only was he supposed to be under arrest, but she hadn't been aware that he even knew that number. Fortunately, she'd rigged the landline several months ago to roll over to her cell phone. And apparently her charade had worked. That was the good news, the only good news.

The bad news was that whatever Eric had found was taking him to France. That could mean Diego and Marie-Claire, or it could mean Durand. The first two would draw him a blank. But Durand was different. If Eric talked to Durand or, worse, went to the man's villa, he'd quickly discover she'd been lying to him. Durand wasn't destitute. His pool was not a pea soup of algae. His Picassos and Miros still hung on the walls. If Eric went there, she'd be fucked.

She cursed herself that it was *she* who had constantly steered him toward Durand. She'd never thought Eric, in his financial condition, would actually fly to France to confront the old fart. All she'd wanted to do at first was deflect suspicion from herself. Later, when it became clear Eric wasn't going to drop this thing, Durand still seemed like the best scapegoat. If Eric could convince that detective guy, then maybe Interpol or the Sûreté would get involved. Visions of Durand being humiliated by a police inquiry had been too succulent to resist.

But what could Eric have found in the shop that would actually point him to Durand? She stared out the window, seeing not the aircraft but the dealer's office. Concentrating, she scanned every item—the desk, the computer, the papers. Was there something in the papers? Was it possible Durand had gotten interested in Balquees and corresponded with the dealer about purchasing some oud?

Dammit, Eric shouldn't have had time to look through those papers. The cops should have shown up first. Calm down, she told herself. What's done is done. You're still in control, still ahead of the game. Steeling herself to think like a chess player, she began planning her moves. Subtlety and deceit were critical. But most important was anticipation. If this, then that.

At last, she turned from the window. With a smile, she walked back to the lounge's service bar and rewarded herself with a fresh vodka. In the end, it all hinged on one opening move. Regardless of what Eric had found, if he was going to Durand, she had to get there first.

❧

With its siren hee-hawing, the police Land Rover careened through the streets, rocking Eric and Tanya back and forth on a steel bench that ran down one side in the rear. Plastic lock-bands bound their wrists behind their backs. Eric's dug into him so tightly his hands were numb.

On the facing bench, separated from them only by Eric's and Tanya's luggage, sat two cops armed with pistols. The younger one had a close-cropped beard and looked uneasy, casting only furtive glances at Tanya. Eric suspected he was devout, the type of Muslim man who felt uncomfortable around Western women and would keep his distance from her. But the older guy, a bruiser with a black front tooth, fondled Tanya's leather purse in his lap and leered at her like a crocodile appraising a tethered lamb.

"I'm scared," she mouthed.

Eric knew. The pungent smell of her fear filled the cabin almost as strongly as the stench of lust rising from the bruiser. Eric was scared, too. But in an effort to appear strong, he pressed his shoulder reassuringly against hers.

"All we have to do," he said, "is answer their questions."

"I just don't want them to … touch me."

Eric cringed inside, knowing full well he would be powerless to protect her. "That's not going to happen."

The big cop grinned, confidence oozing from him like oil from his pores. He lowered his eyes to Tanya's breasts and slowly squeezed her purse.

Suddenly the Land Rover swerved and its siren shut off. Eric peered out the window as they slowed at a gateway manned by a guard, then entered a walled parking lot and stopped by a metal door in a stone-block building.

The rat-faced cop who'd held his pistol to Eric's forehead opened the rear of the vehicle. "Out."

"We're innocent," Eric told him for the umpteenth time. "I demand to call the American embassy."

Ratface grabbed Eric's arm, yanked him sideways, and tumbled him to the bare dirt.

Tucking his head, Eric managed to protect his broken nose, but the impact knocked the wind out of him. As he struggled to his feet, he saw the bruiser kick their luggage onto the ground, then climb out of the Land Rover and take Tanya's elbow. But the moment she stepped down, the guy reached from behind and groped her breasts.

Tanya spun around. "Keep your filthy hands off me."

The young cop rolled his lips in, apparently repulsed by Tanya's mistreatment but too low in the pecking order to voice a protest.

After a brief smirk, Ratface barked a command and the bruiser stepped back.

Eric strained at his wristlocks. He wanted to kill these bastards. But he couldn't even feel his hands.

"Come," Ratface growled.

Eric waited for Tanya to pass, then stepped in behind her so the bruiser couldn't grab her again. They crunched across the parched ground, waited for Ratface to open the steel door, and followed him inside.

The door slammed with a heavy clank. At the sound of it, the last vestiges of Eric's hope drained out of him. They had disappeared from the outside world. No one knew they were here. No help was coming.

Ratface stopped at a desk manned by another cop. The two of them conversed, the seated one writing in a hardbound ledger before pushing a button that buzzed open a second metal door.

As Ratface pulled it open, a scream split the air. Then a dull *whack* and another scream.

"We're not going in there," Eric shouted.

A blow to the kidney dropped him to his knees. Pain speared up his spine, a shockwave that racked his whole body. His vision went black, then dull red. He sucked for air.

Tanya's voice came through the fog. "Eric. Eric!"

Rough hands hoisted him to his feet. Eric staggered. The agony brought tears to his eyes. But through his tears he could at least see again. The bruiser gripped Eric's arm and drove him forward, marching him behind Tanya who kept looking back desperately. The guy's breath stank of rot, like putrefied apples. His grinning face, too close to Eric's, seemed to say, *We're going to enjoy you two.*

They descended stone steps into a basement where the screams and whacks grew steadily louder. A long corridor stretched ahead of them, lined on both sides with more steel doors, some open, some closed. At a closed one, Ratface stopped and pointed through a barred window.

Tanya turned her head away, but Eric couldn't help looking. A naked man hung upside down, saliva dripping from his mouth, his legs splayed, his genitals swollen and purple, bound with wire. As Eric watched, a man in a blood-spattered lab coat slammed down on the victim's crotch with a length of hose. No response. The man pressed a stethoscope to his victim's chest, then threw a bucket of water in the poor guy's face.

"We're innocent," Eric yelled.

The sadist in the lab coat turned toward the door, his eyes drilling into Eric's. The eyes were dead, the same color as cold grease.

"The doctor," Ratface said with a mirthless smile. "You may meet him." Then he led the way to yet another steel door at the end of the corridor. When he opened it and switched on the lights, about a thousand cockroaches skittered across the floor, disappearing into cracks in the concrete walls.

The room reeked of urine and stale cigarette smoke. Straight ahead stood a long metal table, to the right a desk and chair. On the wall behind the chair hung a photograph of a man, presumably Yemen's president, looking smugly self-confident in a tailored blue suit.

Ratface enthroned himself at the desk, slapped down Eric's and Tanya's passports, and laid his pistol across them. "Why did you kill that man?"

"We didn't kill him. I already told you, he was dead when we got there."

A zip and a snap made Eric turn his head. The other two cops stood at the table, laying open his shoulder bag and Tanya's suitcase. Like jackals ripping out intestines, they tore through the clothing, tossed it aside, and dived in for more. The bruiser held up a pair of black lace panties, stretching them like an accordion.

"Where is the murder weapon?" Ratface shouted at Eric.

"I don't know." Aching everywhere, Eric watched the young cop riffle through the pages of his book on Arab perfumes, then throw it on the floor and start emptying pill bottles. The bruiser squeezed out Tanya's toothpaste in long glops that fell back into her bag. When he finished with that, he took a knife from his pocket and sliced through the suitcase's lining.

"Murder weapon! I ask you one time more. Then I give you to the doctor."

"I went to ask questions," Eric said. "It was my idea. Tanya had nothing to do with it. Let her go, and I'll tell you everything you want to know."

"Eric, stop it. I'm not leaving here without you."

"I see now." A cruel grin twisted Ratface's mouth. "You hide the weapon on *her.* So you want her to leave." His gaze switched to Tanya. "I think we find it under your clothes."

"She doesn't have any weapons. *I* don't have any weapons. We didn't do it. Can't you get that through your thick skull?"

Ratface sprang to his feet, knocking over the metal chair. "Confess!"

Eric shut his eyes. What was he going to do? Confess and face execution, or let Tanya be strip-searched and God only knew what else?

"Yusuf," Ratface barked.

The bruiser dropped Tanya's tattered suitcase and came forward.

After a few words that made Yusuf beam like a slobbering idiot, Ratface turned to Eric. "He will help her undress."

"No!" Tanya scrambled into a corner and huddled down with her back to the wall.

Whipping around to Yusuf, Eric snarled, "If you touch her—"

Yusuf punched him in the gut.

Eric crumpled to his knees, heaving vomit.

"Confess," Ratface repeated.

Slowly Eric raised his head, seeing first Yusuf's scruffy boots, then his olive-drab trousers patched at one knee, then the metal desk with Ratface standing behind it and the photo of the president. Eric spat out the remnants of vomit in his mouth.

With a satisfied smirk, Yusuf cracked his knuckles and headed toward Tanya.

"I'm on my period," she blurted.

Brilliant. A menstruating woman was unclean, untouchable.

When Ratface looked at her questioningly, she pointed to her lap. "I'm bleeding. Down there."

Ratface blanched, then growled something. Yusuf stopped in his tracks. The young cop looked at his own hands and wiped them vigorously on his trousers.

Eric knew she was lying, but these guys didn't. *Thank God.* Maybe now—

A knock sounded at the door.

It opened to reveal two women in black Arab garb that covered them head-to-toe except for their faces. Both had heavy eyebrows. One wore black-rimmed eyeglasses.

Ratface uttered a word that sounded like an expletive.

The two women walked to Tanya, where the one in glasses held out a hand. "Come with us."

"Why?"

"You prefer to be questioned by men?"

Tanya darted her eyes to Eric.

"Go with them," he said. "It's got to be better than this."

"But what about you?"

Suddenly Ratface snatched up their passports. "Cole and Foster. You are not married?"

"No, we're not married," Tanya said as though offended.

"So you are a whore! The penalty for that is stoning."

"I am not a whore."

"Yet you fornicate with Mister Foster."

"I don't fornicate with anyone."

"So, you are a virgin?" His rodent eyes beamed. "I might believe that, if you stay here. But if you go with these women, I promise when you return I will bring the doctor. He will see if you are a virgin."

Chapter 36

Still on his knees, Eric stared at the door, the last place he'd seen Tanya as the two women ushered her out. There were stains on the door, dried remains of what looked like blood and something yellowish. If the "doctor" ever got to her …

Eric looked away. What now?

Ratface had re-seated himself behind the desk. Yusuf and the younger cop sat on the edge of the long metal table. All three of them smoked cigarettes, vile things that stank like a mixture of bat shit and seaweed. The contents of Eric's and Tanya's luggage lay strewn on the floor.

Yusuf puffed up his cigarette until the ash glowed red hot. Then he came over to Eric, his eyes saying, *I'm going to burn you in places you never knew you had.*

"Confess," Ratface hissed.

"How many times do I have to tell you? I didn't do it. *We* didn't do it. We flew in this morning. You can see that in our passports. We took a cab from the airport to the hotel. Wait a minute. I have the driver's card right here." Eric fished with bound hands in his rear pockets, but couldn't find the card. "It must be in a front pocket. Untie me and I'll find it. We got to the dealer's shop a little after seven, and he'd already been dead for at least three hours. The driver can tell you. His card's—"

"Who says he is dead three hours?" Ratface's eyes narrowed to slits.

"Tanya. She's a—" Suddenly it struck him. "Tanya Cole is a police officer. She and I both work for the New York Police Department."

"Lies."

"I can prove it," he said, praying that was true. At the crime lab, Tanya had taken a photo-ID card from her purse, used it to open the doors, and later had worn it on a lanyard around her neck. He could picture the card now, just as clearly as he could see the exact same purse lying on the table. "Check her purse."

For the first time, Ratface displayed a hint of uncertainty. He said something in Arabic, and the younger cop shook Tanya's purse upside down.

"Empty," Ratface said.

"Look on the floor. A plastic card with a cord running through it and her picture."

Frowning, Ratface got up from the desk and kicked a booted foot through the debris on the floor. Then he paused, glanced at Eric, and picked up the ID badge.

"That's it!" The blessed card with NYPD emblazoned across the top in big black letters. Hope pounded in Eric's chest. "New York Police Department."

Ratface examined the card, front and back, rubbing it between his fingers as if feeling for evidence of forgery. For a moment, he seemed undecided. Then he stomped out of the room.

Please, God, let this be our key to freedom.

The two remaining cops looked bewildered. The younger one asked something. Yusuf shrugged, flicked his cigarette across the room, and sidled over to the table where he picked up Tanya's purse and buried his face in it the way a hyperventilating person would do with a paper bag.

Eric knew precisely what smells the guy was inhaling, the leathery, powdery, lead-pencil scents common to most women's handbags, mixed with the vetiver-Diorella combination that was characteristically Tanya. That this asshole was sucking them in felt like a violation—an invasion of her most private moments, of intimate things only Eric knew about her.

"Leave her stuff alone."

Turning toward Eric, Yusuf fondled the soft leather. He

rubbed it to his cheek, ran it down the front of his uniform, and pressed it against his crotch.

Pig. Eric was trying to find some consolation in the fact that the creep was getting off on her purse, instead of doing his worst to her, when the door opened and he turned to see a bald, stocky man in a tan suit.

"Mister Foster." The man entered, followed by Ratface and enveloped in a cloud of lavender scent so strong he must have bathed in the stuff. "You are a police officer?"

Eric got up off the floor. "I'm a consultant with the New York Police Department."

"What kind of consultant?"

"I identify scents at crime scenes."

"Scents?"

"Significant odors." In a flash of clarity, Eric pointed his chin at Yusuf, recalling the stink of the guy's breath. "Like, for instance, *that* asshole has both diabetes and stomach cancer." The telltale odors, originally jumbled in Eric's mind as putrefying apples, had resolved into smells that were almost diagnostic of the two diseases, sweet apple for the former, fermentation for the latter. "I can smell it."

With a skeptical squint, the bald man turned to Yusuf and asked something in a stern tone.

Yusuf's mouth fell open. He backed a pace, stammering out words that sounded like denial. But soon his protest petered out, replaced by an I'll-kill-you glare at Eric.

The bald guy glowered before shifting his gaze back to Eric. Holding up Tanya's ID card he said, "And this woman?"

"She's a forensic chemist in the NYPD crime lab. One of the best."

"We shall see." Pensively, the man pulled a lollipop from his breast pocket, unwrapped it, and stuck it in his mouth.

Whoa. Bald head, lollipop. Eric's hopes skyrocketed. "I know your father. He drove us from the airport to the hotel. He can tell you we didn't kill the dealer."

The man scowled. "You think my father is a taxi driver?"

"He told us about you. You love Kojak."

"Eric!" Tanya stood in the doorway, flanked by the two

women who'd taken her away. Her blouse was misbuttoned, her hands still behind her. "They don't believe me."

"Look who's here. It's Kojak."

"What? Oh, my God, you're right. Mister ... What's his real name?"

Eric's mind shot back to the driver's business card. "Salah."

"Mister Salah, you can help us, can't you?"

Kojak said something to Ratface, then told Tanya and Eric, "You will go with this man."

In Kojak's office, hung with photographs and certificates, Eric and Tanya sat facing him across a wooden desk, their fingertips blackened with the stains of printing ink. At least their lock-bands had been removed. Ratface, who'd not only supervised their booking but had also given them wet towels to clean themselves up, stood behind them now, close enough to strike. The office stank of lavender, and a rotating table fan beside the closed window only made it worse. Eric, unable to find a position that eased his back pain, squirmed on his wooden chair as he recounted every detail of their few hours in Yemen. He ended with, "And that's when you walked into the room."

Kojak sat steeple-fingered. He'd listened wordlessly while sucking on the lollipop, its white stick switching every few minutes from one side to the other. One of the photographs on his wall showed Telly Savalas in a gray herringbone suit coat and tinted glasses with a bulge in his cheek and a similar white stick protruding from his mouth. The likeness wasn't perfect, but it was close.

"The beatings you mention did not happen," he said at last. "We treat our prisoners humanely."

"Didn't happen?"

"I see no evidence."

Suddenly Eric realized that Yusuf's punches to the kidney and stomach were designed not to leave marks or draw blood. "You may not be able to see it, but I hurt like—"

"Silence! Do not speak, unless and until I say so." Kojak

removed the stick from his mouth, the candy part now mostly gone. "Why," he asked Tanya, "do you think the victim was dead for three hours?"

"Three hours or less. No rigor mortis, and the body was still slightly warm."

A sinking feeling filled Eric's gut. He'd remembered it wrong. He'd told the cops *more* than three hours. Less than three hours incriminated them, or at least didn't absolve them. He looked at Kojak and could practically see the same thought forming in the man's mind.

"So you lied," Kojak said to Eric.

"I didn't lie. I—"

"You lied." Kojak pointed the stick at Eric. "The man's liver temperature confirms it."

Eric slumped in his chair, but a stab of pain from the kidney punch made him sit upright again. "I made a mistake."

"One of many." He bent the stick in two, as though snapping Eric's spine. "What did you do with the stun gun?"

"Stun gun? I don't have a stun gun. I've never had one."

Kojak eyed him skeptically, then turned his gaze on Tanya. "So it's yours?"

"I don't know what you're talking about," she told him. "The man was suffocated. Look at his neck. If the killer used a stun gun first, I—"

"Twice. The marks are on his back."

"That proves we didn't do it," Eric said, hope rising again. "You've searched our luggage, and I assume you've searched the crime scene. Neither of us—"

"Did I not tell you? Speak only when asked."

Eric felt body heat behind him and knew Ratface had moved closer, ready to bash him in the head if he didn't obey.

Regarding them balefully, Kojak twisted the broken lollipop stick between two fingers. Ominous silence filled the room. Then the phone rang.

Eric jumped at the sound.

Kojak answered, uttered a few words in Arabic, and hung up.

A moment later, the office door opened to reveal their cab driver.

"Mister Salah." Eric jumped to his feet. "Thank God, you're here."

"Sit down," Kojak barked. Ratface grabbed Eric's shoulders and forced him back onto the chair.

Coming around from his desk, Kojak stepped up to the driver.

Eric watched as father and son spoke, father animated, son deadly serious. The conversation seemed to go on forever before the two embraced and the father, without so much as a parting glance at Eric or Tanya, left the office.

Not a glance.

Kojak walked to the window, crossed his arms, and peered out. In the harsh sunlight, he stood rigidly, feet apart, only his jaw muscles moving and, above them, a vein that pulsed angrily in his temple. His bald head seemed to redden, as if fury were building inside him.

Finally he uncrossed his arms, tugged down the cuffs of his suit coat, and turned to them. "Go. My father will take you to the airport. Do *not* come back to Yemen."

Never more relieved in his whole life, Eric angled his face to the sun as he and Tanya stood beside the open trunk of Mr. Salah's taxi, waiting for what was left of their luggage to come out of the police station. His back still ached. His stomach ached. But they were free, or would be, as soon as Salah drove them out of the walled parking lot and deposited them at the airport.

"He is good son, yes?" Salah said.

Eric looked at the man's proud face, then at Tanya who was gnawing a fingernail anxiously. "Good" was not something Eric was willing to concede. But something had made Kojak release them. "What did you tell him?"

"I say I take you to Rock Hotel. We arrive to there at six forty-five. He say man is dead two hours before. He say, I am sure the time? I say yes." Salah held up his wrist and pointed to the watch. "Timex. American. I am always sure the time."

The steel door opened, and a cop they hadn't seen before came out with their luggage. Part of a blouse protruded like a tongue from Tanya's suitcase. The cop threw their bags in the trunk.

When Eric and Tanya had climbed into the cab and Salah had secured his door with the bungee cord, he turned to Eric in the back. "Please say you did not tell him Kojak is dead."

"No, sir, I didn't tell him. And I never will."

Chapter 37

Half a mile from Durand's villa, on a winding road flanked by low stone walls and towering trees, Abby braked to a halt. She was missing something. What were Eric's exact words? She shut her eyes and strained to recall. "Catching the first plane to France." Yes, he'd said that. And "close to nailing the person behind SF." That was all. Nothing more specific.

Opening her eyes, she looked seaward through breaks in the trees where red-tile roofs and an occasional flash of sunlight off a swimming pool were all you could see of the mansions in this hillside enclave of old money. What if she'd made the wrong assumption? Sure, Durand lived in France, and she'd pushed him as the most likely maker of SF. But now that she was two minutes from his house, the notion that Durand had actually contacted the Yemeni dealer and that Eric had found some correspondence between them made far less sense than it had in Aden airport.

Someone honked behind her.

In her rearview mirror, she saw a white BMW with its top down and a platinum blonde in the driver's seat.

The woman hit her horn again, a longer, more insistent blare.

Abby started to give her the finger but decided making a scene would only draw unneeded attention to herself. Instead, she pulled to the side and watched the Beemer accelerate past, its tight-skinned matron no doubt late for another round of plastic surgery.

Good luck, bitch. You need it.

What Abby needed, as she sat there chewing her lip, was a reason Eric might come to France if it were *not* to confront Durand. Diego and Marie-Claire? Diego had always topped Eric's list of potential "culprits." Had Diego contacted the dealer? Unlikely. Near as she knew, Diego had never had access to Eric's notebook, the only place Eric kept the dealer's email address.

Did something else tie the dealer's shop to France?

Oh, no. The dealer shipped oud to EDG. All those ledger books on his shelves, they'd surely contain records of the shipments. If Eric had found those records, even one of them, he could be headed to Marseilles.

Abby whipped out her cell phone. She'd text the factory's owner and alert him to the possibility that someone could come snooping around about SF. But as she poised her thumbs, ready to type, she realized a text message from her cell phone would compromise her anonymity. *Think.* How to get a message to EDG without identifying herself?

There were so-called anonymous ISPs. But she didn't trust them, and it would take forever to check out one from her cell phone. She flipped the phone closed. There had to be another way.

An Internet cafe. But where? The nearest one had to be … in Nice. Back the way she'd just come. Why hadn't she thought of this when she landed there? Never mind. Her instinct said get this done. Now.

Abby put the car in gear, swung a U-turn, and burned rubber.

Marseilles held only bad memories for Eric. The one time he'd been here before, to prowl the Arab and African spice markets, his pocket had been picked and he'd narrowly escaped getting mugged. The city stank of oil refineries and dead fish. But now, as he and Tanya sped down the A55 past cargo ships and container yards, he felt fired with anticipation. "How far to Avenue du Cap Pinède?"

"Just a minute." She fought with the Michelin map they'd bought at the airport, a big sheet of paper that rattled in the breeze from her partially open window and half-blocked her view of the highway ahead. Finally she beat it into submission. "Okay, looks like about—"

"One kilometer." He pointed out the windshield at a green sign zooming by overhead.

Tanya slapped the map onto her knees. "You know, if you weren't so cheap, you'd have a data plan with your cell phone. Then we could navigate by GPS."

He refrained from reminding her that, if she'd thought to check her possessions before they left the police station in Aden, then she'd have her own cell phone with all its whiz-bang extras. "Real maps are better."

"Says who?"

The set of her jaw made him smile. The old Tanya was definitely back.

Physically, he could not say the same for himself. The pain in his kidney was constant. Four Tylenol every two hours did little to help. But at least there was no blood in his urine, which meant no serious damage.

At the off-ramp, he exited out of Saturday morning traffic onto a curve that took them to Avenue du Cap Pinède. He turned left, away from the waterfront, and continued past a railway yard where the street changed names to Boulevard Capitaine Gèze and entered an area of warehouses and small factories. "We're close. The address on the crate was number forty-two."

"There." She pointed to the right.

He stopped. Forty-two was embossed on a small, blue-and white oval plate affixed to a coral-colored cinderblock wall beside the open gate. Beyond the gate lay a parking lot with one car in it and a silvery corrugated-metal building with a door and small window in front. A white placard next to the door proclaimed in black lettering, "Encens du Globe."

"What does it mean in English?" Tanya asked.

"Incense of the Globe. We'd probably say something more like Global Incense or Worldwide Incense." Whatever way you translated the words, the sight of them turned Eric's excitement to first-date jitters. Could he pull this off, cast a net of lies that would capture the name of the person behind SF? Crossing his fingers, he drove their little Renault a few feet past the gate, parked at the curb, and took a deep breath. "Ready?"

"What are we going to say?"

He'd pondered that during their long hours in cramped airline seats and had settled on due diligence. "We're potential buyers. The owner of SF wants to sell. We're interested, but we need to inspect the operation before signing a contract."

"What if *these* people are the owners, or part owners?"

"Everything we know about SF says it's based in Switzerland."

"But all your suspects are in France. Except the one in New York."

"Abby's not a suspect."

"So you say. Still, there's no reason these people couldn't be partners."

"And you pick *now* to bring this up?"

"You only told me your plan two minutes ago. Was I supposed to read your mind?"

He shifted in his seat to relieve the back pain. At least that Neanderthal, Yusuf—may he die a slow and agonizing death—hadn't hit him in the nose. "Well, I don't have any other ideas. Do you?"

"Not really."

"Then that's our story. If it doesn't fly, we'll just have to wing it."

"Wing it?"

He got out of the car, turned toward the open gateway, and stood for a moment sampling the exotic mix of aromas that spilled from the factory. Sandalwood, valerian, real cinnamon. The gingery-camphory smell of galangal root. The sweet sharpness of hyssop leaves. Palo Santo wood, with its rosy-woodsy fragrance.

These guys were good. Or at least they used good ingredients.

So, how were they fucking up his formula? That was the other thing he needed to find out.

"Let's go." He walked with her across the parking lot and entered the building, where a young Arab-looking man wearing wire-rimmed glasses sat at a computer behind the service counter. Tanya hesitated, and Eric was sure he knew why. After Yemen, the prospect of facing another Arab didn't sit well with either of them. He knew it was foolish but couldn't help being uncomfortable. Then he noticed a wooden crucifix hanging on the wall and felt ashamed that it eased his tension.

"*Bonjour, Monsieur,*" the man said.

"*Bonjour,*" Eric replied and asked, for Tanya's sake, "Do you speak English?"

"Yes." He rose from the chair, revealing a well-fed paunch beneath his pullover sweater. "May I help you?"

Eric introduced Tanya as Doctor Kay and himself as Ron Fisk. The Kay was for Kansas. Ron Fisk was the junior high school bully whose girlfriend Eric had stolen with a custom-made perfume. "We're here to speak with the owner about a discreet matter."

"My uncle is not available. You may speak with me." He had a vaguely British accent. "I am Basem Fezza."

Uncertain whether it was worth talking to the nephew but having little choice, Eric dropped his opening bombshell. "We're thinking of purchasing the SF brand."

Fezza's eyebrows rose, a clear sign that SF was no secret to him.

With that confirmation, Eric said, "But before we do, we need to inspect the operation."

"What do you mean, inspect it?"

"The production process, quality control, that sort of thing. It shouldn't take long."

Fezza took a step closer to the door behind the counter, the move of a guardian blocking entry. "I was not informed."

"My apologies, but that was our intention." Eric felt perspiration dripping from his armpits. He still didn't know if the uncle was a partner. Nor could he think of a way to broach the subject without blowing their cover. For the time being, he had to stay neutral. "A surprise visit is the only way to be sure that we see things exactly as they are."

With suspicious eyes, Fezza looked from Eric to Tanya and back. He took another protective step toward the door. "This is highly irregular."

"But essential," Eric told him. "Especially if we're going to finance a major expansion of your business."

"Expansion?" A crack appeared in Fezza's stone wall as he rubbed his lips with a chubby hand.

"For increased production," Tanya chimed in. "And possibly new perfumes."

Good hook. To which Eric added, "And of course, bonuses for you and your uncle."

Dollar signs flashed in Fezza's eyes. Then he turned crafty. "What you propose would require a substantial infusion of capital. We would need new equipment, more employees, additional space."

Infusion of capital? Had the guy gone to Harvard? Never mind. He was fishing, and Eric, seeing an opening, pretended to take the bait. "We're prepared to pay for new equipment and personnel. But we assumed you would already have room for expansion. How much space are you currently using to make SF? We'd like to see."

Come on, dammit, let us behind that door.

Fezza looked at his watch as though expecting someone, possibly the uncle. "As you said, SF is a discreet matter. The person who instructs us has been very specific about that."

In a heartbeat, Eric's angst vanished. "The person who instructs us" said it all. These guys had no stake in the ownership of SF. They were simply manufacturers who followed instructions. But Fezza's stubbornness remained to be overcome.

"I've had it." Tanya made a slicing gesture across her throat. "If this is the kind of cooperation we're going to get, then I think we should move production to another company."

Whoa! Giant gamble. Should he backpedal or play along? Friendly persuasion had gotten them nowhere. So ... go with it.

"I'm afraid you're right," Eric said and turned as if to leave.

"No, wait!" A sheen of sweat had appeared on Fezza's forehead. He glanced again at his watch. "I can show you."

Eric looked at Tanya. "What do you think?"

"I think it's about time."

Seeing Fezza shift nervously from one foot to the other, Eric tried now to put him at ease. "You've made the right decision. And by the way, I'm impressed with your business sense."

"London School of Economics," Fezza said proudly. "I just returned last year."

"A fine university." To open him up a little more and convey an interest in him personally, Eric decided on a mild provocation. "But England can be a difficult place for foreigners. The prejudice and all."

"Better than here. French people hate Algerians. All Muslims." He pointed to the crucifix and grinned. "So I fool them with the cross."

"Clever idea. And cleverness is what we're looking for in a business partner." Eric returned the smile. "Shall we proceed?"

"Yes, of course." Fezza waved them around the counter, opened the door behind, and ushered them inside.

The factory was a huge space with a thickly aromatic atmosphere and about forty or fifty workers. The workers, who all looked Arab, were either women or barely adolescent girls and boys. A few glanced up at them. Most kept their heads down.

With his own nerves on high alert, Eric found the intensity of fragrances almost overpowering. He had to breathe through his mouth as he followed Fezza down the central aisle and tried to take in the scope of EDG's operation.

Raw ingredients in boxes, bags, and bottles filled shelves along the left-hand wall. Finished products in cellophane-wrapped packages filled shelving on the right. In between, the workforce ground ingredients for the various types of incense, mixed them into slurries and pastes, dipped bundles of sticks into the slurries, and pressed the pastes into molds that produced various sizes of cones, pucks, and rectangular blocks. Toward the back were drying ovens and packaging machinery and a side room with a sign that read, *Défense d'entrer.* No Entry.

Fezza stopped at the door to this room. "You can see we are already crowded. But the building next door is for sale."

Eric asked Tanya, "Are you prepared to pay for an entire building?"

"If necessary, to accomplish our objectives."

Another smile crossed Fezza's face before he unlocked the door. "This is where we make SF."

The instant he stepped inside, Eric smelled something wrong. "You use alcohol?"

"For extracting the wood. To make the perfume, we use water, according to the formula."

"Does the formula say to extract with alcohol?"

"Yes."

Wondering what other changes the counterfeiter might have made, Eric studied the row of extraction vessels—round-bottomed glass flasks, half-filled with wood chips and alcohol, bubbling away over Bunsen burners and attached to coiled condenser columns that sloped down to drip the extract into collection bottles. All normal, except that the alcohol, turning black from the wood, should have been water.

"What's wrong?" Tanya asked.

"Let me think a minute." Alcohol would extract all of the organic compounds that water would, but it would extract other compounds, as well. This was the difference between SF and Balquees. The alcohol brought out something dangerous, the Agent X he'd searched for in Tanya's lab.

And suddenly he knew what it was.

The prized substance of the oud tree was a black exudate the tree produced to fight off fungal infection—effectively a natural pesticide. That's what he'd smelled in his apartment, the slightly acidic ghost note that reminded him of something in his grandmother's garden shed. Not a fertilizer. A pesticide. A compound that could have bad effects on people who were highly sensitive to chemicals—like people with severe allergies.

He thought back to the crime scene on Central Park South, the apartment where the woman had strangled her boyfriend. In her bathroom, Fawcett had found Naprosyn and allergy meds.

And Tanya had said Patrick was deathly allergic to pesticides.

Eric whipped around to her. "I know what killed those people."

"Killed who?" Fezza asked with a look of astonishment.

"Nothing. Sorry. I was thinking about killing the competition. You know, cornering the market." With an effort to control his exhilaration, Eric again scanned the line of bubbling vessels. "Do you mind if I smell some of the extract?"

Appearing to have regained his composure after the "killed" comment, Fezza walked to the end of the table with the extraction vessels and selected one of several aluminum bottles. "Please be careful. It causes … you know. That's why we let only one man work in here. Very old."

"I understand." Eric unscrewed the bottle and took a short, hard whiff. There it was, the acidic ghost note. Still deeply buried among other notes, like the shoulder on the gas chromatogram, but now definitely detectable.

Tanya held her hand out. "Let me smell."

"Are you sure?" Eric said. "This is the concentrated stuff. Everything else in SF is just filler."

"Give it to me."

He handed her the bottle and watched anxiously as she took a deep inhalation. Jesus, where was the chemist in her? Chemists never stuck their noses in a bottle. They used a hand to wave the smell toward their noses, minimizing the concentration, in case the chemical was dangerous.

Tanya's eyes widened "Wow, that's powerful."

"Please, Madame." Fezza reached for the bottle. "It makes women … immodest."

Eric took the bottle from her and gave it to Fezza. "Thank you. We're finished here." But they still had to identify the perpetrator, a name they could surely find in EDG's records. "I think we can now address the business side."

Taking the cue, Tanya said, "Yes. We need to see the books."

When Fezza hesitated, Eric jumped in with, "Nothing financial. We know you make a profit and expect you'll make more when we take over. What Doctor Kay meant was, we need to look at the Shipping and Receiving details. We might be able to spot some opportunities for improved efficiency."

"We receive the oud by sea freight from Yemen. The other ingredients come from wholesalers in Grasse."

"What about the bottles?" Tanya asked.

Excellent question.

"My brother. He has a glass business." Fezza pointed at some metal shelving in one corner where at least a hundred of the black bottles, each labeled SF in gold script, stood in neat rows.

A hundred bottles of poison. Eric wanted to smash them all, but forced himself to remain calm. Okay, Receiving was a dead end. "Where do you *ship* the final product?"

"To the customers."

"You ship directly from here?"

"Yes."

Damn. If the bottle Eric ordered had arrived before he left, he would have known this. But that would only have told him who EDG was. It wouldn't have solved the mystery of Agent X. Or the mystery of who was running things. "How do you know where to ship? The customers' names and addresses?"

"We receive them by email. From Switzerland."

Bingo! A lead at last. "We'd like to see one."

Fezza frowned.

"So we can understand the communication chain," Eric said. "As I'm sure you know, communications are critical to operating a successful—and expanding—business."

After seeming to mull this for a moment, Fezza beckoned them to follow and led them back through the factory to the reception area where he sat in the chair and pulled up an email on his computer.

Looking over Fezza's shoulder, Eric saw a list of names with addresses in places ranging from South America and New Zealand to Europe and the U.S. But what interested him was the email address of the sender: kontakt@sf.ch. About as anonymous as you could get.

"You see?" Fezza turned in his chair. "Very efficient."

Behind the guy, a new email appeared on the computer screen.

Its first two words, in all caps, grabbed Eric's attention. *PRENEZ GARDE!* Beware. The rest of the title, also in French, froze his eyes to the screen. "Thieves want to steal SF." Who in the world could have sent that? The sender's name meant nothing to him, and he dared not ask. But he did have to keep Fezza from seeing it before they left.

Extending his hand, Eric said, "Mister Fezza, you've been very helpful. I think we're going to have an excellent relationship. But I've just noticed the time. Doctor Kay and I need to catch a plane."

"What are you doing?" Tanya whispered.

"We need to get going."

"Why?"

The front door opened. A big man wearing sunglasses and a black sport coat stepped inside.

"*Oncle*." Fezza leapt to his feet and spoke rapidly in Arabic. His tone sounded enthusiastic but became uncertain, then defensive as Uncle listened with a deepening scowl.

Damn. Now they had to blow off the boss, too. Eric took Tanya's elbow and walked her out from behind the counter where, in Uncle's view, they were surely trespassing. "Sir, I'm Ron Fisk. This is Doctor Kay. We're here to—"

"Show me identification." Uncle's voice was gravelly, like Marlon Brando's in *The Godfather*.

"Our wallets are in the car," Eric told him.

Uncle marched past them, picked up the phone, and stabbed the number buttons as though poking out eyes. In French he said, "I have a problem at the factory. Send Poing and Ali immediately."

Poing, French for fist, was all Eric needed to hear. He grabbed Tanya's hand and hustled her out the door, up the street, and into their car. As he tromped the gas, he saw Fezza in the rearview mirror. The guy was writing furiously on a piece of paper.

Chapter 38

At the first intersection, Eric made a snap decision and turned left, opposite the direction he ultimately wanted to go. If Fezza saw them turn, he'd think they were heading north. "Help me here. What's the fastest route to any major highway?"

"I don't get it." Instead of picking up the map, Tanya stared at him. "Why the big rush to get out of there?"

"The uncle was calling in muscle, and Fezza got our license number. Just find me a highway."

"You mean muscle, like mob guys?" She started fumbling with the map.

"We're going north on Boulevard Gay Lussac." Factories and huge warehouses lined both sides. Semis crowded loading docks. Not a single cross street in sight.

"Eric, are you sure?"

"Gay Lussac. G-A-Y—"

"No, dammit. About the muscle."

"One of the guys he asked for is named Fist."

"Oh, Jesus." With a karate chop, she folded the map in two, then folded it again.

Up ahead, the street forked. Eric veered left. More factories and warehouses. Still no cross streets. God, he hated this town.

"Okay, I think I've got it. Do you see a roundabout?"

"Up ahead. Just past that cement plant." He checked the rearview mirror for anyone pursuing them. "I'm going left."

"No! Go straight. It curves around to the A-Seven."

Two minutes later, as they merged onto the A7 south, Eric wished he'd rented a bigger car. Heavy clouds had rolled in and, on the elevated highway, gusting winds buffeted their tiny Renault like a cat batting a toy mouse. He had to constantly correct the steering just to stay in their lane. But at least they were moving in the right direction. "Now, can you get us back to the A-Fifty? The road we came in on."

"Do you really think they're chasing us?"

"I don't want to take chances. By all accounts, the Algerian mafia in Marseilles is seriously bad." With one eye on the rearview mirror, he told her what he'd read on the subject line of the email that came in just before Uncle showed up. "My guess is that stealing from those guys carries a broken-bones penalty. Minimum."

When she didn't respond, Eric looked at her.

Tanya's face was ashen. "Then what's the penalty for finding out they make SF?"

"Probably nothing. Since SF isn't illegal, they're not doing anything wrong. Except using underage workers. But we're obviously not French police, so we're no threat to them on the employment issue. I think attempted theft is our only so-called crime."

"Small comfort." She peered at the map, which she'd finally folded into a manageable size. "Okay, A-Fifty to the airport."

"No, we're not going to the airport."

"We sure as hell are. Next plane to anywhere."

"We're in a rental car. The airport's the first place they'll look for us." He changed lanes, pulled up next to a semi, and let it run interference for them against the strengthening crosswind. Overhead, the clouds had turned black. "Besides, we're not done here."

"I am. Another run-in with angry Arabs holds no appeal whatsoever."

Eric thought a moment. She'd already been through a lot more than either of them had bargained for. "You're right. There's no reason you have to stay. I'll drop you at the airport, and you should be fine. They're looking for a couple, not a single woman."

Silence, except for the road noise and wind. Finally she said, "Just like that?"

"You want to go to the airport, I'll take you."

She crushed the map in her hands. "You *want* me to go."

"I didn't say that. You did."

"And you're staying here?"

"I have unfinished business."

"Where?"

"Grasse, the town where Marie-Claire lives. With Diego."

"Oh, for God's sake."

"It *has* to be them. Fezza as much as said so when he told us he got all the ingredients, except the oud, from Grasse. There are lots of cheaper places he could buy them. But Marie-Claire's family has lived in Grasse for at least a century, and she thinks it's the be-all and end-all of the French perfume industry. No one but her would specify Grasse."

"You're forgetting Yemen. The only person who knew we were going there is Abby."

"She's in New York. We already established that."

Tanya slumped back in her seat. "I think you're blind."

"No, I'm not." With a clap of thunder, rain started pelting their windshield. "Why would you say that?"

"You might try turning on the wipers."

He smacked the wiper lever to high. "Why am I blind?"

Crossing her arms, she said in a disgusted tone, "Because you're in love with her."

&

At Toulon, a French naval base with even less charm than Marseilles, Eric turned inland, leaving behind the last remnants of the storm that seemed to have followed them for the past half-hour. They'd driven in silence after her comment about Abby. Either Tanya was jealous, which was interesting but unlikely, or she really did think his feelings for Abby were clouding his judgment, which was a slap in the face and just plain wrong. His feelings hadn't stopped him from suspecting her before. He'd said as much in Tanya's apartment, and it was Tanya who'd ruled her out.

He stole a look at her. She still stared straight ahead, as though *he* were the one who'd offended *her*. Ironically, midday sun highlighted her hair in a sort of blonde halo. Yeah, a real angel. Horns would be more appropriate.

Out of the blue she said, "What did you mean, back there in the factory, that you know what killed those people?"

Careful not to mention the shoulder on the gas chromatogram or anything else she might interpret as "I told you so," he explained his reasoning—the alcohol extraction, the oud's natural pesticide. As he spoke, he could see the puzzle pieces coming together in her mind.

When he finished, she said, "Patrick's allergic to pesticides. It used to drive me crazy because he has bedbugs, and he refused to get his apartment sprayed."

"Yeah, you mentioned that at my place, the morning after he beat the hell out of you."

Tanya looked out her side window.

They were doing seventy miles an hour through farmland on their right and forested hills on their left. But Eric doubted she saw the scenery.

She touched her cheekbone, where there was still a hint of bruising. "At least I know now that it wasn't his fault."

"That's splitting hairs. He has a major-league violent streak. SF just brought it out. I hope that doesn't mean you forgive him."

She turned back to him. "What difference would it make to *you*?"

"Well … You know. I just …" *Damn.* "All I meant was, you can do better."

"So now you're going to advise me on dating? You, whose roommate is a three-legged dog?" She rolled her eyes. "Oh, lucky me."

❧

At the roundabout entering Grasse, a sense of composure came over Eric. Like a well-prepared fighter entering the ring for a rematch, he felt confident, ready, poised to finally take back his life.

Having visited Marie-Claire once before, he navigated from

memory up the winding streets that led to her family's hillside estate. Despite the time of year, well before the growing season, the crystalline air carried fragrances of orange flower, jasmine, and mimosa. Residents could be forgiven for likening the place to heaven.

Halfway along one of the switchbacks, Eric turned hard right and gunned their Renault up a long driveway. At the top, he circled a fountain with a life-sized marble maiden pouring water from an amphora and stopped in front of Marie-Claire's home. It could have been featured on postcards, a quintessential Mediterranean mansion in cream-colored stone and terracotta tile.

"Wow," Tanya breathed. "I've never been to a place like this."

"The grandfather built it, back when Grasse was mostly flower fields." Eric got out and straightened slowly to avoid a sudden strike of pain in his kidney. "In more recent times, fortune hasn't smiled so favorably. They had to sell off most of the property, and her father now supplements the business by making custom perfumes for private clients. SF is no doubt Marie-Claire's way of contributing to the family income."

Tanya, who'd already told him she thought he was barking up the wrong tree, looked skeptical again as she accompanied him up the broad steps.

At the door, a massive fortification made of carved oak, Eric rapped three times with the dolphin-shaped knocker. He waited and was about to knock again, when the speakeasy-type portal behind a small iron grille opened and he heard, "Eric! *Mon Dieu.*"

The door swung wide and Marie-Claire beamed at him. "I cannot believe this. You have answered my prayers."

What prayers, he had no idea. But he quickly introduced Tanya, then said, "We need to talk."

"Yes, of course. Please come in."

True to tradition, the receiving room boasted high ceilings, tiled floors, and arched windows with views over Grasse and the distant sea beyond. But the musty old furniture was sun-faded, and one of the doilies on the upholstered arms had slipped to the floor, revealing stuffing under the threadbare fabric.

"Is Diego here?" Eric asked.

Marie-Claire's face wilted. "I thought you knew. I thought you bring me … how do you say … the good news."

"I'm not sure what you mean."

Glumly she sank into an overstuffed armchair. "I do not see Diego since I leave New York. Only he tells me there is another woman."

"Tells you?"

"By the telephone. He says he cannot help himself."

"So it's an older woman."

"Like before." Marie-Claire seemed to deflate. "When I see you, I think you come to say he is sorry. He wants me again."

Had she lost her grip on reality? How could she imagine that Diego would send an emissary or that he, Eric, would ever agree to be one? It was the sort of fantasy you might expect from a high-school girl. Yet that by itself, the sheer innocence of it, touched a sympathetic string.

Which irked him. The last thing he needed was for compassion to blunt his edge. But maybe in her despair, she would now come clean. "The reason I'm here is that I need you to answer a question. You're making SF, aren't you?"

"Eric! Leave her alone." Tanya went to Marie-Claire's side, sat on the arm of the chair, and put a consoling hand on Marie-Claire's shoulder. "Can't you see how distraught she is?"

"With those Algerians in Marseilles," he persisted. "Encens du Globe."

"Algerians?" Marie-Claire spat out the word like a piece of bad meat. "Algerians are filth."

Damn. He should have realized she was too racist to do business with foreigners. "Then Diego's the one who gave them the formula."

"What formula? Is this about your perfume again?"

"You know it is. It's about whose family needs income and would benefit nicely from stealing my formula."

"If somebody has steal your formula, look at Abby. She is the pervert. She serves only Satan."

"Bull. Why don't you stop playing games? All I want is the truth."

Marie-Claire buried her face in her hands. "I think you come to tell me good news, but you kill my heart. Just like Diego. Are there no good men?"

"Not in *this* room." Tanya stood, her eyes burning into Eric's. "I told you it was Abby."

Eric looked past her to Marie-Claire. "Maybe you wouldn't deal with Algerians, but give me one good reason why Diego wouldn't." When she didn't answer, he dug into a deeper vein than he could have stomached if he weren't so desperate. "Remember your faith. Lying is a mortal sin."

She clutched the crucifix hanging from her neck, a duplicate of the one she'd given him when he was expelled. "Before God, I swear Diego makes nothing. Only lies. He says he loves me. He tells to my parents he loves me. All is lies. Even in my bed, we do not make love. Only we do sex. I pretend to myself, but I know he is not thinking of me. It is lies!" She raised her eyes heavenward. *"Mon Dieu, pardonne-moi."*

Eric felt like dirt. He'd had no intention of dredging up anything remotely this personal. But her oath before God confirmed one thing. She was telling the truth. Or rather, the truth as she saw it. Which still left the possibility that Diego was operating behind her back. "How often does he go to Marseilles?"

"Goddammit, Eric." Tanya planted herself squarely in front of him.

"Do not blaspheme in my house." Marie-Claire rose from the chair and came up to face him, also. "Diego cannot go to Marseilles. My parents will not let him drive our cars. I was blind. But they see him for a ... *charlatan.*"

"Then he conducts the business by email." In fact, that made more sense. EDG's orders for SF all came by email.

She shook her head. In a tone now coldly matter-of-fact, she said, "He does not have a computer. Our family computer is in my father's office. Diego cannot go in there."

No car. No computer. The guy had been a prisoner in a gilded cage. But surely he could walk into town. "Then he used an Internet café in Grasse."

"Non!" Marie-Claire's face clouded again. Fidgeting with her hands, she glanced over her shoulder as if expecting help to arrive. The powdery scent of her skin rose in heated waves. Then something within seemed to steel her. "Wait here."

When Marie-Claire had left the room, Tanya hissed, "You're a bastard."

With an effort, he stopped himself from telling her to butt out. Instead, he turned away and looked out the windows. A million-dollar view, but stagnant. Unchanging. The kind of view that quickly became boring, neglected like the windows themselves which showed the streaks and smears of perfunctory cleaning. Diego, the dashing Spaniard, would have grown to loathe this place. SF would have been his release, his connection with the wider world, his rebellion against his father. And the source of a hefty bankroll accumulating in Switzerland and ultimately funding his escape.

He had to be the one.

At the sound of footsteps, Eric turned back to see Marie-Claire coming toward him.

"I found this in one of his pockets." She handed him a piece of paper that had obviously been wadded up at some stage but was now folded in half. "I kept it because … I don't know."

Eric opened it, and his legs almost buckled. It was a receipt from Encens du Globe for one bottle of SF, dated three months ago and made out to Diego Alvarez.

"So you see," she said.

When Tanya reached for it, Eric didn't resist. He had no resistance left. A person in the business of making SF would never have to pay for a bottle.

Dropping to a couch, Eric blinked to clear his vision. Only one possibility remained.

"Your face is white," Marie-Claire said. "Do you want some water?"

He barely heard her. Sure, he'd once had suspicions. But at one time or another he'd suspected almost everyone he knew at ISIPCA. Staring at the floor, he racked his brain for even the slightest hint he might have missed. Nothing. And he'd eliminated everyone else.

Pain filled his heart as the face appeared before him like a specter through swirling mist. He just couldn't believe it.

Jacques Durand.

Chapter 39

Partway down the slope of his driveway, Durand braked to a stop. A woman he didn't recognize leaned against one of the columns flanking his front door. Obviously hearing his approach, she straightened and faced him. An Asian woman who now seemed vaguely familiar. ISIPCA. A close friend of Eric's. Abby something. Hong? Han? That was it, Abby Han.

Why was *she* here?

Durand eased his Facel Vega along the remainder of the drive and parked under the *porte-cochère*, out of the afternoon sun, as a few details about her came back to him. A student in the flavors curriculum. The best student, according to some. She'd been here at the weekend party he hosted two years ago, a somewhat distant woman who spoke mediocre French with an appalling accent.

"Miss Han," he said, climbing out of his car. "To what do I owe this pleasure?"

She came forward and extended her hand. *"Monsieur,* I apologize for arriving unexpectedly. But I need your help."

Perplexed, he looked around. "You came by foot?"

"No. I parked my car on the street, up above. Can we talk?"

He detected a feral odor—gratifying for its confirmation that his sense of smell was recovering, now that he'd canceled his treatments with those Swiss vultures. But also slightly disquieting, as though this woman he barely knew had tracked him down like an animal with ill intent.

More curious than he might have been before his life descended into the boredom of complete retirement, he led her inside to the library and gestured her toward a sofa near the fireplace. *"Aperitif?"*

"I'd prefer a vodka. Neat."

A stiff drink for this time of day. Apparently the "help" she needed was serious, at least to her. At the sideboard, he poured her vodka and mixed a Ricard and water for himself.

Turning back, he glanced around the room, feeling suddenly self-conscious about its appearance after so many months without visitors. Sunlight from the windows illuminated the carved desk where he spent much of his time and the thousand-odd volumes that rose floor-to-ceiling on either side of the fireplace. But papers littered the floor around his desk. Dust motes hovered in the light. And the rest of the room was spiritually bleak, with its daggers and swords arranged in fans on one wall, the two suits of armor, the portraits of ancestors who seemed to scowl in the knowledge that he'd killed off their line by letting his son die in that motorcycle accident.

"Is something wrong?" Miss Han asked.

Only the depth to which I've let myself sink. He handed her the glass of vodka and sat on the facing sofa. *"Santé."*

"Thank you. But it's *your* health I'm worried about. And Eric's."

Durand halted his glass halfway to his mouth. Did she know about his stomach, his useless treatments in Switzerland? No, she couldn't. So why say such a thing?

"My health is fine." Then her last sentence struck home. "Is something wrong with Eric?"

"Not physically. But in his mind."

"Nonsense. Eric has a superb mind."

"He used to." She hesitated. "I don't know how to tell you this."

"English will be fine." *Then drink up and get out.* He had no time for whatever game this woman was playing.

"It's a long story, but the bottom line is, I think Eric is coming here. Today or tomorrow. And if he does, it's for one reason only. To kill you."

"Absurd!" He got to his feet and glared down at her. "I don't know what you think you are doing, but—"

"It's true," she exclaimed. "Believe me, I would not have come here if it weren't. I love him, and I fear for both of you."

❧

Speeding along the inland highway, *La Provençale*, Eric barely noticed the road in front of him. All he saw was Durand's saddened face on the day of Eric's expulsion as the man prepared to drive off. "You have broken my heart," Durand had said.

Well, the feeling is mutual. Durand had been a second father to him, as critical yet caring as his own father, the mentor he'd deeply respected and tried always to please. The thought of confronting him made his hands cold, his mouth dry. Like he was already dying inside. Would he even be able to say the words?

A *pop* jolted his attention to the road. The car veered sharply to the right as a new *flop, flop, flop* sound told him he'd blown the right front tire. "Dammit." He pulled as far as he could off the pavement, which was only half the width of their car, then set the brake and sat there. Durand's image came back, not sad, disappointed.

Eric put his forehead on the steering wheel. "I can't do this."

"Change a tire?" Tanya said. "It's easy."

"I can't confront him."

"Then don't. I'm tired of following you around on this wild goose chase. Let's just fix the tire and go home."

Could he do that? No good would come from facing Durand and saying, *"J'accuse."* Even with a full confession, he would never turn in this man to any police agency. Why go through the agony and embarrassment of a verbal shoot-out? "Maybe you're right."

"I know I am."

A passing semi blared its horn as its slipstream rocked their little Renault. Two more cars followed in quick succession, then there was a break in traffic. Eric got out, opened the rear hatch, and lifted the mat to find one of those micro-sized emergency tires.

Tanya came up beside him. "You know how to do this?"

Did she think he was stupid?

A minute or so later, he'd loosened two lug nuts on the stricken wheel and was fighting the third when she said behind him, "So, what's this about Abby being a pervert?"

The wrench slipped. Eric's knuckles scraped the ground with a burst of pain that made him wince.

"You sure you know how to do this?"

"Abby's not a pervert." He fitted the tire iron again, put his back into it, and loosened the third nut. The fourth nut broke loose more easily.

"Don't take them all the way off."

"I know!" Jesus, he'd changed a tire before. He put the jack in place and started cranking up the car.

"So why did Marie-Claire say she was?"

"Forget it."

"Oooh. Must be bad."

He removed the four nuts, pulled off the wheel, and replaced it with the pint-sized substitute. Strangely, squatting like this eased the ache in his kidney.

"You know I'm going to hound you until you tell me," Tanya said.

That was probably true. After threading on the four lug nuts, he decided it was no big secret. "Abby's bisexual."

A noise halfway between a gasp and a sharp laugh erupted from Tanya's throat. "Oh, that's rich. You're in love with a woman who fucks women."

Eric laid into the lug nuts like he was tightening a garrote. He was sick and tired of being dumped on by everyone—his Nazi boss at Rheinhold-Laroche, detective ass-wipe Darrell Fawcett, know-it-all Tanya. Worst of all, Jacques Durand, the root cause of everything else.

Eric felt a flush of heat as his anger rose. The man had betrayed his trust, stabbed him in the back, then acted like *he* was the wounded party. The need for justice, for revenge, tightened Eric's grip on the tire iron. Maybe he had no legal grounds for turning the man in, but he could expose him, destroy his hard-won reputation. All he had to do was get a pocket tape recorder, which he could buy in Nice on their way to Cap d'Ail.

"What happened to your knuckles?" Tanya asked behind him.

He threw the tire iron in the trunk and slammed the lid. "Come on. I have to get to Nice before the shops close."

"Nice? I thought we were—"

"We're nailing Durand."

♫

This wasn't going well. Abby watched Durand as he alternately paced the library and stood over her, scowling like her father had done when he caught her out in a lie. She kicked herself mentally for not anticipating Durand's reluctance to believe anything bad about Eric. She had to get out of here before Eric arrived—if he arrived. But she couldn't leave until she'd convinced Durand of Eric's "ill intent."

Locking her fingers together to keep from fidgeting, she tried to come up with something that would jolt the old fart out of his disbelief.

The oud. That could work. But she had to sneak up on it, slip it in with a rehash of things she'd already told him or implied.

In a grave tone, she said, "Eric has never been the same since he was expelled. He hates the job you got him in New York. He's depressed all the time. And now there's a perfume called SF, and he thinks it's a counterfeit of Balquees, the perfume he made with the oud he stole from ISIPCA."

Durand stopped in mid-pace. "Are you saying he actually stole that oud?"

Hook set, thank her stars. Now reel in gently. "He still has it. He only ever used a few shavings."

For the first time since she'd arrived, Durand looked pained.

"*Monsieur*, I'm sorry. I thought you knew."

"I suspected at the time. But later I thought I must be wrong. He denied it so strongly."

"I tried to throw it out once, but he got furious. He said it reminds him of how much he hates you."

Durand winced. A gleam of moisture appeared in his eyes.

Progress at last. Abby took another sip of vodka, gathering strength from its fire. Since Eric would surely mention SF, she wanted to make sure Durand knew exactly what it was. "Things got worse in New York when the police tied SF to a series of murders they're calling crimes of passion. They say it drives people wild with lust. So wild that some of them kill their lovers."

"Murders from a perfume? Impossible."

"You know that, and I know that. But the police do not."

"Then I will tell them."

"They won't believe you. They have a whole series of murders and assaults with only one common link. They all involved SF." She watched with secret amusement as Durand's resolve withered. "So when Eric said SF was his, meaning a reproduction of Balquees, the police naturally interrogated him as a potential killer."

"They accuse him of murder? I don't believe it."

"I couldn't believe it either. But it's true, and Eric is scared to death. The cops threaten him with prison, or worse. They say if he didn't do it, then he knows who did, and that makes him equally guilty. He's getting no sleep. He's become obsessed with finding *and* punishing the person who is making SF." Abby bit her lip for effect, then added, "He went through everyone else he knows and finally concluded that the only person with a nose good enough to duplicate Balquees is you."

Durand's eyes hardened. "Miss Han, I have never even smelled it."

Uh-oh. How could she have known that? Stealing an anxious glance at her watch, Abby searched for a way out. "He thinks you have. There were several bottles of it floating around ISIPCA."

"Why would I want to duplicate a *student's* perfume?"

"Because it works. Everyone who's tried it wants more. People all around the world are buying SF as fast as they can."

Durand peered at her skeptically, then rubbed his chin and started pacing again. In a barely audible voice, he muttered, "A true aphrodisiac?"

For some reason, that got him. She wasn't sure why, but it didn't matter. Now was the time to reel in hard and clobber him in the head with … what?

Love. As a Frenchman, he'd buy that. And it gave her a reason for coming all this way to warn him. "*Monsieur*, there's something I haven't told you. Eric and I are engaged to be married."

He spun around to face her, but no words came from his

open mouth.

"And because of that," she continued, "I may be to blame for the danger you're in."

"Explain yourself."

Quickly she fabricated a story. "I had to come to Paris on a business trip, so I asked him to come with me. He's always loved Paris, and I thought being there might restore his perspective. But even before we landed, he started muttering, 'I have to deliver the head of the thief. The head of the thief.' I was so frightened that I canceled my business meeting the moment we got to our hotel."

Go, girl. You're on a roll here. "I insisted on ordering room service for dinner, so I could keep him confined until I managed to change our return flights. But when I woke up this morning, he was gone. And when I looked at our dinner cart, his steak knife was missing."

"Do you honestly believe he means me harm?"

"I'm certain of it. And if he does, I'm certain he will be caught by French authorities. *Monsieur,* you must help me. Please talk some sense into him."

Seeming to ponder this, Durand suddenly frowned. "If he left Paris before you, how did you get here first?"

Damn, another blunder. Why would it take Eric longer? "I called for a taxi to the airport. Maybe he took the train, or a shuttle bus. He doesn't have much money."

The doorbells chimed.

Abby sprang from the couch. "Oh, God. If that's him, I can't be here. He'll go ballistic."

Still frowning, Durand told her, "Stay in this room." Then he walked to his desk, withdrew a small revolver from a side drawer, and slipped the pistol into his front pocket.

Abby's heart pounded so hard she could barely stand it. As soon as Durand walked out and closed the library doors behind him, she raced to the windows behind his desk. No way to climb down and too far to jump. She turned around and stared at the doors. *Get a grip.* This was no time to panic.

Okay, either they came in here, or they didn't. If they did, she'd stick to her story. It was her word against Eric's whether they were actually engaged and how they'd come to be here. He'd lose his temper. If her luck held ... oooh. A tingle coursed through her like sexual arousal. If her luck held, there'd be a fight and Durand would shoot the bastard.

And if they didn't come in? They could fight in the hallway. Durand could still shoot Eric. And she could at least be a voyeur at the climax.

Either way, I win.

Licking her lips, she tiptoed across the room and pressed her ear to the crack between the doors.

Eric switched on the digital voice-recorder pen in his shirt pocket, a surprise find at the electronics shop in Nice. But now that he and Tanya faced Durand's front door, his bravado bled out of him. His hands trembled. He had another case of dry-mouth and saliva too thick to moisten his throat. "This can only end badly."

"Just get it over with," Tanya said.

He heard the door handle turn and braced himself. He'd do this in a rational way, get it over with, and get out. All he wanted was an admission of the truth.

The door opened. Durand glanced at him, arched his eyebrows at Tanya, then fixed his gaze on Eric.

Weird. They hadn't seen each other in a year, yet Durand regarded him with less reaction than he'd have for the mailman. Suddenly Eric felt like unwitting prey about to check in at the Bates Motel. "Were you expecting us?

"I had a premonition."

If Durand had premonitions, it was news to Eric. News that made his skin crawl. Trying to create a semblance of normality, he said, "I'd like to introduce a friend of mine, Tanya Cole."

"*Mademoiselle.*" Durand shook her hand, then looked at Eric with a mystified expression. "I ... imagined you would come alone."

What was going on here? Why should Durand "imagine" anything? Searching for an advantage of some sort, Eric came up with, "Tanya is with the New York Police Department."

Durand's eyes popped.

At last they were getting somewhere. "Show him your ID," Eric told her.

She cast Eric a sidelong glance, then produced her identity badge, held it up for Durand to see, and replaced it in her purse.

Seeming confused now, Durand stood aside to let them enter.

Eric, pleased at finally shaking up the man, took Tanya's hand and led her inside. But they'd walked only a few steps when he halted. All the paintings he remembered from his previous visit— the Chagall, the Miro, two Picassos—still hung on the hallway walls, exactly where they'd been before. Abby had said he sold them.

The front door closed with a heavy thud.

"You don't look well," Durand said.

Eric released Tanya's hand and turned to him. "I'm fine."

"When was the last time you bathed?"

What was this, an interrogation by his mother? Granted, he hadn't showered or changed his clothes since leaving New York. But that was beside the point. "We need to talk about SF."

No visible surprise. No guardedness, or response whatsoever. It was almost as though the man hadn't heard him.

"I believe you have been under a lot of stress," Durand said. "Perhaps I can help."

"Are you deaf?" In exasperation, Eric half-shouted, "We're going to talk about SF. About an old man who claimed honor was the most important thing, and then turned around and stole my formula. A two-faced hypocrite who posed as my friend, then wrecked my life."

Tanya grabbed Eric's arm, but he jerked it away.

"You are wrong about me," Durand said evenly. "I have never done anything dishonorable toward you or—"

"Bullshit. You—"

"And *yet!*" Durand's eyes blazed, two flamethrowers aimed straight at Eric. "And yet, you bring to my house an officer of the police. *Your* police."

So, that did bother him. As coldly as he could, Eric said, "The Sûreté won't be far behind. Crimes have been committed in New York *and* France *and* in a lot of other countries. Crimes caused by that sleazy counterfeit of yours."

Durand shook his head sadly, the fire within him evidently snuffed out. "I swear on my son's grave, I know nothing about this SF."

"Eric, I believe him," Tanya said.

"You don't even know him. You don't know what it's like to be really good, and then in a blink have nothing. I do. And so does he. It makes you do desperate things."

She glared at him with a look that said, *I'm about to walk out.*

She couldn't do that. He needed her help. Her police status was the one thing that might jar the truth out of this obstinate old man. Backing up a few steps, Eric took a deep breath to calm his temper and—*What was that?*

He couldn't believe it. No way that smell could be here. He blew out his breath and sniffed again. Oh, my God in Heaven. Only one thing smelled like cream with a hint of violet. Abby's skin.

Her face filled his vision, and he knew beyond doubt she had been here. Right where he was standing at this very moment.

Then a vague memory took form in his head. The dealer's shop. A smell that had seemed out of place. The one he hadn't been able to identify at the time because it was swamped by so many other aromas. It was Abby.

His knees felt weak. Abby had been there before him. Which could only mean one thing.

"Eric, what's wrong? You look like you're going to be sick."

He blinked and saw Tanya standing two feet in front of him, her expression alarmed. "You were right all along."

"About what?"

"Abby." He swallowed hard, barely able to speak the words. "Abby killed the dealer."

"How do you know?"

"Her smell."

Durand stalked up to him. "What nonsense is this about Abby killing a dealer? What dealer?"

"In Yemen," Tanya told him. "We just came from there and—"

"She's also been *here*. Today!" Was she still here? Were she and

Durand in this together? He glared at the man. "Where is she?"

Stony silence.

Eric's temper flashed. Durand was protecting her. Abby had stood right here, then gone … Where?

He looked around. To his left, the dining room doors stood open, revealing a long table flanked with chairs. He dashed in. Nobody. But there was another door, centered in one of the side walls. He ran to it and threw it open. A butler's pantry.

"Eric," Tanya shouted.

Beyond the pantry lay a huge kitchen. And more doors. Yanking them open, he found food pantries, linens, flatware. No one hiding. A glassed-in breakfast room on the far side commanded views of the sea—and stood empty.

"Stop this," Durand growled.

Eric whipped around. "Where is she?"

Durand looked outraged. Beside him, Tanya stood wide-eyed.

"Tell me now," Eric said, "or I'll find her myself."

When Durand came toward him, Eric ducked through a pair of swinging doors that took him onto the terrace. At the balustrade, he looked down. The pool was full, its water crystal-clear. He saw nobody on the patio.

The kitchen doors banged open. Durand stood there, his face livid. "I demand you stop this madness."

Panting, Eric peered up at the outside of the house. The place was huge. Another floor above this one, a partial floor below, and probably a wine cellar and storage rooms below that. She could be anywhere.

"Eric, please," Tanya said.

Wait. When he called Abby's landline in New York, she'd answered. But she couldn't have been there. Pulling the cell phone from his pocket, he charged back into the hallway to the spot where he'd smelled her. He punched her number again. *Come on, come, on.* He strained his ears. Two pairs of footsteps came down the hall behind him. He turned to see Tanya and Durand, neither of them any help.

Then he heard it. Faintly, from behind the doors to the library, came the opening notes of "La Marseillaise." Abby's ring tone for him.

Storming the doors, he bashed them open.

"Hey!" Abby lurched backward. "Watch what you're doing."

He gaped in shock, suddenly realizing that he'd hoped to be wrong, hoped she wouldn't really be here, that there'd be some other explanation for all of this.

"Sweetheart, close your mouth." She shoved her cell phone into her pocket. "I've told *Monsieur* Durand everything, and we both want to help you. But you have to calm down. It doesn't matter if he betrayed you. Or not. That's all in the past."

Eric ached inside, ached so badly he barely heard her words. After everything they'd been through. "How could you?"

"How could I what, my love?"

"We …" His voice caught. "We were friends. More than friends."

"We still are."

Moisture blurred his vision. He blinked to clear it. They'd shared so much. He'd trusted her, poured out his heart to her, told her things he'd never told anyone else. And all that time she'd been utterly false.

"Earth to Eric," she said.

He stared at her. The same face. The same voice. But the woman in front of him? "You're not Abby. Not the Abby I loved."

"Dear, you're talking gibberish."

Feeling the presence of Durand and Tanya in the doorway behind him, Eric took a few steps into the library. This was between Abby and himself.

At his advance, she retreated, tempering her move with an uneasy smile. She was trying to act calm, but the scent of her skin rose in heated waves that revealed her anxiety.

Which brought him no sense of triumph, no relief. All it brought was a hollow sadness. And the ultimate question. "Why did you do it?"

"Do what?"

"I would have given you the formula. Then no one would have had to die."

The teardrop-shaped birthmark below her left ear reddened. "I don't know what you're talking about."

"Just tell me why. You owe me that much."

Her eyes flicked slightly to the left, an obvious glance over his shoulder. "I see you brought Miss Cole. I'm sure you want to avenge her beating. That's what you want. To get back at the man whose counterfeit drove her boyfriend to pound the hell out of her."

"Stop trying to shift the blame. *You* counterfeited my perfume. But you screwed up the formula." He took another step toward her. "You knew your knock-off was killing people, but you kept on selling it."

"Don't come any closer."

He stepped forward again. "When you found out I was going to Yemen, you got there first, and you murdered your own supplier. Murdered him in cold blood."

"You're crazy. I've never been to Yemen." Beads of sweat rose on her forehead. "*Monsieur* Durand, you have to believe—"

"I *smelled* you. I smelled your skin in the dealer's shop. Just like I can smell it now."

She clenched her fists. Her eyes darted around the room, the eyes of a cornered animal desperately searching for escape.

"It's over," he said.

"For you." In a burst of speed, she sprinted to the nearest wall, ripped down a dagger, and charged him.

For an instant, Eric stood paralyzed. Then he grabbed a table lamp to fend her off. She slashed at him. He jabbed the lamp at her chest.

Out of nowhere, Tanya came flying, arms wide like a linebacker diving for the tackle.

With a sidestep, Abby sliced downward.

Tanya screamed and crumpled, her arm scored with an ugly gash.

"No!" Eric cocked the lamp like a baseball bat, about to swing it at Abby's head, when a gunshot cracked behind him.

"Drop the dagger," Durand bellowed.

Falling plaster clattered down on the parquet floor.

Abby quickly knelt, pulled Tanya's head back by the hair, and held the knife across Tanya's throat. "Screw you, old man. You drop the gun."

Dead silence filled the room, except for the thumping pulse in

Eric's ears. How in God's name had things come to this? He was powerless. So was Tanya, her eyes wild with fear. Durand stood still, obviously wavering.

"I said drop it," Abby snarled.

Slowly Durand bent down and placed his revolver—wherever that had come from—on the floor.

"Kick it over here."

After a moment of hesitation, Durand kicked the pistol.

Eric lunged as it slid across the floor. Snatching it in both hands, he rolled onto his back and aimed it at Abby's face.

"Aren't you brave?" Abby yanked back harder on Tanya's hair.

"Hurt her and I'll blow your head off."

"You don't have the balls. You've never had balls. You want to know why I make SF? That's the reason. Because you didn't have the balls to do it yourself. You and that fossil over there." She cocked her chin at Durand. "Both of you are stuck in the past. No one wants romance anymore. They want guaranteed sex. And that's what I give them. SF, a sure fuck."

"You're sick."

"And you're a loser."

Still aiming the pistol, Eric got to his feet. His hands shook. "Let Tanya go. This is between you and me."

"Careful what you wish for."

He needed to get her away from Tanya, make her so angry she'd focus completely on him.

Her father.

"I should have seen it before," Eric said. "The reason you're sick is that you're still a child. A little girl with a pathetic father fixation. 'Oh, daddy, why don't you love me?'"

"Go fuck yourself."

"But he hated you. He paraded you naked in front of his doped-up friends."

"You son of a bitch."

"That's why you made SF. To seduce your father. To make him love his twisted little girl."

Abby leapt up. "You're going to die for that."

Eric backpedaled. He pointed the gun at her heart. "Don't do it."

With bared teeth, she raised the knife and charged.
"Stop," he yelled.
But she didn't stop. The knife came down.
Eric pulled the trigger.

Chapter 40

Still half-dazed, Eric stared at the blanket covering Abby's body. It was an old wool blanket, the drab brown of a monk's robe, with frayed satin binding at each end. The sort of blanket that probably itched. He wished Durand had used a softer one, or put a sheet over her first.

Durand, who seemed born to take charge, was now talking on the phone at his desk while Eric and Tanya sat on one of the sofas in the library. And Abby ...

Eric looked again at the blanket. It was idiotic, he knew, but he kept hoping for the slightest movement beneath the hills and valleys of the fabric, the faintest hint that Durand had been wrong in pronouncing her dead. Finally giving up, Eric shut his eyes and tried to imagine Abby looking peaceful in repose. But all he saw was the shock on her face when he fired that pistol. The unbelieving astonishment. An instant of horrified realization, as stunning as his own.

God, forgive me.

That he'd actually done such a thing—done it to Abby—made him sick. Made him want to throw up and purge himself.

If only he could turn back the clock. Do something different. Smarter. Find a way that didn't end in death.

It was just a perfume, for Christ's sake. If she wanted it so badly, he would have given her the lousy formula. All she had to do was ask. But no. She stole it. And when the two of them could have worked out something here, she resorted to violence. Why did she always have to do the wrong thing when the right thing would have been so much easier? Why did she force him to shoot?

He heard ice cubes rattling and looked down at the glass of Scotch in his hand. He wished the shaking would go away.

Beside him, Tanya took his glass, her right forearm wrapped elbow-to-wrist in white gauze. "Maybe you need to walk around a little."

"I shouldn't have goaded her."

"If you hadn't, that would be me under the blanket."

"Don't say that." In a heart-stopping flashback, he saw the dagger at Tanya's throat. It filled him with a dread so cold he shoved his hands under his thighs for warmth. He'd *had* to save her. First Tanya, then himself. But, dammit, he shouldn't have had to "save" anybody.

Across the room, Durand hung up the phone. "He will be here in an hour."

"He" was the police captain in Nice. Durand's hunting partner. The man Durand had said would take care of everything. But Eric's recent experiences told him never to trust a cop.

"Relax." Durand took a handkerchief from his pocket and began wiping down the revolver. "Just tell him what I said."

Durand's story, pressed on them with unnerving calm, was a mixed bag of half-truths and outright lies. Abby had come here, deranged, the spurned woman in a love triangle. She'd hoped to win back Eric by killing Tanya, had assaulted her with the dagger, and had left Durand no choice but to stop her. Open and shut. No serious investigation. No legal repercussions.

And one hell of a gamble. You never knew what a cop might do. Durand could end up in prison. Scared as Eric was of being caged in any jail, he'd rather it be him than the man who'd been his second father.

"Sir, please. You didn't do it. I shot—"

"Do not be a fool." Durand's eyes bored into Eric. "The captain is *my* friend, not yours."

Eric slouched back in the sofa, too exhausted to protest any further.

With a look that said, *That's better*, Durand gripped the revolver in his right hand, obviously pressing his own fingerprints where Eric's had been. Then he laid the pistol on a side table. "I think we are finished here. Let's wait on the terrace, where the air is fresher."

A whole hour. Eric reckoned it would be the longest wait of his—*Hang on.* He wasn't eager to see the captain, but, "An hour? Nice is only fifteen minutes away. Twenty, tops."

"There is no rush." Durand poured himself a Ricard and water. "Miss Han is going nowhere. And the captain has some errands to run before the shops close."

Tanya turned to Eric with a faintest of smiles. "Toto, we're not in New York anymore." Then she stood and handed him his drink.

A brilliant sunset flamed across the horizon, fanned by a cool Mediterranean breeze. But the beauty of the setting did little to lift Eric's spirits. Standing at the balustrade, he couldn't help poring over his years with Abby and how blind he'd been.

"It will help to talk about it," Durand said, apparently divining Eric's thoughts. "Not the shooting, but what came before."

Maybe he was right. Setting his drink on the stone rail, Eric took a fortifying breath. "It goes all the way back to ISIPCA. She loved Balquees, said it was a goldmine and I should go commercial with it."

He walked them through the whole story, augmenting the facts with the painful realizations he'd come to just today—all the way from her stealing the oud to killing the dealer.

"Even up to Yemen, I might have been able to forgive her. Her impoverished childhood, the abuse, no love at all until … until me." *Which she never truly returned.* "But none of that could justify murdering a perfectly innocent man."

"That is the outside story," Durand said. "You have not mentioned anything about the inside story."

"And I'm not going to."

"I think you should," Tanya told him.

"You want me to say I was a fool? That the woman I loved never existed?"

"Not only say it, but believe it." She faced him squarely, her eyes sympathetic but resolute. "You shot someone you didn't even know until thirty minutes beforehand. A cold-blooded killer who was about to kill again."

He turned away. The sunset had faded to a thin red streak. The breeze now carried the biting chill of a March night. In the distance below him, waves hissed against the stony shore. Everything Tanya said was true. Maybe by the time they got home, he'd be able to accept it.

Home. That sure sounded good. He'd get Daisy and— "Holy shit! Abby was supposed to be taking care of Daisy."

"Oh, no," Tanya gasped. "How long has it been? Three days?"

Eric pulled out his cell phone. "I have to call someone." He thought a second. "Fawcett."

"I have his number somewhere," Tanya offered, her voice as urgent as the pounding in Eric's chest.

He punched it from memory.

"Who is Daisy?" Durand asked.

"His dog," she said softly.

Finally a click, then, "Fawcett."

"This is Eric. I need you to do something. Immediately!"

"Where the hell are you, asshole? I've been calling you for—"

"Please, you need to go to Abby Han's apartment. Break down the door. She's not there. Daisy's inside. She's been there for days, probably with no food or water. You've got to get her to a vet." *If she's still alive.*

"I said, where are you?"

Dammit. Fawcett wasn't going to give without receiving. "I'm in France. Abby was behind SF. She's dead. I'll explain it all later."

Tanya tapped the pen in his shirt pocket.

Of course. "I've got everything on a voice recorder. I'll give it to you. Just go get Daisy. I beg you."

"Are you fucking with me? About SF? 'Cause if you are—"

"I'm not. I swear it. Please hurry."

After a moment of silence, the line went dead.

Eric closed his eyes and saw Daisy lying on her side on Abby's kitchen floor, her gaze unfocused, her breathing labored. Watching helplessly, he heard her last conscious thought: *Why did you punish me? I tried to be a good dog.*

He felt a lump in his throat, then the gentle touch of a hand on his shoulder.

"She'll be all right," Tanya said with genuine concern.

He wished he could believe that, wished there was anything he could still believe in. But he couldn't even believe in himself.

He'd been a terrible judge of character, trusting Abby when he shouldn't, not listening to Tanya when he should. And Durand. How in the world could he have imagined a man like Durand would stoop to counterfeiting Balquees?

Eric turned to face his old mentor. "*Monsieur*, I apologize. My suspicions of you were unforgivable. I've disgraced myself."

"No, it is I who must apologize. Against my own heart, I doubted you." He rolled his lips in. "The heart is always right."

Reaching out, Eric took hold of Tanya's hand. "I can't thank you enough for putting up with me through all this."

"I'm getting used to it."

The doorbells chimed.

"Wait here until I call you," Durand said. "And remember, you were two sides of a love triangle." His eyes twinkled. "I think you can manage that."

Suddenly self-conscious, Eric released Tanya's hand. He took a sip of Scotch, then rested his forearms on the balustrade's rail and looked out at the darkened sea.

Tanya stood silently beside him as the sky slowly filled with stars.

He'd dreamed of having a place like this. But it was hard to enjoy with his nerves numbed by uncertainty. Daisy. The police captain. He was powerless on both counts, nothing he could do but wait.

He glanced at his watch. Barely fifteen minutes had passed since Fawcett hung up. Unable to stand still, Eric paced the terrace, willing Fawcett to hurry. He would. Crusty as he acted, the guy had a soft spot for Daisy. He'd already saved her life once by foisting her off on Eric.

He went back to stand by Tanya, and for a while, they watched the stars brighten.

Then she pointed to her left. "Look."

The moon had peeked over the horizon, sending a silvery path across the water like a tentative feeler testing the rippled surface.

Eric's cell phone buzzed. He yanked it from his pocket and saw Fawcett's number on the screen. He punched Talk. "Please tell me she's okay."

"Your dog is smarter than you are. She chewed her way through the leash, went down the fire escape as far as she could, and sat there on the landing."

"Abby tied her on the fucking fire escape?"

"No food or water, but it didn't matter. The people on the second floor saw her out there, couldn't find an owner, and took her in. She's been living like a queen. Much nicer apartment than your joint."

A rush of relief washed over Eric. "Thank God."

"Thank the couple in Two-A. Now, tell me what happened."

Eric saw Durand beckoning him from inside but held up his hand in a "wait" gesture as he gave Fawcett the salient details.

At the end, Fawcett burst out, "*You* shot her?"

"I had to."

After a pause that stank of disbelief, "I want that voice recorder you talked about."

"You'll have it as soon as I get back."

"Which is when?"

"In a day or two."

"Better be." Fawcett paused again, then said with the tiniest trace of wonder, "Maybe you're not such an asshole, after all."

To Eric's amazement, the police interview took less than twenty minutes. The captain, a mustachioed gentleman in a dark blue suit, directed most of his questions to Tanya, who fielded them with the skill of an actress. Eric's only role was to corroborate, since he'd supposedly been nothing more than a bystander in shock. He felt guilty that Tanya took the heat, but the heat was barely tepid.

During the course of "interrogation," men in coveralls lifted Abby's body onto a gurney and wheeled it out. When Durand offered to hand over his revolver, the captain waved it off dismissively.

And that was that.

Eric heard good nights being exchanged at the front door, then a single set of footsteps coming back down the hall.

"Well done." Durand poured snifters of cognac and handed them out. "To the triumph of justice. May we never doubt her."

"Or me," Tanya said as she clinked her glass against Eric's.

Durand took a seat across from them. "Now, if you don't mind, Eric, there is something I must ask you. This Balquees. Is it truly an aphrodisiac?"

Taken aback, Eric simply said, "Yes."

"And it does not have the bad side effects of this ... SF?"

"No. Why do you ask?"

"I was just thinking." Durand set his glass down and rubbed his chin. "Retirement does not suit me. Nor, as I understand it, does your current job suit you."

"So?" He looked at Tanya to see if she knew where this was going, but she seemed focused on Durand.

Durand smiled at her. "Did I mention, *Mademoiselle*, that the captain has need of a fresh mind in his forensic department?"

Eric sat up straight. "What are you getting at?"

"Just idle thoughts of an old man."

Baloney. The wily fox was up to something.

But before Eric could say anything, Durand yawned. "It's late. If you'll excuse me, I think I shall retire for the night. Should you decide to stay, there are twelve bedrooms upstairs. Choose any you like. Except mine, of course, which is above the kitchen." He got up, walked to the doors, then turned. "*Bonne nuit.*"

When he'd left, Tanya said, "I think we should take him up on his offer. Of rooms."

"Do you know what he was talking about?" Eric had suspicions, but they were more like fantastic dreams than anything he dared hope for.

"I know the thought of bed sounds good. It's been an awfully long day."

Leaving their cognac barely touched, they climbed one of two curved staircases to the upper floor. At the top, Eric pointed toward the sea-view side of the house. In the corridor there, they saw five doors, the rightmost one with light glowing under it.

He led her to the left. "Take the corner room. It's probably bigger."

"And you?"

The fragrances of her body seemed suddenly stronger. The remnant scent of vetiver from the last time she'd bathed, the chamomile of her hair, the tang of her dried perspiration. Maybe it was the confines of the hallway that intensified her scent. Or the minor exertion of climbing the stairs. Or maybe …

He shook off the last thought and played it safe. "I'll take the one next to it."

She gave him an expression he couldn't read, then walked to her door and disappeared inside.

In his own room, Eric found a double bed, an *en suite* bathroom, and French doors that gave onto a balcony. He opened the doors wide, then stripped off his shirt and threw it in a corner. He could use a shower, but the cool breeze from outside lured him with its soothing aromas of pine and cypress trees and the flinty scent of wet rocks.

Walking onto the balcony, he saw that it extended across to Tanya's room.

And there she stood. At the railing on the far side of her doors, a vision bathed in moonlight, gazing out to sea.

For a long moment, he just watched her. The breeze ruffling her hair. The moon filling it with silvery highlights.

Then, as if sensing his presence, she turned to face him. Her eyes questioned his.

And his doubt vanished.

ABOUT THE AUTHOR

John Oehler is an award-winning author of three novels. He lives in Houston with his wife, Dorothy, and their Old English Sheepdog, Elfie. Dorothy is a member of the Mars Science Team, which operates and analyzes data from NASA's Curiosity rover.

You are invited to visit John's website, where you will find photographs and behind-the-scenes descriptions of the making of *Aphrodesia*. You can also download excerpts and see reviews of his two forthcoming novels, *Papyrus* and *Tepui*. In addition, there is an author biography, a blog for questions and answers, and contact information.

www.johnoehler.com

COMING SOON

Papyrus

Rika Teferi, a young Eritrean woman, is working on her doctorate in the Cairo Museum when an accidental tea spill uncovers hidden writing on a papyrus written by Queen Tiye to her youngest son, Tutankhamun. Horrified at the spill but aching to read the entire secret text, Rika reluctantly agrees to let a visiting remote-sensing expert, David Chamberlain, smuggle the priceless papyrus out of the museum and scan it with instruments on his specialized aircraft.

The results are stunning. They show Tiye to have been the power behind the thrones of her husband and sons. They show her to have been the architect of Egypt's only monotheistic religion, the religion of Aten, the sun god. They reveal that her tomb is not in Egypt, but in modern-day Sudan. And they indicate that, instead of being embalmed, she had herself buried alive in a coffin filled with restorative oils from which she expected to waken, rejuvenated.

Rika and David devise a risky plan to find Tiye's tomb. But a major in the Secret Police misconstrues their activities as part of a fundamentalist plot to overthrow the Egyptian government. He vows to kill them.

Reared in revolution, as a sharpshooter in Eritrea's war for independence, Rika feels a spiritual bond with Queen Tiye, a Nubian commoner who married Pharaoh and revolutionized Egyptian society by introducing a monotheistic religion that freed Egypt from the tyranny of the Amun priests. Rika's quest to find Tiye's tomb parallels the queen's last journey up the Nile, three thousand years before. Throughout the story, Rika is torn between her passion for Tiye and her love of country. If she finds the tomb, should she be satisfied with knowledge only, or should she take the most valuable artifacts and sell them to buy arms that could tip the balance in Eritrea's continuing battle against genocide? In her growing love of David, she is also torn by the fear that he could never live in her culture, nor she in his. These quandaries plague her until the shocking end.

Tepui

In 1559, forty-nine Spaniards exploring a tributary of the Orinoco River, in modern-day Venezuela, reached a sheer-sided, cloud-capped mountain called Tepui Zupay. When they tried to climb it, all but six of them were slaughtered by Amazons. Or so claimed Friar Sylvestre, the expedition's chronicler. But Sylvestre made many bizarre claims: rivers of blood, plants that lead to gold.

Jerry Pace, a burn-scarred botanist struggling for tenure at UCLA, thinks the friar was high on mushrooms. Jerry's best friend, Hector, the historian who has just acquired Sylvestre's journal, disagrees. Hector plans to retrace the expedition's footsteps and wants Jerry to come with him. Jerry refuses, until he spots a stain between the journal's pages—an impression made by a plant that supposedly died out with the dinosaurs. Finding a living specimen of that plant would make headlines and skyrocket Jerry's faltering career. When the patron who funded the journal's purchase sends his representative, a seductive blond, to accompany them, Jerry's interest heats up even higher.

But the Venezuelan wilderness does not forgive intruders. Their canoe capsizes, they lose their gear, a deranged Dutchman vows to slit their throats. And their trip has just begun. Battered and broken, they reach a remote Catholic orphanage where the old prioress warns of death awaiting any who would venture farther. It appears they've come all this way for nothing, until one of the orphans, an exotic Indian girl who sees Jerry's scars as a sign of strength and virility, offers secretly to guide them on. She leads the way through piranha-infested rivers and jungles teaming with poisonous plants, to Tepui Zupay—the forbidden mountain no outsider has set eyes on since the Spaniards met their doom.

OEHLE   MNT
Oehler, John.
Aphrodesia /

MONTROSE
01/14

24955899R00193

Made in the USA
Charleston, SC
11 December 2013